THE BEAUTIFUL ASHES OF GOMEZ GOMEZ

Ballads of Paradise
The Beautiful Ashes of Gomez Gomez
The Sound the Sun Makes
Venus Sings the Blues

Ballads of Paradise · 1

THE BEAUTIFUL ASHES OF GOMEZ GOMEZ

BUCK STORM

KREGEL
PUBLICATIONS

Library of Congress Cataloging-in-Publication Data
Names: Storm, Buck, author.
Title: The beautiful ashes of Gomez Gomez : a novel / Buck Storm.
Description: Grand Rapids, MI : Kregel Publications, [2020] | Series: Ballads of paradise ; book 1
Identifiers: LCCN 2020003625 (print) | LCCN 2020003626 (ebook)
Classification: LCC PS3619.T69274 B43 2020 (print) | LCC PS3619.T69274 (ebook) | DDC 813/.6--dc23
LC record available at https://lccn.loc.gov/2020003625
LC ebook record available at https://lccn.loc.gov/2020003626

ISBN 978-0-8254-4637-5, print
ISBN 978-0-8254-7643-3, epub

Printed in the United States of America
20 21 22 23 24 25 26 27 28 29 / 5 4 3 2 1

CHAPTER ONE

GOMEZ GOMEZ TALKED TO SNAKES. Something many might've found odd had the subject in question not been Gomez Gomez. Even as a kid he was considered a half bubble off plumb.

Their loss, he figured. A simple problem—people didn't know how to listen. He couldn't blame them, of course. The world at large, the ones outside the glass looking in, had no way of knowing. No, it wasn't their fault. They had no real perspective. No foundation in the exceptional.

Not like him. He understood the exceptional. He'd breached the glass. After all, he'd been married to Angel. At least before she'd learned how to die.

The other thing they didn't understand—couldn't understand—was that Gomez Gomez never initiated the conversation.

And the thing about snakes, they always had a lot to say.

The shrill phrases of the garter snakes, the machine-gun staccato of the red racers—you couldn't get a word in edgewise with those guys—the coughing rasp of the gopher snake. The big rattler, five feet at least, scared him with his dusty slur, but his stories were by far the most interesting.

This afternoon a huge king snake stretched himself out on the log under the mesquite tree and regaled Gomez Gomez with tales of the hunt in his comfortable, booming baritone.

Gomez Gomez sipped from a paper bag–wrapped Thunderbird wine bottle then arched an eyebrow at the big king. "You told me that one before."

"Did I?" the snake said.

"You told me most of these before. You have a bad habit of repeating yourself."

"You know you're cranky when you drink?"

"Then I'm always cranky."

"Good point."

"And don't judge me."

"Why would I? Still, you must know you're killing yourself."

"Not fast enough, you ask me." Gomez Gomez took another pull. "Besides, Thunderbird is first-rate snake-hearing juice. Nothin' like it. Seems like that's something you'd be all for."

"Maybe, but I worry. What would Angel say?"

"She don't say nothing anymore. She never does. Can't even dream about her. And leave her out of it, anyway."

"I'm just saying that some ghosts have heavier footsteps than others."

"You don't know what you're talking about."

The snake lifted his head, flicked his tongue against the clear Arizona autumn air. "So what's on the paper?"

"What paper?"

"The one in your hand that has you so upset."

Gomez Gomez squinted an eye down at the notice. "I was trying to forget about it."

"How's that working out?"

"Your reminding me doesn't help."

"Call me curious. Sue me."

Gomez Gomez held the sheet up to the blue sky. The sun shining through the print made it unreadable. He wished it would burst into flame. "It's an eviction notice."

"A what notice?"

"Eviction. I'm evicted. I'm an evictee. Somebody stapled it to the front door. Means I'm supposed to leave."

"What front door?"

"My front door. What front door do you think?"

The snake's eyes were glassy black beads. "You call that a front door?"

Gomez Gomez turned and studied his makeshift shack.

"It's a cracked piece of old plywood with some ratty tarp hanging on it," the snake said.

"Well, you know what they say, right? One man's castle and all that."

"So . . . are you going to? Evict or whatever?"

Gomez Gomez took another slug from the bottle. "I ain't going nowhere. I got no plans of evicting in the near or distant future."

"What if they arrest you and put you in prison? Or wherever they put crazy people. What then?"

"You're a real ray of sunshine, you know that?"

"What are friends for?"

"I said I ain't going nowhere."

"Well, I am. It's getting late."

"I ain't keeping you."

"Couldn't if you tried, buddy." Another flick and the king slid off into the brush.

Gomez Gomez offered a lazy wave. "Adios then."

He dozed into the afternoon. Let the shadows grow. The dozing helped him forget about the notice—and the rocks.

The rocks came at ten minutes after three, right on schedule. Not big rocks—they couldn't throw big rocks all the way down from the road—but big enough to hurt if one connected. And one did. A light flashed in his skull. He put his hand to his forehead. Blood oozed through his fingers and dripped into his eye. Normally he'd have crawled into the plywood-and-tarp shack that served as home at the sound of the last school bell. But the sun and booze . . . too late now. Thankfully the other rocks pelted into the pine trees around his camp then stopped.

Adolescent laughter rang through the trees and moved on up the road.

"You missed, you little freaks!" Gomez Gomez shouted toward the sound.

More laughter.

"Try coming down here sometime, how about?" Gomez Gomez touched his forehead again and winced. "You missed . . ."

The daily ritual. He could picture it. Get out of school, shell the wino with rocks, then head home to homework, supper, family, and normal.

To the snakeless life on the other side of the glass.

"You're bleeding."

The voice made Gomez Gomez jump. Then again he was jumpy these days. Mostly 'cause the rattlesnake had a way of sneaking up on a guy.

Not the rattlesnake this time, though. A kid. Hard to tell his age. Maybe thirteen? Whatever that gawky, pimple-faced age was—yeah, thirteen sounded about right. He wore heavy work boots, jeans, and a faded Brad Paisley concert tee. Feathery-looking brown hair, unevenly cropped, stuck out from his head at a dozen different angles.

The kid blinked owl eyes at him from behind thick plastic-framed glasses. "You're bleeding."

"You already said that."

"From the rocks."

Gomez Gomez considered. "Anyone ever tell you you have a keen sense of the obvious?"

The owl eyes blinked again. "No. Not really, I don't think."

"You know what that means? Keen sense of the obvious?"

"I'm not stupid. It means I'm good at recognizing what's right in front of my face. Are you the guy who talks to snakes?"

Gomez paused. "That depends."

"On what?"

"On if I'm in a talking mood. Sometimes I just listen. Who are you? One of the rock throwers?"

"No, that's Travis Gart."

"Travis Gart throws a lot of rocks for one person."

The kid shrugged, his shoulders bony beneath his tee. "He has followers. It comes down to the same thing. They wouldn't do it if he didn't."

"And you're not a follower?"

"No."

"What are you then?"

"They say you're a drunk. Are you?"

Gomez Gomez scratched his chin stubble. "I imagine. At least drinking's what I mostly do."

"Are you drunk right now?"

He took inventory. "Hard to tell. Most likely. What's your name?"

A second of hesitation. "Bones."

"Bones? What kind of name is that?"

"It's what people call me. You got a problem with it?"

"What does your mom call you? She call you Bones?"

The kid shrugged again. "She don't call me nothing. What do they say to you? The snakes?"

"All kinds of things. They're very unpredictable animals. And fairly good conversationalists."

Bones stood and turned his face to the sun, closing his eyes. He stayed that way for a long moment, then spoke, eyes still closed. "They're kicking you out. Did you know that?"

"The snakes?"

"No, the city. 'Cause of Sonny Harmon."

Confused anger picked at the edges of the Thunderbird numbness. "Yeah, I got a paper on my door. But that don't mean anything."

The kid turned his owl eyes back. "Harmon Chevrolet wants to expand. That means you have to go somewhere else. Or else."

"Sonny Harmon can shove his car lot where the Arizona sun don't shine. Anyway, I can't go somewhere else. There is nowhere else. I have to be here."

"Because your wife died here, right? That's what people say."

"I have to be here, that's all." Gomez Gomez said.

"They also say you're crazy."

"Maybe they're crazy. You ever think of that? Maybe you're crazy."

"Nah, I think it's you."

Gomez Gomez sighed, squinted down the neck of his T-bird bottle, then took a swig. "Yeah, you're probably right."

The kid gazed down at him. "Anyway, they're gonna make you go. If Sonny Harmon wants this place, he's gonna get it. And he says you're just a drunk."

"Nobody's just nothin'."

"Maybe not. Still, you don't matter to Sonny Harmon. Nobody matters to Sonny Harmon. Doesn't matter if you're the president of the United States or the baby Jesus."

"Well I ain't either one. And I ain't going nowhere, neither. You tell them that."

"Not up to me to tell anybody anything, man. Plus Sonny wouldn't listen no matter who talked to him. What Sonny wants, Sonny gets. And you're a drunk. A homeless. A nobody."

"I ain't homeless. I live here."

Bones looked around. "It ain't bad, actually. Nobody telling you what to do, right?"

"Right."

"Except Sonny Harmon, I guess."

Gomez Gomez crumpled the notice and tossed it on the smoldering ashes of his campfire. It smoked but didn't catch. "Yeah, except Sonny Harmon."

Bones picked his nose and looked at his finger. "Anyway, you want those guys to quit throwing rocks?"

The change of subject caught Gomez Gomez off guard. "Why? You gonna stop them?"

"Maybe. If I want to. You know, if I feel like it."

Gomez Gomez ran an eye over the boy's thin frame. "How you gonna do that? You can't weigh more than a duck. Maybe half a duck."

The lopsided grin that came to the boy's face didn't touch his eyes. "Because I'm Bones, man."

He left in the opposite direction of the king snake.

CHAPTER TWO

FATHER JAKE MORALES WAS NOT a sudden man. When change came knocking, if it wanted to stay it had to earn its keep. Water through granite, carting away sediment in tiny increments as it whittled the canyons of his heart.

Paradise, Arizona, fit his slow burn like an old pair of boots.

Habanero peppers, coffee, sunrise over the mountains. The sun's slow track across the sky before it cast its last color across the desert below. Starlight flickering through rodeo dust. A neon goddess standing watch over the Venus Motel out on Highway 30, her light fading as it reached pastel fingers down a stretch of empty road . . .

Yeah, Paradise fit Jake fine. The town lay along a highway that wound along an out-of-the-way mountain range in the southeast part of the state. Scrub oak, sage, and pine competed for real estate. Cowboys and hippies, young and old for the most part got along, the soundtrack supplied by Lightnin' Hopkins country blues picked out on Willie's old Spanish guitar.

Jake sighed and looked out his office window, deep-set high in the thick adobe wall of the Jardin de Dios Mission, at a view he'd taken in a thousand times. Autumn shone bright and the warmth of the Arizona sun almost broke through his cloud-shrouded thoughts—almost. There'd been a time he'd been comfortable with his own company. Years and another lifetime ago. Back *before*. These days he tended to shove everything into a locked room in the back of his brain. Maybe not the healthiest choice but a guy did what he had to do in the name of survival.

His window faced the rear of the mission, away from the old downtown. Sun glinted off an elderly Airstream trailer below, polished bright by sun and wind. Beyond the trailer, a dust devil whipped across the dirt baseball field. Pine trees peppered up the mountain beneath an expanse of blue, broken only by a distant streak of white jet exhaust.

Jake loved his town. He loved the way it loitered and lazed in the afternoon stillness. Loved the way it smelled, sounded, and breathed a life of its own. His family had made this place their home for generations.

Then why do I feel homeless?

He closed his eyes and listened. Plane engines rumbled just under the predictable drone of insects and birdsong.

Post-industrial Earth—a planet devoid of silence. Where had he read that? Some article somewhere. Even in the middle of the ocean, they said, you couldn't be free from the insistent aural press of mechanized progress.

Then again, Jake wouldn't know. He'd been to rodeo arenas across the country, yes, but never the middle of the ocean. Maybe he'd ask Doc next time they talked. Doc was probably in the middle of the ocean this very moment. The thought of his brother brought a needed smile. He missed the guy. But Doc and his new wife were off sailing somewhere in the Caribbean, a long, long way away.

His stomach growled. He should go to Shorty's and get something to eat. Or maybe not—Honey would be there and she'd already been too much on his mind.

Jake shifted his focus outward again with effort. By the ball field, a couple of teenagers rattled up on bikes and leaned them against the chain-link dugout. One said something and the other laughed, but they were too far away to make out any words. Thirty seconds later they were joined by a cloud of dust with a primer-gray Toyota pickup wrapped in the middle. The truck skidded to a stop behind the backstop, and wind pushed the dust on across the field. A couple of guys tumbled out and grabbed a bat bag and gloves out of the truck bed. Looked like the on-again, off-again afternoon ball game was on again. Jake would most likely join them after a while. They'd laugh about him playing ball in his cassock and battered old cowboy hat, but they'd be glad to have him. Probably even fight over whose team he'd be on. Not that he was Doc. Or anywhere near as good. Doc had taken the skill and passion he'd developed on that dirt field all the way to Fenway Park and the major leagues. Jake shared his little brother's athleticism and passion, but he'd chosen to channel it into a fairly successful rodeo career, touring the rodeo grounds of America on the top deck of a saddle bronc. He had a scrapbook of X-rays to prove it. But, hey, no regrets.

Behind him, his office door banged open with a dull thump of pine. Jake didn't need to turn. "What's up, Early?"

"*Detective* Early to you, amigo." The voice rough but cheerful, a wool blanket of smoker's gravel around the edges.

"But you still can't say *Father* Jake?"

A low chuckle. "How'd you know it was me? You have some kind of spiritual super-vision or something?"

"Don't need it. You're the only one who doesn't knock. Even Father Enzo knocks."

On the field the boys started throwing a ball around.

A chair squeaked as Early sat. "So I'll come to confession. You can give me penance or that rosary deal. Take me over your knee and spank me, whatever it is you spooky old crows do."

Jake sank into his desk chair. Across from him, Early grinned his raggedy Early grin—same one Jake had seen since kindergarten, one incisor tooth turned at an angle. His friend laced his fingers behind his head and stretched the considerable length of his legs out in front of him. Early Pines, carved by desert wind out of wood and leather. Six foot five without his boots on, lean, muscular, and hard as nails. A quarter Navajo but he looked more. Dark hair to his shoulders. An old scar tracing up from one corner of his mouth, giving the illusion of a perpetual smirk. His hawk nose, flattened more than once during his life, angled to the left. Jake could remember at least two of the occasions of injury. One a headbutt from an angry steer and another a parking lot fight behind an Amarillo bar. Jake didn't like to think about that fight. Early'd left the place with a busted face, but the huge drunk cowboy who'd challenged him barely left at all.

"Old crow?" Jake said.

"I say that in the most loving way. I heard Old Crow whiskey was named after a priest."

"No, you didn't."

"Yeah, I didn't. So what's up in God's world?"

"Talked to Doc last week. He's gonna be a dad, can you picture that?"

Early grunted a laugh and scratched his chin. "Uncle Jake . . . Who would have thought?"

"He said if it's a boy they're gonna name him after me."

"I don't know, 'Old Crow' just sets the kid up for ridicule."

"You ever consider taking your act on the road?"

"You'd miss me too much. Hey, if it's a girl maybe they can call her Earlyina."

"Uh-huh. Because Earlyina is just beautiful."

"Well, *I'm* beautiful. What can I say?" Early shifted his boots up to Jake's desk, resting one on top of the other. "Anyway, we need to talk."

"You comfortable?"

"Very."

"All right, I want you to be happy. What are we talking about?"

Early's dark eyes glittered above flat, pock-scarred cheeks. He took his trucker's hat off his head and tossed it onto the toe of his boot. The logo settled facing Jake. *Kiss Me, I'm Baptist.*

"Why d'you look like that?" Early said.

"Since when are you a Baptist?"

Early shrugged. "Since the Catholics don't give out free hats. Now, why do you look like that?"

Jake walked over to a battered pine sideboard and poured two cups from the same Mr. Coffee maker he'd had since college. He dumped a liberal amount of sugar into one and handed it to Early. He kept the black for himself and dropped back into his chair. "You know you've gotten all cocky since you made detective?"

"Do I get a spoon?"

"Use your finger."

Early did. "I wasn't cocky before?"

Jake sipped. "You got a point."

"You gonna answer my question?"

Jake sighed. "Why do I look like what, Detective Pines?"

"I don't know, man, old."

"I'm thirty-one, same as you."

"Uh-huh. But you look old and whipped."

"Thanks for the boost, buddy."

"I'm taking confession today, amigo. Special deal for priests. You get half off. Talk to me."

Jake rubbed the bridge of his nose. "It's nothing. Just the past tapping me on the shoulder, that's all. What's up? You didn't come here to talk about me."

"Looks to me like the past roundhouse kicked you to the back of your head. You thinking about Gomez Gomez?"

"You really want to know?"

"I already know, but yeah."

"I'm pretty much always thinking about Gomez Gomez. But I've been thinking about Honey too."

"Honey? As in you-see-her-at-Shorty's-all-the-time-and-act-like-you-never-practically-got-married-to-her Honey?"

"That would be the one, yes."

"Why're you thinking about her? Daydreaming about women can't be healthy in your line of work."

"It's way past stupid. The other day she brushed my hand when she was pouring my coffee."

"So?"

"So . . . It's hard to explain. It brought back memories for some reason. Old times and all that."

"You miss her. It's natural. Honey's cool. And beautiful."

"You have to say that out loud?"

"Sorry, man. Facts are facts. I proposed to her just this morning."

"How many times is that now?"

"Never say die."

"I don't know. I still feel bad the way it all happened. Feel bad for her."

"Uh-huh. And yourself, I'm thinking. Look, nobody questions why you became a priest. Maybe I think you're a little crazy, but I don't question. You got your reasons and you gotta do what you gotta do. I'm sure Honey feels the same, you know?"

"Maybe she does. Thing is, we never talk about it."

"What's done is done. What good would it do to talk about it?"

"You're right. Forget I even brought it up."

"Listen, man, I'm just saying you got friends when you need us, Honey included, that's all."

"I know. And I appreciate it."

"You sure?"

"Sure that I appreciate it?"

"Sure that you *know* it."

"I know it. I'm telling you, I'm fine."

"If you say so. So now for the bad news. Speaking of the past, you need to go with me to talk to Gomez Gomez."

Jake paused. "What's up with Gomez Gomez?"

"Town council wants to kick him out of the bushes."

"What do you mean kick him out?"

"I mean Sonny Harmon wants to expand his stupid car lot and Gomez Gomez is in the way."

"That land is publicly owned. Sonny can't have it just because he wants it."

"If the place is a car lot, it generates property taxes. If it's vacant land, it generates snakes and dust. One's good for the town's bottom line, and the other's only good for Gomez Gomez. Guess who wins? I'm sure they're happy to shuffle the fine print if it makes a few bucks. And as far as they're concerned, it's Gomez Gomez. Who cares about him?"

"Everybody cares about him. Because everybody loved Angel."

"It is what it is, man. Angel's gone. And Gomez Gomez is . . . well, he's Gomez Gomez."

"I don't know what I can do. You know I've been trying to talk to him for years. He doesn't even acknowledge I exist unless it's to cuss me out or throw something at me."

Early sipped his coffee and grimaced. "But he's never been being kicked out before. He needs his friends right now."

Jake picked up a paper clip, studied it without seeing it, then dropped it back onto the desk. "He's been down there a long time. Maybe this is finally a way to end it."

"Maybe. What's it been? Four, five years since Angel?"

"Five. Long time to be living alone in that shack."

"And it's a long time for you to beat yourself up for something that was an accident."

Jake met Early's gaze. "So you my therapist now?"

"Nah, man. But sometimes I think guilt has got you buried."

"Maybe it's not guilt. Maybe it's honor."

"And maybe with you there's a blurry line between the two."

"Why can't you talk to him? You're his best friend."

Early threw the Early grin. "Nope, I'm your best friend. And I am going to talk to him. You and me together are gonna talk to him."

"Why me?"

"Because he always listened to you. Even when you were just plain old Jake. Busting broncs instead of saving souls."

"You were there too. Plus that was then, this is now. These days he'd rather stick a knife in my chest and laugh while I bleed than let me buy him a cup of coffee."

Early shrugged. "Maybe we all traveled together, but you were always the smart one. The thinker of the bunch. Gomez Gomez got what little brains he started out with pounded out on the bulls, and us bulldoggers aren't especially known for our essay-writing skills."

"That's not true. Besides, those were different times. You're a detective now. You have authority."

"Not so different when it comes to the three of us."

"A *lot* different. Have you seen him lately?"

Early nodded. "I go in there and talk to him. Take him a little cash sometimes, a little food. He's mostly drunk or on his way to drunk. Says he talks to snakes all day. You know the Navajos say snakes are bad luck? I'm pretty sure I agree with them. And even if they're not bad luck, it's just plain weird. He probably talks to Angel too. Guy's losing it—or lost it already."

"We're talking about Gomez Gomez here. I'm not sure he ever had it to lose."

Early's chair squeaked as he shifted. "Look, man, that whole Angel thing was a bad deal, but what can you do? When you gonna move on?"

"I don't know. Maybe when Gomez Gomez gets his world back. I've tried—I'm trying."

"Well, right now he's down at that camp of his scratching around in the dirt for Angel's ghost."

"Don't you know I think about that every day?"

"So here's your chance to help fix it—maybe fix yourself in the process. Go talk to him with me. It could be good for both of you."

"You know I'd do anything I could to help him, but the only thing he really wants is Angel back, and that's something I can't give him."

"Nobody can. All I'm asking is you go over there and help me try to talk him out of the bushes. You don't need to call fire from heaven or turn water to wine, just be there, man."

"That shack is all Gomez Gomez has got left. Sonny Harmon already owns half this town. Why can't the guy leave well enough alone?"

"Because he's Sonny Harmon, what more do you need? So you gonna come or sit here and daydream about Honey?"

"Of course I'm gonna come. You knew I would before you asked."

A tap sounded at the doorjamb. Jake glanced over. "Father Enzo, come in."

"Join the party, father, there's gonna be clowns," Early said.

Only a few years shy of eighty, Father Enzo's lanky frame, still mostly black hair, and smooth brown face belied his age. He moved with the limber ease of a man half his age as he entered Jake's office carrying a worn notebook and dropped into a chair next to Early. Though he'd been in the States for years, he'd never quite shaken his Italian accent. "I never really understood clowns. They scare the children."

"Nobody understands clowns," Early said. "We would have had dancing girls, but this being a church and all . . ."

Father Enzo chuckled and patted Early's knee. "How's police work? You busy shaking down small-business owners and pestering old women with parking tickets?"

"Somebody's got to do it. Jake's busy polishing his halo, and I'm sure eating Jell-O and watching *Matlock* reruns sucks up all the hours in your day."

Father Enzo laughed. "I'm going to pray for your soul, boy."

"I won't pretend it doesn't need it." Early indicated the notebook in the priest's lap. "Are you a fan of the Man of Steel?"

Father Enzo glanced down. "Ah yes, Superman . . . Just a little project of mine. I found the notebook in the donation bin."

"Father, would you like coffee?" Jake said.

"No, no. I was only coming to talk to you about . . . that thing we talked about."

"Sounds serious," Early said. "Should I step out?"

"Oh no! Nothing serious. Just an old man's indulgence. I wanted to read something to Jake, but it can wait. We'll do it tonight, yes?"

"You bet," Jake said. "I'll look forward to it."

"Sermon notes?" Early said.

The old priest shifted and offered a rueful grin. "Nothing so weighty as that. Just a story. Something I do to pass the evenings. But who knows? I'm a priest after all. Maybe someone will find a little comfort in the words I write. And Father Jake is an excellent sounding board." He tapped the notebook with an index finger. "This is a new one."

"You write stories?" Early said.

"Father Enzo is a budding novelist," Jake said.

"No joke? Paradise's own Louis L'Amour?"

"Who is Louis L'Amour?" Father Enzo said.

"He wrote cowboy stuff mostly," Jake said. "Only books Early's ever read."

"Not true. Well, kind of true."

Father Enzo patted his notebook. "This story is about two boys who grow up on Corfu—a beautiful island in the Ionian Sea. They are best friends, but very, very competitive. Much like you two in fact."

"Let me guess, they fall for the same girl," Early said.

"If I tell you that, it will ruin the story," Father Enzo said. "But many things happen to these boys. There is a big fish." He winked. "Maybe a girl too."

"Where's the Ionian Sea?" Early said.

"Ah, the Ionian Sea! So beautiful! Between Italy and Greece."

"Corfu . . . I like it," Early said. "What time should I be here?"

"Be here for what?" Jake said.

"To hear the story, genius. What do you think? Expand my horizons. Get a little culture." Early scratched at his chin, eyes drifting a bit. "Maybe something to take our minds off stinking Sonny trying to bulldoze our friend's shack." He shifted back to Jake. "And off certain waitresses."

"Waitresses?" Father Enzo said. "Your face is troubled, Father Jake. I would help if possible."

Early answered for him. "Honey touched Jake's hand."

Jake sighed. "Early . . . don't."

Father Enzo steepled his fingers. Lines formed between his eyes. "Honey Hicks touched your hand . . ."

"Don't listen to Early. He likes to stir the pot when he's bored."

"Honey is a beautiful girl," Father Enzo said.

"It's really nothing, father. Please, ignore him."

Father Enzo's brown eyes lingered on Jake, then he nodded. "All right, then what's this about Sonny and bulldozers?"

Jake explained.

The old priest leaned back in his chair, craggy face thoughtful. "When did you hear about this deal with Sonny Harmon?"

Early leaned forward for his hat, rubbed at a spot on his boot, then put the hat on his head. "This morning. Town council met. The mayor told Matthias they wanted Gomez Gomez out of his snake hole and Matthias punted it to me. He's probably scared of snakes."

"Matthias is your boss. It seems to me he can tell you to do whatever he wants," Father Enzo said.

"Yeah, but I'm *definitely* scared of snakes."

"Getting Gomez Gomez out and getting his head straight is the right thing, Sonny Harmon or not." Father Enzo rose. "I will pray our God leads you in His wisdom. Go with blessing. And tonight, Corfu."

"Tonight, Corfu!" Early said. "The Ionian sea and a big fish."

"But no cowboys," Father Enzo said.

"I'll suffer. But I'll live," Early said.

"Excellent. Now, you both go do what you have to do. And, Early, get your feet off the desk." The old priest closed the door behind him.

Early dropped his boots to the floor. "The guy's really not bad for an old crow."

"I'm pretty sure you're going to hell."

"Naw. God smiles on Baptists."

"You know, for his own good, you really should just go order Gomez Gomez out. Get him in some kind of facility."

"Maybe. But my gut says it needs to be slow. He'll lose it if he's pushed. Maybe even hurt himself. Plus the guy's our friend. I can't just go drag him out."

"Or because he's our friend that might be exactly what you should to do."

"Let's just go feel the dude out. Then we'll talk about it."

Jake stood. "Fine, let's go. But let's at least get something to eat first. I'm starving."

"Shorty's?"

"That's what I was thinking. Aunt Katie's cooking today."

"Your Aunt Katie's always cooking. And we never go anyplace else anyway. You know Honey's working, right?"

"I've been avoiding her for a week. Enough's enough."

"Over bumping your hand?"

"Just leave it alone."

Early got up, wincing at some old leftover rodeo pain. "You're the one that was sitting here all moony eyed. You thinking of hanging up the robe, amigo? That the deal?"

"You know it doesn't work that way."

Early laughed. "Well, pontiff, you better straighten out that halo. It's looking a little crooked."

CHAPTER THREE

"THE THING IS—MAYBE YOU don't realize—you look like a lunatic the way you carry that can around," the big rattlesnake slurred from the snake log.

Gomez Gomez stood and stretched, working a kink out of his back.

"It's not a can, it's Angel."

"Earth to GG . . . It's a Folgers coffee can."

"It's Angel."

"It's a bunch of ashes—charcoal, dude. What a moron."

"You're a snake, what do you know about death anyway?"

"Um, you ever heard of a little joint called Eden?"

Gomez Gomez looked down at the Folgers can. Clutched like a football, tight as a wide receiver five yards from the end zone. "You know what's weird? I can't hardly drink when I'm holding her."

"Why not? Who's gonna know?"

"I don't know, nobody. But I can't."

"You're a real psycho, homey."

Gomez Gomez didn't argue the point. After all, he *was* talking to a rattlesnake. He set the Folgers can on a flat rock with gingered finesse, well away from the firepit, then picked up a Thunderbird bottle. He held it up. Almost a quarter of the liquid happiness remained. "What do you think about that Bones kid?"

"You seriously have to set her down first? Just to take a drink?"

"It's easier. I already told you."

"That Bones kid . . . I think he's as much of a crackpot as you are. You two are made for each other."

"You feel that way, why don't you just bite me and get it over with?"

The snake slithered out of his coil and flattened himself against the sun. He offered a tired sigh. "I'm not in the mood. Besides, I find you mildly entertaining."

"In other words, you're not bored with me yet."

"I guess not."

Gomez Gomez tipped the bottle to the sky and took long gulps, draining it. He set it on the flat rock next to the Folgers can and studied the pair. He picked the bottle back up and tossed it deep into the brush. The snake didn't move. Lying there like a stick pretending to be asleep. Stupid thing always did that.

"I know you're not asleep. Don't start fake snoring either."

The snake might as well have been dead. Better for everybody if it was.

"You're faking," Gomez Gomez said.

"No, I'm not."

"Your eyes are open."

"Snakes don't have eyelids. Didn't you ever take biology?"

"You don't? And you say I'm the freak?" A dangerous way to talk to the rattlesnake but the alcohol put Gomez Gomez in a mood. He picked up the Folgers can and ducked into his shack where he sat on a dented aluminum lawn chair and stared down at the makeshift urn in his lap.

The rattlesnake appeared in the doorway. "Why don't you ever open it?"

"I already know what's in it. I don't need to see it again."

"Yeah, a bunch of charcoal."

"No. She's beautiful."

"Whatever. Anyway, I'm gonna split."

"See ya," Gomez Gomez said.

"I'm really leaving."

"So you said."

"Weirdo." The snake slithered off toward the bushes.

"Lidless freak," Gomez Gomez called after him.

He leaned down and set the Folgers can in its usual place, a shrine constructed of flat shale he'd carried up piece by piece from an old rockslide down by the river. He took a plastic Bic out of his coat pocket and lit the scattering of burned-down candles. He pulled a trucker's wallet from under his dirty mattress and stared numbly at it. The hand tooling on its sides nearly worn away. Stitching frayed. With great care he opened it and pulled out a photo. A flat sunbeam slanted down through a crack between a plank wall and the plywood roof of the shack. In it tiny dust particles danced in perfect choreographed synchronicity, humming the tune to "The Lion Sleeps Tonight." He'd always liked that song. He moved the photo into the beam. Angel's smiling face both warmed and wrecked him. He remembered the day he'd taken it—her twenty-fifth birthday. They'd driven to Flagstaff and spent the night, then got up early to see the Grand Canyon, one of Angel's bucket list wishes. The photo caught her in candid motion as she turned toward him, a second or two after her first glimpse over the canyon rim. Pure Angel. Pure joy. Pure perfection. Tears breached his lids and caught in his beard.

"Stupid snake. Lidless freak. What does he know anyway? You're beautiful, Angel. The most beautiful thing I ever saw."

Angel smiled.

He gave a ragged laugh then coughed into his sleeve, carefully away from the photo. "Hey, do you remember that time down in Nogales? That was some kind of something, wasn't it? Remember that Tejano band? How we danced? Man, you loved to dance. I guess I did too . . . At least I used to 'cause it was with you." He smiled and wiped his eyes with the back of his hand. The dust particles slowed as they switched tunes—Freddy Fender's Tex-Mex "Before the Next Teardrop Falls." Gomez Gomez traced the edge of the photo with a finger. "Look at me, right? I'm a broken record. We just talked about Nogales yesterday. But, man . . . that Tejano band, they were something. You were something . . ."

Outside a single dove cooed, thickening the lonesome of the afternoon. Stinking doves made it hard to breathe sometimes.

Angel smiled.

"You knew how to die, didn't you?"

The dove again.

"You are so beautiful, Angel. I couldn't believe you chose me, you know? Crazy bull rider Gomez Gomez . . ." The dust particles stopped humming Freddy Fender and hung still and silent, maybe waiting for the dove. "Remember the nights? At our old place? Sometimes we'd just lie there and hold each other. I know you remember too. I hit the lottery with you, man, but better. A million times better. What's more than a million? A gazillion? I wish . . ." He shook off tears and looked up at the sunbeam. The stupid tears made everything blur. "Anyway, that Tejano band, right?" The particles hummed again, low and soulful, a tune Gomez Gomez didn't recognize. "I hear everything now, Angel, did you know that? No kidding, everything. I hear the snakes—they never shut up. I hear the river laughing at me. I hear the sun . . . scraping across the sky like sand on a flat rock. Then, when it goes down it hisses like hot metal in water. And after it's gone the stars start singing. I hear it all. The world is so stinking loud." He looked at the photo. "But not *you*, Angel. I never hear you. The only thing I want to hear, but I never hear you. No matter how much I want, how much I hope, how much I drink . . . I never hear you. Talk to me, Angel. Please talk to me."

The particles hung. The dove cooed. Then just the wind in the trees and the distant scrape of sand across flat rock.

And Angel smiling, fresh from the canyon.

Gomez Gomez stuck the photo back in the wallet, dropped to his knees, and shoved it deep under the mattress. Then, clutching the Folgers can of ashes to his chest, he curled up in his own filth and let himself weep.

CHAPTER FOUR

HONEY HICKS'S SLIM BODY ACHED hair to toenails. The tray piled with taco specials balanced on her right arm weighed roughly the same as her Aunt Holly—a considerable amount even after the free Weight Watchers trial promo. The coffeepot in her left hand didn't feel much lighter. On top of it all, no matter where she went in the Shorty's Café dining room, Matthias Galt's eyes never failed to find her.

Although, come to think of it, Matthias's attention might not be a bad thing. The jury was still out on that one.

At a window table she delivered the taco plates, filled a couple of coffee mugs, and offered the ready smile and usual pleasantries that came naturally to her. Delivery accomplished, she navigated back through the tables and around the counter toward the swinging door that led to the peaceful refuge of the kitchen. Matthias started to say something as she passed, but she pretended not to hear. Better not to give the guy the wrong idea.

Katie Morales, Jake's aunt and most recent in a long line of Shorty's Café matriarchs, hovered over the wide stainless steel cooktop. "So you talk to him?" Her Mexican accent thick.

"Talk to who?" Honey said.

"Don't give me *who*. Matthias Galt, that's who. Would it kill you to be nice to him? Maybe go out with him once?"

"I *am* nice to him."

"So go out with him."

"There's a big difference between being nice and going out. Maybe he's not my type."

"Maybe he's not your type? Nice. Makes good conversation, good job? And he's crazy about you, obviously. What's the matter with you? You like being lonely? He's been asking you out ever since he got to town. What's that, six months now? And he's handsome! I'm about to go out with him myself."

"I think Lou would have something to say about that."

"What the ball and chain doesn't know won't kill him."

"Dating customers is categorically frowned upon in the employee handbook."

"We don't have an employee handbook."

"Well, we should. Hey, I serve. I smile. I make small talk. What more do you want?"

Katie tucked a bottle-black curl behind her ear then dabbed her forehead with a kitchen towel. "I want you to not be lonely. I want you to be happy."

"I'm happy enough."

Katie snorted. "Enough doesn't count, *mija*."

Honey had to smile when her boss called her "daughter." Being everyone's mother was Katie's way.

"Let me ask you—what are you doing here anyway?" Katie said.

"Um, I think I'm picking up a carne asada burrito plate for Charles Faulks."

"Exactly my point. Here you are working as a waitress. You have a college degree. You should be doing more."

"I have an associate's degree. From Paradise Community College. Not ASU . . . or Harvard. It hardly even counts."

"A whatever degree. It's still a degree. You started a career. Traveled."

"I did social work in Honduras. I don't think that counts as a career either."

"And almost got married to that doctor down there. Marrying a doctor definitely counts as a career where I come from."

"I grew up three doors down from you. And almost got married isn't exactly a high point on a job application. What are you saying? You don't want me here?"

"Don't be dense. I love you here."

"Then what?"

Katie tapped her acrylic nails on a stove knob and flipped the tortilla. "I don't know, mija. Put down some roots. Live. Realize your potential."

"Now you sound like a self-help book."

"That's because you could use some self-help."

"I think my roots are growing fine. I got a cat. Did I tell you? How about that for roots?"

"You got a cat?"

"A big orange one."

"What's this cat's name?"

"Are you saying you don't believe I got a cat?"

"I'm saying what's his name?"

Honey paused. "His name is Charles Faulks."

"Charles Faulks as in the Charles Faulks you just waited on?"

"So? I like Charles Faulks. If I want to name my cat after him it's my business. Besides, it's a common enough name."

Katie shook her head. "You don't have a cat."

"You can't prove I don't have a cat."

"You don't have a cat, mija."

"Well, I'm getting a cat. At least I'm probably getting a cat."

"Matthias Galt is a nice boy. Solid. Plus he's good-looking. Go out with him."

"I thought we were talking about cats."

"Which is exactly your problem. You need to stop talking about cats."

"Matthias is too good-looking. It's suspicious. The guy probably drowns cats. Or hates old people. And what's with the New York accent? Is he in the Mafia?"

"Call me crazy, but it might have something to do with the fact he's from New York."

"And why is a guy from New York, a guy like that, in Paradise, Arizona? I bet he's in witness protection or something shady."

"Because witness protection people usually become police chiefs. He's a nice boy," Katie repeated.

"One thing I can say, he's a man, not a boy. Maybe he's too old for me." Katie flipped the tortilla again. "At least you noticed he's a man. He's thirty-nine and you're thirty. That's not too old for you."

"How do you know how old he is?"

"I asked him. You sure weren't gonna do it."

"Thirty-nine . . . Well, he's too young for you."

"Debatable. True love knows no age."

"I can't believe you asked him how old he is."

"I like to know things, okay?" She tossed the tortilla on the counter and spooned strips of grilled steak, shredded lettuce, sour cream, red salsa, and guacamole onto it. With pursed lips she rolled a fat, tight burrito, fingers moving with the ease of years of repetition. "He's a man and you're a woman. Perfect match. End of story. Or are you thinking of becoming a nun like my idiot nephew?"

Honey grabbed a hot pad and took a plate from the warming oven. She scooped generous portions of lettuce, rice, and refried beans onto it, sprinkling the beans with cheese then adding the burrito when Katie handed it to her. Sadness nudged at the mention of Jake, but she shook it off. That ship had long sailed. She'd even sort of gotten semi-used to seeing him on a regular basis again, priest garb and all.

"The whole Jake thing is complicated. Nuns are still women, by the way. And Jake's a priest, not a nun. Don't act like you don't love him either. You spoil the guy rotten."

Katie shrugged. "Priests, nuns, what's the difference? Same depressing black clothes and same love life—zero. Sure, I love the idiot, but that doesn't make him less of an idiot. He could have had you, right? But he let you run off to some third-world backwater and almost get married to someone else."

"He didn't let me go. He went to seminary, remember? And the doctor came later. Long after Jake."

"Same difference. Would you have left if he didn't go to seminary?"

"He did go to seminary. Doesn't matter now, it's all in the past. The point is I like being a waitress. And I like being one at Shorty's."

"You sure you don't like it here 'cause you get to see Jake practically every day? You need to move on, girl. It's pathetic."

Jake . . . Everything always came around to Jake.

"I have moved on. Jake—Father Jake—didn't leave me much choice, did he? Could we please talk about Charles Faulks the cat again?"

"No cats, we're talking about Matthias Galt."

"I'm telling you, a guy like that won't like Charles Faulks the cat."

"You're hopeless. Quit gabbing and get out there. Get busy or you're fired."

"You can't fire me now. I have Charles Faulks the cat to support."

"Watch me."

Honey rolled her eyes as she slid the plate onto her tray and headed for the dining room. "You couldn't live without me," she said over her shoulder.

"Don't bet on it."

Matthias sat on a stool at the counter working on his four-hundredth cup of coffee, give or take a few. He smiled at her again as she passed. The guy was nice to look at, Katie was right about that. Tan, sun-lined face, gray eyes, a few days' worth of stubble on his chin. His sandy-brown hair reminded her of the desert, and the badge pinned to his khaki uniform shirt gave him an official air—solid and real. The shirt tucked into Wrangler jeans . . . all in all the guy looked like he belonged on the cover of one of Katie's ridiculous romance novels. The Western kind, where the beautiful 1890s rancher's daughter with windblown movie-star hair is falling into the arms of the misunderstood outlaw with a heart of gold, his shirt half torn off and a bandage on his arm.

Yeah, he was nice to look at.

Honey slid the carne asada burrito plate in front of Charles Faulks—the man, not the cat—a skinny tow truck driver in greasy coveralls with his name stitched over the right breast pocket in blue thread.

A Paradise fixture, Charles Faulks liked to talk, especially if talking involved correcting someone. His name was one of his favorite points of contention. Don't dare call him Charlie or Chuck. Only Charles Faulks, first and last, would do.

"One carne asada burrito plate, Charles Faulks. More Coke?"

"Pepsi."

"Excuse me?"

"It's Pepsi, not Coke."

"Right, well, Coke in the generic sense."

"You can't say Coke in a generic sense. Coke is distributed by The Coca-Cola Company. It's very specific. Pepsi is distributed by Pepsi-Co. I'm struggling to see why you can't understand the difference."

"How about if I just call it soda? That work?"

"I'd rather you didn't."

"Okay . . ."

"And I'm done arguing the point. Arguing makes me nervous. You know that."

Honey gave a decisive nod knowing full well how much Charles Faulks loved to argue. "Me too. I think it's a good idea we just drop the whole thing. I'll consider it a lesson learned."

"Good. Yes, by the way."

"Yes what?"

"The answer to your question. Yes, I would like more Pepsi."

Honey smiled. "Out of Pepsi, only have Coke today."

"Was that a joke?"

Honey showed a narrow gap between her thumb and finger. "Sorry. A very tiny one."

"Oh, okay. Very nice, very funny. I like jokes."

"Me too. I'll get you that Pepsi."

"Okay . . . Yes, that was very funny." He muttered something about Pepsi under his breath as she walked away.

Once Charles Faulks was properly re-Pepsied, she headed around the counter and picked up the coffeepot to make the rounds. Shorty's jangled with conversation, laughter, and rattling silverware. Honey let her body navigate the cluttered waters of the dining room on autopilot. On the radio behind the counter, Chris Stapleton explained the difference between "Whiskey and You" in his earthy baritone. Sun poured in through the big windows facing the town square. Honey loved this place. Shorty's Restaurant and Café—a Paradise staple for more than a hundred years. Even listed as a landmark by the National Register of Historic Places. Though his moniker graced the sign out front, Shorty, whoever he'd been, languished in the dim and misty recesses of yesteryear. As far as the locals were concerned or could remember, the place had always belonged to some generation of the Morales family—Katie and her husband, Lou, for the last two decades. The vintage clock above the pie cabinet sported a rotund, hand-painted Mexican man with a sombrero and drooping mustache. His disjointed arms and hands circumnavigated the numbers pointing out the time. At the moment Mario, as he was affectionately referred to by the staff, indicated with somber gravity that Honey's shift would be over in twenty minutes. She offered him a silent gracias on behalf of her throbbing feet.

She paused in front of Matthias Galt's empty cup and raised one eyebrow in an unspoken question.

"Yes, please," he said.

"You really want more?"

"Is that a problem?"

"Maybe. Columbia called. They're running low and asked if you could cut back."

Matthias smiled then nodded toward the tow truck driver across the room. "How's old Charlie?"

"You mean Charles Faulks?" Honey said the name with her best low-whispered Charles Faulks impersonation. "I don't get it. He eats the same carne asada burrito plate at least five days a week, drinks a gallon of Pepsi—not Coke, by the way—and he's still skinny as a dry beanpole. How does that work?"

"Must be genetic. Lucky. How about tonight?"

"How about tonight what?"

"You and me. Us. We go to Spur's, have a nice meal. Talk. You know, things people do when they're dating. Plan our life. Start our future."

Honey filled his cup. "So we're dating now?"

"I figure we spend enough time together. Might as well make it official."

"By time together you mean you sitting here drinking coffee while I run burritos over to Charles Faulks?"

Matthias blew on his coffee then sipped. "I guess that's one way to look at it."

"That's the only way to look at it. Do you ever give up?"

He scratched the back of his head and grinned. "Not to my recent recollection."

She looked him in the eye but didn't smile. "Can I ask you a question? Why do you wear Wranglers if you're from New York?"

"I like to fit in with the locals. What can I say?"

"Honestly, did you always secretly dream of being a cowboy or something? Read Zane Grey under your covers with a flashlight at night in your Manhattan apartment?"

"I'm from the Bronx. And no way, I hate big animals. Horses, cows, elephants, doesn't matter. Cowboys got a screw loose."

"I wouldn't say that too loud in here."

Matthias glanced around. "You're probably right about that. So what do you say? Come out to dinner with me."

"Do you like cats?"

"Absolutely not. I hate cats."

"I knew it. Not even kittens?"

"Maybe kittens, if they're other people's kittens. Tonight?"

She paused. "I'll think about it."

His face broke into a Dentyne commercial. "Really? What time should I pick you up?"

"I didn't say yes. I said I'd think about it."

"But that's good, right? It's more than you ever said before."

"Don't push it." She moved down the counter, turning her back to him.

"Yes, ma'am," he said.

The bell over the front door jangled.

And Jake walked in . . .

Jake with Early Pines on his heels, a sight familiar to Honey since grade school. Jake's gaze swept the room then landed on her, holding warmth and distance at the same time. For a second she thought he'd come over to her, but instead they headed for the counter and took stools next to Matthias.

Matthias said something to Early and Early shook his head.

Jake . . . More than a year now since she had come back from Honduras—more than five since they dated—and the guy still stirred something inside her.

She'd been around priests her whole life and for some reason never really thought of them as actual men. More like another species altogether, somber, mysterious aliens. But Jake was, well . . . *Jake.* Robe and collar, sure, but Jake. Tall. His dark hair curling at the ends. Those wide-set eyes, a blend of serious and kind.

Had it really been that many years since they'd been together? She'd traveled, met another man, even come close to getting married. But when she saw Jake, it all seemed like yesterday. She'd been approached by plenty of men since her return—with waitressing, it went with the territory—and she'd been tempted to say yes a time or two. But in the end . . . *Ugh—in the end nobody's Jake.*

Jake, quiet and serious. How those dark eyes of his looked right into you. How such hard hands could be so gentle. How sometimes he'd break his stoic shell and say something funny when you least expected it. And best of all, always knowing he was a man who would have your back, no matter what came, no matter how hard life bucked. *What happened, Jake?*

Early grinned as she approached. "Hey, Honey, want to marry me and have nine kids since Jake's a priest now?"

Same old Early, smile so contagious Honey couldn't help returning it. "You've been asking me that since I was in second grade. Come to think of it, you asked me when you were here an hour ago. The answer's still the same—a very solid maybe. How about some coffee instead?"

"Just remember, I was asking back when the pope here didn't even know you were alive." He held his arms out wide. "Look what you missed, lady. I'm pretty. Some lucky woman is gonna snatch me up any minute. You better come to your senses before it's too late."

"Uh-huh. You want coffee or not?"

"Always."

Honey reached under the counter and pulled out a couple of ceramic mugs. She slid one in front of Early and poured. "If you tell me to stir it with my finger to make it sweeter, I swear I'll punch you in the neck."

"You already said it for me," Early said.

"How about you, Jake? You want coffee?"

Jake nodded. "I could use some. How're you doing, Honey?"

Honey tried to read his face but couldn't. She poured for him, shaking her head. "Great. Everything's perfect. All good."

"How's your grandma?"

She put on her neutral, talking-to-Jake face. "Still good. You ask me that every time you come in. You need some new material, buddy."

The corner of his mouth rose a fraction. "I'll work on it."

Maybe it was the way he said her name. Maybe the fresh fingerprints of her kitchen conversation with Katie. Or some star she'd never heard of aligned with some other star as it slid through the cosmic shadows . . . Or maybe it was just the new lines she saw around his eyes. The man who wore his duty, honor, and commitment like a lead X-ray apron and always would. He was Jake. No, Father Jake, like it or not. And Katie was right—Honey needed to let go.

And Matthias wasn't a bad guy . . .

In fact, he was a pretty good guy. He was nice . . . solid. And all that coffee he'd poured down himself just to be near her . . . *At least give the guy a chance. One date never hurt anybody, right?*

Matthias's coffee cup still sat three-quarters full. Honey put her pot down next to it with a thump. "Let me ask you something. What kind of person doesn't like cats?"

"What?" Matthias said.

"Cats. Did I stutter?"

"No."

"Do you have a hearing problem?"

"Not as of my last physical."

"Then answer the question."

He scratched his chin. "Lots of kinds?"

"Do you like old people?"

"They're passable, unless they have cats."

"Okay then. Seven o'clock," she said.

All three of the men looked at her.

"What?" Matthias said.

"For our date. Pick me up at seven. How hard is that to understand? Don't you solve crimes for a living? Lord, help this town." She turned and headed for the kitchen.

CHAPTER FIVE

JAKE WATCHED THE KITCHEN DOOR swing back and forth a couple times then settle. He had to smile. *Same old Honey.*

"So that was strange," Matthias said.

"Nope, that was classic Honey. Wasn't it, Father Jake?"

Jake kept his face neutral. "Don't call me father."

"I thought I was supposed to. You said it was respectful."

"Not the way you say it."

"Nah, man. I'm the wind beneath your robes, amigo. Anyway, I'm a Baptist. I don't know how to behave around you Catholics. You gotta cut me some slack."

"Baptist . . . Give me a break."

Early shrugged. "I hear they have a good softball team. Spank you Catholics every time."

"What's with you guys?" Matthias said.

"He's just mad because we get to wear pants," Early said. "So, you're gonna go out with Honey?"

"Looks like it. About time too. I've had so much coffee the last few weeks I can hardly look at the stuff anymore."

Early blew across his own cup and took a sip. "How 'bout that, Father Jake? Matthias is going out with Honey."

"Let me ask you something, Early. What would you do if she ever said yes to one of your proposals?" Jake said.

"I'd marry her in a hot second, man. I'm not stupid and I'm not wearing a dress."

"I'm the one with the date, don't forget," Matthias said.

"The man has a point," Early said.

Matthias looked Early up and down. "What's with the hat? Is there ever going to be any way to get you to wear an actual uniform?"

"Probably not. But check it out, boss, I do have my badge on."

"I'm deeply impressed. When did you last shave? I can't tell if you're a detective or a Hells Angel," Matthias said.

"Can't find my razor."

"Since when, last spring?"

"And I have my gun. Don't forget that," Early said.

Matthias glanced down at Early's pearl-handled Colt .45 in its worn leather holster. "The weird cowboy gun. You know a department issue Glock 23 holds thirteen rounds, right?"

Early sipped. "Why would I need thirteen? I hit what I aim at."

"You hit what you aim at . . . Remind me to give you a raise."

"I don't remind you enough already?"

"True, forget I said anything."

Early leaned forward on the counter, arms framing his mug. "Besides, it's my day off. I'm only working because you asked me to go talk to Gomez Gomez."

"Uh-huh, and tomorrow when it's your day on it'll be different? Nice clean uniform? A shave?"

Early stood and stretched. "My cue to hit the head. Keep my stool warm, boys."

Early rounded the end of the counter and had to duck when he reached the hallway leading to the restrooms.

Matthias turned. "You know that buddy of yours drives me nuts?"

Jake sipped his coffee. "It's his special gift. Born with it, I think. I notice you keep him around."

"How long did it take you to get used to him?"

"I've known him all my life. When it happens I'll let you know."

"Yeah, I keep him around. Unfortunately, in addition to being annoying, he's also the best detective I have. Not that I have many—only him actually. But he's good. Big mouth and all, he always gets the job done."

"Just don't ask him how he did it, right?"

Matthias lifted his cup. "I'll drink to that. One thing I've learned out here in the Wild West, when it comes to Early Pines, ignorance is bliss."

Jake lifted his own cup. "Amen."

"So this is probably a dumb question. About Honey—I know you two have history. But, I mean, you're a priest, right? I'm not stepping on any toes here? I kind of get a vibe."

"A vibe?"

"Yeah. When you come in here there's a definite vibe with her."

"Honey and I were a long time ago. Another life."

"I can appreciate that. So we're good?"

"About what?"

"Honey . . . and me . . . The date."

"We're good."

Early returned and slid onto his stool. "You miss me, boss?"

"It's pure suffering to be apart. Did you wash your hands?"

Katie banged out of the kitchen, hair askew, plump body poured into her yellow waitress uniform. "Hey, the Lone Ranger and Tonto. You boys want to eat?"

"Absolutely, Aunt Katie, I'm starving," Jake said.

Early raised an eyebrow. "Which is which? Who's the Ranger and who's Tonto?"

Katie shrugged. "You got the pearl-handled *pistola*. You be the Lone Ranger and let my nephew be Mexican Tonto, I don't care."

Early grinned his crooked grin. "Nah, Tonto was cooler. Plus it'd be a crime to hide this face behind a mask."

"Good call. Tonto was better looking," Katie said. "Jay Silverheels. I had a huge crush on him."

"Who's Jay Silverheels?" Matthias said.

42

"The actor who played Tonto," Katie said.

"I thought that was Johnny Depp," Matthias said.

Katie shook her head. "That's the remake. I mean the real one. The black-and-white. But Johnny Depp is pretty good-looking too, for a pirate. So what're you heroes of the Wild West eating?"

"Whatever's easy. Just me, I guess," Jake said.

"Hold your big white horse there, kimosabe. Maybe I'm hungry too," Early said.

"Didn't you just eat? Here?" Jake said.

"So what? I'm a growing Indian."

Katie tapped her pen on the counter in front of Early. "What'chu gonna have then, Mr. Depp?"

"Two adobada tortas, beans, rice, and a Coke. On Jake's tab."

"My tab?" Jake said.

"You're a man of the cloth, dude, don't be stingy."

"You want chips and salsa?" Katie said.

"Load me up, sister."

Katie reached over and patted Early on the head. "Know what? You're not such a bad-looking Tonto yourself."

"That's what I'm always telling everybody," Early said. "I might want that on my tombstone."

"And you're old enough to be his mother," Jake said.

"Relax, padre, I know his mother, remember? I'm older," Katie said.

Early winked at Katie. "Stay out of it, kimosabe. Maybe I like older women."

Katie laughed and headed for the kitchen. Turning around, she pushed open the swinging door with her ample behind. "Don't get ahead of yourself, Tonto. Maybe you got muscles but you ain't no Jay Silverheels."

"You're really going to eat two tortas after you just ate an hour ago?" Matthias said.

"They're small," Early said.

"They're not small," Jake said.

Early shrugged.

"When are you going to talk to Gomez Gomez?" Matthias said.

"After we eat. Jake's going with me."

"So Early told you about our little relocation issue?"

"Uh-huh. He told me Sonny Harmon wants to spread his wings."

"And the unwritten law of Paradise, Arizona, clearly states, what Sonny wants Sonny gets. The council says Gomez Gomez is out. As in yesterday."

"Where do they expect him to go? They have any suggestions about that?" Jake said.

"I don't think Sonny cares. In fact I know he doesn't. And officially there's a law against vagrancy so out he goes." Matthias glanced at Early. "Nothing anybody can do."

"He's been there five years, man. Nobody ever said anything about a vagrancy law all that time," Early said.

"Well, Sonny's bringing it up now," Matthias said.

"Sonny's a piece of work. One of these days somebody needs to tell him the word no," Early said.

Matthias shrugged. "Not anybody who wants to keep their job. Gomez Gomez is a vagrant. Sonny wants what he wants and *gets* what he wants."

"I wouldn't really call him a vagrant," Jake said.

"He's homeless. What else do you call that?" Matthias said.

Early shook his head. "He's got a shack down there. That kind of counts as a home."

"But it's not his land. He's squatting," Matthias said.

"It's everybody's land. And nobody ever cared about it before. People around here loved Angel. They feel sorry for him—take him food, clothes, everything he needs. He's part of the community."

"You know about Angel, right?" Jake said to Matthias.

"His wife? A little. Just that she was killed in a head-on and Gomez Gomez went off the deep end over it."

Jake caught Early's reflection watching him in the mirror behind the pie cabinet.

"It was a bad day for the town. For all of us," Jake said.

Somewhere across the room, a man mumbled something and a woman laughed. Silverware rattled. A couple of ranchers argued about the weather. *Angel . . .* Everywhere, life went on. *But not for you, Angel.* Jake's hand shook, making tiny ripples in his coffee. He set the cup down and flattened his hands on the counter.

"Gomez Gomez was born off the deep end, man. Angel dying just moved it along," Early said.

Jake tried the coffee cup again. Still rippling. He set it down. "We used to travel together. On the rodeo circuit. Me, Early, and Gomez Gomez. We were close back then, like brothers. He met Angel on one of those trips."

"*Were* close? You're not now?" Matthias said.

"Early still sees him." Jake ran his fingers through his hair. Took a breath—centered. "Maybe you already know, but I was in the accident that killed Angel. And yes, we hit head-on. Gomez Gomez never forgave me. Whenever I've tried to talk to him since, he shuts me out completely."

Matthias looked thoughtful. "You were in the accident? I hadn't heard that."

"I woke up in the hospital. That's when they told me about Angel."

"Ouch. That's a rough one. Look, I understand why you feel bad for him. I feel bad for him and I've never even met the guy. Problem is, accident or not, the council didn't leave any gray area about getting him out. He plain old has to go."

"He's got to have rights," Early said.

Matthias shrugged. "Sonny Harmon owns the land now, and the council dances to his tune. That includes the mayor. It's not personal. It's politics. We do our job."

"Our job . . . I never liked Sonny Harmon," Early said.

"Early's right," Jake said. "Maybe Gomez Gomez is an inconvenience to Sonny, but he's still a person, a human being, just like anyone else. The council should know that."

"I think Sonny is an inconvenience," Early said.

"Yeah, but he's a rich, influential inconvenience," Matthias said.

"The worst kind," Jake said.

On the radio behind the counter, Guy Clark jumped off the garage with his flour-sack cape. The café breathed.

Matthias sipped and made a face. "I seriously don't know if I'll ever be able to look another cup of coffee in the eye again." He put the cup down and slid it away. "Why do they call him Gomez Gomez, anyway? Why not just Gomez?"

"It's just who he is," Early said. "First time I heard it was in sixth grade when we got in a fight over a bag of Fritos. They had us waiting for the principal after, and I said, 'What's your name, anyway?' He said, 'Gomez Gomez' and punched me in the eye. Right from his chair, man. Dude never was big but he was always scrappy."

Matthias waited. When Early didn't offer anything further he said, "So? What did you do?"

"I punched him back, what do you think I did?"

"What's any of that have to do with why his name is Gomez twice?"

Early shrugged. "Gomez Gomez is different, man. His mom was too. She used to make yard art out of old doll heads and tires and stuff. Lady was freaky Friday. I never met his dad 'cause he went back to Mexico when Gomez Gomez was a kid, but his mom always said he was named after a bad bull out of Patagonia, down on the border near Tucson. A *really* bad bull, big deal on the circuit back in the sixties."

"They named their kid after a bad bull? You cowboys are out there, you know that?"

Katie banged through the door with a tray of plates and a couple of baskets of tortilla chips. She slid the lot in front of Jake and Early. "Tortas for Tonto and carnitas for *el* Lone Ranger." She poured salsa out of a red plastic pitcher into a small bowl and set it down by Early's chips. "Mild, right?"

"That's right, gorgeous."

"Mild?" Matthias said.

"I have a sensitive palate," Early said.

"There's nothing sensitive about you," Jake said.

"Amen to that," Matthias said.

Katie placed the other bowl in front of Jake. "And *caliente* for the nephew."

"Thanks, Aunt Katie."

Early picked up one of the tortas and doused it in salsa. He took a huge bite and a stream of meat juice dripped down his wrist. Early set down the torta and wiped his hand and beard with a napkin.

"I still can't get used to the way you eat," Matthias said.

"How do I eat?" Early picked up the sandwich and took another bite. Same results.

"Like a caveman waking up from a coma."

Early gave a closed-mouth shrug, still chewing.

Matthias looked at Jake. "Why do you want to get involved in this Gomez Gomez thing when the guy doesn't want anything to do with you?"

Jake swallowed a bite of carnitas and thought. "I guess it's just the right thing to do. I don't know if he'll talk to me, or listen, but I've known him a long time. He's still my friend."

"All right. It doesn't matter to me as long as you two get him gone."

"The thing to keep in mind is, Gomez Gomez is fragile. He needs decompression," Early said.

"Decom-what?" Matthias said.

"Decompression. Like those deep-sea divers on the Discovery Channel. Go down real deep for a long time and you have to come up slow. You have to stop and wait once in a while or you get an air embolism and die. Gomez Gomez's been on the bottom five years, man. He needs to come up slow for sure. Real slow."

"An air embolism?" Jake said.

"Cable TV. Pretty smart for a Baptist, huh?" Early said.

Honey stopped in front of them. She took out her pad and scribbled, tore the page and dropped it in front of Matthias. "My address. See you at seven. Now switch to herbal tea for a while. Or at least decaf." She moved on before he could answer.

Matthias stood, fishing for his billfold. "So I guess I'm an herbal tea man now. Okay, Early, I asked you to take care of this Gomez deal because you know the guy. Take Father Jake and go talk to him. Maybe I can stall Sonny Harmon for a day or two, maybe not. But Gomez Gomez needs to move. No decom-whatever. Sonny's not gonna wait long, if he waits at all." He laid a couple of bills on the counter. "And put on a uniform shirt, would you?"

Mouth full, Early nodded and gave a thumbs-up. Matthias headed for the door.

Early swallowed. "How're the carnitas?"

"Always good," Jake said. "You gonna put on a uniform shirt?"

"Absolutely not. Polyester. Those things itch. You ready to go talk to snakes?"

Jake sighed, wiped his mouth, and tossed the napkin on his empty plate. "All right, let's get it over with."

CHAPTER SIX

GOMEZ GOMEZ'S CAMPFIRE SMOLDERED. MOSTLY coals now. Wood gone, almost out. From the other side of the pit, Bones eyed him through opaque wisps of smoke. Two days and no rocks raining down from the road. The kid'd actually pulled it off somehow.

Gomez Gomez drew in a slow breath through his nose. Sage and pine in the late afternoon air, thin, clean, and turpentine sharp. Last night had been cold. Not chilly. Not crisp. Plain old cold. And judging by the hard-cut shadows cast by the rocks and trees around his camp, tonight would be more of the same.

"How'd you get those kids to stop throwing rocks?" Gomez Gomez said.

Bones scratched his armpit. "How long you lived here?"

"I don't know. Years, I think. Three, four, five . . . a hundred maybe? However long it's been since Angel left."

"Why do you say she left? Why don't you just say died?"

"Angels don't die, kid. Don't you know anything?"

"More than you, maybe."

"Yeah, maybe. But Angel left. She flew on."

"Left as in she's still alive? Like life after death and all that crap? Like the *alive in your heart* junk they spew at you when your grandma dies or something?"

"It's not crap. A person like Angel is too big to die. Angel found

49

Jesus, man. She knew. She prayed, talked about heaven a lot. That's where she is for sure."

"How do you know for sure? You ever see her now? Talk to her? Like to her ghost or something?"

"Nah. I want to but I don't think that's the way it works. I dream about her sometimes but she never talks. I just mostly talk to the snakes. And you, right now."

Bones poked at the coals with a stick. "Then how do you know? Do you pray too? You believe in that stuff?"

"Angel knew. She showed me. I believe it for sure."

"Then why are you like you are?"

"Like what? What am I like?"

"Living down here in a shack. A drunk and all that."

Gomez Gomez thought. "I guess I'm what you'd call an imperfect believer."

"So you and Angel got religion. What if you're wrong? What if when you die, you just die? Like a piece of meat? What if nothing comes after?"

"Is that what you think?"

Bones shrugged. "Maybe. Yeah. I'm probably an atheist."

"Probably? You're not sure?"

"Nah, I guess I'm sure. That's what they say in school. And I don't see no God out there in the universe. Just a bunch of nothin' other than the stars and planets and crap."

"Have you *been* everywhere in the universe?"

Bones looked up at the sky. "No. Nobody has."

"Not those school people either?"

"Nobody has, man. You know that."

"Then I guess there ain't nobody well traveled enough to be an atheist. Best you can say is you don't know. But I know Angel's in heaven."

"That's actually kind of true. I ain't been everywhere."

"So now you at least know you don't know."

"Whatever. You're still crazy, man. You talk to snakes."

"Yeah, probably I am."

Bones sniffled and wiped his nose with the back of his hand. "I like talking to you though. Hey, you want me to bring you some money? For whiskey or beer or whatever it is you drink?"

"You can get money?" Gomez Gomez said.

"Any time I want. I can get lots of stuff."

"You steal it?"

"You care?"

Gomez Gomez thought about Angel up in heaven. "I think I care a little bit."

"Nah, man. I don't steal nothing. You know you're a real straight arrow for a drunk guy?"

"I guess. Yeah, I could use some dough. You ever gonna answer my question? About how you got them kids to quit throwing them rocks?"

"Maybe I'll bring some food too. What do you like to eat?"

"How about fillet mignon? Not too rare. Roast duck, apple pie . . . waffles? That cool?"

Bones laughed. "You're weird, man. I'll find you something. What are you gonna do about Sonny Harmon?"

Gomez Gomez shook his head. "You're kind of like talking to a radio, you know that? It's a little one-sided."

Bones shrugged and wiped his nose again.

"You sick or what?" Gomez Gomez said.

"Nah, I'm cool."

Gomez Gomez eyed the kid's thin shirt. "Don't you have a coat?"

"I'm cool."

"You say that a lot. Don't your mom and dad care you're out running around all the time?"

Bones's stick caught fire. He blew it out and watched the smoke curl up. "Nah, they're cool too."

"Where do you live anyway?"

"Why do you care? I said I'd get you some money. What else do you want?"

"I'm just curious. What does it matter if I know where you live?"

"On a street. In a neighborhood."

"What neighborhood."

"Man . . . Okay, I live in the trailer park out off Rural Route Five. My dad fixes cars. My mom's a housewife and makes the best chocolate chip cookies in the world. Both of them tuck me in at night. Sing me songs while I fall asleep. You happy now?"

"You lying?"

"All right, so they don't sing me songs."

"The rest of it?"

"They're cool. I told you."

"You gonna bring some of those cookies?"

"Sure."

"Seems to me like parents like that would want you to wear a coat."

"Fine, I'll wear a coat and bring cookies, okay?"

"Okay. For now I'll just get the fire going better."

"Don't worry about it. I got to go anyway." Bones dropped his stick next to the firepit and stood. His head disappeared into the bright autumn sun. Gomez Gomez squinted up at the head silhouette and shielded his eyes with his hand. Sunlight radiated through the kid's ears and Gomez Gomez could make out tiny veins running through them.

"Your head reaches all the way to the sun, man," Gomez Gomez said.

"Yeah?"

"Yeah, right into space. Right to the sun. What a trip. Bones the spaceman. Where you going, Bones the Spaceman? You looking for God up there?"

"You're freaky, dude. It's cool. Probably nowhere. Just around. I'll get you that money."

"And cookies."

"Best in the world."

"Why you gonna get me money? What did I ever do for you?"

"Because that's what friends do—help each other out."

"That what we are? Friends?"

"Yeah. I don't have no others. You're it, man. The crazy drunk guy. Pretty pathetic, huh? You got any friends?"

"Not really. I don't do friends real good. Early, guy I used to rodeo with, he might be my friend still. And sometimes people bring me stuff—but they're just remembering Angel so that doesn't count. Other than that it's just the snakes. But not the rattler—he ain't nobody's friend. Bones the Spaceman."

"So we friends then?"

"We'll see, Spaceman. Don't get your hopes up. I'm an imperfect believer, remember?"

"I'll still get you some money."

"Cool."

"Spaceman. That's cool. Anyway, I'm gonna go."

"Ground control to Major Tom . . ."

"Who's Major Tom?"

"Before your time, kid. Don't get burned up there in the sun." The words rolled through the air before getting caught in the updraft of heat from the waning coals and sailing upward. Gomez Gomez started to point them out, but the kid was gone.

He looked around for something burnable to throw on the fire to start it going again. He found a bottle with a little Thunderbird in the bottom instead, emptied it in a swallow, and felt the familiar downward burn.

Bones . . . Spaceman. The kid was a serious trip. But friends? How could anyone be his friend?

He tossed the empty bottle onto the embers. The label bubbled and curled in the heat like a thousand others before it.

Up the hill footsteps crunched, coming this way. Maybe the Spaceman forgot his moon rover. Major Tom back from looking for God on the sun.

Not the Spaceman, though. A cowboy hat floated above the sage. Then a man under it. Loose black robe. Stinking Jake. Early behind him.

"What are you doing here, Jake? How many times I tell you to stay away from me and Angel?"

"Knock it off, man. Jake's here to help. He's your friend," Early said.

"I don't need no help from him. He's done enough helping. And he ain't my friend."

"We only want to talk to you. It won't take long. Then I'll go," Jake said.

Gomez Gomez stared into his firepit. "You guys slumming or what?" Jake squatted across from Gomez Gomez and poked at the coals with Bones's discarded stick. Early sat on the snake log, rays of sun like mini machine-gun bullets dancing off his badge.

"You want a drink, Early?" Gomez Gomez said.

"C'mon, man. You know I don't do that anymore. Three years sober now."

"Oh yeah, AA. Hello, my name is Early . . . Hi, Early . . . What a load of crap."

"You're a real upper, buddy," Early said. "Maybe we should let the snakes eat you."

Gomez Gomez indicated Jake with a dirty finger. "How 'bout you, killer? You want a snort?"

"No, thanks."

"Well, I do. 'Cept I'm clean out. Some kid is gonna bring me money for more. So that's cool."

"What kid?" Early said.

Gomez Gomez ran a hand through his long, stringy hair. "Just a kid. A spaceman kid. What're you doing here anyway, Jake? I told you to stay away about a thousand times at least. I thought we had an understanding. Thought we were clear."

"We haven't been clear in five years. And I've told you I'm sorry a thousand times."

"She's been gone five years, man," Early said. "Time to get yourself together, amigo. I'm sick of telling you. We both want to help."

"So this is an intervention? Six, seven, *eighty* years it'll still be the same. She'll still be gone. And a thousand million I'm sorrys from Jake ain't gonna bring her back."

"Neither is living out here talking to the snakes like an hombre loco," Early said.

Gomez Gomez's stomach lurched. He badly needed more booze.

"You here official, Early? You here about stupid Sonny Harmon?"

"You heard about Sonny?" Early said.

"Yeah. He sent me a love letter."

"We're here because we care about what happens to you," Jake said.

"Care all you want. I'm not leaving. I ain't going nowhere."

"We know you don't want to leave, but Sonny or no Sonny, it's really for the best for you," Jake said.

"You killed her."

"I know. And as much as I'd like to, I can't bring her back. How've you been, Gomez Gomez? Besides mad at me?"

Stupid Jake. How had he been? Angry. Lonesome. Depressed. Drunk. Wishing he was drunk. Maybe crazy like Early and Bones said . . . "I'll tell you how I've been. I've been Angel-less. You have any idea what it's like to be Angel-less?"

"I know you have," Jake said. "And I'm still sorry. More than you can imagine. That's one thousand and one, and I'll keep going."

A dove cooed somewhere up the ravine, answered by another. Peaceful, beautiful. Sad. Gomez Gomez drew in a thick, difficult breath. "You believe in God, Early?"

"I think so. The fact the three of us are still alive after all our craziness tends to point in that direction."

"You got a point about that," Gomez Gomez said.

"How about you, Gomez Gomez? You believe?" Jake said.

Gomez Gomez looked him in the eye. "I really hate you, Jake."

"I know you do."

"Give me a break," Early said. "It wasn't Jake's fault. Everyone knows Angel drove too fast. She always did. Her car swerved and Jake was lucky to get out alive. And you've been down here getting wasted for five years while he's been beating himself up every day. I'm sick of it. You're both my friends. It's time for this insanity to stop. Sometimes things just happen, man. We got to deal with it and move on."

Early's words caught the draft and chased the Thunderbird label ashes. Insects buzzed in the tree branches.

"That right, Jake? You feel lucky?" Gomez Gomez said.

"No, I don't feel lucky."

Gomez Gomez stared at the smoldering coals. "Move on . . . I'm not mad at you for saying that, Early. It's actually good to hear her name. Nobody ever says her name anymore."

Early's words lost some edge. "We all miss her, man. But c'mon, enough is enough. This really is out of control. Look at yourself."

Jake didn't say anything at all.

In the old days, that had been the thing Gomez Gomez liked most about Jake. A person didn't have to talk much around him. He was quiet. Not like the snakes. Maybe that made him a good priest. That and the guilt he carried around like a suitcase full of rocks. *Good.*

Jake scraped up some twigs and leaves. The coals smoked, then a lick of flame appeared. He stood. "Being mad at me won't bring her back. I'll tell you this, if I could trade places with her, I would. In a heartbeat."

Gomez Gomez looked down at his clenched fists. Grief and bile rose in the back of his throat. The words almost choked him. "If you could trade places with her, I'd let you in a heartbeat."

"I'll find some wood." Jake moved off into the brush.

"I'll help. Gonna be cold tonight," Early said.

Good, Gomez Gomez thought. It would give him time to gather his thoughts. The men reappeared a few minutes later, both of their arms full. Gomez Gomez made a thorough check and found his thoughts still decidedly ungathered.

"This should last the night," Early said.

"The thing is, Gomez Gomez, Sonny or no Sonny, it's time to come out," Jake said.

"Thanks for the wood," Gomez Gomez said.

"You're welcome," Jake said.

"I kinda wish I had a dog," Gomez Gomez said.

Jake added a couple of small branches and stoked the fire. "A dog?"

"I don't know where I'd get one though."

"What's it like in your brain, man? That's gotta be a dark and scary place in there," Early said.

Gomez Gomez felt a strange, momentary gratitude for the realignment of the conversation. "Yeah, a dog maybe. I don't know . . ."

"We all miss Angel," Jake said.

Gomez Gomez crushed his eyeballs with the dirty, calloused heels of his hands. He looked around for a bottle, his mouth dry and acidic. Pure reflex. Human animals—the lack of something never stopped eyes from searching and hands from reaching.

"You killed her," Gomez Gomez said. "You took her. I might get a dog . . ."

"I miss Angel and think about her all the time," Jake said.

Angel. Gomez Gomez grabbed her name from the air before the heat took it up, holding it tight in his fist. Just in time—already warm to the touch. "Why does everyone talk around her, never about her? It's all just words, man. Static, you know? Everything is so noisy."

"I do know," Jake said.

Gomez Gomez found Jake's eyes. "Why is that? Why do they gush a bunch of meaningless noise and then act like everything's cool when everything's not cool? Everything's dead. Dry. Used up. Dead and over. Completely over."

"I'm sorry," Jake said.

"One thousand and two," Gomez Gomez said.

"And I'll keep them coming."

Gomez Gomez opened his mouth but his words stuck in his chest. Air was too thick. Stinking doves.

Jake added a bigger chunk of wood to the fire. Low flames licked the air. "Nothing's over. We can talk about Angel all you want."

"You only say that because you're a priest. It's your job."

"I was your friend a long time before I was a priest."

"And because you feel guilty."

"Maybe. But I'm still your friend. It's good to talk about her."

Gomez Gomez gasped a deep, much-needed breath. He tried to muster anger, his trusted bodyguard, but only sad reported for duty. "We had some times, didn't we? The three of us?"

"Yeah, man, good times," Early said.

Gomez Gomez pointed to the log Early sat on. "You know that's where the snakes sit?"

Early looked around him. "You got to knock it off, man. Snakes are bad juju."

"I tell 'em that too. All the time. Don't bother you, though, huh, Jake?"

"I don't buy into bad medicine."

"Us Baptists do," Early said.

"You a Baptist now?" Gomez Gomez said.

"Don't listen to him," Jake said.

"Maybe priests are worse medicine than snakes, huh, Jake?" Gomez Gomez said.

"Could be," Jake said.

Gomez Gomez tried to spit into the fire but his mouth was too dry. "Hey, Early, 'member that time in Yuma? When we were on the road?"

"I remember the place was crazy hot, that's about it."

"But the beer was cold, remember?"

"Yeah, I remember that too."

Gomez Gomez scratched at his beard. "They had that steer in that tent. World's biggest steer, right? Big as a house, man. Crazy big."

"And the fat lady," Jake said.

"Oh, yeah. Not as big as the steer, but close," Gomez Gomez said.

Early stood and moved to the fire. "I remember Jake won big that weekend."

"Big surprise. Jake always won big. Yuma's where you punched that horse, remember?"

"The one that bit me," Early said. "That sucker had it coming."

"That mouthy redneck was riding him. Big old roan horse. Sixteen, seventeen hands at least. Caballo took a chunk out of your shoulder."

"Still got the scar," Early said.

"And that redneck started laughing." Gomez Gomez poked the fire. A nice blaze burned now, updraft catching words and zipping them toward the sky.

"I feared for the man's life. I thought Early would drag him off and stomp him to death," Jake said.

Gomez Gomez laughed. "Yeah, but he punched that roan instead. Right between the eyes. Lights out, man! Never seen anything like it. Redneck rolled off, yanked his leg free, and ran like a jackrabbit with his butt on fire. Spurs all jangly and chaps all flappy. Then later you iced that roan's head like it was a sick kid with a fever. Remember? Big old horse stood there like a scolded puppy."

Early grunted a laugh and watched the fire. "I still feel kind of bad about hitting that horse. Lost my temper."

"You're one big, mean hombre," Gomez Gomez said.

"Nah, man, I'm a lover. Peace-loving Baptist. Just don't bite me."

Jake pushed in another stick then looked at Gomez Gomez. Jake had a way of looking right through a guy. Made you feel bare.

Jake's eyes returned to the fire, releasing him.

Smoke wafted toward Early and he shuffled over a few feet.

The dove cooed again—definitely leaning more sad than peaceful.

Finally Gomez Gomez said, "We met Angel on that trip, remember?"

"I remember," Jake said, his tone indicating he'd expected this turn.

Gomez Gomez kept to the trail. "On I-8. At the Space Age Lodge. Gila Bend. She asked us for a ride to Phoenix."

Early stared at the fire.

"I never saw a girl like that before." The memory drifted like a life ring. Gomez Gomez grabbed and clung, a drowning man in bad water. "I mean, she wasn't no model or nothin'. At least most people wouldn't think. But she was beautiful, man. Something about her, right?"

Jake looked at him again but kept his eyes gentle. Not all X-ray vision–Superman. "Yup, something about her."

"She was good luck too. I took first in Phoenix. I swear that bull wanted to apologize and buy me a Corona after. I coulda led that dude home on a leash. Early bulldogged pretty good too. Second or third, I think."

"Second. Bloody shoulder and all," Early said.

"There wasn't much luck for me that weekend. I got piled on my head. Busted some ribs," Jake said.

"Something about her . . ." Gomez Gomez said. "I never could

59

figure it. Jake all Gregory Peck super cowboy, and big tough guy Early always making the ladies laugh. But Angel picked me. Never even looked at you guys twice, man. Just me."

"You're hard on yourself," Jake said.

"Nah, I'm realistic. I was nothin' but a skinny, little, broken bull rider. Maybe she wasn't no model but she *sure* coulda done better than me. But she didn't. That woman made me ten feet tall."

"I remember for sure. Like you were made for each other," Early said.

Gomez Gomez stuck the toe of his boot toward the fire. Flame licked around it. He pulled it back. "Got married right there in Phoenix. Only knew each other a week."

"Yup," Jake said.

"Remember that preacher? Dressed like Elvis? Sure you guys don't want a drink?"

"Three years," Early said.

Jake said nothing.

"She wore a red dress. Crazy Angel wore a red dress on her wedding day."

"She was beautiful," Jake said.

"Oh well, I don't have no liquor, anyway. Dry county around here today, yeah? You remember that Elvis preacher?"

"Early was best man," Jake said.

"Angel *loved* Elvis. Knew all his songs. She'd curl up her lip, shake her hips—really belt it out. Just a little thing too, with all that crazy blonde hair. She was pretty, right?"

"She was," Jake said.

"But no model, I guess," Gomez Gomez said.

"She was beautiful." Jake didn't look up.

A tear rolled down Gomez Gomez's face and into his beard. It itched as it caught but he didn't scratch, thankful Jake and Early kept their eyes on the fire.

The fire wheezed, crackled, and spit a shower of sparks. An ember landed on Gomez Gomez's hand. He stared at it but didn't brush it off. It burned and he focused on the pain. Pain equaled gravity. Pain and gravity, the only things keeping him earthbound. Keeping him from spinning right off the planet with the words out toward Bones's sun-head. He watched the ember till it turned gray, then he stood and with slow deliberation moved into the shack and picked up the Folgers can. He didn't have to search for it. On the shrine like always. It was the *one* thing—the solid thing. He always knew where it was. The can was center. Gomez Gomez, Jake, Early, whoever—all the rest of humanity—were nothing but inconsequential planets, satellites, and bits of broken space junk floating around Angel in meaningless circles.

Gomez Gomez set the can on the flat rock. "Angel."

"I know," Jake said.

"I just like to say her name."

"I know," Jake said again.

Gomez Gomez ran a hand over his beard. Angel had never liked him unshaven. "The thing is, she liked Yuban, not Folgers. Elvis and Yuban. I'm so stupid, man. Couldn't even do her ashes right. A Folgers can? Stupid."

"Not stupid, amigo. You loved her well," Jake said.

Anger. Sadness. Bones. Doves . . . *Angel.*

"You killed her," Gomez Gomez said.

"I know," Jake said.

Gomez Gomez shook his head. "I didn't love her well. I loved her wrong. She loved me right. See, she knew how to die. Even before she died, she knew how. I wish I had something to drink, man. All this not drinking really messes with my head."

Jake's eyes pinned him. "It's time to come out, Gomez Gomez. You can't stay here. Would you come out? Come home? We'll help you. Let me make it up to you. Let me make it up to Angel."

"Eye for an eye, man. You can't make nothing up." Gomez Gomez picked up the Folgers can and held it to his chest. Panic rose. "Angel left from here. I'm not leaving Angel. Early, you tell Sonny where he can shove his car lot."

"It's not about Sonny. It's about you," Jake said.

"Just tell them all to stay away from me. You owe me that."

"He don't owe you anything," Early said. "He's trying to help you. That's all he's ever done."

"He owes me everything," Gomez Gomez said.

"Look, man. You're my friend, but I got a job to do," Early said. "I'm trying to buy time but you got to come out. Think about it, okay? Just get used to the idea."

"I can't," Gomez Gomez said.

"You don't have a choice. Just think about it. You ready to go, Jake?"

"I'll meet you up top. Give me and Gomez Gomez a second."

Early stood. "All right. See ya, Gomez Gomez. Don't get bit."

"By the dog?"

"No, man, the snakes."

"Yeah, no promises there," Gomez Gomez said.

Early headed up the path. "I'll be in the truck," he called back.

When Early's footsteps faded Jake stood and brushed dust off his cassock with his cowboy hat. "I do owe you. Tell you what, I'll talk to Sonny. I can't promise anything but I'll try. It's really good to talk to you."

"Don't get used to it."

"I won't. But I miss you, man."

Jake turned and started up the path.

"Hey, Jake," Gomez Gomez said.

Jake paused.

"Angel, man . . ."

Jake sighed. "I know."

"I'm scared."

"Of what?"

"I'm an imperfect believer, man. I always was, even before, when she was here. Now she's gone and I'll never see her again."

Jake considered him. "We're all imperfect believers."

"You don't know the things I said to God. Bad things."

"We've all said things one time or another. You'll see her again."

"You think?"

"I know."

Gomez Gomez sat unmoving for a long time after the crunch of boots on the dirt path faded. Then he stood and rummaged around camp for a bottle. There had to be one somewhere. Something to hide behind. Something to shelter his soul, hanging exposed and wet and stinging in the chill evening air.

CHAPTER SEVEN

HONEY REACHED UP AND PULLED down the passenger-side sun visor of Matthias Galt's Cadillac Escalade. She flipped up the mirror and gave herself a quick once-over. Blonde hair loose and holding its light curl—her natural blonde, not the too blonde Katie always suggested. Makeup . . . check. Wait a minute, maybe a little lipstick touch-up. She spoke through open fish lips while she applied it. "Spur's Tavern, huh? Kind of spendy for a first date." The sentence slurred since she couldn't bring her lips together and *Spur's* and *spendy* sounded more like *Sur's* and *sendy*.

Matthias smiled. Was white the brightest shade teeth could get? *Because those teeth are a little whiter than white.*

"Depends on what you order." Matthias spoke loud over the whine of the Escalade's oversized tires.

"Oh, there's no question about that. Surf and turf. And champagne. The expensive kind—Don what's-his-name."

"I think it's *Dom* what's-his-name."

"Whatever. Still costs the same no matter what his name is."

Those teeth again. "Low blow to the wallet. Maybe I should rethink this."

"Relax, I don't drink anyway. And I can always do a kid's grilled cheese if you're tight for cash. Don't want you to get your lights turned off."

"You order whatever you want. I've been saving up in case you ever said yes. I could retire on what I've got stashed in the bank. Or buy an island somewhere. Or Yankees season tickets."

"Yankees tickets cost as much as an island?"

"More."

"You know what they say, good things come to those who wait."

"They do say that. Besides, this isn't just any first date," Matthias said.

"No?"

"This is *our* first date."

She glanced at him. "Are you really this cheesy?"

"I save it up for special occasions."

"At least I'll get Katie off my back."

"Katie?"

"You wouldn't believe it if I told you. That woman is a broken record."

Matthias turned into Spur's parking lot, tires popping gravel. "So that's why you finally caved? Katie wore you down? I knew there was a reason I liked that woman besides the tacos."

Jake's face pressed into Honey's brain. She gave it a Three Stooges eye poke. "I don't know. Maybe it's just time to get out and *do* something. It's been a long time for me."

"Could you at least lie and let me think I had something to do with it? I promise I'll believe you."

Honey dropped the lipstick into her purse and snapped it shut. "It wouldn't be a lie. Putting down as much coffee as you did shows determination and stamina. Character stuff."

"Maybe I just like coffee that much."

"Do you?"

"Not a chance."

"Listen, I came with you tonight because I wanted to, okay?"

"Man, you're good. I almost believe you."

"You should."

Matthias climbed down and walked around to her door. He opened it and reached up a hand. Honey took it. "Chief of police, cover model, and a gentleman to boot."

"Cover model? Like *Sports Illustrated*?"

"Like those cheesy romance books. Katie leaves them around the kitchen."

"Hey, if the money's good, count me in. I got surf and turf to pay for, right? And get used to having doors opened for you. My folks raised me to respect. I always open the door for a lady."

"What if I'm a feminist?"

"Are you?"

"Nah, I'm just a waitress. And a Presbyterian, I think. Either way, I like men to open doors. It makes me feel special."

"You are special. Here, take my arm. You look shaky in those heels."

"Gravel parking lots aren't really geared for these, are they?"

"Doesn't seem like it, but then again I've never tried."

She took his offered arm. "I should have worn more sensible shoes."

"Absolutely not. Helping you is much better."

Like Shorty's, Spur's was another longtime Paradise institution. Wide, low, and rambling, the mismatched wood, stone, and even tin additions jutted in all directions from the original structure. The tavern edged a steep cliff that dropped away to the desert floor a million miles below. The legendary view drew diners and drinkers from as far away as Tucson and Phoenix. Matthias waved down a hostess outfitted in a cowgirl blouse, cutoff Levi's, boots, and a holster and went to speak to her.

It'd been a long while since Honey had been here. When? With Jake? *Don't go there.* The place hadn't changed at all. It probably hadn't changed in close to a century. The main room sprawled out wide and deep. Doors and archways led to other rooms. No recognizable architectural order to be seen. Across the room near a huge stone fireplace, three Viking-bearded bikers talked and laughed around a pool table. At the bar a stunning brunette in a black evening dress clinked cocktail glasses with a man in a pinstripe suit and James Dean haircut. Above the couple hung a gilded-framed life-size portrait of a cowboy painted circa 1940. A bronze plaque beneath it read "Stumps Parker—World Champion All-Around Cowboy and Local Legend."

"Local legend, huh?" Matthias said.

"You never heard of Stumps Parker?"

"Should I have?"

"Maybe not in New York, but if you've been in Paradise longer than five minutes, yeah."

"Okay. Who is he?"

"Was. Been gone awhile now. But I met him when I was a kid. He used to sign autographs at the used car lot, next to the free hot dogs and one-man band. Stumps won All-Around Cowboy back in the thirties or something. National title."

"Ah. More cowboys. Of course."

"They gave him a parade when he got home. He got ahold of a bottle of Cuervo and drank it to the worm. Rode right in here on Mr. Peaches."

"Now I'm curious. Who or what is Mr. Peaches?"

"His favorite roping horse."

"He rode it in here?"

"Right where you're standing."

He laughed and she liked the way his eyes crinkled. "That wasn't the thing, really. Mr. Peaches wasn't the first horse inside Spur's. But Stumps decided to rope a waitress. The owner tossed him out. Said Stumps was drunk and Mr. Peaches was underage."

Matthias laughed out loud. "And this is a true story?"

"Cross my heart."

Levi's-cutoffs girl approached and they followed her to a table for two right on the edge of the back deck. The girl smiled, eyes lingering on Matthias longer than necessary, and handed them menus. She took their drink orders—Diet Coke for Honey, coffee for Matthias—then, showing off her Levi's, sauntered off. Honey glanced at Matthias to see if he noticed the exaggerated catwalk, but his gaze was fixed on her. He smiled, and her cheeks heated. *What are you, sixteen on your first date?* She covered by looking out over the desert. She'd forgotten how breathtaking the view from Spur's back patio was. Under her left elbow, the cliff fell away to the desert floor. Looking down at the drop made her dizzy. West, across the immense stretch of valley, the sun worked its way slowly down to the horizon.

"If this is meant to impress me, you're doing a good job."

"Good."

"You take all your dates here?" She asked.

"I don't date a lot."

"What's not a lot?"

"Let's see. I've had exactly two dates in the last three years and zero here in Paradise. They say this is the best place in Paradise to take someone. So far, so good."

"Is that a jab at Shorty's, pal?"

That smile again. "Did you want me to take you out to dinner where you work?"

"Katie would absolutely love it, I'll tell you that much."

Cutoffs returned with their coffee and Coke, then told them about the specials, all smiles and "hons."

When she'd left Honey said, "Is she old enough to call us hon?"

"I'm not sure she's even old enough to serve beer. But, hey, what are you gonna do?"

"Call the cops?"

"No way. Early might show up and propose to you again."

"Well, she's flirting with you, hon."

"I doubt it."

Honey laughed. "Oh yeah, she is."

"Maybe, but if she is, she's wasting her time. I'm out with Honey from Shorty's."

"That's right, Honey from Shorty's, coffee pourer to cover-model police chiefs. But I don't call people hon. And my uniform is yellow polyester. Not cutoff short shorts and a pretend pistol."

He lifted his coffee. "Too bad, but you do polyester well. Here's to first dates."

Honey clinked. "Okay, officer. Here's to 'em."

CHAPTER EIGHT

MOST GOOD CATHOLIC RESIDENTS OF Paradise never ventured farther than the deep, vaulted adobe and stone first floor of the Jardin de Dios Mission. Never saw more than the nave, sanctuary, and choir loft. Decades ago, no less than four priests, several curates, and at least twenty nuns staffed Jardin de Dios—a time when the church represented not only spiritual health but fellowship, family, and all things community. But in this world, change is the only constant. These days the mission staffed exactly three people: Father Enzo, the parish priest; Jake, his assistant pastor; and Lucille Plunkett, the church secretary. Maintenance, grounds keeping, and a bevy of other tasks were handled by a rotation of devoted attendees.

Along with a library and offices, the second floor of the mission contained separate rectories for Jake and Father Enzo as well as a small, well-appointed room for Lucille, a longtime widow who found living at the mission preferable to keeping up a house in town. A communal living room updated sometime around the Bing and Bob era came complete with thick rugs, a fireplace, a couple of worn recliners, and a lumpy couch. Recently—due to a 40-inch to 64-inch television upgrade in a parishioner's recreation room—a new used flat-screen television had been donated, replacing the old tube and rabbit-ear unit. A happy turn of events had it not set in motion a perpetual verbal wrestling match over the remote. Lucille was strictly British dramas. And Father Enzo, of all things, a '70s television junkie.

Tuesdays were toughest, pitting *Downton Abbey* on PBS against *Starsky & Hutch* on eighty-seven. But Lucille could pull a mean double leg takedown, and *Downton Abbey* usually prevailed.

Tonight was Thursday, so no riveting hour in the English countryside with the Crawley family. Instead, Lucy slouched on the couch playing Trivia Crack on her smartphone, while Father Enzo sat in the worn recliner with his Superman notebook.

"Knock knock." The door opened and Early lanked in. He bent and tapped Lucille's leg. She shifted over with a smile, and Early settled his long frame next to her, dropping an arm around her shoulders.

"And it's not even *Downton Abbey* night," Jake said. "You bring popcorn?"

"Nope, just my stellar personality," Early said. "And don't knock *Downton*. It's cultural."

"Even without cowboys?" Jake said.

"Mmm, a cowboy or two could be interesting."

Lucille patted Early's leg without taking her eyes off her screen. "You're always welcome here, handsome."

Early looked at Jake. "At least some people appreciate my presence."

"We *Downton*-ers have to stick together," Lucille said.

Father Enzo shifted in his recliner and set the notebook on a side table. "You're a police officer, Early. You should watch *Starsky & Hutch*. Perps and busts instead of Lord Grantham and Mary bickering about sheep."

"There's always baseball," Jake said.

"That Mary is too pinched," Father Enzo said.

"She's regal," Lucille replied with Texas-accented matter-of-factness.

"She looks like the Ghost of Christmas Pale. What that girl needs is a couple of weeks in Hawaii and a cheeseburger," Father Enzo said.

"She's in mourning," Lucille said.

"She lost Matthew, man. She's in pain," Early added.

"Are you kidding me?" Jake said.

Early shrugged and grinned. "It's a Baptist thing. We're sensitive."

Lucille patted Early's leg again. "Don't listen to them, they're jealous because you're cultured." She threw Jake a wink and he couldn't help but smile. Good old Lucille. Tall, round, white verging on pink—a big, soft, fluffy woman, Texas to the bone and without filter. Jake couldn't imagine the place without her.

With Father Enzo making a few last-minute adjustments in his notebook and Lucille and Early discussing the finer plot points of *Downton,* Jake's mind wandered, walking a high wire between Gomez Gomez's haunted eyes and Honey's date with Matthias Galt, the first a colossal knot he felt powerless to untangle and the second something that shouldn't bother him at all but made him want to climb the walls.

Matthias Galt seemed like a decent guy . . .

And Honey deserved to be happy . . .

So knock it off.

But Honey's face wouldn't retreat.

Lucille rose, went into the kitchen, and returned with a half-gallon container of mint chocolate chip ice cream and a handful of spoons. "Anyone?"

Father Enzo and Jake declined, but Early took a spoon and dug a bite from the container.

"Here we go. Countdown to Early's ice cream headache," Lucille said.

Early winced. "Yeah. Too big of a bite."

"You do it every time," Jake said.

"Put your tongue against the roof of your mouth," Father Enzo said, his Italian accent making the word *tongue* sound like *a-tong-a.*

Lucille plopped the container on the coffee table and scooped. Halfway to her mouth her bite escaped her spoon and rolled down the front of her caftan. She gave it a not-too-concerned look and re-spooned it off her lap. This time the bite made it to her mouth without mishap. She didn't wipe the dribble. Lucille wasn't much on appearance. She licked her spoon and looked at Father Enzo. "We're all here. Quit scribbling and let's here this tale of yours. We're on pins and needles."

Enzo picked up Superman. "You are sure? Father Jake could just . . ."

"Wouldn't miss it," Lucille said.

"C'mon, padre. Give us the big fish," Early said.

Father Enzo rustled pages.

Jake glanced at the clock. Five after eight. *Matthias Galt* . . . What were they talking about? Was she smiling? Laughing? He made a concerted effort to retreat behind his stone wall of cassock and collar. Problem was, the mortar was chipping.

Father Enzo adjusted his reading glasses. "Please bear in mind it is a work in progress."

"Don't have to be no Hemingway," Lucille said. "It'll be great."

"Or Louis L'Amour," Early said.

"Please excuse the accent," Father Enzo said.

Lucille scooped more mint chip. "Read on, boy."

Father Enzo cleared his throat.

Corfu, Greece—1961

He'd heard about mermaids all his life. His grandfather—out with the rising sun on his tiny fishing boat most days—kept a thousand stories at ready disposal, many of them anchored by those beautiful sirens of the sea. And everyone in Greece knew Alexander the Great's sister Thessalonike had retreated to a life of watery immortality in the depths of the Aegean after the death of her brother. But hearing about mermaids, no matter how often or how ingrained the stories became in a person's mind, could never prepare them for the moment they actually met one. And that's exactly what happened to Erasmo Petrakis on a bright summer afternoon in 1961, fifteen feet beneath the clear waters of Paleokastritsa Bay, Island of Corfu, Greece.

Lucille arched a brow. "Mermaids, Enzo?"

"Shh," Early said. "This is good. Keep going, father."

Father Enzo gave a noncommittal cough and continued.

Erasmo had been after the fish for weeks. Hercules: the huge and crafty old grouper sure to fetch a good price at the fish market should Erasmo's spear ever find its mark. But the money was secondary. The prestige, the glory—this was the bread that nourished. He'd be the talk of the island. And on a young man's scale, pride outweighed riches, stone to feather.

Fabrizio, his best friend and greatest rival, claimed to have seen the fish and taken a shot, but then again Fabrizio claimed a lot of things, among them being the first-best spear fisherman in the Greek Islands. And Fabrizio's boast might have been almost true if it hadn't been for Erasmo. Erasmo's existence made Fabrizio second best, although this difference of opinion proved a source of continual good-natured conflict between the two friends.

Still, bringing in Hercules before Fabrizio would be better than Christmas morning. And it was imagining the look on Fabrizio's face that sent spirits of delight radiating through Erasmo's body as he hung fifteen feet down, suspended in liquid space, and lined up his spear with Hercules's eye. He willed himself to be calm, trying to slow his heart as his finger tightened on the trigger.

But at the last split second, with a rush Hercules jerked sideways, amazing speed for his size, and disappeared into the rocks. Erasmo had no time to contemplate either his disappointment or confusion. Because at almost the same instant the fish vanished, he caught movement in as much of his peripheral vision as his dive mask allowed. A rush of flowing blonde hair, a sweep of fishy tale—and it was gone. Erasmo forgot he was fifteen feet under the sea and gasped, sucking in salty seawater. Gagging, he bolted for the surface. He coughed as he treaded water, rotating in a circle, scanning the horizon.

Nothing surfaced on the bay's calm surface.

He made quick time to the beach, head spinning. Hercules would have to wait another day to die. Mermaids? Impossible.

Mermaids were nothing but fairy tales for children and doddering old people. He carried his flippers, mask, and speargun across the beach and up to the road, still struggling to make sense of what he'd seen.

Skidding tires made him jump back. He looked up to see Fabrizio straddling his new Vespa and grinning at him.

Fabrizio turned off the engine. "Watch where you're going, I almost killed you."

"You'd like that, wouldn't you? Then you'd finally be the first-best spear fisherman on the island."

"Keep telling yourself that, vlakas. Maybe one day you'll believe it. I see you're not carrying Hercules on your spear, eh? Too smart for you. Too smart for anybody. Like I told you, nobody will ever get Hercules."

"Wait a second. What's a vlakas?" Early said.

"Probably a knucklehead or something," Lucille said. "That close, Enzo?"

"Knucklehead . . . Yes, that is close enough," Father Enzo said.

"I already don't like this Fabrizio dude. Name sounds like an odor spray."

"Go on, Enzo. This isn't bad for a *Starsky & Hutch* guy," Lucille said.

Erasmo considered telling his friend about the mermaid but decided against it. Something in him knew the memory, the experience, should be his and his alone for a while. Yes, the thought felt right.

"Where're you going, vlakas?" Fabrizio said.

"Call me all the names you want. It still doesn't make you first best, too bad for you."

Fabrizio laughed. "The world is full of dreamers these days. So answer me, where are you going?"

"Home. My grandmother asked me to bring milk. And I'm tired of fishing."

Fabrizio made his eyes suspicious. "Since when do you get tired of fishing?"

"Wait," Jake said. "What do you mean by 'made his eyes suspicious'?"
"Like this." Father Enzo demonstrated.
"Ah, you mean narrowed his eyes," Jake said.
"Yes, yes. Narrowed . . . Very good." Enzo scribbled.

Fabrizio narrowed his eyes. "Since when do you get tired of fishing?"
"Since now. What about it?"
"You're walking?"
"I forgot to bring my Alfa Romeo, what was I thinking? Of course I'm walking."
"You need a Vespa. Maybe you'll finally get a girlfriend. A real girl instead of a picture of Brigitte Bardot you tore out of a magazine."

"Yeah, this guy's a real jerk," Early said.
Father Enzo's smile spoke of answers to questions that hadn't been asked.

"Do I look rich like you? Can I afford a Vespa?"
Fabrizio laughed, pushing dark curls out of his eyes. "Not as rich, not as handsome, and no Old Man. How sad for the second-best fisherman."
"Not as handsome? Without your papa's money you'd probably have to marry your cousin. The fat one with the wart and bad breath."
Fabrizio shrugged, still grinning. "At least she would be flesh and blood, not a picture I tore out of a magazine at the barbershop. Besides, I do have my dad's money, so it doesn't matter. The girls are lining up, my friend. Be nice. If you are, maybe I'll introduce you to my cousin."

"Tell her to brush her teeth first."

Fabrizio kicked the Vespa to life and raised his voice over the motor. "You should be so lucky. Quit griping. Get on, let's go for a drink."

Holding his mask and fins in one hand and his speargun in the other, Erasmo threw a leg over the seat and perched behind his friend. Both leaned into the momentum as Fabrizio gunned the scooter.

"No one will ever get Hercules," Fabrizio shouted back.

The sun felt good on Erasmo's shoulders. As the beach shrunk behind them, the blue sky danced sparkles on the ocean, a shiny subterfuge to hide the mermaids swirling beneath.

Father Enzo closed the notebook and looked up.

Jake shifted in his seat. *Flowing blonde hair* . . . Honey in the passenger seat of his old pickup, windows open to the setting sun, trying unsuccessfully to tuck stray strands behind her ears . . . He shoved the picture to the back of his mind.

"That's it?" Early said.

Father Enzo lifted a shoulder. "A work in progress. There is more to come. Chapter two."

"I think it's beautiful," Lucille said.

Early rested his elbows on his knees. "But what about the mermaid?"

"I'm getting to it. Next time."

"Story time with Father Enzo. I'd better get invited to the next installment," Early said.

Lucille picked up her phone and thumbed the surface. "I want to see where Corfu is."

Early moved back so he could see the screen.

Jake kicked off the recliner and headed into the little kitchen. He opened the refrigerator door and stared at the contents. Gomez Gomez. Honey and Matthias Galt. *You're a priest, man. You chose this.*

You committed. Snap out of it. He closed his eyes, hand still on the open door of the refrigerator.

"Are you okay, Father Jake?" Father Enzo stood in the doorway.

"I'm fine. I like the story. You're a fine writer, father."

"I'm just an old man with too much imagination."

"No, I mean it. It's a good start."

"Tell me something, does anyone say a penny for your thoughts anymore?"

"I haven't heard it in a while."

"Well, I'm a priest. It's all I can afford. Tell me, are you trying to stare that food to death? I have milk in there I'm somewhat attached to."

Jake took one last glance into the fridge and let the door fall shut. "Just a little preoccupied."

Father Enzo crossed the room and opened the freezer. He dug around and came out with two Eskimo Pies. He handed one to Jake then pulled out a chair and sat.

"These are Lucille's," Jake said.

The old priest peeled the wrapper off his ice cream and took a bite. His mouth full of ice cream paired with his accent made understanding difficult. "She will survive. We need our strength, eh? Sit. Talk to me."

Jake sat.

Father Enzo smiled. "I'm telling you, those Eskimos are on to something very nice indeed."

Jake peeled the foil back and took a bite.

"Can I ask you a question?" Father Enzo said.

"Of course, father."

"Are you in love with Honey Hicks?"

Jake stared. "I'm surprised you even know who Honey is. She's not part of the parish."

The old priest shrugged. "I know a lot of things. But you didn't answer my question."

Jake searched for words. He couldn't lie. "I'm praying about it, father. I can get past it."

"So you do love her."

"I'm sorry."

"Why are you sorry?"

"For letting you down. The church. God."

Father Enzo's face registered surprise. "You have let God down?"

"I'm trying not to love her, father."

"Trying not to love . . ." Father Enzo took another bite. "So in your opinion, love disappoints God?"

"When a man is a priest? Doesn't it?"

"We all wrestle with things, Father Jake. No human is immune to this, whether we wear a collar, a habit, or a waitress uniform. None of it surprises God."

Jake set his half-eaten Eskimo Pie on the table. "It shouldn't bother me, I know, but she's out on a date tonight."

"This explains your preoccupation."

"I thought it'd be easier. The priesthood, all of it. I thought I'd forget what it used to be like between us. Then some little thing happens and it all rushes back."

"What did it use to be?"

"How can I say it? I'd never known someone like her before and I haven't since. I'm not much of a talker, you know that, not like Early, but Honey never minded my quiet. It was almost like we read each other's minds. Sometimes we'd go out on the cliffs and just sit for hours. Watch the sunset, then the stars . . . Didn't have to say a word. Like there was already so much between us we didn't have to fill it with anything."

"It sounds beautiful. What happened?"

"I asked her to marry me. I gave her my mother's ring."

"And she said no?"

"She said yes. But that was the morning . . . that day . . ."

"That day? Ah! The day of the accident? Angel Gomez . . ."

"Yes."

Father Enzo nodded slowly. "I remember that day very well. I was at the hospital."

"I don't remember seeing you."

"You wouldn't have. I was in with Angel. Strange I've never told you before this."

"Some things are hard to talk about. You were with her when she died?"

"Yes. Maybe you died that day too, eh? But Angel was at peace. She knew where her next breath would be. She was ready to go be with her God."

"Her husband wasn't ready to lose her."

"We all walk a path. We all have a time. There are no accidents with God."

"What am I supposed to do, father?"

"That's not an easy question. Let me tell you, we will pray. You will pray. I will pray. And we will listen, eh? But other than that, you simply need to start knowing."

"Knowing what?"

"That the One who knows your rising up and your lying down is never *ever* disappointed with love."

CHAPTER NINE

THE BACK DECK OF SPUR's Tavern diffused the night with a warm bubble of light. Patio lanterns splashed color beneath strings of bright clear bulbs crisscrossing every compass point. Moths hummed and bats flitted. To the west, the sun had long dropped behind the Chiricahua mountain range.

Honey looked down at her now empty plate. "Surf and turf. Man, that was every bit as good as I thought it would be."

"Yeah, but there goes my island," Matthias said.

"I notice you ate all yours too."

"They do a good steak here. Worth two islands."

Honey gazed out at the inky night. "You know, I've seen the sun set a thousand times, but it looked better from here for some reason. Brighter. More intense."

"I'd say it's the company, but I think I'd risk you calling me cheesy again."

Honey shifted her eyes back to him. She smiled. "Pretty sharp for a police guy. But you can say it if you want to."

"You know *police guy* isn't an actual term, right?"

"Okay, *officer* then. So what's up with the Wranglers, man? I still can't figure that out. You sure you don't want to be a cowboy?"

Matthias took a sip of coffee and shrugged. "What can I say? I like Wranglers. Want to know a secret? I went as a cowboy for Halloween when I was six. I dug the hats. Little cowboy going door to door in the

Bronx. Then on my birthday my dad took me to a rodeo at the Garden. Scared me to death. Those guys are one-hundred-percent crazy."

"Yeah, maybe. Look at Early."

"Case in point. He used to jump off horses and wrestle steers to the ground, right?"

"It's called bulldogging."

"It's called insane. By the way, what's up with the marriage proposals every time he sees you?"

"That's just Early. He started proposing when we were in second grade. Never stopped."

"That's because you never said yes. Early might be crazy but he's not stupid. Second grade? I'm trying to picture him as a kid."

"Not much different. Same long hair, same black eyes, head taller than everyone else. Same attitude too. A good guy to have on your side."

"And a bad one to have as an enemy?"

"I could tell you stories."

"Nah, I have to work with him. Less I know the better. He's definitely on your side, that's for sure."

"Well, he's Early. I'm glad."

"Not so sure he's always on mine. Anyway," Matthias lifted his mug, "here's to Early."

"And to bulldoggers everywhere." Honey clinked his cup with her Coke glass. "How about country music?"

"How about it?"

"They have country music in the Bronx?"

"I'm more of a rock guy. I like some of the new country stuff though. Not so twangy."

"New as in drive your lifted pickup down to the lake, drink beer, and watch girls dance in the headlights country?"

"I guess. It's pretty good. Sounds like a good idea too. I'd probably have to skip the beer—never know when I might get called in. At least it keeps the beer calories off. And I don't have a pickup, but we could always take the Escalade."

"I don't think an Escalade would have the same effect. Haven't you noticed all those bro-country songs are kind of the same?"

"I don't listen that close to the words. Besides, I'm a bro. What can I say?"

"How about Johnny Cash? You like him?"

"I think so. The prison guy, right?"

Honey shook her head in mock wonder. "You *think* so? You're killing me."

"Okay, what about you? Justin Bieber? Boy bands? Miley Cyrus?"

"Never. I like the good stuff. Old country, classic rock . . ."

"Jazz?"

"Sure. I love swing too."

"Like Rat Pack? Aren't you young for all that?"

Honey shrugged. "My parents always loved music. Plus I have two much-older brothers. I was a late-in-life accident. And no one is too young for Rat Pack."

"Older brothers. Should I be worried?"

"Definitely. Career navy and army. One's in San Diego and the other at Fort Bragg."

"Parents?"

"They moved to San Diego a long, long time ago. When my brother and his wife had kids."

"Rat Pack, huh? How about Sinatra?"

"C'mon, everybody loves Sinatra. That's a given."

Matthias looked out toward the desert. The guy really did have rugged hero type written all over him. Faint sun lines creased the corners of his eyes. His hair kind of forties—buzzed short on the sides and longer on top. *People* magazine movie star all the way. She realized she'd judged him for it. But talking tonight, he had depth. Sincerity. And on top of it, he made her laugh.

Matthias's eyes came back to her. "What's going on in your head?"

"Nothing. Just how much I like the view."

"And old country music."

"Twangier the better, pal."

The waitress with the tight shorts appeared, taking their plates. "Refill on the coffee?"

"Why not?" Matthias said.

The girl smiled, her dimples a foot deep. "I'll make sure they brew it fresh. How 'bout you, hon? Another Coke?"

"No thanks, hon," Honey said. "I'm Coke-ed out."

The girl moved on and Matthias laughed.

"The funny thing is, hon is short for honey and that's actually my name, so it sort of works."

"It's not my name, and she calls me hon too."

"Here's something we need to clear up. By rock do you mean heavy metal or what?"

Matthias scratched his cheek. The guy made the smallest things look good. "I don't know. Just what's on the radio, I guess."

"Like? Give me a name."

"Seriously? You give *me* a name, Miss Old Stuff. Am I being judged here?"

"Definitely. Okay, Lefty Frizzell, Merle Haggard, Willie, The Stones . . . Now your turn."

"Man, okay . . . How about Mötley Crüe?"

"Mötley Crüe? So you're talking rock as in eighties hair bands? Spandex pants and Aqua Net hair spray and all that?"

"Pearl Jam? Coldplay? U2?"

"Would you please just say Skynyrd or Zeppelin so I can feel better?"

"Definitely Skynyrd and Zeppelin. Oh, and the Beatles."

"All right then, *hon*. U2 . . . They did one song with Johnny Cash at least."

"And I'm from New York, so it's in my genes to like Sinatra. Don't forget we have Frank in common."

"Doesn't count. Everybody likes Sinatra. Plus I already told you I liked him, so it seems like you're just trying to kiss up."

"All right. I'm pretty sure I like Hank Williams."

"Senior, Junior, or the Third?"

"Are you kidding me? There's three of them?"

"You're completely hopeless."

"Well, I like Sinatra no matter what you say. No kissing up involved."

"Tell you what, I'll give you Frank. Let's call that common ground and leave it alone."

"Sounds good. And hey, I have an open mind. Bring on the twang. You might win me over."

Levi's Shorts came back with Matthias's coffee, flashed her dimples at him, and moved on.

Matthias poured in sugar and stirred. "Let me ask you something. What's the deal with you and Father Jake?"

"Deal?"

"Yeah. What's the deal?"

"You don't beat around the bush, do you? Why do you ask?"

"Early said some things today . . ."

"Leave it to Early. I think we just left cute first date banter and went straight to 'that's a little personal.'"

"Want to talk about Van Halen instead?"

"Roth or Hagar?"

He reached across the table and touched her hand. "I just want to get to know you, that's all. It seems like hearing about you and Father Jake might be a big part of doing that. I know there's history there."

Honey edged her hand away. "Yeah, there's history there. Everybody west of the Mississippi River knows there's history there."

"I'd like to hear about it."

He isn't going to drop it. "It's nothing, believe me. Not anymore. It's in the past, water under the bridge, yesterday's news—pick a cliché and apply it." *Now just believe it yourself, sister.* If there *had* been a bridge, Jake had burned it down to the water and walked away from the ashes years ago, so what was the point?

"You still with me?" Matthias said.

"Of course . . . It's just more than I planned on talking about tonight."

The corner of his mouth turned up, and for a moment Honey could picture him as a little boy. "You figured we'd stick close to the surface?

Look, I know it's a nonissue. He's a priest, right? Tell you what, forget it. I don't know why I said anything in the first place."

Insects buzzed in the overhead lights and a band tuned up in the bar. Honey swirled the ice in her glass.

Matthias picked up his coffee, then set it back down. "Hey, come back. I'm sorry. I spoke out of turn, okay? It's our first date and I definitely don't want it to be the last. Can you please rewind and ignore?"

"Only if you're talking about a Mötley Crüe cassette."

"I'm serious."

Honey took a sip from her water glass, considered, then took another. "What the heck. You want the short or long story?"

"You sure?"

"Absolutely not. Long or short?"

"Your call."

"How about medium?"

"Okay, medium."

Honey looked out over the rail and caught the tail end of an "I'm So Lonesome I Could Cry" falling star. Hank Senior would be proud. "All right. So I've known Jake most of my life. He was a couple of years ahead of me in school. The strong, quiet type. Still the strong, quiet type. Every girl in town had a crush on him. I used to go with my friends to watch him and Doc—Doc's his brother—play baseball on the field out behind the mission. Seems so long ago now. Like another lifetime."

"*The* Doc Morales, right? The Red Sox?"

"One and only. He married an actress. Now she's his first mate, or maybe he's hers. Anyway they're sailing somewhere in the Caribbean on a big old boat."

"Sounds very Jimmy Buffett."

"Another long story, I'll tell you sometime."

"*Promise?*" *Man, this guy would be a lot easier to talk to if he had a bag over his head . . .*

"So Jake went to junior college on a rodeo scholarship, then got his philosophy degree from U of A."

"A cowboy with a philosophy degree. And what about you? Are you in this story?"

"I graduated high school, then went to Paradise Community College. Riveting stuff, huh?"

"Very. And you were dating Jake then?"

"Nope. I'm not sure he even knew I existed. Jake came home to spend Christmas break with Doc his senior year at U of A—their parents died when they were young, and Jake pretty much raised Doc. I was working part-time at Shorty's. Some things never change, right? Jake and Doc came in. I guess I'd blossomed. Isn't that what they call it?"

"I can well imagine."

"But no Levi's cutoffs."

"Just yellow polyester."

"Take it easy . . . So Jake asked me out and, I won't lie, it was head over heels stuff pretty much immediately. He finished up school but came home every weekend. Then he graduated, and we were inseparable. We both wanted to be in Paradise, but there's not much call here for a saddle-bronc rider with a philosophy degree. Or anywhere, I guess. Jake worked at a couple of ranches and broke horses on the side, but he made most of his living traveling the rodeo. Actually he did really well at that. Made a chunk. He went all over with Gomez Gomez and Early. He was really good."

"Did you talk marriage?"

"Man, are you writing a report or something?"

"Sorry. Let's talk music instead. I'll name eighties hair bands and you can make fun of me."

Honey absently slid her water glass around on the table, forming the letter H in invisible ink. H for *history*. "Marriage. Yup. That was the plan, Stan."

"So what happened?"

"Well, officer, thanks for asking. What happened was we broke up. Jake decided to take a left turn. He went to seminary. I went to Honduras and did social work at a hospital in the mountains, and now here we are watching bats eat bugs on Spur's patio while girls in short shorts call us hon. Ain't life grand?"

"That's the medium version? I think you meant short. Why did you break up?"

"Because we broke up and now he's a priest, over and out, the end. Can we change the subject now, please?"

"The end?"

"Look, maybe another night, okay? These are things that are hard to talk about."

Matthias nodded. "Of course. I'm sorry. But does that mean there'll be another night?"

Honey smiled. "On another note, did I mention I got engaged to a doctor in Honduras and left him standing at the altar?"

"I think I'll get some more coffee."

CHAPTER TEN

GOMEZ GOMEZ WANTED BADLY TO doze but the rattlesnake wasn't to be trusted. Oh, he talked a good game, like he was all good intentions, but still, keep one eye open as a general rule.

"He left them on a tree?" The rattler's voice slid smooth, with just the softest slur.

"Uh-huh. Stuck 'em on with a thumbtack. Never even heard the dude. That tree right over there." Gomez Gomez tipped his bottle toward a big pine standing on the edge of the firelight. "Two good old Ben Franklins. Hundred-dollar bills. Kid's golden. And loaded, I guess."

"Well, GG, the Bennies explain the fresh bottles of T-bird." The rattlesnake was big on abbreviations and street slang.

Gomez Gomez kicked over an empty. Several other full bottles stood at attention beside him, flickering reflected campfire. "One dead soldier. Somebody blow reveille."

"I think you're thinking of taps."

Gomez Gomez squinted at his liquid army. "No, sir. Reveille. We're just getting started."

The sun had long gone but the fire raged high, throwing sparks up into the gloom. Above the sparks Venus danced, first to push through the dark with narcissistic insistence, demanding center stage, showing off. Good old Lady Venus, loudest singer in the star choir and jockeying for a solo. Gomez Gomez lifted another bottle of Thunderbird toward the watery orb and unscrewed the cap using only his thumb.

The snake adjusted itself on the log. "So what are you going to do about Sonny Harmon? Will you be leaving us soon?"

Bottle hand still high in the air, Gomez Gomez lifted his free hand in the direction of the car lot and offered a one-fingered salute.

"You're in a mood," the rattlesnake said.

"Why don't you bite him? Solve all my problems."

"Bite old Sonny? It's a thought."

"Maybe I'll sick Bones on him. He stopped the rocks."

"Bones is an interesting dude, no doubt."

"His head reaches to the sun, man. It's a trip."

"Whatever you say, weirdo."

Gomez Gomez grunted and took a pull from the bottle.

The rattlesnake slid to the ground and gathered himself. "Well, general, the hour has arrived and the hunt awaits. Good luck with the battle. May your soldiers all make it home to their loved ones."

"Not a chance. Few of 'em are going down for sure."

"War is hell."

"Your lips to God's ears. I ain't gonna wake up with you in my sleeping bag or nothing, right?"

"Adios, GG. TTYL. Peace out." The rattler slid off, silent as a prayer.

Gomez Gomez watched the sparks mingle with Venus for a while longer then began to float up with them. He reached a hand into the sparks. Tiny needles of pain brought him back down to earth.

From the road at the top of the hill a glow appeared. Stationary, not passing headlights. No noise came to him. No flashing or aliens or Michael the Archangel. The glow hung in the air beyond the brush and pine trees, steadfast und unmoving.

Gomez Gomez turned to his line of full Thunderbird bottles. "Boys, we're being invaded. I say we go meet this glowy so-and-so with whom there is no variableness or shadow of turning head-on. I'm looking for volunteers."

Just as he suspected, every bottle stepped forward. Gomez Gomez stood tall and puffed out his chest. "I'm proud of you, boys. I didn't expect everyone. You're brave to the core. But unfortunately this is a stealth mission. Plus I only have two pockets. I do, however, have one available hand. So that makes room for three of you."

He leaned down, picked up two unopened bottles, and shoved them into his coat pockets, then lifted the bottle already in use toward the glow. "And into immortality . . . The rest of you boys hold down the fort and prepare to care for the wounded upon our return." With this last order he sat down, leaned against a tree, and fell asleep.

He woke with a start, blinking the sand and spiders out of his eyes. He took a slug of T-bird to freshen his breath and calm his nerves. Lady Venus had shifted considerably in the sky. Eleven? Midnight? Whatever. The glow at the top of the hill still glowed. What was that thing?

No time like the present to find out. He struggled to shaky feet.

Halfway up the path a second set of feet scraped dirt, and Bones appeared next to him.

"Ain't it past your bedtime?" Gomez Gomez said.

"These things are flexible."

"My old pop woulda whupped my butt if I was out late like this."

"My dad's overseas right now."

"Fixing cars?"

"Nah, some kind of mine thing. In the jungle. Pretty cool."

"Jungle like Africa or something?"

"Like something, yeah."

"What about your mom? You bring some cookies?"

"Next time."

"Hey, thanks for the dough."

"No prob. Where you going?"

"See the glow. How 'bout you?"

Bones wiped his nose. "You know what's up there?"

"Nope."

"You're not gonna like it."

Gomez Gomez patted a pocket with his free hand. "I'm good. I got backup."

"You might need it."

The path terminated at the edge of the upper road. Not a car in either direction. The glow here, no longer diffused by brush and trees, shone bright and clean.

Bones was right. Gomez Gomez didn't like it. In fact, he didn't like it at all. Above them, plastered to a billboard and shining down like some demented cherub, stood Sonny Harmon. Eight feet tall, dressed in his white cowboy outfit, and lit up by six gazillion-watt spotlights. Yellow lettering in all caps above his hat read FUTURE HOME OF HARMON USED CARS—NO CREDIT? NO PROBLEM!

"I told you," Bones said.

"I feel sick. I think I might puke."

"Cool. Go for it."

Gomez Gomez turned to the bushes and did.

"Feel better?"

"No."

"Maybe you should puke again."

"You're weird."

"Whatever," Bones said.

"This is the place, you know. Where Angel crashed. She left from exactly right here." Gomez Gomez leaned back, arms wide, holding a bottle in each hand for balance. He stumbled. His feet caught themselves. The stars, planets, and satellites spun in a cosmic blur. "Angel!" The heavens gave no reply. "Aaanngel!"

"I don't think she can hear you, man."

"Because Venus is too loud. Stinking Venus won't shut up."

"Sure. That must be it."

"She's up there, man. I'm telling you. Anyone deserves heaven, it's her."

"So you keep saying."

"Stupid Sonny put a picture of himself right on the spot she left from. What kind of person does a thing like that?"

"This might help." Bones held out two cans of black spray paint.

"What you gonna to do with that?"

Bones grinned and pointed to the base of the sign where a workman's ladder still stood. "Sonny Harmon started it, right?"

Gomez Gomez took a long swallow of T-bird. Then another. Then a third just to cover the bases. He set the bottle on the gravel shoulder. "The battle goes to the brave, or the swift, or whatever. Ain't that what they say?"

"Something like that. Sometimes it just goes to who's maddest."

Gomez Gomez eyed the ladder. "That's a long way up there, Spaceman."

"Yeah, but are you mad?"

"Pretty mad. Madder than Sonny, I bet."

"So let's do it, man. I'll hold your hand. It'll be worth it."

"Friends don't let friends climb drunk, right?"

"We're friends?"

"Maybe."

"You drunk?"

"Definitely."

"Just don't look down. It'll be cool."

"You say *cool* a lot."

"You doing this or what?"

Gomez Gomez saluted. "Company . . . charge."

A million rungs later they reached the narrow platform at the base of the sign. Even higher than Gomez Gomez expected. Stars swirled around him up here, streaking, exploding, then bursting back into existence in perfect and pure silence. Venus offered the only sound. He was eye level with her now. Nearly done for the night, her song drifted quiet and low, a breathy moan in the night—dark blues in a minor key.

Bones rattled one of the cans, loud in the quiet. Venus paused her blues, offended.

"I'm going for it," Bones said.

"What you gonna say?" Gomez Gomez said, eyes still on the stars.

"This is her place, right? Before Sonny screwed it up? Sacred ground, man. Like a sacred burial site. We gotta take it back."

"What I was thinking. 'Cept she ain't buried. She's in a Folgers can."

The spray can gave a snaky hiss. Bones made quick work of it, and down the ladder they went. Not as far down as it had been up. Breathing hard and battle-fatigued, the two stood side by side looking up. The work was neat. Thick, bold, and unmistakable.

"What do you think?" Bones said.

Gomez Gomez blinked tears. The shining, heavenly sign moved in and out of focus. "It's perfect." He patted Bones's bony back. "Man, it's really perfect."

"It'll do. 'Cause we're friends, right?"

"We're getting there, amigo. Definitely headed in the right direction."

On the billboard above, in thick black block letters, one word completely ruined Sonny Harmon's white suit. One word with two huge feathered wings protruding from its top.

ANGEL.

CHAPTER ELEVEN

Rolling loose between long, hot summers and frost-filled winters, autumn comes to the mountains of Southeast Arizona lightly sanded and gently worn. Lazy winds rustle the pines and push tumbleweeds and trucker litter across the highway.

This morning, sunlight flooded through the massive plateglass windows that fronted Sonny Harmon's dealership showroom. Sonny wiped beads of sweat from his forehead, though the airplane hangar–size room was temperature controlled and kept at a constant, even seventy degrees no matter the season.

Sonny stared through the thick glass at the lines of new cars without really seeing. "The thing is," he said, "the sign company won't even come back to redo it now. Seven to ten business days, they say. I told 'em every day is a stinking business day for actual non-morons and to get their butts out here pronto, but they're not budging. At least they came and got their ladder so nobody else can get up there. Seven to ten business days . . . That's two weeks! Must be nice to be that busy."

"Must be," Matthias Galt said.

Sonny stood with his back to the police chief, but he could see Matthias's reflection in the glass. Galt crossed his arms and leaned against a brand-new loaded Camaro.

"Would you not lean on the car please?"

Galt stood. "Sorry." He took a small notebook from the front pocket of his uniform shirt. "So you'd like to make a complaint then, Mr. Harmon? About the graffiti?"

Sonny sighed, checking his reflection up and down in the glass. In his fifties now but he still had it. Starched white dress shirt tucked into tight jeans. Okay, maybe a little paunch hanging over the silver turquoise belt buckle—he'd have to work on that, maybe a few extra sit-ups—but still fairly fit for his age. Boots polished. The amber-encased scorpion bolo tie gave him a nice, cool edge. But best of all, the hair. Check out the '77 PHS yearbook pictures, especially the on-one-knee-leaning-on-a-football-helmet one that said *Sonny Harmon—Quarterback* under it, and you could see the same hair in glorious Technicolor. Why change perfection? A little longer than collar length, blond—the cut-and-color girl called it "ash"—and perfectly feathered, brother. Some classics just never went out of style.

And if it ain't broke, don't fix it.

Sonny smoothed his mustache with a finger and a thumb. "There's no use filing anything. I don't care about a complaint. Just go arrest Gomez Gomez and drag his sorry butt out of the bushes. We know he did it. Frankly, boyo, I hold you responsible. You were supposed to have the nutjob out of there yesterday."

"Yeah, sorry about that. In my defense, I was only asked to *do* it yesterday. And Father Jake wanted to talk to him first. I didn't think a little time was unreasonable given the fact we're about to turn the guy's whole world on its head."

"You didn't think? What does Father Jake have to do with the price of tea in China?"

"They were friends. Along with Detective Pines. Thought it might help."

"Help what? The guy's a hobo. There's nothing to help. Do what you're paid to do or we'll find someone else to do your job. This is not rocket science. You like your job here?"

"I'm not complaining."

Sonny turned purposefully. "You think because you're from the big

THE BEAUTIFUL ASHES OF GOMEZ GOMEZ

city you know better than us?" He said "big city" with exaggerated finger quotes.

"No, sir. Nothing like that."

"How's the Escalade working out for you?"

"Fine. It's a very nice car."

"Heck yeah it's a nice car. One I let you drive out of the goodness of my heart. You think you could afford a car like that on what we pay you?"

"Probably not. I appreciate the loan."

Sonny's voice rose of its own volition. "Do you appreciate it enough to do what I tell you once in a while?" *Watch the blood pressure.* He looked up at the ceiling and took a long, slow breath. "Look, just get it done, okay?" He stuck four fingers in each front jeans pocket. Pants too tight to fit the thumbs. "You like that Camaro you keep leaning on? Just like the guys drive on *Hawaii Five-O*, right? You like that show?"

"Not sure I've seen it."

"You never seen *Five-O*? Stinkin' great show. That Danny, man, he's a funny little sucker. You should watch it, what with being a cop and all."

"I'll have to check it out."

"What's your gun?"

"Excuse me?"

"Your gun. What make is it? Glock?"

"Uh, yeah, department issue. Glock 23. Forty caliber."

"Cool. Not quite a .45, but it's got some stopping power. Ever shoot anybody?"

"No, sir."

"Ever want to?"

"I sure hope not."

"Bummer. Remember *Miami Vice*?"

"Sorry, never saw that either."

"Seriously? The one from the eighties? Crockett and Tubbs?"

"I know the show. I've just never watched it."

"Man, how are you even a cop? Don Johnson drove a 1986 Ferrari Testarossa. Second-greatest cop show of all time."

"What was the first?"

"You're kidding me, right?"

"Not kidding."

"C'mon! *After Sunset* with Gregory Jones. Hands down number one. He grew up here, you know. I used to know the guy. Weird dude but great show. Drove a 1967 Shelby Super Cobra on TV. Stinkin' great car."

"I'll have to look it up. So back to Gomez Gomez—"

"Bad boy had a 427 V8 and eight hundred horsepower."

"What?"

"The Shelby Cobra. *After Sunset*. Track with me here, boyo."

"*After Sunset*. Got it."

Sonny pulled a comb out of his back pocket and re-feathered. "A lot of people say I look like Don Johnson, what d'ya think?"

"Sure. So about Gomez Gomez, Detective Pines seems to feel we should bring him out slow. Let him acclimate to the idea."

"Detective Pines seems to feel . . . Early doesn't have a construction deadline. Besides, he's a moron like the rest of the hicks around here."

"He just thinks that—"

"What's Early's last name?"

"Excuse me?"

"Early. What's his last name?"

"Pines. You just said—"

"That's right—Pines. Not Harmon. Look, the rules are simple: if someone's name isn't Harmon, then their opinion doesn't count. My name *is* Harmon, so my opinion counts. Get it?"

"I just think—"

"Your last name Harmon?"

"No, it's not."

"Then why are you thinking? See? Simple rules for simple minds. You're not a social worker. You're not a decision maker. You're a doer. A worker bee. A little fish. That's it. That's how police chiefs in Paradise, Arizona, wind up driving Escalades, *comprende*?"

"All I said was a little slack would be wise. And I thought it'd be good to have Early talk to him. They're friends."

"I'm getting all teary. Look, I don't mind Early running your occasional errand. Or even being a detective. I can see how the guy would put the fear of God into the criminal element. But you got to do this yourself. This town's still all gooey about Angel. You understand?"

"I do, and that's why I thought—"

"Are you even listening to yourself? You *thought* instead of *did*. Which, once again, is clearly against the simple rules. Why are we still talking?"

"It's touchy. People are talking. That's why I let Father Jake go down with Detective Pines. Seemed like the right call."

"Does the nutjob need to confess something first? We're talking about a drunk Mexican or Indian or whatever he is with broken glass for brains. This isn't a 'talk to him' deal. It's a 'tell him.' He's on my land. He needs to leave. End of story."

"Actually that land is city owned. It's public."

"How long've you been here now, Matthias?"

"Six months, give or take."

"Not long. That's why I'm trying to cut you a little slack, but you're wearing me out. See the sign out there? The one that says Harmon Chevrolet and Cadillac? And you remember the Harmon deal, right? Harmon says more than just auto sales. It says that regardless of what some crap paper says down at city hall, if I say it's my land then it's my land. And it also says you do what I say. One more time, simple rules for simple people. That's the way we keep things around here. Streamlined."

"Look, I'm not trying to be difficult. And I do appreciate the Escalade, it's just with the guy losing his wife—"

"When? Like a hundred years ago!" Sonny scanned the lot. "Did you know this is the third-largest Chevrolet dealership in Arizona?"

"No, I didn't."

"No, you didn't. But now you do. And do you know why the third-largest Chevrolet dealership is here in Podunkville?"

"Because you grew up here and inherited it?"

"Well . . . yeah, actually. Exactly. And why do I still live here? Because I want to be able to do what I want to do. Get it? I'm a big fish in a small pond, which I like being. That saying is always used in such a negative way, but that's because most people are little fish. See, us big fish got it made in our small ponds, man. The big fish get to call all the shots. My daddy was a big fish. His daddy was a big fish, and his daddy and so on. We swim around here in our little pond, do what we want, and die fat and happy. We even got a whole big fish section of the cemetery all to ourselves. And I'm telling you—big fish to little fish—to go get Gomez Gomez out of there so I can add ten acres to my used car department because then I'll be the second-largest Chevrolet dealership in Arizona. And I would very much like to be that."

"I—"

"Get-off-the-car!"

Matthias stood again.

Sonny ticked points off his fingers. "Traffic tickets, bar fights, jaywalkers, go for it. We're not micromanaging you. But if you want to think, go do it in Dallas or Tucson or Phoenix. There's plenty of opportunity out there for a young go-getter like you." He rubbed his eyes with his thumb and forefinger. "Look, Galt, just do what I say when I say it and when I need you to do it, capiche? Right now I need you to go get the freaking weirdo out of the bushes. I can't believe he painted on my sign!"

"Here's something to consider—a week or so for him to relocate wouldn't cost you anything, and it'll look good to the community. Generate a little goodwill."

"And you're still standing here. Unbelievable." Sonny eyed Matthias, considering what it'd be like to punch him in the face. Or shoot him with his own gun. But actually, as much as he hated to admit it, the guy was right. Sonny couldn't care less about the dead chick or crazy Goober Gomez, but he *did* have a grand opening to think of. Business was business. "I'll tell you what. I'll give the nutjob a week. But after that I'm going in with earth movers and bulldozers and if he's not gone, I'll scrape him out right along with the cactus and coyotes, got it? You go tell him that. Tell him I'm not fooling around."

"I'll tell him."

"And spread it around town that I'm being nice."

"Will do. Appreciate it."

Sonny turned back to the glass. Across the lot, through the trees, he could just make out the back of his vandalized sign. A movement caught his eye. "What the . . . ? You've got to be kidding me. Somebody's climbing up the sign again."

Sonny let the heavy glass door swing shut behind him as he walked outside to the main lot. Matthias followed.

Both men stood shading their eyes with their hands, looking toward the billboard.

"I'll go check it out," Matthias said.

A maintenance man buzzed by in a golf cart and Sonny stopped him with an upheld hand, then jerked a thumb to motion the guy out. He looked at Matthias. "Nah, I want it done right this time. Hop in, we'll both go. Catch whackadoodle in the act. Lock his butt up. Perfect. I'm sick of hearing about him and his dead wife."

The cart arrived at the sign just as an old pickup truck with a ladder hanging out of its bed peeled away around the corner.

"Last I heard, Gomez Gomez doesn't own a pickup," Matthias said.

Sonny climbed out of the cart and looked up at the billboard. "What kind of crap graffiti is that?"

Underneath ANGEL, slightly smaller and in blue paint someone had sprayed BOUGHT ME GROCERIES.

CHAPTER TWELVE

JAKE'S MORNING UNFOLDED LIKE USUAL. Wake up with the sun, pray, study, breakfast with Father Enzo and Lucille, morning Mass, a couple of hospital visits, an hour or so in the confessional . . . Days chased one another, rollers on the ocean. And now back in his office, thick adobe cool, even as the afternoon outside grew warm. Father Enzo always suggested this time of day be set aside for prayer, and Jake did just that, the names Honey and Gomez Gomez surfacing more than a few times in today's vertical conversation.

"Am I interrupting?" Father Enzo stood in the doorway.

"Father, I didn't hear you. Not at all."

Father Enzo held up the Superman notebook. "I was hoping you had a few minutes."

"Of course." Jake indicated the chair in front of his desk. "Please, sit."

"Excellent! Thank you. I couldn't sleep last night, and I spent some time on the story. Would you mind? It helps me to read it out loud to someone. And I don't want to wait."

"Early and Lucille will be disappointed."

"You flatter me. I can read to them later, but what's the saying? The muse has struck."

Jake leaned back in his chair and laced his fingers behind his head. "The muse must never be denied. Read on. I'm honored."

"*Eccellente!* Thank you for bearing with an old man's fancy." Father

Enzo pulled his bent and glazed reading glasses from his cassock, settled them on his nose, cleared his throat, and began.

Corfu

Fabrizio pulled the Vespa to a stop in front of the Taverna Sophia Loren, one of the many establishments owned by Tavi Bakis, Fabrizio's father. By Erasmo's estimation, Fabrizio's family owned half of Corfu, but the long-lingering island afternoons always found Tavi here at his favorite spot. In ages past the place had been called the Taverna Ampeli, or Tavern of the Vine, but a few years earlier Tavi had seen the Italian film actress on a ferry to Hydra where she was shooting *Boy on a Dolphin*.

Upon his return to Corfu, nearly unrecognizable behind brand-new Hollywood sunglasses, he'd promptly changed the name of his establishment to the Sophia Loren in honor of the beautiful film star. Of course the whole thing infuriated Fabrizio's mother and Tavi wound up sleeping in one of his hotels for a few weeks. Eventually, though, he'd convinced his wife to see the movie with him, even managed to arrange a private screening at the Hi-Lo Film Theater.

"So far a-so good?" Father Enzo said.
Jake gave a thumbs-up. "You have a way with words, father."
"Or they have a way with me, eh?"

A small crowd gathered outside the Hi-Lo that night to watch the aftermath of the showing, an ending they knew promised to be much more explosive than the writers in Hollywood could ever dream up. Bakis domestic squabbles ranked very high as far as local entertainment went. They held their breath as the couple emerged from the building. Imagine their surprise when Mrs. Bakis—a beauty in her own right—raised both hands in mock surrender and proclaimed, "Sophia Loren! Who can blame my idiot husband? Drinks on the house!" Cheers erupted. Tavi let the "idiot" comment pass but had to work hard to bury his dismay over giving away so much free liquor. In the end he counted it a small price to pay to be allowed back into his own bed.

Erasmo followed his friend into the tavern. It was early for the after-work crowd. The Sophia Loren was quiet and nearly empty. Tavi wiped down the bar beneath an oversize movie poster of Sophia, veins standing out against the great muscles of his forearms. He grunted when he saw the friends. "Here they come, hide the liquor and women! So, did you get Hercules today, Erasmo? I have a lot of money riding on you, my young friend."

"Nobody will ever get Hercules," Fabrizio answered for him.

"Don't be bitter, boy. I have money on you too. I'm a man who hedges his bets. That's why I'm rich."

"Fabrizio's probably right," Erasmo said. "But if anyone does get Hercules, it will be me, not Mr. Vespa here."

Tavi shook his head and laughed. "You sound just like your grandfather. How is that old reprobate? Tell him to come see me. I'll trade him a drink for one of his stories. I could use the entertainment."

Fabrizio walked behind the bar and returned with a bottle of retsina and two short glasses. "I told Erasmo he thinks about fish too much. He needs a girlfriend."

"What happened to Brigitte Bardot?" Tavi said.

Erasmo's face reddened. "How do you know about Brigitte Bardot? Isn't anything private on this godforsaken rock?"

Tavi shrugged. "Giorgos told me when he was cutting my hair. He also said you owe him a new magazine."

"I'll never get a haircut again," Erasmo said.

"Don't worry! Who am I to talk, eh? Standing here beneath a picture of Sophia Loren?"

"And it's just one of about a hundred in this place," Fabrizio said.

"Who knows? I bet she'll hear about us and come in sometime to see what all the fuss is about," Tavi said. "How could she not?"

"Because she spends so much time on Corfu," Fabrizio said. Tavi went back to wiping. "You have your mother's mouth, do you know that?"

Erasmo laughed. "Maybe Sophia Loren needs a waitressing job."

Tavi shook his bar rag at him. "You have his mother's mouth too."

Fabrizio pushed the hair from his face with the back of his hand. "Speaking of haircuts, I need one. Maybe I'll steal a picture of Bettie Page while I'm there. Hey, Pop, I told Erasmo I'd fix him up with Agnette if things don't work out with Brigitte Bardot."

Tavi chuckled. "Your cousin is fat and has breath like a sick horse. Better he should stick with Brigitte. Even if he only sees her in his dreams."

Fabrizio walked to a table on the patio and Erasmo followed. Fabrizio poured the retsina and both took a long sip of the bitter pine-flavored wine. The sea shone in the distance.

"I had him today," Erasmo said.

"Had who?"

"Hercules."

"I don't believe you. What happened? You missed?"

Erasmo drank, considering how much to say. "I saw something. It scared him and he ran for the rocks."

"Saw what?"

Erasmo paused, then laughed. "I think it was your cousin. Spouting water."

"That could have been!"

Conversation, laughter, and retsina flowed on within the comfortable confines of old friendship.

But then an engine rumbled and a long red convertible

pulled to the curb in front of the taverna with a tight screech of brakes and a grind of gears. Here was something truly out of the ordinary. The boys paused their talk to watch this new entertainment. A middle-aged man sat at the wheel. Thin, dark mustache and wire-rim glasses. A woman next to him, plump, pretty, and sunburned.

"I told you," the man said. "The Taverna Sophia Loren! Isn't that a gas?"

"It is! Just a gas!" the woman said.

"Matt Hamilton tells me they make the best bourdeto in Corfu. He said we have to try it. Couldn't face him if we don't. I'd never hear the end of it at the club." The man made a puppet mouth with his hand. "Blah blah blah. Matt Hamilton, what a bore!"

The couple spoke English. Not the American kind from the movies but the British tourist kind. The type of tourist that could afford to take their holiday on a Greek island.

Jake held up a hand. "Wait, are you trying to do a British accent?"

"Of course! This family is British."

"Okay . . . It's actually not bad."

"May I continue?"

"Please."

Father Enzo ran his finger over the page. "Where was I? Ah yes, the mother . . ." He slid back to Brit-talian.

The woman scrunched her face. "What's bourdeto?"

The man explained the local fish dish. But it wasn't the middle-aged couple that held Erasmo's attention.

Or the teenage boy in the back seat. The one with dark hair and glasses like his father.

No, it was the girl . . .

She might have been eighteen, beautiful as a summer day. She wore a loose-fitting sundress. Her shoulders were bare and tan. Freckles scattered across her nose. Even from across the patio Erasmo could see her eyes were the blue-green of the ocean and sky—the color of summer. Her hair was long and blonde and still wet from the sea. And Erasmo knew exactly where he'd seen that hair before.

"The mermaid," Jake said.

"Of course. You thought it was a real mermaid?"

"It's your story, father. I wasn't sure."

"My story. Yes . . . On we go."

Erasmo had known Fabrizio since primary school. And his friend never hesitated when it came to the fairer sex. Fabrizio leapt the low patio wall and bowed deep as he opened the car door for the mother, although Erasmo knew for a fact the plump, sunburned woman wasn't the target of the arrow Fabrizio nicked from Cupid.

Erasmo's English was nominal at best. Fabrizio's was better, but even had it not been, it wouldn't have deterred him where pretty tourists were involved. "Lady, lady! Welcome to Sophia Loren. Yes, yes! Bourdeto! A Corfu specialty and Sophia Loren has the best bourdeto in all Corfu. You must try!" He kissed the tips of his fingers for emphasis, a gesture more Italian than Greek, but international lines tended to blur when Fabrizio was in full flirt mode. "Beautiful fish, beautiful sauce, beautiful olive oil, onions! For a beautiful lady!" Fabrizio's eyes flashed to the back seat with this last phrase, and Erasmo felt a sudden and irrational pang of jealousy. The girl with the summer eyes was his mermaid after all.

The mother laughed gaily as she took Fabrizio's hand and stepped out of the car. "Then beautiful bourdeto it is! What a charming young man. This place is such a gas!"

"A gas!" the father repeated, following his wife out of the convertible.

Erasmo sipped the retsina. It burned on the way down and warmed his mood. Jealous pang or not, he couldn't help but watch the show with amused interest. The one consistent thing about Fabrizio—his friend never failed to entertain. The girl's brother hopped over the car door without opening it. Erasmo thought the girl would too—he sensed she wanted to—but Fabrizio would have none of it. He made a great show of helping her down, then offered her his arm to escort her. The girl took it with a gracious smile and they followed her family onto the taverna's patio.

As Fabrizio and the girl passed Erasmo's table, her gaze, for the briefest of moments, locked on him. Cool sea and warm sky eyes that assessed and dismissed and then were gone with a flash of fishy tail. Erasmo told himself it was the retsina that brought the color to his cheeks.

Tavi appeared loaded down with menus and good-natured joviality. He waved the family to a table with extravagant hand gestures and the only English phrases he knew, "Welcome!" and "Jolly good!"

With the guests seated, Fabrizio immediately switched modes to unofficial waiter and tour guide and rattled on in his broken English about the supremacy of Greek food, culture, and all things Corfu. The family laughed, bantered, and seemed altogether delighted. Tavi reappeared with a bottle of ouzo and four glasses, but the mother insisted on lemonade for the juniors of the party and punctuated her instructions with a happy laugh and several exclamations of "What a gas!" Tavi scooted away and returned in short order with a pitcher of lemonade. He poured for the family, then produced a glass from his apron pocket and poured a bit of ouzo for himself. He glared at Fabrizio who, in turn, crossed the patio and retrieved his retsina.

Fabrizio lifted his glass high. "A toast to our guests! Gia mas! To your health!"

"Gia mas!" Tavi repeated. "Welcome, welcome! Jolly good!"

"What does 'gia mas' mean exactly?" the mother asked.

"Gia mas! It means 'what a gas'!" Fabrizio said.

The woman's face lit and the family lifted and proclaimed in imperfect synchronicity, "What a gas!"

Fabrizio inquired where the family was from—London. Where they were staying—The Aegean Hotel. How long they would be on Corfu—at least the summer, maybe longer. As he spoke he occasionally gave the girl's shoulder a light touch.

Erasmo sipped his retsina and listened. The girl glanced his way again. Again his cheeks burned.

Tavi lugged out platters of food. Bourdeto, salads, bread, and more. A bottle of wine appeared and this time the girl accepted a glass. As the afternoon wore on and the food diminished, the family seemed in no hurry to leave. Fabrizio talked on and they plied him with never-ending questions about the taverna, Greek culture, and life on Corfu. Fabrizio, warmed by retsina and spotlight, did his best to satisfy their curiosity. He was an animal in his element, having been invited to pull up a chair and join their cheerful party.

More wine. The sun inched with reluctance into the sea, as it does on Corfu. More patrons arrived and empty tables filled. Lights came on. The Castellanos brothers, faces like old leather, strummed guitars. Tavi dropped into the chair across from Erasmo and helped himself to the retsina bottle, pouring into his glass then refilling Erasmo's. "My son doesn't waste any time, eh? He has his eye on that English crumpet."

"That's Fabrizio for you."

"Ah! His mother spoils him." He gestured around him. "But this will all be his someday. And you? How are the gods treating you?"

Erasmo turned the corners of his mouth down and shrugged. "What's to complain about? I go out on the sea in my grandfather's boat. We catch fish. He tells stories. We have sunshine.

We sell fish. And here I am drinking free retsina and watching the Great Fabrizio Show."

"Ha! True, true! I'm hungry. Tell me, what shall we eat?"

"How about bourdeto? I hear it's the best in Corfu."

Tavi clapped his hands together. "Yes, the best in Corfu!" He waved down a pretty server. "Takisha! Bring us bourdeto and a bottle of white wine, eh?" He clapped Erasmo on the back. "Ha! Bourdeto."

Erasmo clapped him back. "The best in Corfu!"

Conversation and laughter thrummed the patio in the gathering twilight.

Erasmo sipped and stole glances at the girl.

At length the family rose, bid Tavi and Fabrizio a wine-happy goodnight. As they climbed into their convertible, Erasmo willed the girl to glance his direction, but she'd clearly forgotten he was even there, if she ever knew in the first place. The big car's engine rumbled, and its red taillights bounced up the street and faded into the night.

Fabrizio flopped into a chair next to his father with an exhausted ear-to-ear grin.

"Let me guess, you're in love," Tavi said.

"Of course I'm in love! Did you see her?"

"Yes. She was fat and sunburned," Erasmo said.

Fabrizio laughed. "Cassie, you idiot, the daughter. She's like something out of a dream!"

"She's not bad," Erasmo said.

Fabrizio lifted his glass. "Let's drink to Cassie, the most beautiful woman in the world!"

Erasmo lifted and said in his best broken English, "What a gas . . ."

Father Enzo set Superman down.

"All so far?" Jake said.

"All so far."

"Quite the love triangle shaping up."

"Yes, love has many, many lines and angles. Tell me, who should get the girl?"

"Erasmo, of course. If it's going to be a happy ending."

"Would you like it to be a happy ending?"

Jake met the old priest's gaze. "Don't we all?"

Father Enzo smiled as he stood. "I suppose. Maybe so. But every ending, happy or sad, has a sweetness all its own. We'll have to see where the pen goes."

"Well, I have high hopes for Erasmo."

Father Enzo paused at the office door. "I prayed long for you last night, Father Jake. I'll continue to do so."

"You're talking about Honey?"

"Aren't we always?"

"Thank you, father, but you can trust me to do the right thing."

"I question many things in this world. But your honor is not one of them."

Jake stood, reached for his battered old cowboy hat. "That means more than you know. Really. I think I'll head over to Shorty's. Would you like to come?"

"Thank you, no. I have a story in my head that must come out. There are hearts on the line, eh?"

"I suppose there are. But go easy on them, would you? Love is tough."

"Of course not! A writer must never go easy. To lighten the pain is to lessen the joy. Enjoy your meal. See you this evening."

Topped with its towering adobe bell tower, the Jardin de Dios Mission crowned Paradise's town square. A sidewalk ran along the base of its steep steps, fronting businesses in both directions. Across the street, in the center of the square, a massive oak tree spread out its thick branches toward the buildings.

Jake took the sidewalk to the right and turned left at the corner. His long legs made quick work of the fifty yards or so to Shorty's.

Mermaids and big fish . . . Why couldn't real life be like a story? A big Superman notebook in the sky. A cosmic, corny happily ever after.

Arm around the girl, watching the sun set fire to the sky as it sinks into the Greek sea to Spanish guitar. No. In real life there were promises to keep. Vows. Schedules and commitments . . . *God, you know I'll do the right thing. You have my word. But I'm asking a favor—could you just possibly smooth the path a little?*

At the café, he reached for the handle but the door swung open with a jangle before his hand touched it.

And Honey stepped out.

CHAPTER THIRTEEN

"THE THING ABOUT GOPHERS," THE gopher snake was saying, "is that they just don't sit well with me. I'm not sure what it is exactly, but I'm beginning to suspect they might have too much acid."

The gopher snake kept talking—he *always* kept talking—and Gomez Gomez's mind drifted.

"Hello? Are you listening?" the gopher snake said, breaking his self-focused diatribe.

Gravel crunched up on the path.

"Uh-oh, peace out, Girl Scout." The snake dropped off the log and noiselessly slid his five-foot-plus, gopher-stuffed body into the brush.

Gomez Gomez squinted and made out flashes of a khaki shirt coming through the bushes. The shirt grew jeans and boots, then a head on top. A few more gravel crunches and a whole man walked into camp.

Gomez Gomez stared up at him. "You know people never think to knock around here?"

The man looked around. "I knock when there's a door."

"I ain't got no door. Just a gopher snake. I don't know how he hears people coming so good. All he's got for ears are a couple of little holes. Snakes are freaks, man."

"I take it you're Gomez Gomez."

"And I take it by your badge and *pistola* you're Sonny Harmon's messenger boy."

"I don't like to think of it that way."

"And yet, amigo, there it is. What can you do? You want a drink?"

"No, thanks."

"Right, you're on duty and all that TV cop show stuff. So, you came to officially tell me to beat it?"

The man shifted his weight to one leg and crossed his arms. "I was going to say it a little nicer than that. I'm Matthias Galt, by the way."

Gomez twisted a cap and took a slug of T-bird. He pointed the bottle at the man. "You should say *Officer* Matthias Galt. It sounds more official. Carries more weight, you know?"

"All right. I'm Officer Galt, if you like. You know Mr. Harmon wants me to arrest you for defacing his property?"

"And I'd like you to arrest Mr. Harmon for being a general jackass. We don't always get what we want, do we?"

"Afraid not."

"Maybe Sonny does, come to think of it."

"That's true."

"But even if he does, I didn't deface nothin'."

This gave the man pause. "You're saying you didn't spray-paint Mr. Harmon's billboard?"

"That's what I'm saying."

"Do you know who did?"

"Yup."

"Who?"

"This kid with a sun for a head. He forgot the cookies. Sure you don't want a drink?"

"Very sure. What kid are we talking about?"

Gomez Gomez picked up a stick and scratched his back with it.

"I'm talking about writing 'Angel,' not 'bought me groceries.' I know you didn't do that part," Galt said.

"Somebody wrote 'bought me groceries'?"

"Uh-huh. Blue paint. Right under 'Angel.'"

"She bought a lot of people groceries. Could have been anybody. Angel bought a lot of stuff for a lot of people. She was like that. She found Jesus."

The officer looked at the ground, rubbed the back of his head, then looked up again. He sighed. "You mind if I sit down?"

"You want the couch or recliner?"

"How about the log?"

"You're the officer, officer. Sit where you like." Gomez indicated the snake log with the bottle tip.

"Why don't you call me Matthias?"

"Okay, Matthias. You're the boss."

"Actually, and unfortunately, I think Sonny Harmon's the boss."

"Yup. Boss Hog . . . He give you the big fish speech?"

The man raised an eyebrow. "You've heard it?"

"Shoot, man, everybody's heard Sonny's big fish speech."

"Problem is, it's true. This pond is pretty micro."

"I guess. Still a lousy speech."

"Is how he looks like Don Johnson always part of it?"

"He does kind of, don't you think?"

"Yeah, if Don Johnson had a long nose and his eyes in one hole."

Gomez Gomez chuckled. Liking the man just a little.

"Did Father Jake come talk to you? With Detective Pines?"

"*Detective* Pines . . . Funny. I remember when Early used to be Hey-Gomez-Gomez-buy-me-a-beer-I-ain't-got-no-money Pines."

"I know you guys are friends. And Father Jake."

"Jake's the one you should be arresting. You know about Angel?"

"Your wife, right?"

"She was my wife until Jake hit her head-on right where your boss's stupid sign is. I used to put crosses on the side of the road, but somebody kept taking them down so I gave up."

"You think Father Jake caused the accident?"

"He ain't my father. My father's probably drunk in some cantina down in Old Mexico—or dead. Of course Jake caused it. The Lord gaveth and stinking Jake tooketh away. Whatever. He has to live with it now."

"I suppose he does. Life is hard."

"Nah, man, dying is hard. Life was good."

"Is that what you're doing out here? Dying?"

Gomez Gomez drank again, his bottle almost empty. Matthias Galt blurred. Gomez Gomez squinted an eye, trying to bring back a little focus. "Maybe. I hope so."

"Listen, Sonny says he'll give you a week. No more. Then he's starting construction. There are people who can help you. We'll get you something to eat and check you in to a place that can get you straightened out."

"Sonny's a peach. You think I need straightening out?"

"I hear you talk to snakes. That sounds like things have gotten pretty crooked out here."

"You want I should be rude to 'em? Ignore 'em?"

Matthias stood. "A week, okay?"

"You can tell Sonny I ain't leaving Angel. Not in a week. Not in a year. Not in a hundred years."

"Angel's not here. She's gone."

"I feel sorry for you. You don't know nothin'."

"A week, then we'll get you some help. That's the best I can do."

Gomez Gomez waved him off with a hand. "Just tell Sonny what I said. Tell him he can kill me if he wants. I ain't going anywhere."

"Watch those snakes." Matthias moved up the path. "A week, all right? I'll see you then."

"You said that already," Gomez Gomez mumbled.

He picked up his bottle and walked on uneasy feet past his shack down a path leading deeper into the brush. He kept a wary eye on the ground for the rattlesnake, but the sneaky thing didn't show. The rattler was slick, though. He could be anywhere. After a half mile or so he popped out of the brush beside a thick ponderosa pine. A wide swath of smooth, rounded stones lay before him. The shallow river beyond played, danced, and laughed, throwing sun sparkles high into the morning. Bones sat on a driftwood log close to the water's edge. He looked up as Gomez Gomez approached.

"Don't you ever go to school?" Gomez Gomez said.

"It's a holiday."

"What holiday?"

Bones tossed a rock and it splashed into the river.

"You got any of those cookies yet?"

"Nah, my mom's been busy. Pretty soon though."

"What's she busy with?"

"Just house stuff, I guess."

"I thought you lived in a trailer." Gomez Gomez leaned down and picked up a flat stone. He crouched slightly—feet still unsteady—screwed up one eye, held his bottle out with his left hand for balance, and attempted to skip the rock across the water. It bounced off a boulder at the water's edge and hit the river with a chunking sound. "Yeah, man, I skipped it."

"No, you didn't. You bounced it off a rock."

"The rock counts as one skip."

Bones laughed. "That's *zero* skips, man. Skips are on the water. You're such a freak."

"You ever see that movie *Tin Cup*? Where that dude hits the golf ball down the road? One time I skipped a golf ball across a parking lot like a million times."

"That's called bouncing, man, not skipping."

"You say potato I say po-*tah*-to. So hey, Sonny Harmon says I gotta leave in a week now. I got a stay of execution."

"What happens in a week?"

"He's gonna pour asphalt over my cold, dead body, I guess."

"What about Angel?"

"What do you care about Angel? You don't even know her."

"I sprayed her name, man. We're bonded now." Bones got to his feet, bent, and picked up a flat stone. He winged it across the water and counted eight skips out loud before it lost speed and sank. "Eight, dude. *That's* skipping."

"That was pretty good potatoes."

"Because you and me are friends. That's why I care about Angel. We gotta get Sonny Harmon off your back. He's crashing too hard into our world."

"Why you want to be my friend so bad?"

"Someone's gotta teach you how to skip. And help you get Sonny off your back."

"How we gonna do that?"

"I'll help. Don't worry."

"Yeah, but I mean how?"

Bones skipped another rock. "I'm thinking."

CHAPTER FOURTEEN

THE HUGE OAK IN THE middle of the town square never failed to capti-
vate Honey's attention. Its branches twisted, rose, and dipped in every
direction. Legend had it that old Coronado himself rested in the oak's
shade on his quest for his ever-elusive lost city of gold. An amazing
tree, mesmerizing even, and completely to blame, she told herself, for
her colliding into Jake's chest as she rushed out of Shorty's.

Jake stepped back, reaching out to catch her stumble. "Honey! I'm
sorry. I didn't see you coming."

"How could you? I was coming out and I wasn't watching where I
was going. I was looking at the oak."

Jake glanced over his shoulder at the huge tree. Like he wanted an
excuse to break eye contact. "Coronado's oak. Amazing tree . . ."

Honey paused. "Hey, is everything okay with you?"

His eyes tightened as he looked back at her. "I'm fine. Isn't today
your day off?"

"Uh-huh." Honey held up her cell. "Forgot my phone and stopped
by to pick it up. Never know when someone might call, right?"

"You never know."

"Like Publishers Clearing House. Or the president."

"Wouldn't want to miss a call from the president." He watched a
pickup pass. A few silent seconds ticked.

She stuck her phone in her purse. "All right, Mr. Sunshine. What's
with you lately? Are you mad at me or something? I mean, we can

BUCK STORM

still talk, right? You didn't make some new holy vow to Our Lady of
Depression to ignore waitresses, did you?"

His shoulder dropped slightly and he smiled. "I think I've just been
preoccupied. I'll do better."

"Why do you look like you're having a tooth pulled when you say
that?"

His smile found his eyes.

"Look, man, enough. We have history, okay, all that stuff back
there. But it seemed like everything was kind of normal. We'd moved
on, right? Now we're down to nothing but you asking me about my
grandma and me giving you a basket of chips."

"You're right. I'm sorry. I'm not sure what's wrong with me."

She fingered his cassock. "Well, I know what's wrong with me. I
still can't get used to seeing you in a dress."

"Tell you the truth, neither can I."

"Are you coming in to eat?"

"I thought I would. A little slow at the mission today."

"And you knew I was off so you wouldn't run into me, is that it?"

"Cut me a little slack. I come in when you're here all the time."

"No, you thought you'd miss me but I ran into you instead. And
now you're squirming. Tell the truth. Priests aren't supposed to lie."

"Actually, nobody's supposed to lie. Where are you headed?"

"Home."

"Where is that these days?"

"Wow. You know it's so weird you don't know that? Same apartment, believe it or not. Mattie even gave me the same rent when I got
back from Honduras." She studied him. And herself. His proximity
still stirred her, no denying it, but yesterday she'd made a decision to
move on. One too long in coming. And she'd had a good time with
Matthias. He'd been attentive, fun, smart, and genuinely interested.
A good, solid man by any standards. But Jake was Jake. He'd been
a huge part of her life and, even if there could never be a future, she
missed his friendship. No one knew her like Jake. "Look, Jake . . ."

"What is it?"

She took a breath, steeled herself. It would be a good test, right? To make sure she could give her whole attention to Matthias. She owed that much to herself. "If you're not starving to death, why don't you walk me home? Make it up to me for your recent lack of conversation."

Jake scratched his cheek and looked down.

"Or not," she said. "No pressure. I'd just like us to be able to be friends. With nothing weird."

Something shifted behind his eyes. Settled in his mind. "I can walk you if you'd like. I'd like that."

Wide and comfortable sidewalks fronted the buildings ringing Paradise's square. And unlike other towns dangling over the postmodern abyss, Paradise's old downtown remained vibrant and well used. With a fairly moderate temperature most of the year, the mountain town attracted locals and tourists alike. In the past year or so, several vintage stores and art galleries threw their hats in the entrepreneurial ring and prospered. Across the street from the storefronts, a narrower sidewalk skirted the low adobe and iron wall encompassing the grassy park beneath the oak tree. Red-gold tinged the tree's leaves, and autumn sun filtered down through its twisted branches, leaving little patches of leftover summer on the ground.

They passed Ace Hardware and Happy Yogurt in a bubble of awkward silence. *Enough.* Honey stopped in front of Finnegan's Bookstore. "You know what? Buy me a coffee."

"Coffee?"

"It's hot and comes in a cup. You drink it. And sometimes while you drink it you talk. With actual words. Which is something it seems like we could use a little of."

Jake lifted a corner of his mouth. "I think one of the reasons we always got along so well was that you talked enough for both of us."

"Not today. Today it takes two to tango. Coffee or not?"

Jake hesitated. "Okay then. Coffee."

"With words?"

"With words."

Two bay windows framed Finnegan's entryway. Books, new and

used, were on display in both. Scraps of paper taped to the inside of the glass-paned door advertised live music, roommate searches, and book club flyers. A neon-green poster shouted the news about a Saturday night dance at Spur's. Jake held the door open and Honey stepped in. The comfortable aroma of furniture polish, books, and coffee hung in the air.

The shop's owner, Finn O'Gara, glanced up at them over his reading glasses from behind the counter.

"How you doing today, Finn?" Honey said.

"Fair to middling. Same as usual. How about you?"

"Upright, breathing, and moving forward."

"That's a good sign. Could be worse."

"What more can a girl ask for?"

"How's life, Father Jake? Good Mass Sunday."

"Appreciate it. What're you reading there?"

"Somerset Maugham. *The Razor's Edge.* Ever read it?"

"Jake's more of a Zane Grey guy," Honey said.

"Not true. I read *Lonesome Dove* once. I'm well-rounded."

"McMurtry. He won the Pulitzer for that one." Finn went back to his book.

"See? Don't knock the western," Jake said.

Honey gave a what-can-I-say shrug. "I stand corrected. So you're deeper than you look."

"You making coffee today, Finn?" Honey asked.

Finn walked down a few feet to where the checkout counter became a coffee bar. "Always. People tend to buy more coffee than books these days. How can I make you caffeinated and happy?"

"How about a medium coconut mocha?" Honey said.

Finn pulled out a cup. "One cocomocha coming up. What about you, Father Jake?"

"Just coffee for me. Black. Can you do that?"

"Two-shot Americano for the padre. I can do that."

Honey and Jake made their way through shelves of books to the back of the long room.

"I think Doc made me watch the movie version of *The Razor's Edge* in a motel one time," Jake said.

"Leave it to Doc. Did you like it?"

"Sure."

"Remember, priests don't lie."

"I hated it."

"That's better."

Honey led Jake to a small table between a couple of bookshelves. Jake removed his hat and set it crown down on the floor beside him.

"What's an Americano? Finn can't just pour me a cup of coffee?"

"Let's pretend it's pretty much the same thing, you'll never know the diff. And, cowboy, trust me, you're the definition of Americano."

Jake gave a half smile and scanned the books on the shelf beside him.

"So how are Doc and Miss Hollywood, anyway?" Honey said.

"They're gonna have a baby. They were headed for Guadalupe in the Eastern Caribbean last time he called."

"A baby? No kidding. Good for them."

"That's what I told him."

"Crazy Doc."

"Yeah. Crazy Doc."

"He met his match in that girl."

Jake gave a slight affirmative tilt of his head, still studying the books.

"Okay, Jake, enough. Spill it. What's going on? We were close once. Things happened, I get that. And things changed. But you can't even look at me right now. Did I do something wrong?"

"It's not you that's the problem."

"Are you sick or something?"

Jake exhaled, shifted his gaze down to his hands. Finally he looked up again. "I'm not sure what to say. Things have just gotten hard. It's hard to focus on what's right. On what's real."

"What is real?"

He shook his head. "I'm not sure I know anymore."

"You didn't answer. Are you sick?"

"No, it's nothing like that."

"Then what? What things have gotten hard? Priest things?"

He took a long breath and blew it out slowly. "It's just something I have to deal with. And I will."

"You can talk to me, Jake. We're not what we used to be, I know, but it's still me."

Those serious Jake eyes. "I guess the Sonny Harmon and Gomez Gomez situation has brought up some old things. Feelings. Things I thought were in the past."

"You mean Angel?"

"Angel. The accident. That day. Everything . . . And you. Especially you."

Caution tugged. "Look, Jake . . ."

His face settled. Eyes softened. "I think about you all the time. God knows I shouldn't, but I do."

"Jake . . ." Heat came to her face. This couldn't happen. Not now. She'd turned a corner, right? Or at least put her blinker on. "You can't do this."

"You're right. I can't."

Finn approached, a cup in each hand. "Here you go, boys and girls. I'll be up front. Shout if you need anything else."

"You bet, thanks," Jake said.

Finn chugged off, leaving a wake of awkward silence behind him.

Don't do it, Honey. But she heard her voice say, "What is that you think?"

"Everything I shouldn't." A muscle ticked next to his eye. The same muscle that'd tick those rare times he'd talked about losing his parents. Or a friend who'd taken a bad fall off a bull. It broke her heart.

"I think about the way your hair use to catch the sun," he said. "The way you smile when you pour coffee and the way your smell lingers when you walk away. I think about every second of every minute we were together. How we laughed. How we fought. How we made up."

She blinked back tears and looked away. "What are we doing, Jake?"

"You're right. I should shut up."

"We both should. Just the coffee, hold the words."

"I've never told you I was sorry. I am. After Angel, I left. Then you left. And then all this life happened . . . I know it was years ago but we never really talked about it. And I should have."

"I waited a long time. I would've been there for you."

"I wish to God it all had never happened."

"But it did happen."

"And I can't take it back. I can't change it."

"Angel . . . That's why you punished yourself, I know that. But I could never understand why you shut me out, why you disappeared. And then a priest? Why? Why wasn't I enough for you?"

"You were. I wanted to talk to you back then. I wanted to explain."

"Then why didn't you? I had your mother's ring! We were supposed to get married. We were supposed to be there for each other!"

"How could I have married you? How could I have started a life and been happy when I'd taken Angel from Gomez Gomez?"

"You didn't just punish yourself, Jake. I suffered too."

"By the time I could talk about it you were gone."

"I was mad. Can you blame me?"

"I never blamed you. Not for anything."

"But you suddenly want to talk about it now? Now that you're a priest and I've just been on my first real date in a thousand years?"

"I didn't want to talk at all. I wouldn't have. It's just that . . ."

"That what?"

"That you bumped my hand."

"I what?"

"At Shorty's. You bumped my hand."

"What in the world are you talking about?"

"It made me think. I started remembering things, feeling things, I thought I'd buried a long time ago."

She stared at him, then shook her head. "I bumped your hand . . . Did my going out with Matthias have something to do with all this remembering too?"

"If I'm honest, it certainly didn't help."

Years of hurt and frustration swirled. Anger surged. "So what then? I finally have a chance to move on, and you're going to do this now? Unless you're going to ditch the robe and collar, I think it's a few years too late for this conversation, don't you?"

He met her gaze, then leaned back and sighed. "You're right. What am I doing? I'm sorry."

"Ugh, Jake! I . . . Oh, what's the use?" She rubbed her hands over her face, then flattened them on the table and looked up at the stamped tin ceiling. "This is all so pointless! Your mother's ring—it was the happiest moment of my life. You were everything I wanted. When you left that day after you asked me, I pinched myself to make sure I wasn't dreaming. Like I was in some stupid movie. But it was our movie. And then I had to take that memory and shove it in the trash. Convince myself it never happened. That even though I pinched myself, it actually was a dream. Because what's done is done, right? We live and move on. You've left us no other choice. And to tell you the truth, it all makes me want to scream."

"Angel," he said. "I—"

She'd never seen such pain on his face. For some reason it only fed her frustration and anger. She couldn't stop herself. "Angel, I know. And then not a word. You didn't say a word! I went to the hospital. I tried to see you, but you wouldn't even talk to me. You wouldn't talk to Early, Doc, anybody. It was like you died right along with her."

"I wish I had."

She shook her head, openmouthed. "Why do you say that?"

"Because I killed her. Me. I killed Angel. Just like Gomez Gomez says."

"Gomez Gomez? How can you be so thickheaded? Everybody knows it was an accident. Angel swerved into your lane. And even if it was your fault, do you really think Angel would want you to punish yourself? To throw your whole life away?"

"The priesthood isn't throwing my life away."

"Of course not, but—"

His face was the picture of remorse. "You want to know why? I'll tell you why. When I left your place that afternoon, I set my stupid hat on the seat. And just before the big curve, the wind blew it on the floor. I should have left it. I didn't need it. But I unbuckled and leaned down for it. That's the last thing I remember before I woke up in the hospital and they told me Angel was dead. It was my fault, Honey. Mine. Even if she did swerve toward me, I could have avoided it if I hadn't been reaching for that stupid, stupid hat."

Honey stared. "And you never told anyone about it?"

"Of course I told people. I told the police. But just like you they said Angel came into my lane and left it at that. They said there was no way I could've avoided it. It's Paradise. Small town. Everybody knows everybody, and I think they figured I was already wrecked enough, so why add to it? I told Gomez Gomez—I had to. And now I'm telling you. I wanted to see you then—tell you then—but I couldn't. I must've picked up the phone a hundred times. I drove by your apartment . . . but I couldn't stop. I couldn't bring myself to talk to you. Then you were gone and it was too late."

"You broke my heart, Jake. I was a mess. Aunt Holly wanted me to come stay with her in Tucson till I got my head together, so I did. I mean, what was keeping me here? Not you, that's for sure. Guilt? For taking your eyes off the road? Something we've all done a hundred times? This is why you ran away and hid in the church?"

"I wasn't hiding."

"Hiding is exactly what you were doing."

"I took Angel away from him. How could I go on and be happy with you?"

"Did you get the ring? When I mailed it?"

"Yes."

"Do you still have it?"

"Yes."

"You should pawn it. Or give it to somebody who can use it. Which isn't you, is it?"

"That's a low blow."

"I just wish I could swing lower."

"The ring is yours, Honey. It'll always be yours."

"You could have talked to me."

"I know."

They sat drinking their coffee. Neither looking at the other. Finally she said, "I tried to convince myself it was all a lie. That you must have had second thoughts."

"It was never a lie. What we had was the best thing I ever knew. The best thing I'll ever know. I was happy. And . . ."

"And what?"

"You might not like it, but I have to say this. Just this once and I swear I'll leave it alone."

"What?"

"I've only had one love in my life, Honey—you. I loved you then, I love you still, and I always will."

I love you, Honey . . .

The words hung in the air between them, thick and heavy as barroom smoke.

She stared at him. "Do you have any idea what an idiot you are?"

"A pretty good one, yeah."

"You sit there in that stupid robe or whatever you call it and say this? I honestly can't decide whether to walk out or hit you."

"Are those the only two choices?"

"At the moment, yeah."

"Then hit me, I guess."

She did. She slapped his left cheek so hard her palm stung. A red handprint formed on his face. "Shut up, Jake."

"I didn't say anything."

"Just shut up."

"All right."

"I wish I could hit harder."

"You hit pretty hard already."

"You love me? Why are you telling me this now? You're a priest! How am I supposed to react?"

"I don't know. By hitting me, I guess. I'm an idiot for saying anything. But I do need you to know how sorry I am for everything that happened back then. And if you know I'll still be loving you, even if it's from a distance, and even though I don't have any claim to you and never will, well, it's all I can give you. What we had was real. I don't want you to have to leave it in the trash."

"Your timing sucks, man, you know that? All those years . . . Do you know how badly I wanted to hear you say those words? Then I tried to forget you. I'm still trying. Going out on a date with Matthias is me trying. Heck, getting up in the morning is me trying. Do you know I left a guy standing at the altar?"

"I heard that, yes."

"Because of you."

"I didn't know that part."

"What did you think? Of course it was because of you. I looked down the aisle that day—my wedding day! He was standing there and the only thing in my head was, *Why isn't he Jake?* He was a good man. A really good man. But I need to be over you now, Jake. And I've met someone I think I like, you know? Someone I might have a shot with. Finally." Sorrow wrapped cold tentacles around her body. She kicked hard to keep from being dragged under. "I should probably hit you again."

"You can if you want."

A tear slid down her cheek. She made no effort to wipe it away. "I can't love you, Jake. You understand that, don't you? I want to be happy."

"I want you to be happy too."

"All this wasted time. You had to reach for a hat?"

"I wish I could go back and change it."

"So you became a priest."

"For Gomez Gomez and Angel . . . and God."

"I lied a while ago, you know."

"About what?"

"I remember touching your hand."

He let out a long, slow breath. "I know you're moving on, and that's the right thing. Just know how sorry I am for everything that happened."

"And everything that didn't happen."

"That too. Especially that."

"I should go."

"All right."

"I'm not mad at you, Jake. But I need you out of my head. For good. Do you understand?"

"I do."

It felt ridiculous reaching out a hand. "Fine. Friends?"

He took it. "Always."

"But I'm not sorry I hit you."

"I know."

"Bye, Jake."

"Goodbye, Honey."

CHAPTER FIFTEEN

SONNY EXAMINED HIMSELF IN HIS floor-to-ceiling mirror as he talked. He dug the way he looked behind his desk. Seriously powerful. Not Hickville powerful. Big-city stuff. "So it's settled then? Done deal? All dotted and crossed? We got the money?"

Mayor Casper Green sat across the wide expanse of thick, green glass that served as Sonny's desk. Casper's chair squeaked under his considerable weight as he leaned back and laced fingers behind his permed bottle-brown hair, his paunch a basketball beneath polyester polo. He gave a cat-and-canary grin. "Stick a fork in it, Bubba—contract signed. Eight million dollars, not a penny less. All that resort traffic'll funnel off Highway 30 at Juniper Road and turn up the mountain right here on a beautiful brand-new four-lane."

"Through my land."

"Ha! Best part. I still can't believe the council sold you that tract for one dollar."

"Right through my land . . ."

"Yup, but this new contract says part of it belongs to Talbot-West Resort Properties now, Bubba. Two-hundred-foot swath from Juniper to the river. And eight million bucks on the way—done deal. For a dollar investment. Not a bad profit, you ask me."

Sonny shook his head and whistled. *Eight million dollars for an empty stretch of nothing.* "That, my friend, is a seven million nine hundred . . . Well, whatever eight mil minus a buck is. A bunch of profit."

"You ain't blowing smoke, Bubba. And this is just the beginning. It puts you in a prime location with prime traffic. I can't get over it, eight mil for you and me to split."

"Minus the buck."

"Yeah, minus the buck."

"And the council's all good? Nobody suspects anything?"

"Not yet. Been a couple years since the meeting when Talbot-West approached. When nothing came of it right away, they all forgot. Even if they suspected, your billboard's a good ruse. Far as they're concerned you're just expanding your lot."

"I guess it doesn't matter anyway. They'll do what they're told in the end."

"I just don't want anything to sting us legally."

"Since when do we care about legally?"

"Since the payout is eight million bucks. Even those council pantywaists might raise a fuss about that kind of dough." Casper took a comb from the pocket of his golf pants, picked at his perm with nervous excitement. "Man, can you imagine? A ski resort on the mountain's gonna bring a pile of traffic through. I'm thinking about opening up a store. Ski gear with rentals. It'd be a gold mine."

"Okay, I gotta ask, what's with the perm?" Sonny said.

"Lisa's idea. Says it makes me look twenty years younger."

"Maybe, if twenty years ago were 1975 and you were the sound guy for KC and the Sunshine Band. It looks ridiculous."

"Well, Lisa likes it. And she's the one who has to look at it."

"I'm looking at it right now. And frankly I'm not digging it."

Casper shooed him like a fly. "Anyway, what do you think about my store idea?"

"Day late and a dollar short, junior. I've already got it in the works—Harmon's Ski Shack." A total lie but a rental store sounded like a good idea.

"Are you kidding?"

"Sorry, Mac Davis, you snooze you lose."

"Dang it. Oh well . . . I'm buying a boat, did I tell you?"

"Only about six thousand times."

Casper's veined, fleshy face beamed. He had terrible BO and Sonny did a quick shuffle through his brain for an excuse to get the guy out of his office. It paid to keep Casper fat and happy—he was a useful tool and front man—but Sonny's eyes were starting to water. Sonny indicated Casper's yellow polo. The poor thing stretched so tight over the mayor's gut it looked about to rip. Even worse, a few thick gray hairs poked through. *Disgusting.* "Golfing today?"

"No, why? You want to go?"

"Nah, just the clothes."

Casper looked down and scratched his gut. "What about 'em?"

"Golf stuff, right? Figured you might be in a hurry to make a tee time. Don't want to keep you."

"Nope. Hey, you got any of that Old Rip Single Barrel left?"

"You can see it right there on the shelf. You're not blind."

Leave it to Casper to go for the expensive liquor. Two grand a bottle, man!

"C'mon then, Bubba! Share the love. We're celebrating, right? Eight million bucks!"

Sonny sighed. "Yeah, we're celebrating." He focused on breathing through his mouth as he walked over to the liquor cabinet. He poured two fingers of the Rip Van Winkle for himself and, checking to make sure Casper's back was to him, a quick shot of Old Crow he kept in a separate decanter for the mayor. Hillbilly idiot would never know the diff, biff. He refused to waste good—no, *great*—bourbon on a fat slob like Casper Green. Still, the dude could come in handy. At least until the construction was underway and the town quit whining about all the extra traffic, crowds, and noise that would come parcel and post with the resort road. And they would whine, the sorry carcasses. Sonny could already hear it. The small-minded Paradise bumpkins loved their hick town. That's what came from having absolutely no vision. When it all hit the fan with the rubes, Casper would be a good fall guy. Let him dream about his boat, he'd never see a penny. As far as Sonny was concerned, stinky Casper could wind up in prison. Or dead in some ditch with Goober Gomez. He handed Casper the Old Crow whiskey, lifted his Rip Van Winkle, and grinned. "Here's to a job well done, buddy."

Casper lifted and clinked. "Here's to you, partner. And big, expensive boats."

"And to boats," Sonny said, wondering if he had an underworld contact that knew how to rig one to explode.

Casper swigged and sighed. "Ah! That's the real stuff."

Then again, it might be a good idea to keep the idiot around for a while. Stink or no stink, the mayor might be good for another backroom deal or three. He had his good points—certain lawyerly skills and questionable moral standards where money was concerned. But, man, that stench!

Sonny returned to his chair. "When will construction start?"

"They'll start surveying next week. Not a problem, is it?"

"Nothing I can't handle. It's just the nutjob's still down there."

Casper swirled his drink then sipped again. "Gomez Gomez? Thought Galt was supposed to vacate him."

"I gave him a week. People still get all mushy and stupid about Angel. I don't need a bunch of sappy idiots starting some Sonny Harmon boycott, getting all riled up against mean old big business over a dead chick. Especially with the lot expansion coming."

"I thought expanding was a red herring?"

"Who knows? Once the road to the resort's in, I can do anything I want. It's what you call location, location, location. I can have the road, Harmon Village, *plus* the biggest Chevy dealership in the Southwest. The whole enchilada."

"Yeah, I guess. Look, Sonny, something you should know, I told Talbot-West the town was dying to have their road through here. A little white lie. I gave 'em my handshake and everything. Their lawyer made it real clear they don't want any bad press for the company. They even put it in the contract. That means you gotta get Gomez Gomez out of there and still placate the folks around here about Angel. We gotta keep 'em happy. Those messages on your sign say something. This could go sideways real quick. Goodbye, enchilada."

"It won't go sideways. No way. Those signs don't mean a thing. People will shut up if I say shut up."

"I wouldn't be so sure, Bubba. You should hear 'em talk. Angel's kind of a folk hero. I think you better do some serious contemplation about old GG and how to deal with him. Get him out, but do it peaceful. Play it right, you come off a hero instead of zero. You need it. We need it."

"You know how many of these hillbillies pay their rent because of me?"

"I'm just saying go easy, that's all."

"Yeah, yeah. I'll go easy. Don't worry, everything's gonna be cool breeze."

When Casper shrugged his turkey neck jiggled. "It's a lot of money. Let's not take chances. That's all I'm saying. You know what happens when you take chances."

Sonny narrowed an eye. "What's that supposed to mean?"

Casper swallowed and grinned. "State championship, man. In the bag."

"That pass was on the money! Johnson dropped it!"

"On the money if Johnson was eighteen feet tall. You shoulda just run the play coach called 'stead of grandstanding like that. You woulda had a state championship on that shelf next to the Old Rip."

"That was over thirty-five years ago. Coach has been dead and buried for twenty. You'd think people would be over it by now."

"Who needs 'em? We got eight mil to split, right? I can't wait to get on that boat."

"Yeah, who needs 'em. That pass was on the money though."

"Sure."

Sonny held up his tumbler. Probably a hundred and fifty bucks' worth of Pappy Van Winkle's Family Reserve. "Anyway, eight mil. And like you said, we're just getting started."

Casper lifted his own fifteen cents. "Amen and pass the pretzels. Here's to the future."

"The future. When the honorable Mayor Casper sails the *Minnow* into the sunset with Ginger and Mary Ann."

"And Lisa."

"Can't forget Lisa. Perm queen of Paradise."

Casper beamed and emptied his glass. He gave another exaggerated, satisfied exhale. "Gilligan, how about a refill?"

"Why not, Skipper?" Sonny breathed through his mouth again as he retrieved the tumbler. Old Crow whiskey. Nah, useful or not, this smelly blob of flesh had to go.

And that pass had been on the money.

At least almost.

CHAPTER SIXTEEN

JAKE STEPPED OUT OF THE bookstore with not a clue about what to do or where to go next. He'd told her he loved her. It was the truth, collar or no collar. She would move on, had to move on, and that was as it should be. But she'd know he was always here for her. That, in his heart at least, he wouldn't abandon her again.

Out here on the sidewalk, the afternoon sun assaulted and he closed his eyes to let them adjust.

Early's gravel cut the afternoon. "Hey, Elijah, you praying or something? Calling fire down to burn up us Baptists?"

Jake cracked an eye to find his friend's old truck parked against the curb.

"And please let it be soon, Lord. Amen."

"Funny guy. Need a taxi when you're done with your intercession?"

"Not sure where I'm going."

"Physically or metaphorically?"

"All of the above."

Early leaned over and pushed the passenger door open. "You and the rest of the world, amigo. Add a train, somebody's mom, and some beer and you got yourself a country hit. Get in if you're gonna, you're on the meter."

Early had right around the same level of appreciation for police vehicles as he did for uniforms. Instead of department issue he opted for his 1972 Chevy pickup. He claimed it saved the department wear and tear. If anyone minded, Jake hadn't heard about it. The truck could use new paint, but the engine ran strong, and Early said his handheld radio and the magnetic police light he could stick on the roof when he needed it made him official enough.

Jake climbed in. "You on duty?"

"Uh-huh, just came on. Look at Mike up there. Guy's gonna kill himself."

A Paradise Fire Department truck was parked parallel to the sidewalk, ladder extended. A man wobbled at the top, struggling to tie off one side of a banner hanging draped across the street.

Early leaned out the driver's side window. "Hey, Mike, you okay?"

The man replied without looking down. "About got 'er whipped."

"Just be careful, would ya? You're making me nervous. I don't want to have to call for an ambulance. Or roll your bloody carcass off the street. I got fairly new boots on."

"I'm good," the man said.

Jake pushed a used coffee cup out of the way with his foot. "You pull people over in this thing?"

"As often as possible."

"They take you seriously?"

"Once in a while." Early pointed at Mike's banner and shook his head. "Miracle Days. Here we go again. A bunch of extra unpaid hours babysitting tourists. These are a few of my favorite things . . ."

"It's not that bad."

"All those vendors and crowds? It's worse than bad, man. Except for the rodeo. Maybe I should bag this cop thing and start bulldogging again. You could come with me. See if you can still ride."

"I can still ride."

"So, you got money for gas? Just stick it in the ashtray."

Jake leaned his head back and closed his eyes.

"You praying again?"

"Nah."

"All right, what's your problem?"

"Honey."

"You been bothering my fiancée?"

"Yeah. If having coffee with words counts. Which I think it does in this case."

"Coffee? So?"

"Wasn't the coffee so much as the words."

"Uh-oh . . . words as in *words* words?"

"Yup. About the bad old days."

"What's the matter with you?"

"Everything probably."

"How'd you leave it?"

"All right, I guess."

Early cranked the engine, checked the rearview mirror, and eased out onto the street. "So where am I taking you? The Vatican?"

"Anywhere. I don't care."

"It was that bad, huh?"

"It was pretty bad."

"What did you say to her?"

"We talked about the crash."

"What about it?"

"How this thing with Gomez Gomez has dragged up a lot of old stuff."

"Like?"

"I told her about her bumping my hand. And that I still loved her."

Early pulled a half tires-screeching U-turn and parked in the shade of the big oak, facing the grass. He threw the truck into drive and killed the engine. "You told her what?"

"Yeah . . ."

The engine ticked. Under the oak a mother watched her toddler drag a toy car on a string. The child made motor noises with his lips, the sound carrying in the still air.

"You do know you're an idiot, right?" Early said.

Jake waited for more. When none came he said, "Yeah, I'm an idiot."

"You want to know *why* you're an idiot?"

"You dying to tell me?"

"Absolutely."

"Okay, why am I an idiot?"

"Because Honey's the best thing that ever happened to you, man. She's the best thing that could ever happen to anybody. And now here you're sitting in my truck, depressed. Worse than that, what do you think she was supposed to say? You're a priest, man."

"I know that."

"So what did she say?"

"She hit me."

This brought Early a smile. "Really?"

"She has a good right hook."

"Good for her. You know you've always got me in your corner, but what were you thinking becoming a priest? Seriously, how could you possibly let her go? You were swimming with mermaids, you know?"

"Of course I know. But you can't tread water forever."

"That just might be the stupidest thing you've ever said. And I've known you long enough to hear you say some pretty stupid things."

"It was a road I had to take, okay?"

"Says who?"

"Me."

"And you're telling me you don't regret it?"

Jake took off his hat and set it on his knee. He gazed out toward the tree. "Maybe I do. Sometimes. What person doesn't question the decisions they've made once in a while? But that doesn't change them. What's done is done."

Early shook his head. "You told her you still loved her . . ."

"Yup."

"And she hit you."

"Yup."

"I should drag you out of this truck and pound you myself, man."

"You should. I don't know, it just came out."

"I mean, of course you still love her. A blind man could see that. But is it fair to her? Fair to the Catholics? Have you thought about leaving it? The priesthood?"

"I took a vow."

"You saying it's never been done? This is your life we're talking about, man."

"I can't expect you to understand."

"Good, because I sure don't."

Jake leaned back, suddenly tired to the bone.

Early started the truck. "I'm sorry, man. It seems simple to me but I'm a simple guy. I shouldn't give you a hard time. You did—you do—what you think is right."

Jake glanced over. "Thanks."

Early stretched his right arm across the seat back and backed out. "But if Honey ever decides she likes big, busted-up, retired bulldoggers, I'm gonna marry her so fast it'll make your head spin. I ain't no priest."

Jake grunted a smile. "Nah, you're a Baptist."

"Free to marry, free to procreate. Like Adam and Eve."

"I think you're gonna have to beat your boss to it."

"True. Dang that Matthias."

The police radio on the seat squawked. Early picked it up. "Go ahead, Arlene. What's the word, beautiful?"

The dispatcher's voice came through with a metallic ring. "Early, would you head over to Sonny Harmon's? He just called. Something's got his tighty whities in a knot again. He says he needs somebody to meet him at that new billboard of his."

"You got it. On my way." Early dropped the stick to drive and headed for the end of the block. "Want to go for a ride?"

"Do I have a choice?"

"Not really."

"Still on the meter?"

"Definitely."

Early headed out of the downtown area. Buildings rolled past. Vaughn's Electric, Circle K, Dairy Queen . . .

Jake kept his view fixed out the passenger window. "What do you think has Sonny riled?"

"We'll see soon enough, but I'll bet you a million bucks it starts with Gomez and ends with Gomez. How did coffee with Honey happen in the first place?"

"I was headed for Shorty's and Honey ran right into me coming out."

"As in literally ran into you?"

"Yup."

"You gonna talk again?"

"I don't know. Not like that anyway. But I'll see her at Shorty's. She said we were friends at the end. Still, probably be good to let it sit a while."

Harmon Chevrolet loomed. Early passed it, veered right, then cranked the wheel left and pulled a U-turn. Gravel popped beneath the tires as the truck came to a stop in front of the billboard.

"Wow," Jake said.

Early leaned his forearms on the steering wheel. "Yeah, I can see why Sonny's so thrilled."

On the billboard, ANGEL still stood out stark against Sonny's white suit. And beneath it BOUGHT ME GROCERIES in blue. But now several pieces of plywood, cardboard, even plastic had been nailed to the billboard's support posts. More messages, each a different color and writing style.

VISITED ME WHEN I WAS SICK

GAVE ME A RIDE

HELPED ME HOPE AGAIN

TOLD ME I WAS SPECIAL

Both men climbed out and walked over to the sign.

"People definitely remember her," Early said.

"And miss her."

Early looked out over Gomez Gomez's vacant lot, took off his hat, and scratched his head. "I came and saw you in the hospital after the crash. You were still under. Did you know that?"

"No, I didn't."

"Then when you finally woke up they said you wouldn't talk to anybody. Since it's been honest day, I'm gonna say something. You checked out that day and you never came back. I know you're a priest now. I know you took whatever vows that entails. But I gotta tell you, I still miss Jake."

Jake kneeled and ran a finger across one spray-painted word— HOPE. "I changed because I killed her."

"C'mon, man. For the thousandth time—"

"No. I told Honey, I'll tell you. I wasn't watching where I was going. The last thing I remember was looking away—reaching down for my hat—and then Angel was dead. I might as well have killed Gomez Gomez too. It was my fault. All of it. I killed them both."

"What are you talking about? What do you mean reaching for your hat?"

"It blew onto the floor. I unbuckled and reached down to get it. I knew better. Wasn't watching the road at all. I probably could've missed her. How am I supposed to live with something like that?" Jake pointed to the makeshift signs. "She was so good. You remember how happy Gomez Gomez was after he met her? She was his life. And I took her away."

"You don't know you could've missed her. The result might've been the same, hat or no hat. Why didn't you tell me about this before?"

"I don't know. I never even told Doc, man."

"But you told Gomez Gomez."

"I had to tell him. It was only right. I thought I was finally doing good. Getting it back together. Then a little thing like Honey touching my hand and it feels like it's all coming apart again. How am I supposed to live with what I did?"

"Look, Jake, I don't know exactly what happened. What would've happened if you'd been watching. But you just live, man. What choice do you have—die? You have to let it go. No matter what, or how it happened, it's over. It's the past. You have friends. You have God, right? You have your work."

"These signs don't make it seem like it's over. Gomez Gomez down there in the trees drunk and talking to snakes doesn't make it seem like it's over."

A whirring sound came from up the road. A golf cart buzzed out of

Sonny's lot and headed toward them, Sonny behind the wheel. Next to him a big man sat wedged into the passenger seat.

"Look at that dude," Early said. "Like an elephant shoved into a football helmet."

The cart stopped next to them, bringing a cloud of dust with it. Sonny hopped out. "About time you showed up."

Early walked toward him. "You're the one just showed up, Sonny. I been standing right here. What's the problem?"

"What do you think's the problem?" Sonny pointed to the sign. "Can you believe these people? Defacing private property? This is vandalism pure and simple."

"They don't mean harm. This is where she died and they miss her. It's their way of saying it," Jake said.

"If I recall, I called 911, not the Vatican," Sonny said.

"Well, whoever you called, Jake's right. They're showing their respect for a very good lady," Early said.

"Yeah? It'd be nice if they could show it in a way that didn't destroy my property. What a bunch of hicks."

"Could be they didn't appreciate you putting a ten-foot picture of yourself looking like Roy Rogers crashed into Liberace on the exact spot she was killed," Early said. "That was real thoughtful of you."

"Whatever. Galt told me you two talked to the nutjob. I gave him a week because I'm a nice guy. Is he out yet or what?"

"I wanted to talk to you about that, Sonny," Jake said. "Gomez Gomez is damaged. Losing Angel was more than he could handle. You can expand your car lot anytime. It's not like it's gonna make or break your business. Why not let us work with Gomez Gomez? Do it right. Bring him out slow. In one piece."

Sonny grunted a laugh. "I'm all broken up. I couldn't care less how many pieces the nutjob comes out in. I want him gone yesterday. A week is me being warm and fuzzy and stuffed full of cotton candy. Life is hard, then you die. Out he comes."

"That nutjob is our friend," Early said. "He lost his wife. You can show a little respect, man."

"So what? A lot of us have lost our wives. Hey, I lost mine! She's probably back in Vegas wearing bunny ears and a little cotton tail selling cigars to Wisconsin businessmen yahoos. And good riddance, I say. You don't see me drunk and crying in the bushes." Sonny motioned the man in the cart. "Milton, grab that bar in the back."

It took effort for the huge man to unwedge himself from the little cart. Once perpendicular, he circled to the rear of the cart and removed a crowbar.

Early glanced at Jake. "Dude's even bigger than me, and that don't happen often."

"My new mechanic," Sonny said. "Got him from the Second Chance Program. Fresh out of the hoosegow. Like I said, I'm full of cotton candy—kind of a benevolent dictator sort."

"And I bet he works cheap," Early said.

"Good help is hard to find," Sonny said.

"How you doing, Milton?" Early said.

Milton looked Jake and Early over but didn't speak. Tattoos covered most of the guy's visible skin. Strands of tangled barbed wire inked his neck. A pair of spiders—one beneath each eye—clung to a web that covered his face and shaved head. A swastika showed above the collar of his T-shirt. Another in the middle of his forehead.

"A mechanic, huh?" Early said.

"Fix anything," Sonny said. "But I got a theory he probably has all kinds of hidden talents. Deterring vandals and maybe dragging drunks out of bushes for example. And right now tearing unwanted signs off my billboard posts. Go ahead, Milton."

Milton started forward but Jake stepped in and blocked him. "Leave the signs alone, Sonny. Just let people pay their respects. They'll be gone soon enough."

"What are you talking about? Early, you're a cop. This is vandalism. Now tell your buddy," Sonny said.

Early shrugged. "Jake's right. Go back to your lot and leave it alone."

Sonny snorted. "You crack me up. You always were a loose cannon. Tell you what, Jake, get out of the way or Milton'll wrap that bar around your head, priest or no priest. Or Early's head, I don't care. Right, Milton?"

Milton blinked but said nothing.

"Put the bar away, Milton. You're not touching the signs," Early said.

Sonny stuck a cigarette between his lips and lit it with a gold lighter. He blew a stream of smoke sideways. "I wouldn't push it, Early. I'm betting from the swastikas painted on his neck old Milton doesn't back easy."

"C'mon, Sonny. That's enough. Let it go. Give it some time," Jake said.

Sonny brushed ash off the sleeve of his sport coat with the back of his hand. "Bet he doesn't like Mexicans either, what d'ya think? Even priest Mexicans. You like Mexicans, Milton?"

A car approached and all four men turned. A maroon Monte Carlo pulled up and parked behind the golf cart. The door swung open and Katie Morales climbed out, a bouquet of flowers in her hand. She took in the group, gaze lingering on Milton and the crowbar. "This looks like a fun party."

"What are you doing here, Aunt Katie?" Jake said.

"Heard about the memorial." Katie lifted the flowers. "Angel loved gladiolus." She walked over and pinched Sonny's cheek. "Thanks for doing this, Sonny."

"Doing what? This isn't a memorial. This is private property!" Sonny said.

Katie walked past him and laid the flowers next to one of the posts. She glanced at Early. "How you doing, Jay Silverheels? Who's your little friend with the crowbar?"

"Heya, Katie. This is Milton. He's real mean according to Sonny."

Katie looked up at Milton. "Nonsense. Are you mean, Milton?"

Milton looked down at Katie, expressionless.

Katie smiled. "You know what? You have a handsome face. Why did you have to go and put spiders on it?"

Milton's cheeks flushed beneath the tattoos.

"Sonny wants him to take the signs down," Jake said.

"After he hits me over the head with the crowbar," Early added.

"So you're telling your aunt on me now? What, am I grounded?" Sonny said.

"Oh, Sonny's just talking. He's still sore about blowing that pass in the championships. Makes up for it with fancy cars and crowbars," Katie said.

Sonny lifted his hands. "Why does . . . That pass was on the money!"

"Anyways," Katie said, "he's not taking down any signs. Not with the newspaper on the way, right, Sonny?"

His forehead furrowed. "What newspaper?"

"Tank's sending a guy out from the *Pioneer*. He told me at Shorty's this morning. Probably gonna make you a hero for remembering Angel like this."

"Dang it, I'm not—"

"Oh, don't be embarrassed." Katie poked Milton's massive arm. "You're a strong one, handsome. But let me tell you, don't mess with Tonto there. That Indian will take your scalp with your own bar." She walked to the car, got in, then leaned out the window. "Adios, *mijos*. See you when I see you."

The Monte Carlo spat gravel.

"It's gonna be on the news. This just gets better and better." Sonny said. "A stinking memorial? Crap. Get back in the cart, Milton."

CHAPTER SEVENTEEN

"Thanks for this," Matthias said.

Honey looked at him across the tiny table. As small as it was, it barely fit on the narrow back deck behind her second-floor apartment. His serious eyes reflected the candlelight. Straight from work and not nearly as put together as he'd been on their Spur's date. Kind of the opposite, in fact. His uniform shirt was covered with grass stains and had a tear in the shoulder. His left eye was beginning to blacken, and a wide bandage covered a cut on his forehead.

"Well, mister, you looked like you could use a friend. Not to mention the healing powers of a little home-cooked food."

"It's been a while on that front. Unless you count microwave dinners. The chicken was delicious by the way."

"Thank you. Nobody counts microwave dinners. Does your eye hurt much?"

He put a hand to his face and winced slightly. "I've had worse. You know, I came out here because I thought it'd be less violent than the city."

"At least you landed on grass instead of concrete."

"There is that."

"Moby Powell, wow. I once saw Moby take out half of Scottsdale Community College's offensive line by himself."

"I believe it."

"And Annie's okay?"

Matthias picked up a cup of coffee from the table and tried to sip through one corner of his mouth. "She's with her mom. Upset but not hurt, at least physically. Thank God it hadn't gotten that far yet. Just a lot of yelling on his part. And a chair through their front window."

"You didn't call Early?"

He grinned. "Ouch. I think that comment hurt worse than Mr. Powell's body slam."

"I'm sorry. You obviously handled it."

"Don't be sorry. I wish there'd been time to get Early over there. But Powell was out of his head drunk. I was afraid he'd hurt her." Matthias sipped again. "Besides, I've had worse from my pop. Not to mention my brothers. And being a beat cop in the Bronx isn't a walk in the park. I've seen women half his size who I guarantee you could take Moby out with one swing."

"I'm glad you're okay. Or okay-ish."

"I'm fine. And now I'm here with you getting sympathy and food, so it was all worth it."

"Speaking of food, I have some pie in the fridge. Cherry, from Katie."

"Never pass up pie. The eleventh commandment."

In the kitchen, she pulled the pie from the refrigerator and grabbed plates and forks.

"It feels different tonight," Matthias said, after she sat again.

"What does?"

"You."

She looked at him. "I seem different? How?"

"I'm not sure. Less guarded maybe. More open. For one thing, you invited me to have dinner."

"You gave me a ride home from Shorty's. And you protected Annie. Dinner's the least I could do."

"Well, I appreciate it. It's nice to see behind the curtain."

"You did come on a little strong."

"I guess I did. But you have a way of doing that to a guy."

"Not all guys."

"The ones with eyes and half a brain."

"You only have half a brain?"

"Maybe not even that after Moby Powell's sack."

She laughed. "I don't know. Maybe things are becoming clearer lately. The past is the past and it's time to look forward, right?"

"Lately as in since Spur's?"

"Let's just say I've had some clarity. It's time to start living. I've kind of been floating for a long time now."

He lifted his coffee cup. "Absolutely. Here's to clarity."

She clinked her water glass against his mug. "Clarity."

"And to our future," he said.

She clinked again. "And to not getting ahead of ourselves."

"Hey, I'm not naming our kids yet. But we're at least friends now, right?"

"At least."

"It's a start. I'll take what I can get."

Honey served the pie. She liked him better like this—not so put together, raw from the day. "Can I ask you a work question?"

"Sure. Not much top secret stuff going on."

"What are you going to do about this thing with Sonny Harmon and Gomez Gomez? It's all I've been hearing about at Shorty's."

Matthias forked a bite of pie and shrugged. "I don't know. I have to get him out of there. Like Sonny says."

"This memorial, or shrine—whatever you call it—for Angel is becoming a big deal."

"Don't call it anything in front of Sonny. He's less than thrilled."

"I feel terrible for Gomez Gomez. He just misses Angel. We all miss Angel. Who died and made Sonny boss anyway?"

Matthias swallowed his bite. "Man, kudos to Katie. Sonny Sr., I guess. It was all made very clear when I took the job. What Sonny says goes, period."

"And you put up with that?"

"I at least pretend to. Small town. Goes with the territory. It's the Wild West, right? It's a good job—benefits, 401(k), the works. Even an Escalade to drive around. Anyway, Sonny mostly leaves me alone to do the job."

"But not about this."

"No, not about this."

Honey couldn't picture Jake in an Escalade. *Stop it.* She mentally chased the image away. "You never knew Angel. She was so happy, so full of life. She was Gomez Gomez's center. His everything. I can't even imagine what it was like for him to lose her."

"There you go. Don't you think it's best for him to get some help?"

"Sonny couldn't care less about helping him. What if Gomez Gomez outright refuses to leave?"

"Then I'll have to cuff him and bring him out."

"You mean just drag the guy out?"

"If I have to. It might be the best thing for him."

"And what if I asked you not to do that?"

Matthias set his coffee cup down. "It hasn't come to that yet, and hopefully it won't. I'll tell you what, I understand everyone's concern, and I'll do my best to make it easy, I promise."

They ate their pie in silence, the night sounds soft around them, forks tinkling against plates. Honey thought of Moby Powell. A wall of human muscle, generally harmless but explosive when he drank. She tried to picture Matthias taking the man down. Not many could have done it and walked away, but Matthias was here, albeit bandaged, and Moby was sobering up in a cell at the police station. But Gomez Gomez was no Moby. And she hoped Matthias would see that. Studying his bruised, sincere face in the candlelight, she decided he would. Still, the whole deal with Sonny . . .

"Tell me about Miracle Days," he said. "It's my first go-around. It's a big deal, right? Town council even has me bringing up a few part-time deputies from Tucson."

"It's the biggest thing that happens all year, at least in Paradise. It's supposed to be a celebration of some miracles that happened here a long time ago. But nowadays it's more of an excuse for bringing in tourists and having a big party. It's a fun time. A big dance, food, and vendors in the square. Except for the atheists."

"Atheists?"

"A bunch of atheists come up here to yell at us."

"Yell at you why?"

"I guess they figure it's a good environment to make their point. They usually bring a news crew and wave signs in front of the mission. Shout at the locals. Some group out of the Midwest even threatened to sue the city if we didn't stop the whole thing. It hasn't gone anywhere yet."

"Sue you for what? How is it their business? It's not their town."

"I never could understand. If they really don't believe in God, what do they care anyway? But they're crazy mad about it."

"What kind of miracles?"

"You haven't heard any of this? My grandma was actually the start of it all. She had this heat rash that cleared up one night at a church service. Town went crazy. You'll see her on a float in the parade. She never misses it. Then a little boy fell out of the oak in the square. They say it killed him. But he came back to life right in front of a huge crowd."

Matthias laughed. "And you believe this?"

"I believe my grandma. And I believe the little boy. He's the pastor at the church that shares the mission building now. Some guy even wrote a book about the whole thing. They sell them over at Finnegan's."

"Maybe I'll have to pick one up. I'll put it in the stack right under the Hank Williams biography I'm reading so I can quit being embarrassed when you quiz me on my knowledge of ancient music."

"Hardly ancient."

"Compared to eighties rock, it is."

"Hank the First, Second, or Third?"

"First. I can now say that with absolute confidence."

"What can I say? I'm a great motivator."

"Miracle Days and atheists," Matthias said. "I think I'm already ready for it to be over."

"You've definitely got your hands full. You gonna go to the rodeo?"

"Are you asking me out?"

"Maybe. If you won't start crying when you see the big scary animals."

"Then I just might have to say yes. I think I can keep myself together."

"Good."

"Have I told you you look beautiful tonight?"

"No, but you just did. Thank you."

Music drifted through the open windows. Hank Williams's lonesome moon went behind a cloud and a rolling guitar riff started.

"'Gringo Honeymoon.' Robert Earl Keen. One of my favorite songs," Honey said.

"Never heard of it."

"That's because Robert Earl Keen isn't from an eighties hair band."

"I'll add him to my list. Hey, I know we're not naming kids, but do you want to dance?"

"What?"

"Dance. Hold each other and move to the rhythm of music."

"You're not serious."

"You said you love this song. Why not?"

"For one thing, my deck is three feet wide if I'm lucky. We'll fall off."

Matthias rose and held out his hand. "I'll be careful. Believe me, I'll hold on tight."

He stood there looking down, grass stained and bandaged, his smile a little crooked from the swelling. *Naming kids might not be the worst thing . . .*

"All right," she said, taking his hand.

He pulled her up and to him. Stars peppered the sky and his cologne mingled with the night-blooming jasmine in the yard below.

It felt good to let go. To do, not think.

Matthias held her close, his heartbeat against her cheek. On the radio inside the honeymoon ended and a commercial came on. Matthias didn't let her go and she didn't pull away.

CHAPTER EIGHTEEN

THEY'D GATHERED IN THE MISSION'S living room again. Usual evening drill—Lucille and Early on the couch, Jake and Father Enzo on the recliners, Father Enzo with his Superman notebook on his lap having brought Lucille and Early up to date on the goings on at the Taverna Sophia Loren.

"I knew there'd be a girl," Early said.

"There's always a girl," Lucille said.

"Even in Louis L'Amour, right, Early?" Jake said.

The detective nodded. "Gotta have the fairer sex. What else you got, padre?"

Father Enzo turned a page. "I worked much of the night last. You would hear more?"

"Read on. I'm sure we're about to get to the car chase, right?" Lucille said.

"You'll have wait and see," Father Enzo said. "Now . . ."

Corfu

The rising sun found Erasmo on the sea. His grandfather's boat bobbed beneath him, the morning air seasoned with gasoline, fish, and tradition. His head throbbed, a result of too much retsina last night, but he would find no sympathy in the tough old man. Erasmo wasn't the first fisherman, Greek or otherwise, to drink too much the night before a long day on the water.

"Fabrizio is trouble," his grandfather was saying. "He gets it from Tavi. It's in the blood. All those Bakises are the same."

Erasmo focused on the net he mended. "Fabrizio is Fabrizio. If I drank too much it's my fault, not his. Besides, I drank alone. He was off flirting with some girl."

His grandfather leaned against the bulwark, bowed legs braced against the roll of the sea, face brown and wrinkled as a walnut. "What kind of girl?"

"A blonde girl. A tourist."

The old man spat over the rail. "Blonde women are trouble—too flighty. So are tourists. Stay away from her."

"I did stay away from her! Fabrizio was the one flirting. I was drinking."

The old man's gaze remained neutral, a sure sign of wheels turning in his shrewd brain. "Whatever you say."

"So like I said, if I drank too much it's my fault."

"I didn't say it wasn't your fault. I only said Fabrizio is trouble. If you want to follow his path, don't cry when you wind up in a thicket of thorns with your horns stuck."

"Who's crying? Tavi says come tell him a story and he'll buy you a drink."

His grandfather grunted and struck a match to his pipe. He sucked the stem a few times to get it going, then blew smoke. "Why do I even talk? You and Fabrizio have been thick as thieves since you were old enough to walk. And you always do what you want. What do I know? I'm just an old man. A story for a drink? Sounds like a good trade."

Erasmo sat up, stretching the muscles in his back. "Don't be foolish. You talk because it's your life's joy to give me a hard time. I love you too, by the way. And why am I the only one working today?"

Another stream of smoke. "Because I'm old and smart and you're young and hungover from wine."

"What does that have to do with anything?"

The old man shrugged and pulled on his pipe.

Erasmo sighed and went back to the net. "What a gas."

The sun crossed the sky with the slow deliberation of a politician in love with his own voice. As always, his grandfather's mood rose and fell with the quality of the fishing. This day the haul was good and the old man smoked, told stories, and sang the old songs. The nets went into the sea, the nets came out. Finally, day far spent, the old man pointed the boat toward shore. They ate a light dinner of cheese, hard salami, and wine as the little craft chugged along.

At the dock, with the fishhold unloaded and the decks scrubbed, the old man slapped Erasmo on the back. "See you at home. Tell your grandmother I'm going for a drink and a game."

This was no mystery. Most nights found his grandfather at a table in some tavern deep into a game of diloti.

"I'll alert the newspaper," Erasmo said.

"And stay away from blonde tourists, eh? Stick to Brigitte Bardot."

"I'm going to kill Giorgos."

"Get a haircut before you do. You look like one of those American beatniks."

"Yeah, yeah. Have fun with your diloti."

"The sea was good to us today. Lady luck is smiling. I can't lose." The man limped off with a laugh and a wave.

Erasmo stretched and rubbed tired muscles. His grandfather was in a good mood. He'd stay up late drinking, playing cards, and swapping sea stories with his friends. Tomorrow he'd sleep the party off, leaving Erasmo free to hunt. A good night's sleep tonight and he'd be in the water with his speargun first thing tomorrow. Hercules would be his. He headed across a patch of dirt and grass and started up the hill toward the small house he shared with his grandparents. Halfway home he heard the familiar whine of Fabrizio's

Vespa. A moment later his friend rounded a turn. Fabrizio's face lit up when he saw Erasmo and he pulled to a stop beside him. Erasmo wasn't surprised to see blonde Cassie perched behind, arms wrapped tightly around his friend.

"There he is, home from the sea!" Fabrizio spoke English for the benefit of his passenger. "Erasmo, meet Cassie, the most beautiful girl Corfu has ever seen. Cassie, meet Erasmo, the second-best fisherman in all of Greece."

Erasmo bowed slightly. The summer-colored eyes appraised him coolly, then her face broke into mirth. "Only second best?"

Erasmo didn't quite trust his English so he gave another slight bow.

Fabrizio laughed. "He dreams of first but we have to be realistic, yes?"

The summer eyes continued to study.

Fabrizio slapped Erasmo on the shoulder. "My friend! You stink like your grandfather's boat. I can't believe that death trap still floats. Go home, get cleaned up, and come down to The Blue Dolphin. There is a big dance tonight by the water. Real rock and roll, a band all the way from Athens. And they're showing a movie up on the wall too. Hurry up!"

Behind Fabrizio, the summer eyes waited for his reply.

Finally Erasmo shook his head. He spoke in Greek. "I'm hunting in the morning. And it's been a long day. I'm tired. But have fun, eh?"

Fabrizio shrugged. "Suit yourself." He winked. "But my cousin will be there."

"Keep her away from the baklava." Erasmo tipped his head to Cassie and started up the road. Let Fabrizio have his fun. Grandfather was right, blondes and tourists—a bad mix.

Erasmo turned and took a few steps backward as he watched the Vespa grumble on down the hill. Cassie's blowing hair caught the last rays of the dying summer sun.

Father Enzo looked up, blinking through his reading glasses. "So far so a-good?"

Early gave a thumbs-up.

"I don't like the girl. She's fickle," Lucille said. "How could she like that Fabrizio? He's obviously a playboy."

"She's on vacation," Early said. "Just having fun. And Fabrizio was the early worm. Erasmo needs to man up if he's gonna get in the game."

"Man up like how you ask Honey to marry you every day?" Jake said. "I don't see how that's worked out too well."

"You're the last guy that should be piping in on that one, don't you think? She's playing hard to get. That's all."

"Uh-huh. For twenty-five years? That's pretty darn hard to get."

"You two are as bad as Fabrizio and Erasmo," Lucille said. "You got more, Enzo?"

"Of course!"

"Then read on, Shakespeare. Let's get Romeo his Juliet."

The next morning the chill of the bay sent bumps across Erasmo's skin as he finned out to deeper water. He dove and swam along the rocky bottom, letting his mind clear of everything above the surface. The water held him, embraced him, calmed him. He couldn't remember a time in his life, even as a small child, that the sea hadn't called. She was his mother, his home, and his protector. He kicked on, in no hurry to surface. From so many years of swimming he could hold his breath for well over five minutes. Not a record, by a long shot, but more than a minute and a half longer than Harry Houdini. Fabrizio had once lasted four minutes and twenty seconds and afterward promptly claimed that was plenty long enough for the first-greatest spear fisherman in Greece and anything more was nothing but grandstanding.

An octopus inked and scooted along the rocks. Erasmo followed him, needing nothing but an occasional lazy dolphin kick to keep up. Rays of sunlight filtered through the blue-green. Fish flitted. All was silence and shadow. All was peace. All was perfect. This was where he belonged.

He felt warm now, his body acclimated. Leaving the octopus to its panicked retreat he changed course with a hard flip of his right foot and followed his internal compass toward a jumbled rock formation—sovereign Hercules territory. He surfaced and gave a sharp exhale to clear his snorkel of water. He took several deep breaths as he kicked forward then dove again. Two more minutes of cruising the bottom and the rocks came into view. He swam through them with slow care, making no jerks or sudden movements. He paused, placed the butt of his speargun against his chest, pulled back the band, and notched it into the spear. Holding the gun in front of him he continued a slow path. An eel with a head as big as both Erasmo's fists poked from a crack in the rocks. An easy shot, but not today. No, today was all about Hercules. Today he would make history, he felt it.

"C'mon, Erasmo. Stick it to that slimy friend of yours," Lucille said.

Dive, swim, repeat . . . This familiar cycle went on for more than an hour with no sign of the big fish. For a long while, Erasmo floated on the surface of the bay above the rocks, breathing slowly. The big rocks below looked close enough to touch although the tops of their peaks were at least fifteen feet below. At length, he took a deep breath, pulled himself into a ball, extended his legs, and allowed their weight to push him down again.

Three good kicks and he drifted down the side of a large, craggy rock formation. A chill ran through his body. He'd been out a long time. After this dive he'd swim to shore, find a nice flat rock to lie on, and let the late morning sun seep through to his muscles, into his bones. At the seafloor he leveled and began another slow pattern through the rocks. Sunlight shifted as waves rolled above. He caught a glimmer, a dull flash in a rocky crag, and froze. He froze and remained motionless, suspended in shadow and liquid for nearly a full minute.

And then Hercules came . . .

With agonizing slowness the huge grouper eased his bulk from his hiding place, a king in his element, and hung, still as a star, four feet above the ocean floor. Erasmo could have practically poked him with his spear without even firing. Slowly, bit by bit, in tiny increments he leveled the gun. Not three feet of ocean separated the tip of the spear from Hercules's eye. Erasmo's finger tightened on the trigger carefully. He expected the fish to jerk away at any second.

But it didn't.

Hercules just stayed there, body blending with perfection into the mottled sea and rock. Three feet long, maybe? More than a hundred pounds, certainly. Eye catching the sunlight like a great silver disc.

It was easy, yes? Pull the trigger! Bagging Hercules would make him the talk of Corfu for years to come . . .

But Erasmo didn't pull.

In that immaculate moment, alone in the world except for this fish, something inside him stilled and settled. Hercules's noble gravity overwhelmed and dwarfed. Erasmo, stark and naked in its spotlight, knew in that instant what it was to be rendered insignificant and childish.

What was pride? Bragging rights with Fabrizio?

Foolishness!

This holy moment outweighed everything else. His grandfather's stories, the Sophia Loren, Brigitte Bardot, and even blonde-haired English tourists. Suspended beneath the glittering surface of the Ionian Sea, Erasmo felt face-to-face with Moses's burning bush. This theater, this stage, belonged to no one but King Hercules. No other actors shared it. No director called cues from the wings.

Erasmo eased his finger and lowered the gun. Hercules remained a painting, motionless in liquid space. Dignified benevolence.

It was enough.

Then the great fish began a slow swim. Not in retreat. Not in the opposite direction as Erasmo had anticipated, but directly toward him. A miracle, really. Too unbelievable to be happening. Yet there it was. Hercules swam by in no hurry, the magnanimous messiah welcoming his newest subject. Conquered to the core, Erasmo put a hand out and let his finger slide down the great fish's side.

And then Hercules was gone.

And Erasmo needed to breath.

A gentle kick pushed his body toward the surface. He saw her then, blonde hair billowing a slow dance in the filtered rays, fish tail barely moving in the water. Her eyes were in shadow but he knew they were the blue-green of sea and sky. She turned, hung there, then with a slow whoosh of wide fin swam away. What had she seen?

Erasmo didn't follow. For a long time he just drifted on the surface, thinking of Hercules, the sea and sky, and blonde hair—wet, cool, and beautiful—drifting in ocean-filtered sunlight.

CHAPTER NINETEEN

GOMEZ GOMEZ WRAPPED THE BULL rope twice around his hand and allowed the familiar surge of adrenaline to pull him deeper into the moment. The world narrowed to the width and length of the rodeo chute, population two. The huge Brahman lunged and lurched beneath him. Pain shot through his knee as it slammed against the closed gate and Gomez Gomez grinned because, after all, pain was gravity and gravity was what he needed to stay on the thing. The bull threw his head sideways and Gomez Gomez looked straight down into the beast's eye. It glowed red with fear and hate and the thrill of coming violence. Gomez Gomez breathed deep through his nose to calm himself, though he knew it to be a lost cause. Sweat and bull and dust filled his nostrils. Another lunge and the chute rattled like it'd come apart. Gomez Gomez let the bull settle then shifted his weight forward over the rope. *Here we go again.* It always came down to this second. This fraction of a second. He got balanced the best he could astride a full ton of rocking, slamming insanity then, heart hammering, he nodded to the chute operators. One pulled the release lever while the other yanked the rope that pulled the gate open.

And the world went blank.

White.

Silent.

Then he was back. Hooves thundering in his ears. The huge bull came up, aiming for the arena lights, then dove down and hard to the left. Gomez Gomez's body rocked back, his head slamming against the animal's hindquarters. The bull lunged up and right, wrenching Gomez Gomez left. The violence and force unbelievable. Never had he encountered an animal like this one. The bull spun, then reversed, then leapt and dove again. Gomez Gomez clung, instinctively knowing if the bull threw him, it'd kill him in a heartbeat.

Eight seconds. Hardly anything, but it might as well have been eight years. There had been rides in the past when time slowed. Everything became clear and perfect. He'd even picked out people in the crowd. The woman with the red, white, and blue sparkles on her cowboy hat . . . The little girl with the cotton candy . . . But this ride was different. The world rushed at him, screaming. Hard, bellowing breath with every slam of the hooves. The packed stands screaming, demanding nothing short of death. Crucify him! The bull snorted and rose higher than Gomez Gomez thought possible. The eight second buzzer sounded but still he clung, terrified to let go.

But then he did.

The bull wrenched left. Gomez Gomez slammed back and right, rope tearing from his hand. His boots flashed above his head, then the ground below, then his boots again as he tumbled.

Jarring impact, then blackness and ringing in his ears.

Then nothing.

"You okay, baby?" The voice foggy and far away but familiar. "Hey down there. On the ground. You okay, baby?"

Gomez Gomez cracked his eyes open, trying to focus. "You a rodeo clown?"

"Not in this life, son. Those cats are eighty-proof crazy."

Gomez Gomez blinked. The voice belonged to a face and the face belonged to a man. He stood looking down at Gomez Gomez, arms crossed. The guy wore a sparkly white jumpsuit and aviator sunglasses, his black hair slicked back into a fifties pompadour.

"Man," Gomez Gomez said. "What're you supposed to be? Elvis or something?"

"Not *supposed to be*, son. I am."

"Not a clown?"

"Not a clown, baby."

"You're saying you're the King . . ."

"You can call me your highness." Elvis reached a hand down and helped Gomez Gomez shakily to his feet.

"That was one bad bull," Gomez Gomez said.

"The *baddest*, baby. That was Gomez Gomez. You did pretty good, son. Better'n most."

"I'm Gomez Gomez too."

"Yeah? You a bad bull too?"

"Maybe."

"One crazy ride! Hey, son." Elvis pointed down the arena. "Check that out."

For the first time Gomez Gomez took stock of his surroundings. Lights shone, illuminating the arena and stands. "Where are all the people?"

"All the people're right down there, baby."

Gomez Gomez sighted down Elvis's finger. A woman stood at the far end of the arena.

A woman in a red dress.

Angel.

"Let me ask you something, baby. Who wears red on her wedding day?"

Angel. She stood there, beautiful and smiling. She held her arms out to him.

"Uh-oh, man . . ." Elvis said.

And Gomez Gomez heard it. A snort, a stomp. The huge Brahman pawed the ground, eyes fixed on Angel.

"No!" Gomez Gomez said.

The bull charged, hooves pounding. Gomez Gomez had never seen an animal move so fast.

"Angel, run!"

But Angel didn't run. She stood there, smiling, arms outstretched.

"This is gonna hurt, baby. What chick wears red to a rodeo?" Elvis said.

The bull lowered his head, his horns catching Angel full in the chest. Her head snapped forward against the bull's skull, then she was lost beneath the dust and two-thousand pounds of raging hell.

"Angel!" Gomez Gomez screamed.

He blinked his eyes, confused. He sat up. The rodeo arena was gone, replaced by his shack and dirty mattress. His alcohol-tinged sweat.

"Geez, man. Must have been some dream."

Gomez Gomez snapped his head around. The scrape of flint on steel sounded loud in the night. Bones sat in the lawn chair opposite Gomez Gomez's old mattress, his face eerily illuminated by the flickering flame of a cigarette lighter.

"Where did you come from?" Gomez Gomez said, still shaken, half here and half back in the arena.

Bones grinned, all teeth and glasses. "The sun, man. You wanna go for a walk?"

"What time is it?" Gomez Gomez said.

He kept an electric camp lantern on a rusty metal TV tray by his mattress. Bones flipped it on. "Two or two thirty maybe? Why?"

"What are you doing out at two in the morning?"

Bones lifted a bony shoulder. "Just hanging."

"You got school, right?"

"I don't need a lot of sleep. I'm gifted like that."

"The stars are quiet tonight," Gomez Gomez said.

"Yeah?"

"They're probably tired. I had a dream about Angel."

"Cool."

"And Elvis."

"Cool."

"But Angel got killed by a bull," Gomez Gomez said.

"That's not cool."

"Nah, man, definitely not cool."

"But it was just a dream. Stuff like that happens in dreams."

"I guess."

"So let's go then."

Gomez Gomez scratched at his beard. "Where?"

"I don't know. Just around. There's nobody out this time of night. We can go anyplace we want."

Gomez Gomez felt through his blankets and fished a bottle of T-bird. He lifted it to the light. "Check this out, Spaceman. What do you think this is? Half full or half empty?"

"I'm definitely in a half-full mood," Bones said.

Gomez Gomez stumbled up, took Angel's ashes off their perch, and tucked the coffee can tight under his arm. He stuck the T-bird in his coat pocket. "Then let's go for a walk."

"Angel coming too?"

"You got objections?"

Bones slung a backpack over his shoulder. "Not me. More the merrier."

The pair moved up the path toward the road without speaking, Bones's feet practically silent and Gomez Gomez scraping along with his usual shuffle. They paused in front of Angel's sign. More plywood and a bunch more messages. The bright lights made them easy to make out.

Gomez Gomez eyed the writing and read out loud, "Took me to church . . . Anybody coulda left that one. She took *everybody* to church."

Bones pointed at a board nailed high on one of the posts. VISITED ME IN PRISON. "Your Angel really got around, man. This place is getting crazy. Look at all the flowers."

"Sometimes in life there just aren't enough billboards," Gomez Gomez said.

"True story. Hey, so you really dreamed about Elvis?"

"Talked to the King just like I'm talking to you."

"That's a trip. What'd he say?"

"Said he wasn't a rodeo clown."

"Cool. I guess he wasn't."

"So where we going on this walk?"

Bones spread his arms. "The world is our backyard, Chachi."

Though neither suggested it aloud, they started toward town. The bright lights above Sonny's car lot turned the night to simulated afternoon, Bones's skin practically translucent in the glare.

"That's a lot of cars, man," Gomez Gomez said.

"Sonny Harmon's loaded. He can drive a different one every day of the year if he wants."

"But it ain't enough for Sonny. Now he wants Angel's place."

"Yup. And what Sonny wants . . ."

"He's the big fish."

"I'll get the pole."

They passed the commercial district and its generic metal buildings. And then the Circle K where Gomez Gomez usually got his T-bird. The joint stayed open twenty-four seven, but they didn't sell liquor between two and six a.m. A skinny, pimple-faced dude lounged behind the counter reading a magazine. He didn't look up when they passed.

Gomez Gomez paused, set down Angel, then took a pull from the bottle. He felt good. Really good, in fact. The dream had rattled him, sure, but it wasn't the first he'd had. Probably wouldn't be the last either. They all ended the same: Angel dying in some bizarre way. Elvis, though—the King was a new twist. Not unwelcome. Like Bones said, Elvis was cool. He'd like to talk to Elvis again sometime. Maybe Elvis was in heaven. Maybe Angel even got to meet him. Wouldn't that be a trip? Angel and Elvis? He stuck the bottle back in his pocket and picked up the Folgers can.

The dark storefront windows along First Street made Gomez Gomez think of eye sockets in a skull and his T-bird-instigated warm fuzzies faded a little. "You were right about one thing, man. Nobody around this time of night. I can see why."

"Yeah, I love it like this."

At the intersection where First Street teed into the square they both stopped. Flags hung from every light pole, still as wraiths in the streetlight glow. Miracle Days banners stretched in intervals across the streets that bordered the square. Booths, food trucks, and trailers filled the park beneath the big oak.

Gomez Gomez gripped Angel's coffee can tight. "Miracle Days. I could use a real miracle right about now. Giant magician with a top hat to make Sonny disappear."

"You believe in miracles?" Bones said.

"I believed in Angel. She was one."

"She could turn water into wine or something?"

"No, but she could turn a lost bull rider into a human being."

"That's pretty miraculous. But that was then, right? Now you're a drunk."

"And you want to be friends? Harsh, dude."

"I'm the kind of friend that tells you what's up. You saying you ain't a drunk?"

"Here, hold Angel." Gomez Gomez handed Bones the can. He sighed and drained the last of the liquor from his bottle. He dropped the empty in a corner trash can, and it hit the bottom with a thud—loud in the still night. "Nah, I ain't saying that I ain't a drunk."

"But you're saying we're friends?"

"You don't need no friend like me, Spaceman, trust me."

Bones scratched his fuzzy hair. "A miracle would be cool though, wouldn't it? Something to get more people thinking about Angel maybe. About you. Show Sonny Harmon for the big jerk he is."

"Yeah, but miracles don't fall out of the sky."

"Let's go to the oak, you want to?"

Gomez Gomez eyed the empty, dark storefronts. "The world is our backyard, right?"

"Exactly."

Plywood and tarps covered the booths in the park. The whole place like a ghost town. Gomez Gomez stuck to the middle of the aisle. "Freaky, man. It reminds me of one of them movies where all the furniture in some old mansion is covered with sheets."

"Yeah, kind of." Bones walked with his head tilted back at a crazy angle. "This tree is a trip."

"I heard it's one of the biggest in the country. Maybe the world."

"For sure. Maybe the universe."

"You would know, Spaceman. It ain't six yet, is it?"

"In the morning? You know it's not. Why?"

"Cause Circle K starts selling again at six."

"They're selling now. Go get a cup of coffee."

"You know what I mean."

"You mean you're a drunk."

The pair reached the oak's huge trunk. Bones put his hand against it. "Maybe the whole universe . . ."

"Maybe." Gomez Gomez dropped onto a bench. Wind brushed his face and oak leaves rattled.

Ain't no clown, baby. I'm the king . . .

"You hear that?" Gomez Gomez said.

"Hear what?"

Peanut butter and banana. Don't forget the bacon, man . . .

"That! Elvis, I think."

"I don't hear nothin' but your crazy brain knocking."

"Weird."

Bones dropped his backpack on the ground, knelt, and began to rummage.

"What are you doing?" Gomez Gomez said.

"Starting a little miracle. Get 'em talking and stuff."

Don't know nothin' about music, man. In my line you don't have to. Ha . . .

"You didn't hear that either, right?" Gomez Gomez said.

Bones pulled a can of spray paint from his pack. "Nope."

"How you gonna do a miracle?"

"I didn't say I was. I said I was gonna *start* one. Kind of."

"Cool."

Bones walked to a gleaming white food trailer. A sign above it said ELEPHANT EARS. He rattled the can, then it hissed in the night. When he'd finished he stepped back. Black dripping letters marred the white aluminum: ANGEL LIVES.

That oughta do it, baby. Go cat go . . .

CHAPTER TWENTY

JAKE TOSSED HIS COWBOY HAT onto the hat rack next to his office door. Three hospital visits, a turn in the confessional, and a catechism class so far, and it was only two in the afternoon. He dropped into his chair and opened his laptop. He had a few hours before he was expected at evening Mass. Might as well spend the time studying. His eyes scanned a passage from the apostle Paul's two-thousand-year-old epistle to the believers in Ephesus, but his mind wandered more recent roads.

Two days now since he'd seen Honey. He'd filled them with busyness, a useless attempt to distract himself. Was she doing the same? Or had Matthias stepped in and rescued her damaged heart? At night, in the quiet of his quarters, Jake prayed deeply for hours, trying without success to summon sleep. All this time—years now—he and Honey had an unspoken truce. At times it had even come close to friendship. Now he'd told her the things he kept buried. Opened the door and spilled it all. She'd accused him of hiding behind his collar. Early had essentially said it too. And it hurt. Why? Maybe, if he was honest with himself, because he'd thought the same more often than he liked to admit. He looked at the ceiling. "Are you still here? Because I'm starting to wonder."

Nada. Maybe heaven was closed for Miracle Days.

He pulled his attention back to Paul's words: "For by grace you have been saved through faith. And this is not your own doing; it is the gift of God."

Is that what I'm doing? Trying to save myself?

He snapped the laptop shut, stood, and headed for the door, grabbing his hat off the rack on the way out. Fresh air always helped clear his head. Stepping out onto the sidewalk in front of the mission he took a deep breath. Across the street the square beneath the huge oak thrummed with activity. Booths in various states of completion formed an imperfect grid, transforming the few acres of grass from a peaceful park into a small city. Jake checked for cars then crossed the road. On the grass he passed a shiny silver food trailer topped with a multicolored sign advertising American Indian fry bread. Next to it, a plywood booth, the cheerful banner above it asking, DO YOU KNOW WHERE YOU'LL GO WHEN YOU DIE? Candles, food, jewelry, T-shirts, baby blankets, knives . . . You name it, you could get it at Miracle Days. Without any directive from Jake's brain, his feet found their way to the trunk of the oak at the square's center. A bronze plaque at the base claimed the trunk's circumference measured over thirty feet around. Jake touched the rough bark, something he'd been doing since childhood.

"Quit being an addlepate, please." Father Enzo's voice found him from the other side of the tree.

Jake walked around. Father Enzo and Lucille sat at a folding card table, a chessboard between them.

"Addlepate?" Jake said.

"Simpleton, knucklehead, dimwit—someone who hugs trees in public," Lucille said. "Enzo's calendar word of the day."

"Nice. How did you even know I was here?"

Father Enzo's hand hovered over the board, his brows knit together. He spoke without looking up. "The birds stopped a-singing, the sky clouded up, all the gophers ran for their holes."

"What's that supposed to mean?"

"That you're a walking rain cloud, kid," Lucille said.

Jake chuckled. "You make me feel so loved."

"Happy to help."

"Are you lacking for things to do, Father Jake?" Father Enzo asked.

"Just thought I'd get some air."

The priest's watery brown orbs looked up. "And did you get it? The air?"

"I'm headed back now, father," Jake said.

The old priest smiled. "No, no. There is excellent air today. I can never beat this woman, why is that?"

"All this Texas brain power," Lucille said.

"That must be it," Father Enzo said.

"Hey, it's my book club, back together again." Early walked up. His *Kiss Me, I'm Baptist* hat propped back and a diet Dr Pepper in his hand.

"Patrolling the food trucks?" Jake said.

"I'm what you might call overseeing today." Early sipped his soda. "Bunch of mall-cop temps on the job. Matthias has me babysitting. Not much to do." He dropped onto a bench. "Good news is the first batch of fry bread is almost done."

Jake sat down beside him. "Fry bread sounds good. Especially if you're buying."

"It's your turn."

"How do you figure that?"

"Because it's always your turn. It's our thing."

"We have a thing?"

"Checkmate." Lucille leaned back, smiling.

"I don't believe it," Father Enzo said. "Set it up again."

"Hey, padre." Early pointed to Superman, lying next to Father Enzo's feet. "Any more progress? You kind of left us hanging."

"Ah! Much progress, yes. I believe I even have an ending for the story now."

"Well, we've got twenty minutes till Jake buys me fry bread. How about a chapter?"

"It would be better than losing another game. Are you sure?"

"You bet. It's a beautiful day. Lay it on us," Lucille said.

Father Enzo picked up the notebook and thumbed through. "Where were we?"

"Erasmo didn't kill Hercules," Jake said.

Father Enzo found his spot. "Ah yes, how sometimes the right thing does not always appear to be the right thing."

"And I think Cassie saw it all," Lucille added.

"Good stuff, padre. Read on," Early said.

Corfu

Twenty minutes after his encounter with the Old Man, Erasmo pushed his tired legs the last few feet as he trudged out of the sea and onto the shore at the edge of the bay. The sun hung high in the sky now, hot, laughing at ice cream cones and cold drinks. Tourists sprawled on towels and chairs and huddled under the beach umbrellas popping up from the sand, fairy-tale mushrooms down the length of the beach.

She was there, at the water's edge.

"I'm glad you didn't kill him," she said, summer-colored eyes taking him in with cool interest. She leaned back, her elbows in the sand behind her and the mermaid tail stretched in front. He stared at it.

She laughed. "Don't worry. It's not real or anything. It's made of rubber. My father bought it in Paris of all places. Wild, huh? I think it's a gas. I love the water. I always have. I can hardly stay out of it."

Erasmo marveled at the rapid-fire string of words. She hardly needed to breathe. Maybe she was a mermaid after all. He considered answering but instead opted for a serious nod. She was too beautiful, that was the problem. How could one speak to someone so beautiful? She stole his words. His heart pounded in his ears. If he opened his mouth she would hear it too.

"Do you ever talk at all?" she said.

He swallowed hard, and said, "Yes. I talk at all."

Her nose wrinkled when she smiled. He noticed her freckles. "I love your accent."

"What a gas," he said.

She patted the sand next to her, indicating for him to sit. He did. One didn't deny a girl like that.

"I'm glad you didn't kill him. But why didn't you take the shot?"

How could a man even begin to explain the moment a fish's dignity suddenly weighs more than pride? "Where is Fabrizio?" he said instead.

"Him? Don't worry. It's not serious between us or anything. He's just a friend. Like you, I hope. Can we be friends?"

"Yes."

"You don't say much, do you? Not like him. He never stops saying things."

"Yes," he said. "Never."

"You're so graceful in the water. I could watch you for hours."

"What a gas."

She studied him, serious. "It would be for me." She turned on her side and propped her head on her hand. "Do you go out farther? Deeper?"

"Sometimes."

"I'd love to go with you. Would you take me?"

There was no mocking in her summer eyes. They danced like sunlight filtered through water.

"Yes," he replied.

"Today?"

He shook his head. "Not today. Tomorrow perhaps. If I do not fish with my grandfather."

She laid back on the sand and Erasmo did the same. It seemed strange and not a little miraculous that they both looked up at the same sky.

"Why didn't you come to The Blue Dolphin last night?" she said.

"I was tired. I fished all day."

"I hoped you would come."

He looked at her but she kept her eyes fixed upward.

"Cassie!" a masculine voice called from a distance.

Cassie rolled over onto her stomach and held a hand to shade her summer eyes. "It's my father."

"I should go?" Erasmo said.

She laughed. "Of course not. Don't be silly."

Cassie's father approached. Her mother and brother behind him. "We've been looking for you. Time to go, we're meeting the Reynolds for an early dinner." He glanced at Erasmo. "Ah! You're not Fabrizio, are you?"

Erasmo rolled and got to his knees. His hair fell into his eyes. Sand crumbled and rolled down his chest.

Cassie said, "This is Erasmo. The first-greatest spear fisherman in all of Greece."

Cassie's father held out a hand. "Well then, we're in the presence of royalty. It's an honor to meet you, my young friend."

The man's hand was fleshy and soft. Erasmo looked for the right words. "Yes, an honor. No Fabrizio."

The man smiled, brushed Erasmo's transferred sand from his hand, then held it out for Cassie. "The Reynolds?"

Cassie had rolled the mermaid tail off her legs. They were long, lean, and tan. She stood and so did Erasmo. He bowed slightly to her then to the family.

"I'm coming, father. I'll catch up," Cassie said.

Her mother and father started away but her brother held back. "The Reynolds," he said with exaggerated posh. He put his hand out and Erasmo took it. "I'm Charlie. Please save my sister from a night of Reynolds tedium, eh, chum? See you." He trotted after his parents.

The summer eyes looked up at Erasmo. "Charlie's a good sort. I have to go but Fabrizio is taking me to The Blue Dolphin again tonight. Will you come?"

Erasmo lifted a shoulder.

"Please?"

He nodded. "Okay. Yes."

"My man of few words. Who didn't take the shot."

"Okay, yes, I come."

The summer eyes searched his. "You touched him. It was magical."

He knew she spoke of Hercules. "Yes."

"I'll tell you a secret. I loved you a little when you did that."

On tiptoes, she kissed his cheek. Then flipped her mermaid tail over her shoulder and followed after her brother.

CHAPTER TWENTY-ONE

SONNY SIPPED BOURBON AND PRACTICED taking deep, slow breaths, just like the yoga dude on Oprah said to do. Actually the yoga dude hadn't said anything about bourbon but it couldn't hurt in the relaxation department. *And don't tell me Oprah doesn't take a snort or two when no one's looking. Just look at the chick.*

The office was perfectly quiet. Sonny dug his office, loved everything about it. The huge green glass desk, the white shag carpet, the black and chrome furniture, his bull skull wall mount—it all said cool. The kind of cool from back when cool was cool. Before grunge and hip-hop and bip-bop . . . whatever all that noise was called. He even had an original Patrick Nagel he'd picked up at an auction in Phoenix. An illustrated brunette beauty. The whole place was pure 1979 awesomeness—just like Sonny.

Yeah, Sonny loved his office.

What Sonny didn't love was the newspaper taunting him from the top of his desk. Which is exactly what got him going on the breathing and bourbon routine in the first place. And also why he'd called Matthias Galt, who now stood in front of him.

The headline read, "Remembering Angel Gomez."

Sonny slapped the newspaper. "Can you believe this garbage? Did you read it?"

"Yes, I read it," Matthias said.

"Why did I ever have that stupid billboard put up in the first place? Now I'm stuck with it and I can't do anything about the stupid graffiti without coming off like a jerk. They're making her out to be a stinking saint! What am I supposed to do with that? Why didn't you shut this down before it started?"

"Look at the bright side. They also make you out as a hero for not shutting it down. That must be good for business."

"Business is good with or without the headache of some dead loser ghost haunting me. You never knew her. Chick was as batty as her husband." Sonny slapped the paper again. "They even have pictures! Look at this. *Angel* painted right across my suit. Can't you go arrest someone for that? This is clearly a violation of my property and rights. I don't even care who you arrest. Just pick some random hillbilly and lock them up for a few days. Send a message!"

"I could if I caught them in the act, sure. But I think it'd do you more harm than good."

"There you go thinking again. The sun's shining, but it's raining morons."

"There were five or six more signs nailed up sometime last night. Not to mention a ton of flowers. You know this is a reaction to you forcing Gomez Gomez out, right? I tried to warn you. Did you see the letters to the editor section?"

"Oh, I saw it. I practically have the thing memorized. 'Angel Was My Angel' and 'Leave Gomez Gomez Alone'—just two of the letters today. And there'll be more. They're practically electing stinking Goober Goober nutjob weirdo glass-for-brains for governor. It's killing me!" Sonny sipped and breathed.

"Could I talk you into holding off until things die down? Might solve everything."

And risk losing eight million bucks? Not a chance.

"Are you kidding? And let them win? I don't care if every little fish in town writes twenty letters with their tiny little flippers. I get what I want, and within the next few days there'll be the world's largest bulldozer on the edge of that land. I hope for Goober Goober's sake he's not in those bushes. I hope for your sake too. I want you to be able to sleep at night. You get my drift?"

"All right. He'll be out."

Sonny waved him off with a hand. "Just leave now, will ya?"

Matthias started for Sonny's office door.

"And arrest somebody. I don't care who. Anybody."

"We'll see."

Sonny picked up his phone and dialed the garage extension. "Tell Milton to come see me."

Sonny spaced out breaths and sips for three minutes until Milton's huge tattooed head poked through the doorway. Sonny beckoned him in and the big man entered.

"I pay you pretty good, Milton?" Sonny said.

"Yes, sir, pretty good."

"You think that big cop, Early, really could've taken you out with your own crowbar like the lady said?"

Milton shrugged. "I doubt it."

"I need you to do more than doubt it. I need you to tell me there was no way."

"All right. There was no way."

"Have some confidence, man. You look like you eat Hells Angels for breakfast and pick your teeth with their bones for crying out loud."

Milton's grin showed a broken front tooth. "Hells Angels ain't so tough. I ate a few."

"That's better. I got an issue and it ain't mechanical per se. That bum in the bushes over there? I need him gone but I need it quiet. People around here are all gooey over his dead wife, and they have a soft spot for the nutjob. You up for an extracurricular activity?"

"I guess."

"Meet me out front in an hour. We're gonna go make a little mess. Send a message. He's got to leave quiet, but he's got to leave."

"I hear you."

"All right, that's it then. One hour. Shut the door when you leave."

Milton did.

Sonny stared at his Nagel painting. He'd have a chick like that someday. Eight million bucks would see to that. Ten years now since his ex-wife packed up and headed back to Vegas. Back to selling cigars to losers. Couldn't take the small-town life, she'd said. Didn't like the mountain air. Missed the lights. Well, not the next chick! The chick in the painting wouldn't whine. She'd wait on him hand and foot and . . . *Man, that stinkin' pass was on the money! It was . . .*

The woman in the Nagel watched him. Her face the picture of seductive promise. *How come nobody paints like that anymore?*

He lifted his glass to her. "Eight mil, darlin'. What'll all these morons say then? Stupid Casper and his stupid perm. Like he never dropped a football . . ."

He picked up his TV remote off the desk and punched the on button. His huge screen blinked to life—*After Sunset* with Gregory Jones as Detective Matt Gunn. Sonny had all nine seasons on both VHS and DVD in his office closet. But the whole deal was on Netflix now. Push-button instantaneous. In this episode Gunn worked his way through a dark warehouse chasing a perp. Sonny liked the word *perp*. Gunn dodged through dusty, abandoned machinery, his hair feathered perfection. *They don't make shows like this anymore.* Nagel's paintings and *After Sunset*. Whatever happened to real culture? The greats?

Sonny stiffened as a can rattled in a dark corner of the warehouse. Gunn ducked, drawing his trusty Smith & Wesson Model 29. A deadly weapon. Gunn managed to kill three, four people every episode with it—at least the ones he didn't take down with his mad kung fu skills. Sonny opened a desk drawer and pulled out his own Model 29. Chrome .44 magnum just like Gunn's. He pointed it at the TV waiting for the perp to show his head. *Come out, Rusty! We know you killed Fanny. There's nowhere to go!* The can rattled again and Gunn trained his weapon toward the noise. Sonny didn't. Because, unlike Gunn, he'd seen this episode—and every episode—a hundred times. The can was a ruse of course. And big biker Rusty was about to get the drop on Gunn from behind. But another thing Gunn didn't know—Sonny had his back. When biker Rusty stepped out from behind a stack of fifty-gallon oil drums, Sonny was ready. He pointed, closed one eye, and pulled the trigger. The hammer clicked.

"Bang!" Sonny said.

In his mind's eye he saw Rusty's brains splatter over the wall of the warehouse. *Except Rusty looks a little like the nutjob today . . .* Gunn turned and gave Sonny a grateful thumbs-up. Sonny returned it, set the gun on his desk, and pulled his comb from his back pocket. He pointed it in the direction of the Nagel painting. "That, darlin', is how you do things when you're the big fish." He re-feathered his hair and replaced the comb. Lifting the gun again, he squinted down the barrel.

What would it be like to really shoot somebody? He was a good shot. He could knock a line of cans off a fence without missing once. He'd even killed a couple of coyotes. And then there was that time his neighbor's dog kept yapping—little freak of nature had it coming. Bang! But never a person . . . What would that be like? A human person? Not the first time the thought had come to him—far from it—but he'd always laughed it away. But now . . . now he had a real problem. A glass-for-brains problem that needed to keep his mouth shut. Needed to stop existing. Sonny eyed the pistol. Could he do it? Why not? Maybe he'd even be doing people a favor? Alcoholics could be dangerous and unpredictable. Maybe the guy was even on drugs. And, in the end, would anybody really miss a homeless whack job who spent his days talking to snakes? He picked up the pistol and pulled back the hammer.

Click.

That pass was on the money, man . . .

CHAPTER TWENTY-TWO

"You been up to Angel's sign today?" Bones said.

Gomez Gomez glanced back at the kid as the pair walked single file up the path from the river to Gomez Gomez's camp. Today, along with cutoff jeans, ratty Converse high-tops with no socks, and a dirty tank top, Bones sported a tall green-and-white trucker hat with *Your Logo Here* printed on the front.

"What's that hat supposed to mean? Your logo here?" Gomez Gomez said.

"Whatever you want, man, dealer's choice. You been up to Angel's sign?"

"Yeah, this morning. More messages about her all the time. More flowers too."

"Somebody wrote 'was beautiful.' That's cool."

"And 'helped me find God.'"

"I guess that's cool too. And there's a stuffed giraffe, but its neck is all limp."

The trees grew thick along this part of the path and sunlight filtered through them making random patterns on the ground. Birds flitted. Doves cooed.

Gomez Gomez stopped with an upheld hand. "Be quiet a minute."

"I wasn't saying nothing."

"Shh."

"What?"

"Listen to the doves, man. They don't sound as sad as usual, do they?" Bones turned in a slow circle, cocking his head. "I thought doves were supposed represent peace and crap, not be sad."

"Not the ones down here. They're the sad kind."

"Maybe they're changing their attitudes. Got on some meds. Everybody's on somethin' these days."

"Something. They're definitely cheering up."

"Maybe it's the Angel signs."

The thought comforted. "Yeah, man. Could be. Angel always made things happier."

"'Helped me find God' . . . What a trip. Did you hear that more Angel Lives tags are popping up?"

"By 'popping up' you mean you illegally sprayed more stuff?"

"All over town. It's a crazy miracle."

"Uh-huh. A miracle called Spaceman." Gomez Gomez sat down on a large boulder and unscrewed the cap from a Thunderbird bottle. He took a long swallow then belched loudly.

"God bless you," Bones said.

"I wish. You know, I ain't seen the rattlesnake in a couple of days."

"You worried about him?"

"Worried he's hiding in my shack or something. I don't trust that dude. Gopher snake's been around but no rattler."

A bar of sun came through the pine tree behind Bones, silhouetting his head again.

"So, you're supposed to be out in a few days, right? What're you gonna do?" Bones said.

"Nothing to do. Ain't leaving Angel." Gomez cocked his head. "Them doves are definitely happier."

"What if Sonny runs your house over with a bulldozer like he says he's gonna?"

Gomez Gomez squinted at the label on the T-bird bottle. "Tell you the truth, I probably wouldn't even know the difference."

"You still think Angel's in heaven?"

"I know she is."

"So you still think you'll go be with her if Sonny Harmon runs you over with a bulldozer?"

Now Gomez Gomez squinted at Bones instead of the bottle. "Yeah. Angel showed me Jesus, man. The way, the truth, and the life and all that."

"How come you never killed yourself then?"

"What the heck kind of question is that?"

"Just curious. Seems reasonable."

"I don't know. Maybe I'm doing it the slow way 'cause I'm chicken."

"Least you're honest."

"Call me Abe."

"So you think Angel's just up there waiting?"

"I always figured. Like that captain guy from *The Ghost and Mrs. Muir*."

"What's that?"

"This movie my mom used to watch all the time. The captain dude was cool. Had this crazy cool beard and pointy mustache. Wore all that captain crap."

Bones pushed his trucker hat back. "What if Jesus don't know you? What if you wind up in the opposite place than her? The bad place?"

Gomez Gomez considered this and a little ice formed inside him. The doves sounded kind of scared now.

Bones pressed. "What if, man? The bad place . . . That would suck. What if Jesus don't take drunks? Turns 'em back at the gate?"

"Well, shoot. Maybe . . . One thing's for sure. I ain't gonna let Sonny run over me if Angel ain't waiting at wherever I'm going."

"Only one solution."

"What's that? Don't be a drunk?"

"That a possibility?"

Gomez Gomez eyed his bottle. "I doubt it."

"Then you gotta stop Sonny Harmon before he creams you."

"How? You got a cannon or a bazooka or something that'll take out a bulldozer?"

"Nope. But I'll put my mind to it. Anyway, I'll be back tonight. Maybe we'll think of something by then."

"Yeah, or maybe not. Bring them cookies, man."

"For sure. See you."

"Yeah, see you."

Bones headed back down the path toward the river.

"Hey, Bones," Gomez called.

Bones paused. "Yeah?"

"Where'd you get that stupid hat anyway?"

"From your mom." Bones turned and continued down the path.

Gomez Gomez's feet knew every inch of the path so he leaned back into daydreams and let them carry him along. *The bad place* . . . That didn't sound good. Dark, scary, and eternally Angel-less. Maybe stinking Jake could help, him being a priest and all. *Nah, forget it.*

"Forget what?" a voice slurred.

"Where did you come from?" The pulse in Gomez Gomez's neck accelerated.

The rattlesnake sunned himself in a coil on a tall stump eye level with Gomez Gomez.

"Everywhere. You scared? I thought we were friends, buddy," the snake said.

"Just haven't seen you in a while. You made me jump."

"I've seen *you*, homey."

"That make me feel a whole lot better."

"Good deal, lemon peel." The rattler buzzed a quick rattle and Gomez Gomez took an involuntary step back. "Beautiful day today. Good hunting tonight, I think."

"Yeah. Really nice."

"You headed for camp?"

"Yeah."

"Trouble there, I hear. I'd walk slow."

"You mean Sonny Harmon kicking me out? Old news."

"No, I mean right now. There's trouble at your camp. I'm saying watch your step."

"What kind of trouble?"

"Me to know and you to find out." The rattlesnake slid down the log and slithered down the path in Bones's direction.

Gomez Gomez waited for his heartbeat to slow. The rattler at eye level was freaky. Those little black eyes, all that stuff behind 'em . . . Trouble at camp? What did that mean?

Angel. I wish you were here . . . You could tell me about Jesus again. Tell me about heaven. She wouldn't want him to be a drunk. Somehow he had to stop. *Helped me find God. . .* Angel went to church, or churches, but she never beat anyone up about it. She never got all preachy-sounding when she prayed like most people, just talked to God like she knew him or something—friendly. But she did talk about him a lot too. Before Angel, Gomez Gomez always kind of lumped God in with his dad, who'd basically split the scene without looking back. But after Angel . . . Angel had showed him God was real every day. Just by being Angel.

Helped me find God . . . Yeah, that was Angel.

A quarter of a mile, a couple of snakes, and several more God thoughts later he neared the camp. He slowed, listening. Only the doves—sad again, but curious too. He crept up on what he doubted, but hoped, were quiet feet. He made it to the snake log, lifted his head up, and peeked over with the greatest care. The rattler hadn't been lying. Trouble, sure enough. Bottles kicked over, some broken. His small stack of firewood scattered. The plastic tarp that made up part of his shack had been slashed and ripped, the plywood knocked over. His structure lay flat and sorrowful, reminding him of a donkey piñata his mother bought him for his tenth birthday after it got smacked, beat, stomped, and disemboweled of its candy guts.

Sometimes horrible thoughts hit you so hard you know they gotta be true. He crept on hands and knees to the wreckage. His hands shook as he pulled up a tattered plastic flap and peeked beneath. He sucked in a breath. His vision tunneled as the heavens roared. Somewhere far away a great tsunami rolled beneath the sea. The ground shook and he reached out a hand to catch himself.

Spinning. No center of the universe remained.

Angel was gone.

CHAPTER TWENTY-THREE

THE FLAT SCREEN IN THE upstairs mission living room was on but muted. A golden retriever mouthed something to the camera with CGI lips.

As the dog headed for a bowl of dog food, Jake said, "I can't imagine they actually got Gomez Gomez to talk on camera."

"Eight o'clock news. We'll know in half an hour," Early said. "Rosa said he was pretty out of it. But they got him."

"I hope Rosa went easy on him," Jake said.

"Rosa and Angel were pretty close. I'm sure she was cool."

"I don't know, when Rosa started newscasting she got all investigative reporter. I think she thinks she's Wolf Blitzer now," Jake said.

"I remember when she used to wipe her boogers under her desk," Early said. "So, padre, you got a chapter in you while we wait for the news?"

Father Enzo looked up from the Superman notebook and stuck his pencil behind his ear. "Yes! I was hoping to read you some more tonight."

Lucille set down Trivia Crack. "Twenty-five minutes, Enzo. Let us have it. Last I remember, the mermaid invited Erasmo to The Blue Dolphin and he said he would go."

"Yes, The Blue Dolphin, a wonderful place . . ." Father Enzo said. "You will love it."

Corfu

The Blue Dolphin was more than a taverna. For the younger Corfu set, the place represented a small escape to excitement. A slice of the outside world. Inside the small white-faced building men and women gathered to play cards and swap domestic news. But outside music bounced off the sea cliff, hanging lanterns competed with stars, and laughter rang. Tables and chairs lined the top of the seawall that doubled as a wide patio. Just over the rail everything from rusty fishing boats to million-dollar yachts bobbed on the harbor.

The action was already in full swing by the time Erasmo arrived. Beyond the lights a three-quarter moon cast a shimmering trail across the sea. Guitars and tambourines thumped rhythm and a clarinet blew melody into the salty air.

Erasmo took a bottle of red wine and a glass to a shadowed table close to the water and settled down to watch the dancing. He poured, then drained half the glass, self-conscious in his father's old black suit and polished shoes. The very things his father had worn the day he married Erasmo's mother, two years before the bus accident in Athens. Erasmo had paid Agatha—neighbor, part-time grumbler, and full-time island gossip—to iron his best white shirt. A little frayed around the collar and cuffs but still serviceable. He drank and pulled at his tie. He scanned the dancers and other occupied tables. More than a few tourists mingled with the locals, some of them even blonde, but no sign of Fabrizio or Cassie.

His eyes wandered out to the sea. Hercules was out there somewhere, probably tucked into his rock crack. Hercules—born again. Did fish dream? Sleepy visions of the dark depths or maybe the mysterious light that filtered down through their watery sky? His grandfather swore that one night, many years ago, he'd seen a whale turned on its side and swimming along the ocean's surface, the animal's black eye—big as a dinner plate—staring up at the night full of stars. Maybe he was navigating, his grandfather had conjectured. Or maybe he was praying . . . It was all connected somehow in a way Erasmo couldn't explain. Hercules, the whale, the stars . . . And he too was connected on some deep, molecular level. Often when he dove he felt an irresistible pull to ignore his lung's demand for oxygen and continue down. Down past the rocks and the wall where the island shelf dropped off to deep water. Past the filtered, probing sunlight. Drift down, down, down to where every color faded and the song of whales vibrated the soul. Down there, he told himself, he wouldn't drown at all but be welcomed by mermaids and mermen and great beasts of the depths, with countenances and words too wonderful for human lips to describe.

Or maybe this was only the rambling spew of a lovesick brain both dulled and stimulated by half a bottle of red wine, music, and the reflection of stars on water.

Still no Cassie. What had he been thinking to be seduced by a siren of the sea? But was he any greater than Odysseus, who commanded his crew to fill their ears with wax and then had them lash him to the mast as he sailed past the Pillars of Hercules? Come to The Blue Dolphin, the siren had sung. So come to The Blue Dolphin he had, powerless to resist her song.

Erasmo jerked his tie looser, then off all together. A girl approached and asked him to dance—a Greek girl he knew well. Pretty enough but he waved her off. Just let him drown himself in his cups. Yes, what had he been thinking?

Eventually the moon sank into the sea. The dancers thinned then disappeared altogether. The band packed up their instruments. A couple of old men stumbled through the taverna's door. Their slurry laughter bounced off the housefronts as they made their way arm in arm up the street.

His grandfather would want to fish tomorrow. He stood—and heard the familiar whine of Fabrizio's Vespa. He sat again and watched his friend park his scooter on the street and hold out a hand to help Cassie off. Fabrizio put an arm around her. He talked low—an intimate tone—and she laughed easily as they walked toward the Dolphin.

Cassie's mouth turned down when she saw the empty patio. "Is the party over?"

"When you're with Fabrizio the party is never over!" Fabrizio said. "Let's get a drink, yes?"

Storms and the blue sea in her eyes. "I told you I wanted to come earlier. I invited Erasmo!"

Fabrizio spotted Erasmo even as she said it. "And look who it is! He came. I told you the party wasn't over. Come, come! Sit with my friend while I get us a bottle. Hey, you don't look happy, Erasmo. We lost track of time, eh? But I'll make it up to you. All the wine you can drink! Cassie, please, sit with Mr. Gloomy while I go fetch a bottle." He pulled a chair out for her and she sat. He trotted off toward the taverna.

When they were alone Cassie shook her head. "You came . . . He said you wouldn't."

Erasmo shrugged. "It's nothing, yes? I come for drink. Nothing more."

She glanced at the tie next to the wine bottle but didn't mention it.

"I feel just awful. Fabrizio asked me to go for a ride, and I suppose we did lose track of time."

"My grandfather say time is a slippery thing. An eel. It is nothing. I come for drink."

"Yes, yes, exactly. Time is slippery."

Erasmo stood. "I must go. I fish tomorrow."

"Oh no! Please don't. We just got here and Fabrizio is getting wine. Erasmo, I was stupid . . ."

"I have had wine."

She reached for his arm, her hand warm through his suit coat. "Will you take me tomorrow? To the deep water?"

He paused. "No. Tomorrow I fish with my grandfather."

Fabrizio trotted back with a bottle and glasses. "Here we are! I told you the party is never over with Fabrizio. Where are you going, Erasmo? I'm in love, no? We need to celebrate. A toast!"

"I have to fish tomorrow. I have to go," Erasmo spoke in Greek.

Fabrizio waved a hand. "Tomorrow! Tomorrow will come whether you drink with us or not. Sit down!" He laughed. "Where did you get that ridiculous old suit?"

"I told you I have to fish."

Fabrizio poured for himself and Cassie. He switched back to English. "You always fish. But when do you live?"

He held his glass up to Cassie, not even noticing she didn't return the gesture. "But then again, for our man Erasmo, fishing is life, eh? But no Hercules, right, my friend? No Hercules. Ha! Too bad for you!"

"Yes," Erasmo said. He looked down at Cassie. "No Hercules. No one will ever get the Hercules."

He left the tie on the table beside his empty bottle because he'd never be stupid enough to need it again. He felt her eyes press his back as he left the patio and allowed the Ionian night to swallow him.

"Ugh! That little tramp," Lucille said. "I could strangle her."

"Oh no," Father Enzo said. "She is only young. And on holiday. She has a very good heart. She only doesn't understand how she affects these Greek boys. They are full of passion. Full of the island. Full of the sea. You will see."

"I'd better. You show us the heart, Enzo."

Jake rubbed the back of his neck and sighed. "It's a story. She can be whatever Father Enzo says she is."

"As opposed to real life?" Early said.

Jake shrugged. "The guy loves her and he can't do anything about it. That's the whole problem, right? The good news is Father Enzo can write them a happy ending, and we can all sleep like babies."

Father Enzo smiled. "Maybe I will. Or maybe not. The very good stories often turn our eyes inward, I think."

"If you have pockets in that dress you might keep an eraser or two handy, Jake," Early said. "You could stand a rewrite of your own."

"Just leave it alone, all right?" Jake said. "It's a story, that's all."

"Is it? That's all?" Early said.

"Leave it," Jake said.

Early shrugged. "Consider it left."

Jake pointed. "Anyway, the news is starting."

Early picked up the remote and unmuted the TV.

Staccato music led the broadcast, fading as Rosa Perez's pretty face filled the screen. She jumped in with her practiced reporter-ese. "In the news tonight the mayor of Phoenix is in hot water with the school district. New regulations on Indian gambling and how that might affect our area. And the late Angel Gomez gets a delayed tribute from a *lot* of local admirers. I was able to talk to Angel's widower, Gomez Gomez, earlier today. That and more right after this . . ."

The feed switched to a commercial—a dating website for ranchers and farmers.

They waited through the Indian gambling story, then the mayor of Phoenix. Weather and sports came and went. Two more commercials—Vaughn's Electric and the Arizona Lottery. Finally the screen flashed to Sonny Harmon's billboard plastered with graffiti and signs of all shapes and sizes, each a memory of Angel. Dimpled Rosa flashed perfect white teeth.

"Good evening, Paradise. As most of you know, Miracle Days is right around the corner. Well, I'm here on the outskirts of Paradise this afternoon to bring you a small miracle in its own right. South Street and Eleventh Avenue to be exact. What the locals sometimes refer to as the big curve. As you can see, I'm standing next to a billboard on the east side of the road close to Harmon Chevrolet. A billboard originally intended to advertise Harmon's expansion into this"—she turned and held a raised hand as the camera followed her—"vacant piece of property. But it seems some folks here have a very different plan."

The camera panned to the billboard. The wooden support posts now held signs from the ground to the billboard's platform itself. Different colors and sizes, but all celebrating a blessing someone had received from Angel. MADE ME LAUGH, ALWAYS SMILED, BOUGHT ME GAS, TOLD ME THE TRUTH. Even SAVED MY LIFE.

The camera zoomed in on the name Angel with feathered wings protruding from the top.

Rosa's voice off camera: "Angel Gomez, friend to all, a woman truly loved in this town, was killed tragically in an automobile accident on this very spot five years ago. A familiar story to many, Angel's widower, Mr. Gomez Gomez, now lives in a makeshift structure in the trees right here behind me. A sad and touching tribute to his departed wife. But today, tensions are brewing as the owner of Harmon Chevrolet, Sonny Harmon, has vowed to begin clearing the land for construction as early as next week. This includes Mr. Gomez's home. Now as we were setting up for this broadcast earlier, Mr. Gomez came over to see what we were up to. He has agreed to talk with us and has graciously been standing by."

The camera panned right and fixed on a bearded, bleary-eyed Gomez Gomez. A leaf stuck in his long, stringy hair.

"He looks like John the Baptist," Father Enzo said.

"Yeah, it's not great," Jake said.

Rosa edged into the screen at Gomez Gomez's elbow, microphone in hand. "Mr. Gomez, first let me say how sorry we are about your loss."

Gomez Gomez nodded, eyes swimming.

"Can you tell our viewers how you feel about this outpouring of love for your late wife by this community?"

Gomez Gomez tugged at his beard. His voice shook with nerves. "Angel was good. She always knew how to die. All them things on those signs are true. She helped people. She helped me. Now she's gone. Stole away by Sonny Harmon."

"Okay, I'm a little confused. Are you talking about the accident or the construction project?"

Gomez Gomez's dirty face turned to Rosa. He blinked as if seeing her for the first time. "I'm talking about Sonny stole her."

"Yes, I understand your wife was killed here five years ago in a car accident."

"I ain't talking about that. Don't you know, man? Can't you tell? She was the center. She was gravity. You can feel it plain on this side of the glass. She was in a Folgers can. But Sonny stole her."

"A Folgers can?"

"Exactly. That's what I'm saying."

"Oh, man," Jake mumbled. "What did you do, Sonny?"

"Wait, I think I understand. Are you saying someone stole your late wife's ashes?"

"Not somebody. Sonny Harmon. And Sonny Harmon ain't nobody but a thief." Gomez Gomez looked directly at the camera. "I know you're watching, Sonny, you stinkin' thief. You don't steal somebody without going to hell, you know. You'll be there with the snakes and Jake and everyone else who has blood on their hands. And I ain't never gonna let you rest, never." Gomez Gomez turned and disappeared into the trees.

Rosa paused, at a rare loss for words. "A theft? We don't know for sure. I suppose there will be more to come on this developing story. I'm Rosa Perez, KPTV News, reporting from the big curve here in Paradise."

Early switched off the screen.

"He's worse than I thought. Way worse," Lucille said. "He's saying somebody took Angel's ashes? He had them down there?"

"He kept them in a Folgers can," Early said. "Sonny Harmon might go that far to mess with Gomez Gomez. It'd be like him."

Later that night, Jake sat in his small bedroom staring at page twenty-one of *The Razor's Edge* but not seeing it.

Father Enzo appeared at the open door. "I thought you might be awake."

"He said I was going to hell because I killed Angel. I don't know how to help him."

Father Enzo leaned against the doorjamb, arms crossed. "I don't know about Angel, but I do know your friend Gomez Gomez is a lost soul. He is hurting badly. I believe you have to help him find his way. God has put this path before you."

"I can't even find my own way right now."

"The psalmist says it is God who makes known to us the paths of life. Sometimes you have to just walk. The light will come."

"I'm trying."

"You've been here a while now, Father Jake. And the man I've come to know and admire would never let a bully run roughshod over a friend. Even if he's struggling to find his own path."

Jake gave a reluctant smile. "A little like our boy Erasmo."

"Erasmo will find his way as well. Endings, father. Remember endings. Happy or sad, Love will win. Grace will have His way."

"I talked to Honey. You should know. I told her I'd always love her. But I know my duty."

The old priest nodded. "Then always love her well. That's what we do, yes? Good night."

"Good night, father. And thank you."

"It is nothing. Now I think I'll go see what I can do with our Erasmo, eh?"

Jake smiled. "Give him a happy ending, will you?"

"We will see. But he will be all right, whatever the ending brings. Happy isn't always what we think it is."

Jake lay back on his narrow bed, fingers laced behind his head. *Always love her well . . .* Honey was in the past now. He'd said what he'd had to say and she'd moved on. It was as it should be. But Father Enzo was right. If he was going to find his own path he had to get up and start walking. He'd wasted time. Gomez Gomez was a fight he could understand. And whether his friend hated him or not they'd seen a lot of miles together.

If Gomez Gomez went down, Jake would be at his side, come hell or high water.

CHAPTER TWENTY-FOUR

A FINGERNAIL MOON HUNG ABOVE the tree line. Dry lightning lit the firmament. Burnt ozone and pine permeated the night. Venus moaned, low and painful on the autumn wind.

Doves were silent.

God was silent.

Angel was gone.

Gomez Gomez had done his best to drink his way to unconsciousness after talking to the reporter. But tonight, stars swirling a riot above him, oblivion ducked and dodged, just out of reach.

Angel . . .

"So you were on TV." Bones sat on the snake log drinking a Red Bull.

"Yeah. I'm a star. How long you been sitting there?"

"Long enough."

"I didn't hear you 'cause Venus is so loud."

Bones squinted at the sky. "Whatever. You looked totally whacked on the news, man. I told you I'd come tonight, remember?"

Gomez Gomez made an okay sign with his free hand. "Man of your word, Spaceman. Can't argue with punctuality. Cookies?"

"No cookies. My mom took off a long time ago."

"Took off? When?"

Bones lifted his thin shoulders. "I don't know. I hardly remember her."

"You lied?"

"A little."

"I kinda thought you might be. Never brought no cookies."

"Sometimes I just pretend she's around. Sometimes I even believe it a little. Anyway, I don't feel like pretending tonight."

"Neither do I."

"Sonny Harmon says you gotta go. Time to put up or shut up."

Gomez Gomez let his head fall back against his rock pillow and grunted. "I already chose drink up."

"Nah. I got something that might help."

Gomez Gomez rolled and propped himself on his elbow. "You bring me an army?"

"No army."

"Not even a small one?"

"Nope."

"How about a *federale* with a slingshot? I'll take anything I can get."

"I got this. Check it out." Bones rummaged through his pack and came up with a short, wicked-looking pistol. "Trust me. This is the only thing that'll get Sonny Harmon's attention."

Gomez sat up. "Crap! Where'd you get that?"

"It's a snub nose .38. It's loaded too. All you gotta do is point it and pull the trigger."

"You know Elvis sometimes carried like five guns on him? Point it at what?"

"Sonny Harmon, I guess."

"Shoot him, huh?"

"I was kind of thinking you could just scare him a little."

Gomez Gomez slumped back. "Or I could just point it at me. That might solve everything."

"Thought you were chicken?"

"What I oughta do though."

Bones approached and stood over him, offering a hand. Gomez Gomez took it, got slowly to one knee, paused, waiting for the earth to level, then made it to his feet on shaky legs.

Bones held the gun just out of reach. "I ain't giving it unless you promise to quit saying crap like that. Don't point it at yourself, man. Never do that, okay?"

"Okay."

"Promise?"

"Cross my heart and hope to die."

"That ain't the right thing to say."

"Okay, okay, I promise. I might be crazy, Spaceman, but I ain't *that* far gone."

Bones handed him the pistol. "Cool. Elvis really carried five guns?"

"What they say. I read it somewhere."

"Crazy. They're heavy. And you can only shoot one at a time."

"Two if you're like Billy the Kid or somebody."

Bones considered. "Yeah, maybe two if you're like that."

Gomez Gomez pointed the pistol at Venus. "Shuuut uuup!"

Venus didn't.

"Sorry about your mom," Gomez Gomez said.

"Me too. I could use some cookies sometimes."

"Yeah. Anyway, thanks for the *pistola*, man."

"It's cool. Don't worry about it."

Angel . . . Gomez Gomez started for the road, bottle in one hand and gun in the other. His legs surprised him with uncharacteristic steadiness.

Bones fell in beside him. "Where we going?"

"I figure we'll find out 'bout the time we get there. You're the guy likes to go for walks. But wherever we wind up we're well-heeled, *si, amigo?*" Gomez Gomez held up the pistol.

"Yup. Packin' heat, man."

All quiet at the road. On the billboard, one-dimensional Sonny Harmon stared out at the lightning licking the horizon. Gomez Gomez poked at a bouquet of flowers with the barrel of the pistol.

Angel . . .

HELPED ME FIND GOD.

He remembered their house, their table, their bed. Holding her, listening to her talk in the darkness. *There's so much good in you, Gomez Gomez. So much love . . .*

And now all these signs and messages. This was Angel now. This was her legacy. This was her memory. She didn't belong only to him anymore. Now she belonged to everybody who'd known her and loved her. And Sonny Harmon wanted to destroy all of it. Destroy everything good.

Gomez Gomez pointed the .38 up at Sonny's stupid flat face and said, "Kaboom! Should I shoot up the sign?"

"Putting little holes up there so high up nobody'll see them won't do nothing, man."

Gomez Gomez lowered the gun to his side. "Yeah, ain't gonna waste bullets on a junky woodpecker piece of wood."

"You'd probably miss anyway."

"Maybe. But maybe I'd miss and hit Venus. Get her to shut up for a change." Gomez Gomez squinted at his feet and willed them to move. After a few seconds they grudgingly started into their awkward shuffle and he followed them up the road. They surprised him when they turned right and headed into the Harmon Chevrolet lot. Camaros, Silverados, Tahoes, Impalas—on and on the cars went. Tall light poles lit up the endless lines of shining new vehicles.

Gomez Gomez scanned the sticker in the passenger window of a Corvette. "Financing available . . . That's good news. You think old Sonny would sell me a car?"

"You got credit?"

Gomez Gomez waved the gun. "Nope, just a short nosed *pistola*."

"Snub nosed."

Gomez Gomez turned. "What?"

"Don't point that thing at me. I said it's *snub nosed*. Not short nosed."

"It shoots bullets, don't it?"

"Yeah."

"Then what's the diff?"

"Whatever. So you figure out what you're gonna do with it yet?"

"Kinda. I'm pretty sure I'm gonna shoot Sonny's stinkin' skunk butt. Then me and Elvis are gonna get Angel back."

"Man, you're hammered. I think I should take the gun."

The pair stopped in front of the dealership showroom. Plate glass window a hundred miles in both directions. Though the car lot was brightly lit, the showroom lay in darkness.

Gomez Gomez swigged again, the gun heavy at his side. "Sonny!" His voice reverberated off the glass. "Sonny!"

"I don't think anybody's here," Bones said. "It's the middle of the night, dude."

"Soooonny!" Another hard swig. He waved the bottle over his head. A movement caught his eye. Startled, he lifted the gun. His heart thumped. A man stared at him. A thin, dirty, bearded guy with long matted hair. The dude's clothes hung loose, rags on his thin frame. He screwed up his eyes and tried to focus. There was something vaguely familiar about the wraith. It took several long seconds before he realized it was his own reflection staring at him. Haunted, broken, mocking. Man, how had he come to this?

"The other side of the glass," he mumbled.

"What?" Bones said.

Gomez Gomez pointed the pistol at the demon in the glass. "You! You never loved her right . . . You loved her wrong." The barrel of the gun shook.

"That ain't Sonny, man."

Angel . . .

HELPED ME FIND GOD.

Please, Angel, help me find God . . .

"I'm telling you, I think you better give that thing back till you sober up a little," Bones said.

"You never loved her right. You loved her wrong."

"That ain't a *him*, man. That's just you in the window. A reflection." Bones reached out a hand. "Give me the gun, cool?"

The little pistol sounded like a cannon in the still night. It held exactly six bullets and exactly six bullets blasted through and around the man in the window leaving six holes, cracked spiderwebs of glass lacing away from each.

"Holy crap," Bones said.

"Holy crap," Gomez Gomez said.

"That was *loud*, man."

"Holy crap," Gomez Gomez said again.

"Don't move." A third voice. "Put the gun on the ground."

Bones's retreating footsteps slapped then faded into the night.

"Hey!" Gomez Gomez called.

"I said put the gun on the ground," the voice repeated.

Gomez Gomez turned slowly, searching out the source of the command. His eyes fixed on a large black circle. The circle, he realized after a bit of intense focusing, represented the business end of a shotgun barrel. The gun itself rested in the hands of a tattooed giant.

"Crazy, man. You're a giant. Can I keep the bottle?" Gomez Gomez said.

"I don't care about the bottle. Just put the gun on the ground. Go slow, this shotgun makes big holes."

The pistol slipped from Gomez Gomez's fingers and hit the asphalt with a metallic clatter. Big holes? The idea grabbed his liquor-addled interest and held it. It definitely had merit. A hole where the autumn wind could blow ozone and pine through him. Where Venus could sing the blues.

"How big a hole?" Gomez Gomez said.

"Big enough. I already called the cops, so don't get any ideas about anything stupid."

"I already got holes, man. And lots of stupid ideas." Gomez Gomez raised his bottle in a silent toast to the tattooed monster.

"Like shooting out a window? What good does that do you?"

"I don't know. Like I said, I got lots of stupid ideas."

"Look at yourself. You think Angel would want to see you like this?"

Gomez Gomez rocked slightly and squinted. "What do you know about Angel?"

200

"I hear things. And I read signs. You think this is the way to remember her? 'Cause I think it's pathetic."

Blue and red lights flashed the car lot as a police SUV pulled up next to them. A young officer got out, holding a gun in his shaking hands. "Get on the ground!" he shouted.

"Officer, I'd like to report a theft. Somebody stole Angel," Gomez Gomez said.

"On the ground!"

Gomez Gomez closed his eyes and leaned his head back, still holding the bottle, arms limp at his side. He let Venus's blues wash over him like rain. *Everything's changing, Angel. Show me God. I don't think I can hold on anymore. This giant dude is right. I'm pathetic. I'm full of big enough holes . . .*

CHAPTER TWENTY-FIVE

JAKE HADN'T BEEN INSIDE THE Paradise police station in years. Hadn't changed much. In fact, the place probably hadn't changed in decades. Green squares of commercial-grade tile covered the floor. A dusty plastic ficus plant stood sentinel next to the door. There were three gray metal desks for the officers and dispatcher, though only one was occupied. Bright morning sun slanted through the windows.

Matthias Galt looked up from his paperwork. "You here to see our valued guest?"

"He in the executive suite?"

"Paradise Police Department, we'll leave the light on for ya. We're nothing if not hospitable."

"Thanks for the call. What happened last night?"

"Close as I can tell, our not-so-happy camper decided it'd be a good idea to shoot out the window of Sonny Harmon's showroom. Sonny's new security guard caught him in the act."

"The big guy with the tattoos? Milton?"

"One and only. That guy's something, isn't he? What kind of name is Milton? Kids must have been merciless to him back in the day."

"Probably explains the tattoos and muscles."

"The guy's muscles have muscles."

"Where did Gomez Gomez get a gun? That's what I don't understand. It's not like him. A sledgehammer maybe but not a gun."

Matthias opened a desk drawer and pulled out a plastic evidence bag containing a short pistol. "He's been drinking in the bushes for the last five years. Who knows what is or isn't like him. Smith & Wesson .38 Special. It was stolen out of Mike Noxon's pickup in front of the Circle K two days ago. He stopped to buy a lottery ticket, and when he came back out, his door and glove compartment were hanging open. He called it in right away."

"Did he see Gomez Gomez take it?"

"Did he have to? Milton heard the shots. When he got outside Gomez Gomez was standing there with the gun in his hand. Milton counted six so he knew the thing wasn't loaded when he approached him." Matthias indicated the pistol with a finger tap. "This is Noxon's gun. The same gun Gomez Gomez used."

"What's he charged with exactly?"

"At the moment, theft, vandalism, and discharging a firearm within city limits."

"At the moment?"

"Thing is, Sonny Harmon says Gomez Gomez tried to kill him."

"Was Sonny even there?"

"That part's foggy. Still to be determined."

"You mean Sonny's trying to figure out what story works best for him."

"You said it, pal, not me."

"How does he know what Gomez Gomez intended anyway? Maybe he just shot at a window because he felt like shooting at a window."

"Maybe. Sonny coulda woke up on the wrong side of the bed. Or couldn't get his hair right. Who knows? Either way he's ticked off about the window. Not to mention a bullet hole in a very expensive Camaro, which, in case you didn't know, is apparently the same car they drive on *Hawaii Five-O*. I'm just hoping he'll settle down and forget Gomez Gomez once they finally start bulldozing that land."

"What's Gomez Gomez say? What's his story?"

"He doesn't say anything except for nonstop telling someone named Venus to shut up. Who knows what's going on in the guy's head. It's cobwebs and spiders in there."

"Can I see him?"

Matthias waved a hand toward the door leading to the cells at the back of the building. "Knock yourself out. I'm moving him to the hospital in about an hour. He was pretty loaded when I picked him up last night, and I'm sure withdrawal's gonna kick in hard. Usually happens within forty-eight hours or so. Bottom line, guy needs professional medical care."

"Thanks," Jake said. "I'm glad he's going to get it."

"So am I. It'll also hopefully get him out of Sonny Harmon's craw. Out of sight, out of mind. Best for everybody."

The green tile continued through into the back room. Gray walls gave the place a dreary, institutionalized look. It smelled of old urine covered up by bleach. Three cells lined the back wall. Gomez Gomez slept on a cot in the one on the far left, an arm draped over his face. Sadness tugged at Jake. He remembered this man, stubborn and bulletproof, perched in a chute atop a full ton of muscle and horns. Gomez Gomez, a tough man. A loyal friend. It broke Jake's heart to see him now.

Gomez Gomez had been right when he said Angel had picked him that day at the diner in Gila Bend. She hadn't even glanced at Jake or Early. "Hey, man," she said to Gomez Gomez, "I dig your silver tooth. How'd you get that?" True to form, Early jumped in to explain. Started in on the time Gomez Gomez got his mouth slammed into a metal gate piling off a bull up in Payson. Angel shut him down mid-sentence, saying she was talking to Gomez Gomez—the handsome one with the Elvis vibe. Gomez Gomez melted. He was hers for the taking.

A few folding chairs rested against the wall. Jake grabbed one and flipped it open with a jerk. He placed it in front of Gomez Gomez's cell and sat.

Gomez Gomez dropped his arm to his side with a groan and opened one bloodshot eye a quarter of an inch.

"Morning, sunshine," Jake said.

"Stinkin' Jake . . . I need a drink, man."

Jake pointed to several plastic bottles of water next to the cot. "Looks like you have plenty. Go ahead."

"I'm dying, man. Get me something, please."

"You'll live. It's time to leave the booze."

"I want to report a theft."

"I don't think you're in the position to do that right now."

"I'm sick, man! And I want to report a theft."

"Matthias is taking you to the hospital. Gonna finally get you cleaned up."

Gomez Gomez's voice rumbled like it was filtered through gravel and wet socks. "Yeah? Everybody wants to clean me up. They gonna patch the holes?"

"What holes?"

"The big enough holes, man."

"Are you hurt?"

"Yeah. Bad. I been hurt since you killed her. And now they're gonna wipe out everything. The snakes, Venus, even Angel's ghost. And I can't stop 'em. I'm lying here shot full of big enough holes."

"You're going to be okay now. We're gonna get you some help, amigo."

"Remember that? When we were amigos? I ain't nothin' now. Just holes. Like a piece of cheese. I sure ain't your amigo."

"I should have got you out of there five years ago."

"I ain't going nowhere."

"Doesn't look like you have much choice."

"I shot a window."

Jake shook his head. "Did you really steal that gun? What were you thinking, man? Sonny Harmon says you wanted to shoot him."

"I did want to, kind of."

"I don't believe you'd ever shoot anybody."

"I shot the ghost."

"What happened?"

"They stole Angel, that's what. What do you think it is I want to report?"

"You said that on the news. Somebody really took Angel's ashes?"

"Yeah. Ask the kid."

"What kid do you keep talking about?

"Spaceman. His head reaches the sun. Kid's a trip." Gomez Gomez put his hands over his ears and gave a low moan.

"What's the matter now?"

"Venus, man. She used to only sing at night but now she won't shut up. God help me! Please, man, I need a drink."

"No, you need to get your head clear."

Gomez Gomez sat up. "The thing is, I'm dying, man, and I ain't like her—I don't know how to die. I smell oil and snakes all the time. I hear Venus screaming. Gnashing of teeth . . . That's where I'm going, right? Hell? I'll never see her again."

"You're not dying. You're going to get better. You're going to heal now."

"Death's been following me around for five years, man. I've seen him. I seen the rattler, you know?"

"You're going to get better."

"He's following you too. The rattler knows stuff. Knows about you and Angel."

"We're both going to get better, okay?"

"That's why you're a priest, 'cause you're dying. But you can't hide from the rattler."

"C'mon, man . . ."

"I'm a ghost already. I'm going to hell and she'll be lost to me forever."

"You're talking like a crazy person."

"Help me, Jake. I'm a ghost."

"What do you want from me? How can I help you?"

Gomez Gomez moved with surprising quickness. He stood and stumbled to the bars, gripping them to support his shaking legs. Breath, smoke, old sweat, urine . . . Jake fought the urge to turn his head.

Gomez Gomez's knuckles turned white. "Save me, Jake. I'm full of big enough holes. I'm leaking out all over the place. I have to see her again. Please. Save me. I might be going to the bad place."

"I can't do anything. I'm just a man. Only God can save you."

"But priests forgive sins. Like that big dude said, Angel wouldn't like me like this. I'm full of holes."

"It's not about the holes. You can change. You *will* change. I'll help."

"Are you a priest or not, man? Save me!"

Jake put a hand over Gomez Gomez's. *Am I a priest?*

Gomez Gomez's head fell forward and thumped against a bar. "Help me find God, man. Angel's gone. And I'm full of big enough holes."

"I'll help you. We'll find God, okay?"

"I'm full of holes . . ."

"Me too, amigo. Me too."

CHAPTER TWENTY-SIX

"Town's filling up fast," Charles Faulks said. Honey lifted a fresh Pepsi off her tray and set it on the table in front of him. She could almost see her reflection in his greasy, slicked-back hair. "Miracle Days brings 'em. Can I get you anything else?"

Charles Faulks lifted the drink and sucked the straw. "Maybe more chips?"

"Where do you put all that food, Charles Faulks?"

He answered with another slurp and followed it up with a burp and a lopsided, stubbly smile.

Honey fetched and delivered the chips then wove through the tables with her coffeepot. She made the rounds offering refills, a route her feet knew by heart. Shorty's hummed and rattled, filled to capacity. More visitors today than locals. She paused by the window to watch the action in the square under the old oak. Tents, trucks, people rushing here and there. Tomorrow, when Miracle Days officially started, downtown would be packed shoulder to shoulder. The sun hadn't even reached its midday peak, and people were already staking out their spots on the sidewalk with camp chairs, rope, and reserved signs for tomorrow morning's kickoff parade.

Honey laced her way back across the room and through the swinging door to the kitchen, leaving the noisy clatter behind. She almost collided with Katie's husband, Lou, as he passed her with a tray full of plates and drinks.

"Nice apron," Honey said.

"She tried to get me in one of your yellow dresses, but a guy's got to draw the line somewhere."

Katie's hands danced over the stove. She blew a dark curl from her face as Honey approached.

"Lou in a dress, huh?" Honey said.

"He's got the legs for it."

"Yuck. I've heard enough."

Katie wiped her hands on a towel, picked up a glass of iced tea, and leaned against the counter. "I can't believe it took you this long to tell me my idiot nephew told you he still loved you."

"I probably shouldn't have said anything at all. But I needed to tell somebody. I really just need to ignore the whole thing and try to be his friend. He had a hard time with Angel. It's life, you know? Nobody can rewind it."

"And you told him you were seeing Matthias?"

"I told him I had to move on. He understands. How could he not?"

"Sometimes our brain understands one thing and our heart understands something different. But you're right, what's he gonna do? He made his bed."

"And you know him. He won't ever waver from what he thinks is right. That's one of the things that makes Jake Jake. And one of the things I loved about him. Anyway, he's a priest now. And we're friends."

Katie sipped her tea. "Priest or not, he told you he's still in love with you."

"I'm just glad Matthias doesn't know anything about it."

"You don't think so? Matthias isn't stupid. I'm sure he senses."

"I told him what Jake and I had was in the past, and it is. What more do I need to say?"

"You're saying when Jake told you how he felt you felt nothing?"

"No . . . I felt a lot of things. First I felt mad. I wanted to slap him. I did slap him actually."

"That's the problem. You slapped him because you still love him. Just like he still loves you. Ugh, I might slap him myself."

"Well, I'm moving on. I have to."

"Of course you do. Jake will fade. And Matthias is a solid man. And he's the future. Not the past."

"Last time I was with him it was good. I really felt good. We danced on my patio, Movie stuff, right? Then the very next day my mind got all twisted up again, and I've kind of been avoiding him."

"How much avoiding him?"

"Pretty much totally."

"And you think he won't suspect something is wrong?"

"That's just it, nothing is wrong really."

"If you don't pull your head out of that funk and snatch that man up, I'll take him for myself. Don't think I won't."

"Head is pulled. I'm moving forward."

"I just want you to be happy, mija. And Matthias might be able to make that happen."

"I want to be happy too. I really do."

Lou returned with an empty tray. He turned his droopy eyes on Honey and Katie. "Uh-oh. Looks serious. What are we talking about?"

"Your legs," Honey said.

"That is serious," Lou said.

Katie grabbed a spray bottle, squirted the grill, and scrubbed it with a wire brush. "And how I might leave you for Matthias Galt."

Lou chuckled. "Now's your chance. He's out there at the counter."

"Matthias is here?" Honey said.

"Just sat down."

"I'll make coffee rounds."

Katie smiled. "You do that."

Honey pushed the door to the dining room open and reached for the coffeepot. Sure enough, Matthias watched her from a stool at the counter.

"Hey there," he said. He looked as good as always. Lines etched the corners of his eyes as he smiled. The tightness fisting her heart since she'd told Katie about Jake's confession loosened a bit. Maybe it all really could be okay.

Honey slid a cup in front of him and poured. "Hey yourself. You eating?"

"Yup. Taco plate please. Chicken. I'm on my lunch hour. Not a whole hour though with all the Miracle Days craziness. I tried to call you."

"I saw."

"A few times."

"Sorry about not calling back. It's been busy around here."

"You look like something's on your mind."

She met his eye. "Maybe there has been a little. But not now, okay?"

"That mean I shouldn't ask?"

"That means you should come over for dinner tonight."

"Absolutely not."

Honey set the coffeepot down. "I'm serious. I've been a little out of it but I'm back."

"I'm serious too. I absolutely want to see you tonight. I want to see you every night. But you're not cooking me dinner after you work all day. You pick the restaurant. Burgers or surf and turf, whatever you want."

She smiled. "All right. We'll go out. Now let me get that taco plate before you starve."

"By the look on your face, I'm guessing it went well?" Katie said when Honey returned to the kitchen with Matthias's order.

"He does make me feel . . . I don't know, comfortable somehow."

"Comfortable can be good."

"I'll take it. We're going out tonight."

"Good. Bring me details." Katie slid a plate toward her. "Now go feed the man."

But when Honey returned to the dining room Matthias's stool was empty. Confused, she set the plate of tacos down and noticed a napkin next to his half-drunk coffee. On it was a happy face drawn in blue ink. And under it—*Had to run. See you tonight beautiful.*

CHAPTER TWENTY-SEVEN

SONNY'S INTERCOM PHONE BUZZED, AND a thin voice announced the police chief had arrived. Sonny punched the button and informed his secretary to send Galt back.

Then he punched it again. "Wait, scratch that. Tell him to wait a sec." Sonny leaned back and laced his fingers behind his head. He whistled the theme to *After Sunset* through his teeth for a full minute then punched the button again. "Okay, send him back." Sonny loved his intercom.

Sonny counted to ten before he heard the light knock at the office door.

"Galt, come in," Sonny called.

The door opened a foot and Galt's head poked in. Sonny waved him in. "I said come in."

"Thought so but I wasn't sure."

Sonny indicated a chair in front of his desk. He stood as Galt sat with well-rehearsed timing.

Galt pointed to the .44 magnum on Sonny's desk. "You going hunting?"

Sonny picked up the pistol. "Arizona's an open carry state. Heck, any kind of carry state. Ain't it a great country?" He set the gun on the desk and slid it butt-first to Galt. "Smith & Wesson Model 29. Just like Matt Gunn on *After Sunset*. Killer gun. You can pick it up, it's not loaded."

Galt picked the pistol up and dropped the chamber open. "Uh-huh, nice gun."

Sonny reached for the gun and swung the chamber back into place with a flick of his wrist. "Had to check? Don't trust me?"

"Just habit."

"I get it. We're gun guys." Sonny sighted the pistol on a bird sitting in a bush outside the window.

"So what can I do for you, Mr. Harmon? Dispatch said it was important."

Sonny gave Galt a long stare. Leaving him hanging just long enough to get the nerves jumping.

"How do you like the Escalade so far?" Sonny said.

"Nice. I think I told you that last time."

"It's a great rig. Nice to have friends, right?"

"Friends are nice."

"It'd be hard to afford on your salary without them."

"Like I said, it's a nice rig."

"And I'm a pretty good friend, aren't I?"

"Why do I get the feeling this is headed someplace?"

"Because you've got a brain. You're not either half crazy or a moron like everyone else in this town."

"I'm flattered. What's this about?"

Sonny spun the pistol's chamber. The clicks whirred then slowed. "Here's the deal. I've been thinking about you, and I think you and I need to have a real conversation. We can play at this Boss Hog bad guy versus cowboy cop good guy thing, but it's just gonna keep us winding the engine in low gear. It's cliché. Boring. You know what I mean?"

"Not even remotely."

"Let me put it this way. I want you on my side. But really on my side. Not this whole me giving veiled threats and you grudgingly giving me my way because it's in the unwritten job description deal. The way things are going, I need an actual partner."

"A partner in what?"

"Let's not kid each other. I told you before I was the big fish, blah

blah blah. So I let you drive an Escalade, fine. But I've been thinking. You and me, we could make some real money. That's the benefit of being the big fish. You could be a big fish too. Not as big as me, maybe, but you don't stink. Or have a weird perm."

"I'm confused."

"Yeah, forget the perm part. But not the money part."

Galt sat very still, eyes studying Sonny's face. At length he said, "All right. I'm listening."

"As in really listening? Not all uppity moral guy listening?"

"I said I'm listening. How much cash are we talking?"

"I got something brewing."

"How much cash, Sonny?"

"Sonny? Not Mr. Harmon? That sounds like partner talk."

Galt didn't reply.

"Here's the deal. I told you about wanting to be the second-largest Chevy dealership in the state, right?"

"How could I forget? It's wedged in my little fish brain."

"Well, that wasn't the whole story."

"Enlighten me."

"Did you know the largest Dodge dealer in Northwest America is in a little tiny mountain town just like this? Kellogg, Idaho, to be exact."

"So?"

"So I want to be the biggest. Not fourth. Not even second."

"Good for you. Still, so?"

Sonny sized Galt up. He sounded indifferent but his body language gave him away. The chief was interested.

"You ever heard of Talbot-West Resorts?"

"Of course."

"Talbot-West is building a major ski resort just east of us. We're talking thirty miles—that's it. I've inked a deal for the main access road to come right through Paradise. They'll be doing summer activities too, so we're talking major nonstop traffic through here. And I mean three-hundred-sixty-five days a year. Huge revenue if we play it right, you feel me?"

"Uh-huh, get to the we part."

Sonny punched his intercom button. "Meaghan, hold my calls, will you?"

The thin voice came back. "Um . . . sure, Mr. Harmon. But I doubt—"

"Geez, just hold my calls. It doesn't require a dissertation in reply."

"Calls held."

"Thank you!" Sonny sank into his chair shaking his head. He leaned forward on his elbows and offered his best conspiratorial tone. "Okay, the reason I'm gonna be the number one dealer in the Southwest is because that access road is going to go right through my little corner of the world. Right here. The dealership, yeah, but I'm planning a whole retail community too. Harmon Village. It's going to be huge. Amazing. Bring 'em in from all over the state. Maybe even New Mexico too."

"You're talking about Angel's place. The town's not gonna like that."

"See, that's why you're not a moron—you get it."

"I'm still waiting for an answer."

"To what?"

"Cash. How much?"

"Well, Talbot-West is kicking in a cool backdoor two million for the access land. I figure we split it since we're partners. Fifty-fifty. What do you say?"

"A million dollars? For doing what?"

"Don't think small, Matthias. That's just the start. We'll take this town into the future, you and me. And the future is money, boyo. You tracking?"

"I'm still here, aren't I?"

"Here's the rub. Casper called me an hour ago. I guess these messages spray-painted all over town about Angel have got people thinking. There's a groundswell motion coming up at the next council meeting to make Goober Gomez's backyard stay exactly like it is in Angel's memory. Like a nature sanctuary or something. That can't happen. I need that land available. Talbot-West will bolt if there's any hint of bad publicity. Any hint, you get me?"

"What's Casper got to do with it?"

"Um, he's kind of a partner too. The three of us. What he gets is he gets to stay mayor as long as he plays ball."

"That's it? No money split?"

"He does what I say. But we need to stop this stupid idea before it gets more momentum. Are you in or not?"

"What if I'm not?"

"Then I'm hoping the next chief will be. Get me?"

"Uh-huh, I get you."

"Good."

"So I watched *Hawaii Five-O* last night. You're right, pretty good show."

"And?"

"Those Camaros are cool cars."

Sonny grinned. "Yeah, they are."

"Not my style though."

"No? Why not? Million bucks you could buy a fleet of 'em. Heck, I'll even get 'em for you at cost."

Galt tossed a set of keys onto Sonny's desk with a clatter.

"What's this?" Sonny said.

"Keys to your Escalade. I've realized Escalades aren't my style either. Too many strings hanging on them. See ya around, Sonny. I'll find a ride back to the station."

CHAPTER TWENTY-EIGHT

NAILS, CHAINS, RATTLING BONES . . . GOMEZ Gomez woke with a start, his mouth full of old metal and bitter fumes.

Rattling, rattling. He held his hands against his ears and squeezed his eyes closed. So this was it? Death had finally come for him.

"Get up," Death said.

"I can't," Gomez Gomez said through clenched teeth.

"C'mon, let's go."

"Can't. Too much metal in my mouth."

"Hey! Look at me."

More rattling. Gomez Gomez gave a cautious glance. Bars, concrete, industrial gray paint over brick . . . Officer Galt working his way through a million keys on a ring.

"I thought you were Death," Gomez Gomez said.

"Nope. I'm the tooth fairy. Here to leave a quarter under your pillow if I can ever find the right key. Early!"

Early appeared in the doorway. Officer Galt tossed him the key ring. "What the heck key is it?"

Early picked one and slid it into the lock. The cell door opened with a creak.

"Get him out of here," Officer Galt said.

"I'm taking him?" Early said.

"You're his friend, aren't you? I'd suggest picking up a gas mask though."

Early entered the cell and took Gomez Gomez's arm. "C'mon, amigo. Let's go for a ride."

Gomez Gomez made it to a sitting position. Nausea washed over him. "Wait, man. I'm gonna puke."

Early exited the cell and returned with a bucket. "Make sure and aim."

The nausea receded slightly. "I think I'm good now. Yeah, I'm good."

Gomez Gomez made it to his feet. His stomach lurched again and he hurled, drenching his beard and the front of his coat.

"You missed the bucket," Early said.

"What bucket?"

Officer Galt groaned. "Man, now I think I'm gonna puke. Just get him cleaned up and get him out of here. Right now. They're waiting for him at the hospital."

Early's viselike hand led Gomez Gomez to a bathroom. Early wet a wad of paper towels in the sink and started to work on Gomez Gomez's face and clothes.

"Sorry, man," Gomez Gomez said.

"Don't worry about it. I'm gonna take you to the hospital. They have a room and a bed for you and you're gonna get clean. We'll get you better, amigo. But, yeah, this is nasty."

"Can we get a drink on the way?"

"Man, I'm cleaning puke off you. What part of get clean are you not understanding?"

A young deputy pushing a mop in a rolling bucket passed them as they exited the cell area.

"Sorry, dude," Gomez Gomez said to him.

Matthias held up a hand to stop them as they passed his desk. "Listen, Early, I know he's your buddy, but he did shoot up private property and he's still under arrest. I want him in a hospital bed but I want him restrained. Cuffs, straps, whatever it takes. I do *not* want him walking out of there and making any more trouble for Sonny Harmon. In fact I don't want him anywhere near Sonny Harmon, understand? I'm frankly sick of this whole deal, and I'd like to see it in the rearview mirror."

Early shrugged. "I'll take care of it. I'll keep an eye on him. My responsibility, cool?"

"No, not cool. For once you'll do what I tell you, when I tell you, how I tell you. Unless they've got him doped into a coma, I want restraints and a guard."

Early steered Gomez Gomez toward the door.

"Another thing," Galt said.

"What's that?"

"You see anybody writing *Angel Lives* on anything, anybody with a spray can, Magic Marker, I don't care if it's a second grader with a crayon . . . Anybody even whispering it—arrest them. I've had it up to my ears."

"I'll keep my eyes open."

"Now go get him some help."

A violent sun shone outside the station. Hard, angry sand across stone. Gomez Gomez buried his face in his hands and let himself be led to Early's pickup. The truck door creaked open and Early pushed him up and in. Gomez Gomez relaxed his eyelids and allowed the slightest sliver of light to penetrate. Then a little more once he found he could handle it. Early climbed in on the driver's side and turned the Chevy's engine over.

"Officer Galt's not too happy today," Gomez Gomez said.

"Uh-huh. Look in front of you."

The sun shot lasers through Gomez Gomez's head, but he did as instructed. It took a few seconds to focus, but the smile that came almost made him forget the pounding in his skull. ANGEL LIVES in primer brown was sprayed sloppily across the whitewashed front of the Paradise Police Station.

"Quit grinning or I'll make you scrub it off," Early said.

"Spaceman . . ."

"Uh-huh. Spacemen, aliens, black helicopters, whatever you say.

Hospital time for you, pal. We're gonna get your brain out of your back pocket and into your skull for a change." Early backed out onto the street and began the short drive to Paradise General.

Gomez Gomez saw at least eight more acts of Angel Lives graffiti on the way. Nothing was safe. The bank, the mortuary, stop signs, mailboxes, even a horse trailer hooked to the back of a rusty old Ford station wagon.

"Lucky the horse wasn't in it. He'd've got tagged too," Early said.

"Yeah. Spaceman."

"Quit grinning. All that paint just ticks Matthias off and he takes it out on me."

"Nah. I know you, dude. You don't care if nobody's mad at you."

"It's still a pain."

The one-story brick building that housed Paradise General Hospital loomed on the right, but Early drove straight past it.

Gomez Gomez turned in his seat and watched the hospital get smaller through the back window. "I thought I was getting clean?"

"You are. Just a quick detour then we're headed right back."

"Your boss ain't gonna like it."

"Oh well. What he don't know . . ."

"We getting a drink?" Gomez Gomez felt momentarily hopeful.

"In your dreams."

"Oh yeah, the AA thing. Three years sober, right?"

"Three years." Early drove on, gaze fixed on the windshield.

"You miss it?"

"Sometimes. Not like I used to. But sometimes."

"One day at a time, sweet Jesus . . ."

"Yup, one at a time."

Gomez Gomez pointed to a yard sign. "Check it out. They're everywhere, man. Angel Lives."

"Everywhere enough to get Sonny's shorts in a knot. People are putting those in their yards all over town. Protesting Sonny's expansion."

"Spaceman's miracle."

"Okay."

Five minutes went by as the two rode in silence. Finally Early slowed to a stop, dropped the truck into reverse, and backed onto the gravel shoulder, windshield facing across the street toward the path leading down to Gomez Gomez's demolished shack.

"Check it out," Early said.

Ten-foot Sonny was gone. In his place was a twenty-foot portrait of Angel, offering her smile to all who passed, blonde hair shining in the sun. And rising from behind her—two massive white-feathered wings. Next to her picture, big enough to read from a half mile away, flowing script proclaimed ANGEL'S PLACE.

Gomez Gomez blinked a few times. She was still there. "What happened?"

"Sonny went crazy when you shot his windows out, man. He rattled up the sign company before dawn and made them take down his ruined picture. He trashed all the signs and flowers and other stuff people left too. But it wasn't even a few hours later the sign company came back out and replaced it with this."

"But who paid for it?"

"No clue but Sonny must be flipping. And that thought alone warms my heart."

Even as Early spoke a car pulled up, parked across the road between the pickup and the billboard. An old woman got out. She walked around, opened her trunk, pulled a large plywood board out, and dragged it toward the sign. Her car blocked the view but they could see the top of her gray head as she stood looking down for a long time. Finally she climbed in the car, started it, and pulled onto the road. The woman's plywood contribution leaned against one of the billboard's posts. The rays of the falling sun caught it. It gleamed with fresh paint. In neat block letters it said Bought Me Groceries. A vase of flowers stood next to it.

"Angel lives," Early said.

"Yeah, Angel lives. But Sonny stole her ashes, man."

Early reached over and patted Gomez Gomez's leg. "I know, amigo. But we'll find her. You don't need to worry about that right now."

Gomez Gomez rested back in his seat. "Thanks for bringing me. My eyes feel better."

Early started the truck. "Good. Now let's go get the rest of you better."

CHAPTER TWENTY-NINE

THOUGH THE SUN WAS LONG gone, the mission living space still clung to the heat of the unseasonably warm day. So they gathered on wide mission steps to hear more of Enzo's story. He'd been plugging away and was excited to share.

Jake sat on the top step, watching the action across the street, while Father Enzo made a last-minute correction in his notebook with the stub of a pencil. The oak stood, massive, branches outstretched—a behemoth reaching to heaven and coming close. Beneath it, the temporary Miracle Days city buzzed, a hive of activity. Warm sugar and night-blooming jasmine hung in the air and the sound of a live band playing the "Tennessee Waltz" floated on a slow breeze.

Father Enzo stuck his pencil in his cassock and adjusted his reading glasses. "Okay, I'm ready."

"I'm a-ready," Early said. "I love how you say that. I'm not sure Corfu would be the same without the accent, padre."

Father Enzo looked at him over the top of his readers. "Are you making fun of me?"

Early crossed his heart. "Only in the best way."

"Ignore him," Lucille said. "He loves you."

"Ignoring him can sometimes be the best policy," Jake agreed.

"Read on, padre," Early said. "Let's get our Greek his girl."

"We'll see about it," Father Enzo said. "You know Greeks and Italians both love a good tragedy."

223

"Erasmo walked off into the night pretty beat up. That's pretty tragic," Early said.

"He's due for a little good luck," Lucille agreed.

Father Enzo adjusted the notebook in the porch light.

Corfu

, They are called the lazy days of summer, but in 1961 on the island of Cofu, those stretches of diurnal discourse tumbled over themselves in a race for autumn's finish line.

"Well, listen to that," Lucille said. "Diurnal discourse—say that three times fast."

"Calendar word of the day." Father Enzo's eyes smiled through the readers.

"Diurnal or discourse?" Jake said.

"Diurnal. But discourse was on the same page in my *Webster's Dictionary* and I felt they fit together nicely."

"Like Roy and Dale," Early said.

"Go on, father," Jake said.

The fishing was excellent and brought Erasmo's grandfather an old man's second wind. He and Erasmo fished nearly every day, dawn till dusk, arriving back at the harbor well after the first stars appeared. With the day's work finished, the old man either headed home or found a card game. Erasmo wandered. Often he found himself stopping at an off-the-beaten-path taverna, one far from the Sophia Loren or The Blue Dolphin. A somber establishment known more for serious drinking than conversation.

Fine with Erasmo.

Fabrizio and Cassie seemed to be everywhere. On the beach, swimming and splashing in the sea, buzzing the island on Fabrizio's Vespa . . . Several times they'd approached Erasmo, but he felt in no mood to talk. More than once they asked him to come to The Blue Dolphin. He told them he was tired from work. Fabrizio laughed off his friend's demeanor but Cassie's summer eyes always lingered, concerned and maybe a little sad, though Erasmo convinced himself the sadness was surely the bastard offspring of his inventive imagination coupled with his pride.

Days passed. Then weeks.

A gentle sea rolled and rocked under his grandfather's boat. They hadn't come far today, just motored a bit up the coast and anchored in a turquoise cove. His grandfather claimed it was a day to repair nets, nothing more. A task usually accomplished docked in the harbor. Or on shore. Confused, but not in the mood to argue the point, Erasmo settled down to mending.

The sun was high when his grandfather dropped his end of the net. "Time to eat, boy."

"Why are we out here? We can mend nets in the harbor. We could have saved the fuel."

"Not today! The harbor is for old women and children. Today we belong to the sea. Today we are kings."

Erasmo shrugged. It was hot. He shed his shirt and dove into the sea. He sank deep into the cool stillness, leaving sun and sweat behind. He surfaced and leaned back, treading water.

The old man swallowed a mouthful of bread and washed it down with coffee. He looked down at Erasmo. "It's the girl, yes?"

Erasmo wiped water from his eyes. "What girl? What are you talking about?"

"You know very well what girl and what I'm talking about. The blonde tourist. She's the reason my grandson never speaks anymore. Never laughs. The girl is why you spend every night by yourself drinking at Miko's dump of a taverna."

"Not every night."

"Most nights."

"It's not a bad place."

"It's the girl. Am I right?"

Erasmo sighed. "I can't stop thinking about her. She is kind and beautiful. And she loves the sea. She is much too good to be one of Fabrizio's summer toys."

"So? The way to stop thinking is to start doing. Do something about it."

"I thought blonde women and tourists were trouble?"

"They are—the worst kind! But sometimes a little trouble is the very thing a man needs. Love is trouble by nature. Get back up here, you're not a fish. I'm trying to talk to you."

Erasmo kicked to the boat and hoisted himself on deck in one fluid motion, drying himself with his shirt. "It doesn't matter anyway. She's with Fabrizio."

"Since when do you let Fabrizio stop you from going after what you want? You two have wrestled over everything since you were little boys. Now you're backing down?"

Erasmo crossed his arms and leaned against the wheelhouse. "A woman is different. Besides, she'll be gone in the fall. Everything will go back to normal."

"Maybe, maybe not."

"What does that mean?"

"It means I hear her father is talking to Tavi about buying one of his hotels. I believe the family plans to stay here on Corfu."

Erasmo walked to the rail and stared into the deep blue-green of the water—the color of summer. "Still, I'm just a fisherman on my grandfather's boat. She's a rich man's daughter. The truth is she belongs with someone like Fabrizio."

His grandfather clouted him on the back of the head. Not an easy blow either. "Don't be stupid. And never speak ill of fishermen. We are kings, every one. We are free men. I am a fisherman. You are a fisherman. Jesus was a fisherman."

Erasmo rubbed his head but couldn't help smiling. "I think Jesus was a carpenter."

"Rubbish! He fished. I remember it well."

"I didn't realize you were that old."

The old man lifted a hand to swing again.

Erasmo ducked, laughing. "Okay! He fished."

His grandfather waved an arm to the horizon. "Besides, tell me you'd trade this for any hotel or taverna. For the headaches and hassles of land? What view from any mansion can rival the sunrise at sea with your own boat beneath you?"

"You mean your own boat."

The old man shook his head. "I'm an old man. This boat was my father's. It would've been your father's if he'd lived. Now it will be yours."

"You mean someday it will be mine. You'll live forever. And I'm more than happy fishing with you. You know that."

"As well you should be."

Erasmo grinned. "Because Jesus was a fisherman."

The old man clouted him again before he could duck but there was no power in it. "Show some respect."

His grandfather stepped into the little wheelhouse and returned with an uncorked bottle of wine. He lifted it and took a long swallow, gave a satisfied belch, then handed it to Erasmo. "Drink, Erasmo. Today we celebrate."

Erasmo cast a skeptical eye at the bottle. "What are we celebrating? Net mending? What's gotten into you?"

His grandfather threw an arm around Erasmo's shoulders and showed his tobacco-stained teeth. His black eyes sparkled. "You, Erasmo! We celebrate you. The best spear fisherman in all of Greece, and now the greatest boat captain as well."

"That's all fine and good, except you're the captain, remember?"

"If you're going to be the best, you'll need to read the tide better than you do. Listen! What do you think I've been telling you?" The old man removed his battered old cap, kissed it once, then placed it on Erasmo's head. He took a step back and saluted. "There, it's official. Captain Erasmo!"

"Don't play with me, old man."

His grandfather still grinned but his eyes misted. "I'm not. You were a good boy. The best a grandfather—a father—could ever hope for. Now you're a good man. You have a brave heart. A good heart. A kind heart. This boat is yours. You are the captain now. And I have no doubt you'll own a whole fleet before you're through."

A lump grew in Erasmo's throat and left no room for words. He took the cap off and turned it over in his hands. "But—"

"Put it back on," his grandfather said.

"It's yours. You've never been without it. I can't remember a time."

"I said put it on."

Erasmo did as he was told.

His grandfather adjusted the hat on Erasmo's head to a bit more of an angle, then nodded his approval. He swallowed the last of his bread, checked his battered old pocket watch, and turned the engine.

"What are you doing?" Erasmo said.

"Permit me one last decision as captain, captain. Today we quit early. We celebrate, yes? My decision is final. We're going back in where I will tell all my friends that my grandson, the great Erasmo, owns his own boat. I'm a proud man! Here, take the wheel, captain. Steer us in."

Erasmo put his hands on the worn ship wheel like he had a thousand times before. But today the vibrations felt different. His boat? Could it be? A pair of dolphins finned and leapt out in front of the boat.

His grandfather lifted the wine bottle to them. "See? Dolphins! Good luck. A sign of great things." He slapped Erasmo on the back and shouted to be heard over the chug of the engine. "Captain Erasmo, it occurs to me in this moment that I find myself in need of a job. Are you hiring?"

Erasmo laughed and took the bottle. He drank. "I don't know. What are your qualifications?"

"Ha!" The old man grinned and the dolphins leapt.

"That's better," Lucille said. "I told you he was due. Now let's get him the girl."

"Yes? You would hear more?"

"Let's go," Early said.

"Good, good," Father Enzo said. "We will go on. I think you will be pleased."

"Well, don't ruin it," Lucille said. "Just read."

"It looks like we have a welcoming party," Erasmo's grandfather said as they rounded the jetty and entered the mouth of the harbor.

Erasmo shaded his eyes with his hand. The dock was still a ways off, but there was no mistaking the blonde hair and trim figure. "What did you do, old man?"

"She came to see me. What can I say?"

"And this is why we came back early?"

"What better way to celebrate your new captainship than with a beautiful woman, eh?"

Though the day was hot, Cassie hugged herself as the boat drifted to its berth against the dock.

"Lady!" His grandfather broke into his signature bad English as he stepped onto the dock.

"Hello, Nikolas. The mighty sailors are home from the sea?"

"Yes, yes! And beautiful Cassie waits for us. Meet my new boss, Captain Erasmo."

The summer eyes danced. "Captain now, is it? I like the hat, sir."

His grandfather waved a dismissive hand. "Bah, a relic! A gesture! We get new hat for new captain, yes?"

Cassie laughed. "I think this one is very handsome."

The old man gave a small salute. "Now I go find that lazy Phelix. He owes me a drink. Time to celebrate my retirement! Lady, you keep the captain company, yes? It is big day for him."

Cassie smiled. "Yes. I'll keep him company."

"Grandfather!" Erasmo called to the old man's retreating backside.

The old man turned.

"Thank you!" Erasmo said.

"You've earned it, my son. You are welcome."

"And don't be late for work tomorrow."

The old man saluted and walked off with a laugh.

Cassie approached the rail. "Permission to come aboard, captain?"

"It is an old boat. You will dirty your dress and smell like fish."

"It's a beautiful boat. I've never seen prettier. And I like the smell of fish. May I?"

"Okay, yes. I am sorry. Please." Erasmo held out his hand and helped her aboard, her skin soft and cool.

She smoothed her dress and looked around. "Nikolas told me today would be the day. How does it feel to have your own boat?"

"Nikolas? You know my grandfather by his Christian name?"

"Yes. I found him in the Taverna Sophia Loren. We sat and talked. He loves you very much."

The lump returned to Erasmo's throat. "He has been more father than grandfather."

"I know. And you've been his son. Will you show me around? Give me the grand tour?"

"There is not much." But Erasmo did show her, and with pride. When he was done, she said, "It's beautiful, Erasmo. I'm ready to go."

Her statement confused him. "Go where?"

"You've forgotten? You promised to show me deep water. The first day we met, remember? I've been waiting for you to make good."

"You want to go out to sea?"

"Of course I do. Why do you think I came? Your maiden voyage as captain requires a maiden, don't you think? I, sir, happen to be a maiden."

Erasmo ran his fingers through his hair. "What about Fabrizio?"

"What about him?"

"What will he think? His girl out with another man?"

Her face clouded a squall. "You can be very dense. Has anyone ever told you that?"

"Many people have, I think."

"You call me his girl. As if he owns me. Do I look like a someone who'd allow herself to be owned by another someone?"

Erasmo studied her and admitted she didn't.

"Then show me the deep water."

He smiled. "Okay. Yes. What a gas."

"Ha! Yes. What a gas, captain."

There is a line where the ocean drops off to deep water. Green turns abruptly to blue so deep it's almost black. The wind blew lightly offshore that afternoon. Erasmo dropped the boat's anchor into the green and allowed the craft to drift out over the blue. Cassie surprised him by standing and shedding her dress, revealing a swimsuit beneath.

"You want to swim?" he said.

"Of course I want to swim. You said you'd show me deep water. So show me."

Erasmo pulled fins and masks from a hatch. "The fins should fit."

"You keep them on hand for all the girls you bring out?"

"They were mine when I was a boy."

"Then I'm honored." She donned the gear and saluted as she slipped over the side.

Erasmo followed. They dove together and he was surprised how deep she could go. They surfaced, took breaths, and dove again, kicking hard into the perfect stillness. Down they swam, then deeper still, hovering there in the beautiful nothingness, two particles of flesh and soul, motionless, framed in a wide sunbeam. Far above them the ocean sky danced and shimmered. Beneath them the great light beam disappeared into the inky depths. Cassie reached for his hand and pulled him deeper, following the glowing shaft of light. A large school of fish flashed alongside them, a perfect, flat silver wall. In a blink, a hole broke in the middle and a monk seal cruised through with ballet-like grace. Cassie's excited hand squeezed his.

They dove and surfaced so many times he lost track. The sun worked its tired path across the sky. Once, Erasmo remained on the surface and watched beneath as she thrust down with graceful kicks. She paused and drifted, at least thirty feet below him. A surreal scene, this beautiful woman of the sun hanging in the blue empty, hair drifting out on the slow current. Erasmo held his breath as a pod of dolphins approached and circled her curiously. Cassie reach out a hand and one of the creatures swam closer with tentative motion. It bumped her fingers with its bottlenose then angled, allowing her fingers to run down its side. Then, as quickly as they'd come, with a silent rush they were gone.

Cassie swam upward, the picture of grace, bubbles streaming behind. Her head broke the surface, ribbons of seawater streaming through her hair. She pushed her mask up onto her forehead, excitement and delight transforming her into a child. "Did you see him?"

"Yes. You were beautiful."

"You mean he was beautiful."

"I mean what I say."

They treaded water, face-to-face, the summer eyes alive with sky and sea and the touching of dolphins.

"It's a miracle, isn't it? The boat, the sea, the dolphin—you and me? All of it?"

"Yes. It's a miracle."

She came to him then. Her lips and her cold body pressed against his. He put his arms around her and held her, kicking to keep them both afloat. She pulled her head back, and when the summer eyes spoke her heart, he felt his own would burst.

Father Enzo closed the book and set it down on the step next to him. Low-pedal steel guitar floated over from the square. Moths flitted in the lights.

Jake stood, shoving his clenched hands beneath his cassock. "Thanks, father. I enjoyed it. If you'll excuse me, I think I'll go for a walk."

"Are you all right?" Father Enzo said.

"Yup. Fine. Just a good night for a walk, that's all. Might as well take advantage of it."

"You want some company, amigo?" Early said.

"No, thanks. I'll see you tomorrow."

As Jake left the last step and started up the street he could still hear them talking.

"That was just beautiful," Lucille said into the quiet. "It really was."

"It is a story. A fancy."

"My hind end. I just love it. So this is the end then?"

"The end?" Father Enzo lifted his voice a bit. "Oh no, this is definitely not the end."

CHAPTER THIRTY

"I HAVE HIGH HOPES, BABY. Everything's gonna be cool," Elvis said.

"Yeah, cool breeze," Gomez Gomez replied. Man, Elvis could talk a lot. "Hey, you seen Angel lately? Since that rodeo night when the bull threw me?"

Elvis lounged sideways in a chair next to the hospital room's window, one jumpsuited leg draped over a chair arm. "More than threw you, junior. You got pounded, dude. Yeah, that Angel's one fine filly. Real sweet. Loves to sing."

"Karaoke queen. Loves your stuff especially."

"What other stuff is there, baby?"

"Right. None."

"Yeah, man. Everything's gonna be cool. I feel it in my bones. Deep down in there."

"Hey, did you really carry five guns?"

Elvis pointed a finger at him and pulled an imaginary trigger. "Gotta do what you gotta do, baby."

"Lotta fire power."

"It is what it is."

It was good, Elvis sitting there in his hospital room. The drugs the doctor had pumped into Gomez Gomez stopped the initial shaking, but the tremors had kicked right back in again when the rattler came. He hadn't come alone either. He brought his buddies this time. No gopher snakes or bulls or red racers. Just rattlers. Hundreds of them

until they filled every nook and cranny of the hospital room, buzzing
so loud Gomez Gomez had to shove corners of the hospital blanket
in his ears. Snakes and shakes, angry spirits starting in his hands and
slamming through his body until it felt like his teeth would rattle right
out of his mouth. His skin crawled as the snakes slid under the clean
white sheets and wrapped around his arms and legs. He'd tried to call
out, but one particularly fat diamondback shoved its wedge-shaped
head right into his mouth.

But then Elvis had come. Strolling into the room cool as you please.
Cool as a cucumber. Cool as a morning breeze. Cool as the King. His
mirrored glasses took in the room and he gave his lopsided smile.

"Beat it, man," he said to the snakes. "That's just creepy, baby."

And the snakes did. Slithering back to wherever they came from,
a bunch of snaky ghosts. Elvis had flopped into the chair and started
talking.

And he was still talking.

Yeah, Elvis was just fine with Gomez Gomez.

A nurse came in. Gave Gomez Gomez more pills. She ignored Elvis.

"You'd think she'd freak out seeing you here," Gomez Gomez said.

"Takes all kinds, baby. Ann-Margret was the same way on set."

Elvis started in on a story about an old army buddy. After a while
Gomez Gomez started feeling sleepy.

"Sorry, King. I think I gotta doze. Pills are knocking the wind out
of me."

"You do your thing, baby. I'll do mine. I got good feelings in my
bones."

"Me too."

The King droned on. Gomez Gomez faded. Sometime later his eyes
snapped open. How long had he slept? The room lay in darkness, the
only light seeping in through a crack under the door and moonbeams
through the window. He held up a hand and studied it. It trembled
in the dim light. Glancing at the chair, Elvis had split but a smaller,
thinner figure took his place.

"Heya," Bones said.

"You're not Elvis."

"Nope. Glad to see you're weird as ever. Even off the booze."

"He was sitting right there a while ago."

Bones shifted. "Well, the chair isn't warm or anything."

"How'd you get in here? Isn't there a guard or something?"

"Nah. I sat in the waiting room for a while. I heard a nurse say with all the sleeping pills they're giving you, you won't be going anyplace. I pretty much go anywhere I want anyway. Nobody notices me."

"They did give me a lot of pills. I wish I had a drink."

"It'll get better. The cravings and all."

"How do you know? You're just a kid."

"Nobody's just nothin', remember? Plus I googled it. Got the world at my fingertips, man."

"Oh . . . yeah. That's cool."

"Hey, Angel's place has a new memorial," Bones said.

"I saw it. Early took me by."

"It's pretty cool."

"Early said Sonny's all ticked off about it."

"He's gonna be even more ticked off when he gets his credit card bill and finds out he paid for the whole thing."

"What do you mean?"

Bones reached into his pocket and pulled out a gold card. "Found this lying around. Turns out you can buy all kinds of stuff with it. Even big new signs. All you gotta do is design it on the computer and email it over to the sign company. They're nice peeps."

"You stole his credit card?"

Bones shrugged. "He left it lying around, man. I'm just taking care of it for a while."

"Where'd you get it?"

"In his office during lunchtime. That place is easy. Like I said, nobody really notices me. Probably thought I was some mechanic's kid or something. Like being invisible. It's cool."

"You are some mechanic's kid."

"That's what I mean."

"Okay. Anyways, stinking Sonny."

"Yeah, stinking Sonny."

"Angel lives."

"Angel lives," Bones said.

"You been busy with the paint too."

"I didn't do all of it. People went kind of crazy. Hey, I got some more info for ya. Want to hear it?"

"Nothing else to do. Why not?"

"I heard Sonny's selling Angel's place to some resort company so they can build a road. He's getting eight million bucks for it."

Man, how many bottles of T-bird could a guy buy with eight million bucks? "I thought it was gonna be a car lot?"

"It's gonna be a car lot, a mall, restaurants, all kinds of crap. All built next to a road going to some resort up in the mountains."

"How'd you hear all this?"

"I told you. Nobody notices me."

"But that's Angel's place. Sonny can't do that."

"Sonny Harmon does anything he wants. Anyway, nobody knows about it except him and the mayor."

"And you."

"And now you too."

Gomez Gomez felt hot. He kicked a leg out from underneath his sheet. "I need to find Angel. Everything broke when they took Angel."

"Can't find her from in here, man."

"You said there wasn't a guard, right? I could just leave."

"No guard, but there's a lot of staff walking around. And they'll see you for sure. You move and they'll chain you."

"I need to find Angel," Gomez Gomez said again.

"You really want out?"

"I gotta find her."

"Cool. I got an idea."

"You always do, Spaceman. You got another *pistola*?"

"Nah. This is way more fun."

CHAPTER THIRTY-ONE

MIRACLE DAYS.

Jake walked out onto the mission steps facing the town square. Morning sun lit the spectacle, intensifying color and leaving hard-edged shadows. The door opened and closed behind him. Father Enzo appeared at his elbow.

"Nice day for it," Jake said.

"Beautiful. I see the atheists are back again this year." Father Enzo's accent warmed the morning.

Jake squinted against the sun and pulled his cowboy hat lower over his eyes. "They never like to miss a party. Came in on a school bus about a half hour ago. I'm thinking from Phoenix maybe."

The group of twenty or so protesters loitered on the wide sidewalk in front of the church. A news van—from out of town by the look of it—rolled up and pulled into the alleyway next to the building. The side door slid open and a crew piled out and started unloading equipment. The van's appearance sparked some life into the sleepy protesters and a few signs were hoisted. *Science Is God*, *Hug an Atheist*, *Church and State are Like Beer and Wine—They Don't Mix*, *No Sign from God So I Made This One Myself* . . .

Jake pointed to a slim, bearded young man waving a placard letting everyone within line of sight know Christians were intolerant bigots. "I recognize that guy from last year." Jake waved and the young man gave him the finger.

"It makes for good television holding their signs in front of the mission. It probably makes it even better having priests standing out here," Father Enzo said.

"You want to go inside?"

"Why? It's a good spot to see the parade."

"That's what I was thinking."

Early walked up carrying a cardboard coffee carrier with three cups wedged into it. He handed Jake and Father Enzo each one. "Cream and sugar for padre senior, and black for the junior woodchuck. Do I know my padres or what?"

"God bless you," Father Enzo said just loud enough for the closest protesters to hear. The statement garnered a few dirty looks.

"I believe you did that on purpose," Jake said.

"Do you object?" Father Enzo replied.

"Nope."

Early took the last cup then walked down the steps and wedged his way through the sign wavers to a trash can. He tossed the carrier in. When he came back Jake pointed out his pressed and tucked uniform shirt.

"Nice shirt. And they say miracles don't happen anymore. I bet Matthias is over the moon."

"I'm on foot today. Figure it can't hurt to look a little official."

"Matthias got to you," Jake said.

"All right. He got to me."

Next to the atheists, a hair-sprayed news anchor held a hand to his ear. He crouched slightly, speaking into a camera.

"Look at that dude," Early said. "You'd think he was dodging scuds in Damascus."

The anchor finished what he was saying then stepped back and pointed at the group of protesters. The camera panned over the scene. The little gathering cheered, shouted, and waved their signs. Jake noticed the camera turn his way. What a sight they must have been. Two robed priests, one with a battered, old cowboy hat, and a cop. Jake waved. The camera panned back across the crowd.

Square in the lens, a woman waving a Darwin-fish-with-feet sign stepped toward Jake, her face flushed. "Keep your hands off my body!"

Jake sipped his coffee. "You bet."

Father Enzo took a half step forward. "Of course, child. God bless you."

The woman spat on the ground. "Hater."

"I think they're even madder this year," Early said.

"Does seem like it," Jake said.

Someone started to chant and it was soon picked up by the group. "Keep Jesus in the church! Keep Jesus in the church!"

The bearded young man with the *Christians Are Intolerant Bigots* sign approached Early. "Dude, what are you even doing here? In front of a church? With monks or whatever they are? Haven't you ever heard of separation of church and state?"

Early gave his crooked tooth grin. Friendly enough unless you knew Early. "Have you heard of separation of your teeth from your face?"

The kid's eyes went wide. "You can't say that to me, man! Who do you think you are?"

"Say what?" Early said.

"You threatened me."

"No, I didn't. You hearing voices? Maybe it's God."

"Man, that's hate speech! What's the matter with you?"

"You know what?" Early said. "The rodeo's in town. Maybe they'll let you pet a pony. Try the big ones with horns. They're super cuddly."

Beard guy turned to the crowd. "Hey, this cop is threatening me!"

Cameras still rolling, the crowd grumbled. A simple chant picked up—just the word *intolerant* over and over.

Jake sipped coffee and glanced at Early. "You'll never change, you know that?"

"You want me to?"

"Nah. You're kind of entertaining."

"I can't help it. Every year. They get so worked up if everyone doesn't pander to them. They're fun to mess with."

"Spoken like a true Baptist."

"Amen, brother."

Someone shouted, "Jesus was a homophobe!"

Early nudged Father Enzo. "What do you think, padre? Should I let college beard guy keep his teeth?"

Father Enzo smiled. "It would be the Christlike thing to do."

"What about letting him pet the big pony with the horns?"

"Why not? I believe God does have a sense of humor."

The sound of a marching band lifted above the protest shouts. "Amazing Grace," John Philip Sousa style.

Jake pushed his hat back. "Here comes the parade."

The protesters turned away from the mission and toward the street, hopping, shouting, and waving their signs.

The band passed, followed by a Brownie troop, then the Boy Scouts. Shriners buzzed by doing figure eights in their go-carts. Then a truck pulling a flatbed trailer with a bluegrass band on it. A clown showered the watchers with handfuls of candy from a bucket. Beard guy temporarily dropped his sign to scramble after a Jolly Rancher.

The Harmon Chevrolet float was a huge papier-mâché Corvette. Girls in red, white, and blue sequined bikinis waved from the back seat while Sonny, resplendent in his white fringed cowboy outfit, held the five-foot wheel and pretended to steer. Jake glimpsed Milton's tattooed face through a slit in the fake car's grill, driving whatever actual vehicle propelled the thing.

The sheriff's posse rode by on palomino horses, then more floats and another high school band from Tucson.

"Getting close now," Early said.

Their view blocked by the booths and trailers in the square under the oak, they heard the cheering before they saw the float. When it finally rounded the corner and approached the mission, Jake couldn't suppress his smile. The official Miracle Days float wasn't nearly as glamorous as Sonny's Corvette. In fact it was old and tired-looking and had been for as long as Jake could remember. It didn't matter, this was the highlight of the day. Tradition in its purest form. A flatbed trailer transformed through the magic of imagination, sweat, plywood, and paint into a big King James Bible. A John Deere tractor pulled the Good Book along with plodding insistence. Honey's grandmother, Beauty Hicks, sat in a big padded chair on top of the float, waving gleefully to the cheering crowd. As the Bible pulled even with the atheists, the group erupted into boos and taunts. A couple of them threw things. Beauty grinned and blew the demonstrators a kiss.

This sent the demonstrators into a frenzy.

"Never underestimate the powerful pull of a woman," Father Enzo said.

"Amen, brother," Early said. "Or a mermaid."

Jake wondered where Honey was.

CHAPTER THIRTY-TWO

AFTER A QUICK PHONE CALL to make sure Gomez Gomez was in good enough shape to have a visitor, Jake drove his pickup the few miles across town to Paradise General. The day was bright and beautiful as he pulled into the parking lot. In no particular hurry, he listened to the engine cool and the dry sound of autumn leaves through his open window. He caught his reflection in the side mirror. The weariness surprised him.

The leaves reminded him of Honey. Everything reminded him of Honey. *Will it always be like this?*

He'd had no real choice, had he? After taking Angel from Gomez Gomez? It could never have been right.

And now Honey had moved on. And Jake was a priest. It might be a bitter pill to swallow but his path was simple—keep his feelings to himself from now on, buried deep, and move forward. Let her have a life. Let her be happy. She deserved it.

Gomez Gomez was another story. Jake had become a priest to help people. But at the end of the day he felt powerless to do anything for the one person who really needed his help. He could never give Gomez Gomez Angel back. But he had to do something. And truth be told, if he couldn't help Gomez Gomez, he was lost too. They were two prisoners of life and war, chained together on a sinking ship. If one drowned, both drowned. With a sigh he swung open the truck door and stepped out into the day.

The hospital lobby smelled like antiseptic and sunlight on plastic, conjuring up a pickup load of rodeo-injury memories. He announced himself to the receptionist. She waved him back, saying Gomez Gomez was in room 101. Jake had been to hospitals so big they had colored lines on the floor to follow so a person wouldn't get lost. Not Paradise General. One story, whitewashed brick walls, tired linoleum floors, and no lines.

The door to 101 stood open. Jake knocked lightly and stepped in. Gomez Gomez looked surprisingly good, sitting up with a food tray straddling the bed in front of him.

"Shut the door, would ya? They don't give you any privacy around here," Gomez Gomez said.

Jake did.

Gomez Gomez pointed Jake to a chair by the window. "You here to read me my last rites?"

"You're not in that bad of shape yet. How you feeling?"

"You here as a priest or friend?"

"Friend, I hope. Priest if you need one."

"Better you should be here as a priest."

"Okay."

"They give me lots of pills to make me sleep. I think mostly so I won't run off. Early didn't want 'em to chain me even though I'm a dangerous convict."

"That's good. You need sleep to get better."

"Everybody says that. I'm a drunk. It's not like I was dying."

"Boils down to the same thing. You know that."

Gomez Gomez took a bite of a dinner roll and chewed as he talked. He nudged at a coffee cup on his tray. "They said you were coming. I had 'em bring an extra cup of coffee for you."

Jake reached over and picked it up, a little surprised at the gesture. "Thanks. Appreciate it."

"You look tired."

Jake sipped and made a face. "Definitely not Shorty's. Are they trying to poison you before you get well?"

"It's called hospital food, man. Coffee's the worst. Helps if you dump sugar in it. None left though. I used it all."

"You're all heart."

Gomez Gomez swallowed his bite of roll then took a sip of his own coffee. "Why you here, Jake?"

"Because whatever the history, whether you like it or not, you're still my friend. I won't give up on that."

"You can't change what happened."

Jake sipped again and made another face. "That's true, I can't."

"But you're here whether I like it or not. Man, you're so Jake. You can put on the choir robe and wave the smoke thingy around but you're still Jake."

"I'm not sure what that means."

"It means what it means. I need to find Angel. Early said he would help me."

"Good. We both will."

Gomez Gomez poked at something on his plate covered with dark gravy. "What do you think this is?"

"I wouldn't venture to guess."

"Safe to say it ain't no chile relleno."

"Safe to say." Jake leaned back, weariness covering him like a blanket.

Gomez Gomez pushed the plate away. "I'm having a lot of dreams."

"Yeah? What kind."

"Well, the snakes were here. But I don't think really here. It was probably a dream. Then Elvis came again."

"Again?"

"He's been coming around for a while now. I dreamed about him the other night. I rode Gomez Gomez the bull, man. Trip, right?"

"How'd you do?"

"Made the buzzer but then he slammed me. Elvis helped me up though."

"That's a crazy one."

"Angel too. But then she got plowed by the bull."

Jake winced. "That's horrible."

"Wasn't a bull though. Not in real life, was it? Just a dream."

"Just a dream." Jake drained the rest of his coffee cup, finally getting used to the brutal, acidic aftertaste.

"So Elvis showed up here. In my dream, I think. But maybe not too. Chased the snakes away and sat in your chair there. We talked all night."

Jake set his hat on his knee and leaned his head back. "Must've been cool. Listen, I'm going to talk to Sonny and try to work something out about the window. If I can get this thing to go away, I want you to come stay with me at the mission for a while."

"You don't quit do you, man?"

"You'll come?"

"Nah, I gotta find Angel."

"We will."

"You want me to ask them for an extra plate of whatever this is?"

"I'll pass."

"You want this one?"

"No, thanks."

"Why do you look so tired?"

Jake closed his eyes, his arms feeling heavy. "I guess there's been a lot on my mind lately."

"I guess there would be. How was the parade?"

"You would've liked it. The Elks Lodge guys had a banner that said Angel Lives."

"You seen the new sign? Out at Angel's place?"

"I saw it. The movement is growing fast, I hear. People want to designate the whole place a nature reserve in memory of her."

"But that's the thing. Sonny's lying. He sold road access to a big resort company and he wants to build his own world down there. Big Fish King Sonny Land or something like that. That's why I did it. That and because you killed Angel. I ain't sorry neither."

Jake tried to open his eyes but they were weighted down with anvils. "Did what? Shoot his window?"

"Nah, man, saved up them pills and put 'em in your coffee."

"You did what?" Jake heard himself talking through a long tube. He never heard the answer.

The window was dark when he finally managed to move again. He rubbed his face with both hands, stretched his eyes wide and blinked, trying to knock the sand out of them.

"Sir? Can you hear me?" A female voice.

Jake coughed and looked around. A nurse wearing scrubs and a confused look came slowly into focus.

"What happened?" Jake asked.

"I'm not sure but it definitely must've been interesting." She pointed. He followed her finger and looked down. He had nothing on but boxers and his old cowboy boots.

"I guess it's a good thing you're a nurse," he said.

The corner of her mouth turned up. "I'll admit I've seen worse."

Jake glanced at Gomez Gomez's bed—empty as a pocket. He slumped back in his chair, head feeling like it'd been wedged into a bucket. A swarm of bees hummed in his ears. He coughed again then started to laugh. "The crazy knucklehead even took my hat."

The nurse smiled. "Angel lives."

"Yeah, Angel lives. Hey, you guys got any of those scrubs in an XL?"

CHAPTER THIRTY-THREE

SONNY FUMED. NO, HE BURNED.

No, he *boiled*.

Steam practically came out of his ears like the Coyote in one of those old Road Runner cartoons. He wanted to shoot, smash, pulverize . . . Was there something worse than pulverize? If there was, that's what he wanted to do to someone. He punched the intercom button on his desk phone. His receptionist answered, voice quivering.

"Is he here yet?" Sonny demanded.

"No, sir."

"Send him back here as soon as he is. Understand?"

"Yes, Mr. Harmon. I understand."

She probably wanted to say she still understood since it was the fourth or fifth time he'd barked the same question at her in the last two minutes, but Sonny didn't care. He was surrounded by morons. It was raining idiots. They dropped from the sky like big, ploppy raindrops. They must've injected stupidity into the water system in this godforsaken excuse for a town . . . He had to get out.

Take a breath.

Sonny pressed his hands down hard on his desk. Then even harder until the knuckles turned white. He pounded a fist on the glass.

Morons!

A light tap at the door and Casper stuck his head in. "I'm guessing by the look on your face you saw it?"

"Just get your stupid, fat mayor butt in here!"

Casper sulked in.

"Sit!" Sonny snapped.

Casper sank into a chair. Sonny stood and began to pace. He snatched a newspaper off his desk and shook it at the mayor. "You talked? You opened your big mouth?" His question ramped up to a shout by the last word. He felt his shirt pocket for reading glasses but came up empty, so he opted instead for holding the paper out at full arm's length. "'Dear Editor, what's this about something called Harmon Village being built over Angel's place? Don't we as citizens get a say in this?' And on it goes! Now, only two people in this whole town know about Harmon Village. And one of them, me to be exact, isn't an ab-so-lute moron! I know how to keep my mouth shut."

"I didn't say nothing to anyone," Casper said. "Frankly, I'm more than a little insulted you think I would."

"*Frankly*, you're a moron!"

"It wasn't me! It's gotta be someone else knows."

"You're telling me you haven't said a word?" Sonny slapped the paper back down on his desk.

"Absolutely not. Why would I jeopardize a chance at all that dough? Not to mention my boat?"

"Not even Lisa the perm queen?"

"Not even. She'd blab it down at the salon in a heartbeat. Never."

"I don't get it, man."

"Sonny—"

"Just shut up and let me think."

"Look, I—"

"I said shut up!"

Casper pointed a finger at Sonny. "Listen, Sonny—"

Sonny took a step toward the mayor. "Put that finger away or I swear you'll pull back a bloody stump!"

The two men glared at each other for a full ten seconds.

Finally Sonny broke the stare down. "You're sure? You said nothing?"

"One-hundred-and-ten-percent sure. Could what's-her-name, your receptionist, have heard us talking?"

"Impossible. She's all the way down the hall."

Sonny's original tide of anger abated a bit, yielding a couple feet of neutral shoreline. "Somebody said something. That's all I know. So what's the damage as of now?"

"The damage is that the town is all worked up about that stupid shrine to Angel. And Talbot-West wanted smooth sailing. They demanded it. They don't want any bumps in the road or trouble with the locals. We got to turn this around somehow before it gets back to them."

"Maybe it'll blow over. Morons got short attention spans," Sonny said.

"No way. It's only gonna get worse. We gotta get out ahead of it. And I'm talking yesterday. Somehow we gotta get the town on board. Get 'em on our side."

"I can't believe this. I'm Sonny Harmon for Pete's sake! How can these idiots be causing me trouble like this?"

Casper shook his turkey gobbler. "It's this whole Angel Lives thing. It's just horrible timing. We should have handled Gomez Gomez different. Quieter or something."

"What about a town meeting?" Sonny said. "Talk about the new development? About growth? People have to love new restaurants, stores. A McDonald's, right? Who doesn't love Big Macs? Show them what's coming. We can even do some nod to Angel. A plaque or something. Make it a big deal."

"I don't know . . . If there's one thing this town hates, it's growth. Heck, I ran on a no-growth platform. How do you think I got elected?"

Sonny dropped into his chair. "Give me a break. You got elected because you were the only one running. That and the fact we've known each other since kindergarten and I basically said you were elected."

"Whatever. It don't matter now. What matters is all hell's about to break loose over this. You watch."

Sonny absently studied a pen he tapped on the glass desktop. "I don't see that we have any choice. We have to sell people. I just want to know how it got out there. Now it looks like we were hiding something."

"Well, we are . . . Or we were."

"You know what? I got an idea," Sonny said. "To start with, you spread it around to the council guys that there could be a little bonus of ten grand or so for any of them who gets behind this thing. Call it good faith, an act of kindness, whatever. Most of those greedy idiots would sell their mother for a buck."

"I can do that."

Casper's cell rang and he answered. He listened briefly. "What? How? Look, you find him, you hear? Then let me know when you do."

"What?" Sonny said.

"That was Galt. Gomez Gomez walked out of the hospital a little while ago."

"What do you mean walked out?"

"Galt said he was wearing Father Jake's robe, that's all I know."

"Jake helped him?"

"Wouldn't put it past him. Galt's got men out looking now. He can't have gone far."

"Probably no farther than the closest liquor store." Sonny shook his head. "This just gets better and better. Now they'll turn Goober Gomez into some kind of Robin Hood. I can just see it."

Casper sighed. "That makes you Prince John and me the Sheriff of Nottingham, don't it? So much for Skipper and Gilligan."

"Shut up," Sonny said. "Just go get to it."

CHAPTER THIRTY-FOUR

"It's cold," Gomez Gomez said.

Bones lay on a patch of grass on the riverbank bathed in moonlight, hands behind his head, an unlit cigarette stub stuck to his bottom lip. He cracked an eye. "I told you, if we make a fire they might see it."

"Where did you get that nasty cig? You even know where that thing's been?"

"You got a light?"

"Shut up. You don't smoke."

"Maybe I'll start."

"And maybe I'll run for president. Smoking's bad for you, man."

"Says the guy who downs a million gallons of moonshine a day."

Gomez Gomez scratched a picture of a cigarette in the dirt with a stick. He drew a circle around it and slashed a line across. "Thunderbird, not moonshine. Besides, I'm on the wagon."

"Whatever. Give me a light."

"I'm wearing a stinking priest robe. They don't usually come with lighters."

"I've seen priests smoke before."

"Not Jake."

"It's your own fault. You could've put your clothes on under the robe. They washed them and everything. Not that you'd care about that probably."

"I was in a hurry. I never broke out of jail before."

"It wasn't exactly *Shawshank Redemption*. It was a hospital and no one was even looking. What about Father Jake's stuff? Pants and shirt at least. Don't priests wear clothes under those robes?"

"Yeah, he had clothes but they were way too big. Besides, I tossed 'em in the dumpster behind the hospital soon as I got out." Gomez Gomez laughed. "Oh man, Jake was out like a light. I wish I coulda seen his face when he woke up. Saving those pills for his coffee was genius."

"I'm chock-full of genius ideas." Bones took the butt from his lips with two fingers and blew a long stream of pretend smoke into the late evening air. "Speaking of that, I made up a bunch of pretend advertising flyers for Harmon Village and stuck 'em in people's mailboxes. That'll keep Sonny busy for a while, I bet."

"No joke?"

"Yeah, man. He's gonna freak."

Gomez Gomez waited until Bones stuck the butt back on his lip and closed his eyes. When he was sure the kid wasn't watching he held his hands out flat. They shook as bad as the cottonwood leaves rattling on the branches above. He desperately needed liquor, but what was he supposed to do? Walk into the Circle K in Jake's priest robe and ask them to put it on his tab? He squeezed his eyes shut. No, the important thing now—the only thing—was to find Angel.

"You okay?" The kid was looking now, genuinely concerned.

"I gotta find Angel."

"It's gonna be hard to do, people out looking for you. We oughta go across the river. Deeper in the woods."

"We'd just be going farther away from Angel."

"I'm not sure you appreciate the gravity of the situation."

"You use big words for a little Spaceman. I'm not sure you do."

"They'll look for you at your old place first. Probably already have."

"Probably. I feel sick, man."

"Maybe we should go back to the hospital. You were better off there, huh?"

"But Angel . . . Sonny has her. Dude's always got an angle. I wish I had that short nosed *pistola* again."

"Snub nosed."

"Either one."

A faint shout sounded from far off, and a beam of light touched the top of a distant tree.

Bones stood and craned his neck in the direction of the sound. "They're looking. I told you."

"They won't find us here."

"Sounds like there's a bunch of 'em."

"Yeah, man. We're like Butch Cassidy and the Sundance Kid."

"Not me. They don't even know I'm here. You really think Sonny has Angel?"

"Who else? Don't you?"

"If he does, he's probably got her at his office."

"So?"

"So let's go see," Bones said.

"How we gonna do that?"

"I know a way. We can head along the river and come up the back way to the car lot."

"Then what?"

Another voice echoed through the trees. Closer this time.

"I'm Bones, man, right? Leave it to me." He started off up the river.

Gomez Gomez got to his feet with a low groan. He wasn't sure he told his feet to walk but they started anyway.

A step sounded next to him and Elvis fell in.

"Where'd you come from?" Gomez Gomez said.

"I been everywhere, man. Like that Johnny Cash song. Johnny was a cat. Where we going, baby?"

"Ask Bones. I think we're gonna break into Sonny's office."

"Yeah? Crazy!"

"One thing about the Spaceman, kid gets things done."

Elvis's sequins caught starlight. "Kid's a cat, no doubt."

"It's weird, man, you just showing up all the time. I ain't even drinking right now."

"Could be the not drinking that's doing it," Elvis said.

"That's true. It definitely could be that."

"Or it could be I like your company, baby."

"That's cool. It ain't like I'm complaining or nothing."

"Who you talking to?" Bones said over his shoulder.

"Just Elvis."

"Well, keep it down. Try to keep the crazy to a minimum, would ya?"

"I will, but I can't speak for Elvis. He might kick into song, like the movies. He likes to do that."

"True story, baby. I might get the urge." Elvis hunched his shoulders and shot a leg out sideways.

They walked in silence for a while. Skinny Bones in the lead, Gomez Gomez holding Jake's robe up off the ground so he wouldn't trip on it, and Elvis flashing sequined moonlight. The river flowed on their right, somber and watchful. Stars danced in and out of the trees. Gomez Gomez wondered about the rattler. Probably somewhere close. Then again snakes didn't seem to care for Elvis.

"Tell me again why we're breaking into Sonny's office?" Elvis said.

"I gotta find Angel."

Elvis grabbed a leaf off a scrub oak, rolled it between his fingers, and flicked it away. "Yeah, man, Johnny was a cat. You know what he said one time? He said he was two people. Johnny was the nice one and Cash caused all the trouble. And that they was always fighting."

Gomez Gomez waited but Elvis left it at that. "I feel like you got a point to make."

"Look, baby. You're like Johnny 'cept both of your halves are named Gomez. You quit fighting with yourself and all this Angel stuff will get better. You think finding her dust is gonna make you feel right? Ain't done much for you for the last five years."

"What do you know about it anyway? You died on a toilet."

"That's the story. I'll tell you what, though, Johnny was a cat. But so was Cash."

"You know what? You're crazier than me."

Elvis ripped a kung fu move. "I'm just saying, quit fighting, baby."

"You don't have to come."

"I'm right behind you. Don't worry about the King."

At length the trio ascended a grass-covered hill and tracked along a high chain-link fence.

"Here we go," Bones said, then disappeared.

Approaching the site of Bones's vanishing with caution, Gomez Gomez saw the kid had dropped into a shoulder-deep gully. The chain-link spanned over the top of the cut, leaving almost enough room to walk under it without even ducking.

"Just for us. What do you think?" Bones said.

"Not much on security here, are they?" Gomez Gomez said.

"That big dude might be around. Gotta be careful."

It took some effort for Gomez Gomez to descend the steep wall of the wash in the priest robe but he managed it. He followed Bones up onto the asphalt at the rear of the car lot. The cinder block wall of a big building loomed.

Bones approached a steel door set into the brick. He jiggled the handle. Obviously locked. "Wait here," he whispered, then trotted off into the darkness.

"Where's he going?" Elvis said.

Gomez Gomez shrugged. "He's skinny. Might know a window or something. He's Bones, man. I don't ask."

"Too true, baby. Hey, you okay? You don't look so good."

"Nah, man. I'm singin' the detox blues."

"Hear you loud and clear."

"At least Venus is quiet tonight."

Elvis leaned against the wall and looked up.

"So, if he gets us in, you coming or what?" Gomez Gomez said.

"Whither thou goest, baby . . ."

A rattle and click sounded on the other side of the metal door, then it swung open framing Bones in the dark passage.

"I won't even ask how you did that, Spaceman," Gomez Gomez said.

"You ready?" Bones said.

Gomez Gomez glanced at Elvis, who motioned to the door. "After you, baby."

CHAPTER THIRTY-FIVE

THE STEEL DOOR OPENED INTO a narrow hallway. The dank odor of grease and oil.

Bones indicated a side door. "Need to use the bathroom?"

"I'm cool," Gomez Gomez said. "And I'm pretty sure Elvis has an aversion to toilets."

"Psycho, man," Bones said.

The hallway opened up into a mammoth garage. Lines of lifts, dresser-sized tool chests, air compressors, and work benches. Soft light lit the cavernous space.

"We gonna look in here?" Gomez Gomez said.

"Nah, if he's got Angel she'll be in his office. I bet that's where he keeps everything important," Bones said.

They navigated through the maze of equipment, then through a wide set of double doors. Shelves of auto parts stretched into the darkness. Bones's tennis shoes squeaked on the polished tile floor. A hundred miles later they passed a parts counter and waiting room. Gomez Gomez paused, picking up a magazine off a glass coffee table. *Car and Driver.*

Elvis peered over his shoulder. "They got Cadillacs in there?"

"Probably."

"C'mon!" Bones hissed from up ahead.

Gomez Gomez dropped the mag and continued on.

"Can't beat a Caddy, baby," Elvis said.

Another set of doors. More restrooms. Sales offices. Another waiting room filled with glass and chrome then they were in the showroom. Light filtered in through the massive floor-to-ceiling windows from the acres of cars outside, bathing the showroom in dappled orange and blue. Several vintage and new cars in sight.

"Pretty cool, huh?" Bones said.

"I guess they replaced the window." Gomez Gomez said.

"Hey, man, this ain't too shabby!" Elvis called.

It took Gomez Gomez a minute to locate the King sitting low behind the wheel of a long, gleaming pink Cadillac convertible.

"Nice." Gomez Gomez saw his twin reflection in Elvis's aviator sunglasses as he approached.

"Ridin' with the King, baby. Like that John Hiatt song."

"I don't think I heard it."

"Cool tune. Hiatt's a cat."

Bones headed down another hallway.

"You coming?" Gomez Gomez said to Elvis.

"Nah, man. I'll wait here. Don't let the boogeyman get ya."

"You neither."

"Hey, I'm the original boogie man, baby. I put the boogie in boogie."

Elvis pretended to drop the car into drive. He was making motor noises as Gomez Gomez headed off to find Bones.

The hallway Bones had entered stretched forever. Gomez Gomez's feet made no sound on the thick carpet. "Bones," he whispered.

No answer.

"Bones!"

Bones's face poked out of the last doorway on the left. "Down here. This is it. Sonny's office."

Gomez Gomez padded down and entered. The office spread out, big as most houses. A huge glass-topped desk held nothing but a phone and a single photo in a frame. Gomez Gomez picked it up—a high school football player kneeling on one knee. "Dude's got a picture of himself on his desk."

"C'mon! Let's look for Angel. There's gotta be a security guard around here somewhere, and I don't wanna get shot."

"Big enough holes," Gomez Gomez whispered to himself. He went behind the desk and made quick work of the drawers.

No Angel.

Shelves and cabinets made up one whole wall of the office. Gomez Gomez moved over and opened a cabinet. Folders filled with receipts. The next cabinet was empty. He scanned the shelves. A few trophies. Auto dealership plaques and awards. Pictures—Sonny with the mayor, Sonny with the governor, Sonny with some important-looking couple. Sonny on a beach. Sonny looking starstruck next to Gregory Jones from that *After Sunset* show . . . Sonny, Sonny, Sonny.

But no Angel.

More drawers, more nothing. At the far end of the wall the back half of Bones protruded from a floor-level cabinet.

"You find anything?" Gomez Gomez said.

"Not yet. You?"

"Lots of Sonny but no Angel."

One cabinet held a coffee maker. Another an expensive-looking cigar humidor and a lighter shaped like a jet fighter. Gomez Gomez opened the box and stuck a cigar between his teeth. He picked up the jet. "You still looking for that light?" he slurred around the stogie.

"What?" Bones said.

"Nothing."

Gomez Gomez opened another cabinet. His mouth dropped open. He stood back and saluted. Before him, an army of beautiful bottles stood at attention. He picked up the closest, twisted the top, and drank deep. The alcohol burned and he coughed.

Bones looked up, his glasses opaque circles of dim light. "Are you kidding me?"

Gomez Gomez drank again, finishing with a satisfied sigh. "Mother lode, man. This ain't no T-bird, I'll tell you that."

"I thought you were on the wagon."

"Wagon just went into a ditch."

"Just keep it together, man. I'm telling you, we don't have much time."

Gomez Gomez held out a steady hand. "I'm more than together, kid."

"I thought you were quitting."

"I am. Pretty soon."

"Just keep looking."

"I can work one-handed. I'm an expert, dude." Gomez Gomez opened another cupboard.

The front half of Bones shook its head and disappeared again. A rattle sounded from the hallway and the front half of Bones reappeared. "Did you hear that?"

"Rattling bones. Place is haunted, man."

Another rattle.

"Crap, you know what that is? It's the security guy checking the knobs on the offices!" Bones whispered.

Another rattle.

"He's gonna be here any second. We gotta hide."

"Where?" Gomez Gomez said.

Bones glanced around. "Here, c'mon." He led the way on quick feet to a closet close to the office door.

Three more hallway rattles, each one louder and closer. Then the guard must've seen Sonny's open office door. Gomez Gomez watched through the crack of the closet door as the man entered the office. Not the big guy though. A skinny one. He took his hat off, scratched his greasy hair. He walked to the desk, then to the wall of drawers and cabinets. He gave a quick look around, then opened the liquor cupboard. He selected a bottle, poured a drink, then walked to the window and gazed out at the night as he sipped.

"I got an idea," the kid breathed, his mouth close to Gomez Gomez's ear. Spaceman was a miniature *Mission: Impossible*. "Get ready to move. And be quiet."

As the guard sipped, back to them, Bones swung the door open and stole out on noiseless feet, a golf club in his hand. To whack the guard?

But the kid crept through the open office door into the hallway. Gomez Gomez followed. Bones silently pulled the door closed behind them then wedged the club under the handle and across the doorjamb.

"What the—?" The guard's muffled voice come through the door. Footsteps sounded and the door jiggled. The club flexed but held. Bones was already halfway down the hallway. "Run!" he hissed.

Gomez Gomez did. Down the long hallway, through reception, and into the showroom. Bones was faster, already through the glass double doors and into the parts department.

"Whoa there, man." Elvis still sat behind the wheel of the pink Caddy. "What's the hurry?"

"Guard's on our tail."

"Crazy. That Bones, he's a cat."

"You coming?" Gomez Gomez said.

"You think the King runs out the back door like a scared little schoolgirl, baby?"

"You got a better idea?"

Elvis offered his lopsided grin and slid over to the passenger seat. "Hop in, you're driving."

Gomez Gomez took a long swig off the bottle. Yeah, it was serious quality hooch. He squinted down at Elvis. "Driving where?"

"You ever seen that movie where the chicks drive the car off the cliff?"

"*Thelma & Louise.* Yeah, so?" Gomez dropped into the seat behind the wheel. The liquor warmed him. At least hear the guy out, right? He was Elvis after all. Elvis reached over and turned the key. The Cadillac whined, sputtered, then roared.

"Now what?" Gomez Gomez said.

Elvis made a pistol out of his thumb and forefinger and pointed dead ahead. "I know you got no love for this window, baby."

"You kidding? We'll get cut to ribbons. Let's use a truck."

"Do I look like the truck type?"

The King had a point.

"Besides, man, I got it figured. You get enough speed, we'll blast through like a cannonball, jump the sidewalk, and *bam*, just like that we're gone. You with me?"

Gomez Gomez revved. "Big enough holes . . ."

"Hey!" a voice shouted from the other end of the showroom.

"I guess they don't make golf clubs like they used to," Gomez Gomez said.

"Let's fly, baby."

Gomez Gomez stood on the brake and gas at the same time and dropped the car into gear. Tires squealed on the tile floor. Smoke and burning rubber. He turned to Elvis and shouted, "Ready, Thelma?"

Elvis gave a thumbs-up. "Let her rip, Louise."

The Cadillac leapt forward. Glass shattered and rained a million sparkly little stars, then they were airborne, climbing into the sky like they were riding the jet fighter lighter in Sonny's office. Gomez Gomez smacked Venus a high five and the car crashed into the asphalt, bounced twice, and tore down an aisle lined with shiny new SUVs. A rail fence loomed ahead. The Caddy blasted through it, launched over a berm, and slammed onto the road beyond, sparks flying and tires screeching. Gomez Gomez cranked the wheel. The Caddy fishtailed, straightened, and they were roaring away down the road toward the open desert.

CHAPTER THIRTY-SIX

JAKE STOOD AT THE WINDOW in his mission office, looking out at the night. A shooting star streaked and burned itself out over the mountains. A three-quarter moon threw dull silver and a coyote loped across the old baseball field.

He still wore the scrubs. He'd helped look for Gomez Gomez until the search was called off. It was too dark and Gomez Gomez knew the trees and brush well enough they'd never find him if he didn't want to be found. And with the town full of people for Miracle Days, Matthias and Early had their hands full with more pressing matters.

At least that meant Matthias wasn't out with Honey.

Stop it.

Was this the way it would be? Would his mind always find her no matter how hard he tried to concentrate on other things? Would she marry someday, have a family, and he'd be right here looking out at a half moon wondering what she was doing? If she was happy? With a sigh, he crossed the room and dropped into his desk chair.

His desk lamp cast a glow across the scarred and polished wood, leaving the rest of the room in darkness. He should sleep, but sleep would be elusive tonight. Where was Gomez Gomez? Where was Honey? It was like being on a saddle bronc with no reins to grip. The world bucking beneath him, out of control, and he was powerless to do anything about it.

God, that path Father Enzo talked about . . . I could sure use a little light.

He leaned back and closed his eyes. No voices from heaven. No burning bushes or talking donkeys. No angels with flaming sword. Just the quiet of adobe walls and an Arizona night.

He opened his eyes and leaned forward, forearms on his desk. He pulled over the Superman notebook Father Enzo had left earlier. Picked up the note, though he'd already read it. "Father Jake, I've finished the story, I believe. At least as far as I care to write it. And our pen must follow the path before us, yes? I am very much looking forward to hearing your thoughts on the ending."

Jake sighed.

Better than sitting here dwelling on things I can't change . . .

Inside, Father Enzo's script was neat and precise. No sign of the scribbles and corrections Jake expected. He found the spot where they'd last left off and began.

Corfu

Erasmo took her hand and helped her off the boat and onto the dock. Her blonde tresses, dry now, still held the curl of the sea. She almost tripped and he caught her in his arms. She laughed and his heart sped at the sound.

His girl of the sea.

"Come with me. We'll eat, drink, dance—celebrate tonight," he said.

"Your new captainship?"

"No, your dolphin. He is good luck. We celebrate you and your dolphin. We celebrate you and me."

She stepped back and a cloud crossed her summer face. "I want to. I really do. But we're having dinner with the Bakis family tonight. My father and Mr. Bakis are going into business together. A hotel. My father made me promise I'd be there. I have to go. Please understand."

"With Fabrizio?"

"No! Well, not only Fabrizio. I mean, he'll be there. But it's with his whole family. Our whole families. It's business, that's all. I promise."

"Business . . ."

"Yes. Business."

Erasmo looked down at her. "You do not have to explain to me."

She must have read pain on his face. "You don't understand. In the sea today, what happened between us, it was special. Very special to me and, I know, to you too. A dinner with Fabrizio's family can't take that away." She touched his cheek. "Nothing can ever take it away. Do you understand?"

"Can you meet me later? After?"

Cassie bit her bottom lip. "I don't know for sure. I can try."

"Please, try. I will wait for you at The Blue Dolphin, yes?"

"Okay. Wait for me. I'll try to come. I really will." She stood on her tiptoes and kissed his lips.

As she turned to go he reached for her. He pulled her to himself and kissed her again, tasting the sea on her. "Come to The Blue Dolphin."

She smiled and touched his cheek. Then she was gone.

Erasmo sat on the boat—his boat—and watched the sun drift toward the sea on lover's wings. The sky went orange, then purple, then deep blue. He imagined Cassie floating out there, her hair catching moonlight. He wanted to paint her, to write songs about her. He was no poet, but it felt good to feel ridiculous.

A passing fisherman tossed him a greeting and he returned it with a wave. Cassie would be at dinner by now. The restaurant fancy, much better than a fisherman could afford, even one who owned his own boat. Just another meal to Fabrizio. They would drink. Fabrizio would flirt. Her mother would proclaim everything a gas. But Erasmo hoped against hope Cassie's mind and heart would remember the sea—the deep water. Feeling her hand trail down the side of a miracle. Feeling his lips, his body, pressed against hers.

Jake leaned back and sighed. He started to close the notebook but stopped himself. *It's almost the end.* Father Enzo would ask.

At the house he shared with his grandparents, he cursed himself for leaving his tie behind at The Blue Dolphin that night. He did the best he could with his father's black suit and his white shirt. He stood for a long time looking into the mirror. His height made him duck to see his face. He was dark from the summer sun. His reflection returned scrutiny. Eyes green and serious. He combed his hair back, glossy and black. He stepped back from the mirror to better see the suit, then shook his head. He kept the white shirt but traded the suit coat and pants for a pair of canvas-colored khakis and the polished black shoes for his leather sandals. After all, he was who he was, Erasmo, his grandfather's grandson, captain of his own ship.

Stepping out onto the street he breathed in deep. Bougainvillea and music filled the late-summer evening. The Blue Dolphin was only a mile away, and—a fact well established since the dawn of time—a lover's feet make quick work of distance. In the taverna he bought a bottle of wine and took two glasses to the same outdoor table at which he'd waited before. The patio was quieter, as if the night sensed and offered reserved respect for the monumental events of the day. A lone guitar picked out a few notes and a couple held each other, swaying in slow rhythm.

The darkness breathed and Erasmo wondered if she would come. Special, she had said. The day had been special. Yes, she would come. The deep water, the dolphin, the kiss, the moon—of course she would come.

Except she didn't.

Nor did she come to the docks the next day. Nor was she at the beach in the afternoon. When night came he waited again at The Blue Dolphin, but no Cassie. No girl of the sky and sea. The following morning Erasmo and his grandfather fished the morning tide and rising sun. All day they dropped the nets and pulled them in until Erasmo's muscles ached. He talked little and his grandfather didn't push. By late afternoon the fishhold could hold no more. Erasmo started the engine and pointed the boat for home. Approaching the mouth of the harbor he fought down hopes he'd see her on the dock, hair catching the sun. She had forgotten the deep water.

His heart dropped a beat when he saw the figure from a distance. But as the shore drew closer, the figure wasn't Cassie at all.

It was Fabrizio.

Jake rubbed his eyes with thumb and forefinger. *Of course it is. She's probably back in England with some duke. Or in Honduras marrying a doctor . . .*

Erasmo stepped onto the dock. And Fabrizio swung.

Erasmo blocked the blow and shoved his friend back. "What's the matter with you?"

"What's the matter with me? What's the matter with you?"

"You're waiting here to punch me?"

"To do much more than that. So you own your own boat now. So what? I will own half the island! Maybe more. Can you match that?"

"Of course not. What are you talking about?"

Fabrizio stepped forward, fist clenched to throw another punch.

Erasmo held up open palms. "Wait! What's the matter with you?"

"I love her. I love her, and I'm going to marry her!"

This gave Erasmo pause. "Marry?"

"It's been decided."

"By who?"

"By all of us."

"By her?"

"It's been discussed, yes."

"And she's agreed?"

Fabrizio breathed hard. "I love her, Erasmo. Our families know. Our families are in agreement."

"So it's business? You marry for business?"

"No, I marry for love! Besides, what do you know about business? You own a toy boat, so what? She is a queen. Cassie deserves more. Her family knows it. She knows it. Stay away from her. I demand it."

"You demand? I do what I want. And she can make her own decision."

"Stay away."

"No."

Fabrizio swung, quicker this time. His fist caught Erasmo a glancing blow off the cheek. The shot stung and hot anger surged. Erasmo charged, slamming Fabrizio in the chest with his head. Both men went down hard. Erasmo was up first and his fist connected. Fabrizio stumbled and Erasmo charged again, swinging with both fists. Again they went down. Erasmo connected a couple more blows before Fabrizio shoved up with his legs, tossing Erasmo off. Erasmo started to rise but Fabrizio's hard fist came out of nowhere. His cheek split beneath the blow. Erasmo saw stars and his legs wobbled. He sank to one knee. Fabrizio charged, the light of victory in his eyes. Erasmo shoved himself upward, head catching Fabrizio under the chin. Both went down, then both were up, bleeding and circling warily.

"What's the matter with you?" Cassie's voice hit them both harder than the punches. She stood, openmouthed, staring, some yards away. "Well? Explain!"

"Cassie—" Fabrizio started.

"You're going to marry him?" Erasmo said.

Her face blanched. "Erasmo . . . it's complicated."

"No, it is not! He is rich. Rich makes everything not complicated."

She shook her head. "No, rich makes things very complicated, I'm afraid."

"You love him?" Erasmo said.

"Of course she does. We are to be married!" Fabrizio said.

"Do you love him?" Erasmo repeated, eyes holding her.

"Cassie," Fabrizio said. "We must go. They are waiting."

Cassie stood glued to the ground, her attention fixed on Erasmo, a slow snow beginning to fall in her summer eyes. "Erasmo . . ."

"Cassie!" Fabrizio said.

"Go ahead. I'll follow."

"No! He is nothing but a fisherman. A no one! He can hardly speak English. What could you possibly see in him? He can't even bag the Hercules."

Her eyes remained fixed on Erasmo. "Exactly."

"What is that supposed to mean?" Fabrizio said.

"I'll go with you tonight, you know that. But I told you— I'll be there in a moment."

"They will be waiting."

"I know. I won't be long."

Fabrizio stepped close to Erasmo. He kept his voice low. "She loves me."

Erasmo matched his whisper. "If you believed that you wouldn't be here."

Fabrizio spat on the ground at Erasmo's feet. He turned to Cassie. "Say goodbye to the little fisherman. I'm going to get cleaned up. Then I'll meet you at dinner, yes?"

"Yes," Cassie said.

"Hurry. Don't be long."

"I'll be there."

When Fabrizio had gone Cassie approached.

"I love you," Erasmo said.

"I know you do."

"You love me too. I felt it in the sea."

Her eyes swam. "It's complicated. Things haven't gone well for my father. He's lost a lot of money recently. Old money. Family money. He has everything—our whole future—riding on this hotel. And Mr. Bakis dotes on Fabrizio. He's said it—maybe not in so many words—but an engagement between Fabrizio and me is important to him. I'm stuck, you see? I have no choice. I love my father dearly. I love my family. Can you understand that?"

"And your father would want you to be unhappy?"

"I'll learn to be happy. Fabrizio isn't a bad person. He does love me. And I like him very much. So do you, if you'll admit it to yourself. At least you did like him. You've been best friends for ages. Please don't make this harder than it already is. Please?"

"A miracle. You, me. It was a miracle."

Cassie tiptoed and kissed his cheek. "Yes, it was. Goodbye, Erasmo."

And she was gone. And the world died.

Erasmo put a hand to his bleeding cheek and looked at his grandfather. "You were a lot of help."

The old man puffed his pipe. "Come. We have fish to sell."

"That's all you have to say?"

Another puff. "What do you want me to say? It's all a Greek tragedy, no? The impossible love? The epic battle? Then the hero retreats with his tail between his legs . . . to telos—the end, eh? Too bad. So sad."

"What tail? I gave him more than he gave."

"Bah! The fight is nothing. Two hard heads pounding on each other. So what? Where is the girl? That's the question. I'll tell you where. Right this moment she's headed for the Agatha to announce her engagement to all of Corfu, that's where. And you are here. Unloading fish."

"You heard her. You heard the situation. It's impossible!"

"You're right. It's impossible. Let's go sell fish."

"You're saying I'm wrong?"

"I'm saying let's sell fish. Are you deaf?"

"I know that tone. Don't play with me!"

His grandfather stared at him. "She told me you could've had Hercules. That you had him in your sights but didn't shoot."

Erasmo's cheeks flush. "Yes, so?"

"That, and nothing else, is what makes you the first-greatest spear fisherman in all of Corfu. There are times to hold off. These are the moments that make good boys into good men. But there are other times, son. Times to pull the trigger! And these are the moments that make good men great men. It's impossible, yes, but love is impossible by nature. Love is the world. Love is the heavens! Now, do you want to sell fish?"

"You said the Agatha?"

The old man puffed again. This time around a grin.

Yes, lover's feet make short work of distance. The Agatha was more than two miles away, but Erasmo made it in ten minutes. The tuxedoed maître d's mouth dropped open at the sight of Erasmo's disheveled work clothes and bloody split cheek.

Erasmo gave him no time to recover. "Where is the Bakis party?"

The man's Adam's apple bobbed, but he lifted a thin finger and pointed to a pair of closed double doors at the back of the long dining hall. Conversation came to an abrupt halt as Erasmo strode through the room, looking neither right nor left. When he shoved open the double doors with a bang, two dozen pairs of startled eyes turned toward him. But the only

THE BEAUTIFUL ASHES OF GOMEZ GOMEZ

eyes he cared about were the blue-green color of the sky and sea.

He stood tall. "My name is Erasmo Petrakis. I am the first-greatest spear fisherman in all of Corfu. And I am the captain of my own boat."

And that was all. Jake turned the page. Blank. He closed the notebook and looked at Superman.

"You want to hear my thoughts on the ending? What ending?"

CHAPTER THIRTY-SEVEN

A CHILL IN THE STILLNESS.

All quiet except for the fly.

Gomez Gomez swatted at it but it kept coming back, a tiny kamikaze thumping into his forehead. He swatted again. Another thump, on his cheek this time. Stinking flies.

Somewhere a desert bird warbled. He opened his eyes—just a sliver. Wide blue sky laced with brutal sunlight. Lucidity crept in on tentative feet.

Another little thump on his chin. Then his forehead. He held up a hand to block the angry sunshine and forced his eyes wider. It came back in increments. Bones, Elvis, the window.

The pink Cadillac convertible—he still sat behind the wheel.

A nasty crack stretched the width of the windshield, and a broken-off saguaro cactus stretched crumpled and sad across the pink expanse of the hood.

His eye caught movement in front of the car, and he struggled to bring both brain and sight into clearer focus. Officer Galt stood framed against a backdrop of endless desert, tossing a small pebble up and down. His smile showed straight white teeth. Eyes hidden behind mirrored aviator sunglasses. PPD cap pulled low. Galt brought the small pebble up in front of his face, holding it with thumb and forefinger, then launched the stone with the delicacy of an NBA player on the free throw line. Gomez Gomez tracked the little rock with squinted eyes as it arched, caught a bit of sunlight, perfectly cleared the convertible's windshield, and thumped into his forehead.

"And the crowd goes wild," Galt said.

"Ow," Gomez Gomez said.

Galt walked over to the driver's side door. "Good morning, sir. Can I see your license and registration please?"

Gomez Gomez put his hands on the steering wheel to steady them. "Was I speeding, officer?"

"Funny guy."

"I thought you were flies." Gomez Gomez found the bottle on the seat beside him and picked it up—empty.

"That an open container I see?" Galt said.

"Just an empty one."

"Flies?"

"Yeah, little kamikaze flies crashing into my face."

"Nope, no flies. Just little old me, underdog. Took a while to wake you up."

Gomez Gomez looked down at about a thousand pebbles littering the seat and floor of the Caddy. "Are there any rocks left out there?"

"A couple. Good thing you came around, I was running low. Nothing left but big stuff."

"You couldn't have tapped me on the shoulder or something?"

"Guess I could have. Why didn't I think of that?"

"You're one sadistic chief, you know?"

"You know how much time I've wasted looking for you? You sure seem to have it out for Sonny Harmon's window."

"*Thelma & Louise*. Like the movie, man."

"Uh-huh. Which one are you?"

"Louise, I think. It was Elvis's idea."

"Always is. Can you get out of the car?"

"I'm actually pretty comfortable here."

"Get out of the car, Gomez."

"It's Gomez *Gomez*."

Galt removed his sunglasses and looked up at the blue sky. "Well,

I've been looking for you most of the night. I'm too tired to call you both names. And I'm irritated. So from now on you're just Gomez. Get used to it."

"You weren't too tired to throw a million rocks at me."

"Get out of the car."

"I was looking for Angel. I thought Sonny had, her but I couldn't find her."

"Uh-huh. Maybe she ran off with Elvis."

Gomez Gomez let his head fall back against the seat. The flash of light and pain behind his eyes made him immediately regret the move. "Maybe. I don't think so though. But I dream sometimes and they're together."

Galt looked up and down the length of the Caddy. "You know, you don't look like the pink Cadillac type."

"I told you—"

"Yeah, yeah—Elvis's idea."

"He's definitely the pink Cadillac type."

"I guess he would be." Galt leaned forward and swung the door open. "Enough. Out."

Gomez Gomez told his legs to slide out. It took thirty seconds or so before they obeyed. Finally he pushed himself up and out of the car. A small avalanche of rocks tumbled from the folds of Jake's robe. He wobbled but tried to stand tall and stuck his chest out.

"You hurt anywhere?" Galt said.

"I'm hurt everywhere."

"From anything besides the booze?"

"I don't think so."

"That was some expensive bottle of whiskey you took. I think Sonny's more mad about that than the window or the Cadillac."

"It was definitely better than T-bird."

"Let me guess, Elvis made you take it?"

"Nah. The hooch was all me."

Galt took him by the arm. "C'mon."

"Where we going?"

"Guess. The bright side is I'll let you ride in the front seat."

"Can I play with the siren?"

"No." Galt held Gomez Gomez's head and pushed him into the passenger seat of the Bronco.

"What about Elvis's car?"

"I called it in. They'll send a truck." Galt walked around, opened the driver's side door, and slid in. His gaze tracked the horizon through the windshield. "Man, you picked the place. That's a lot of nothing out there."

"There's a lot of nothing everywhere."

"You a philosopher now?"

"Nah, that's Jake's department. I'm just an imperfect believer."

Galt looked at him. "Elvis? I gotta ask, young and skinny or old and fat?"

"Older, I guess, but not fat."

"Jumpsuit?"

"Yeah, he digs the jumpsuit. It catches starlight."

Galt chuckled. "You're really out there, Gomez."

"So they tell me."

"But to tell you the truth, it'd be cool to see Elvis sometime."

"I could introduce you."

Galt shifted his focus back to the horizon. "You're right. There's a lot of nothing everywhere. You know what? I'm actually kind of starting to see why Father Jake and Early like you. I'm sorry you couldn't find Angel."

"You got a woman, chief?"

"I'm interested. I wouldn't say I have her exactly."

"A live woman?"

Galt grunted a low laugh. "Honey Hicks. Very much alive last time I saw her."

"Uh-oh."

"Uh-oh what?"

Gomez Gomez shrugged. "Her and Jake. You don't know?"

"I know you've been a little off the grid, buddy, but you might have noticed Jake made the decision to become a priest a while back."

"So?"

"What do you mean, *so*? So he's a priest. Automatically out of the picture."

"Yeah, but there are some kinds of love, right? Ain't affected by decisions or life or crap like dying or anything, you know? Jake and Honey are like that. I seen it. Priest don't mean nothin' against love like that."

"You know this for a fact?"

"Anyone with half a brain knows it for a fact, man. Or anyone on this side of the glass."

"And you just happen to have half a brain." A statement, not a question.

"Lucky me."

"Not even dying—like you and Angel, you mean?"

"Yeah, like me and Angel. Love don't stop over stuff like death."

Galt took his hat off and ran his fingers through his hair. "And that's why you need to find her ashes."

"Yeah. Am I going back to jail?"

"No, you're not, Priscilla. Back to the hospital. But with an armed guard this time. Way I told Early to do it in the first place."

"I gotta find her, chief."

"Tell you what. You hang loose, do what the doctors say, and I'll see what I can turn up, cool?"

"I guess I don't have a choice."

"Nope. Some kinds of love, huh?"

"Yeah. Some kinds."

"Well, you're wrong about this one. I think Honey and I have a pretty good shot."

"You're the boss, boss."

Matthias started the Bronco.

"You sure I can't play with the siren?"

"One-hundred-percent."

CHAPTER THIRTY-EIGHT

"I'M JUST SAYING IT BETTER work," Casper was saying.

"I'm telling you I can sell it," Sonny replied. "They'll love it. They're hicks, man."

Casper leaned his bulk against the Escalade, his fat-faced gaze wandering over the makeshift shrine. "'Bought me a taco?' She actually bought somebody a taco and they remember it enough to paint it in tribute?"

"Because they're hicks. Like I said." Sonny ran a comb through his hair, bending to check his reflection in the side-view mirror. "They act like she's the second coming of Jesus or Geraldo or something."

"Except Jesus gave 'em wine or fish or something, not tacos."

"Coulda been fish tacos."

"I guess it coulda been."

Sonny put the comb back in his pocket. "Well, there's a million guys in Old Mexico named Jesus."

"What the heck is that supposed to mean?"

"It means Angel's no big deal. It means I can sell it."

"You better."

"You already said that." Sonny looked at the mayor. *Yeah, this slob has to go as soon as possible.*

"I'm just saying . . ."

"I know what you're saying. Now quit saying it."

"After that call this morning I get the feeling they might back out.

278

I'm getting nervous. I already picked out my boat, you know? Placed the order."

"Stop talking about the boat! I got it all planned. The dance is the perfect time. It'll all be ready. I can sell it. Why do you think I have the third-almost-second-soon-to-be-first Chevy dealership in the Southwest?"

"Because your dad left it to you?"

"Why does everybody keep saying that?"

"Is this gonna be the big fish speech? I don't think I can handle the big fish speech right now. Talbot-West is a bigger fish. They're the Moby Dick of fish. Seriously, the great white whale of fish."

"Just shut up, would ya?"

Casper indicated the shrine with a jut of his turkey chin. "Look at all this crap. 'Bought me groceries,' 'visited me in prison,' 'watched my kids,' 'taught me to read' . . . How you gonna sell it? They love her!"

"I told you to shut up."

"Hey, I'm your partner. You talk to your partner like that? Look at that one. 'Helped me find God.' I'm asking, how are you gonna sell it when she helped somebody find God?"

"Easy, moron. Because at the end of the day people love Outback Steakhouse more than God. This is America for crying out loud! You're panicking. Knock it off."

"That's right, I *am* panicking. I picked out the boat, Sonny! Down payment. Nonrefundable!"

"Seriously, take a breath. You look like you're gonna have a heart attack."

Casper dropped his head and took a long, blubbery breath. "This ain't no football game. This is one pass you can't blow, Sonny."

Sonny closed his eyes and pictured Casper decked out in a Hawaiian shirt and captain's hat behind the wheel of a boat. "What color?"

"What color what?"

"Is the boat?"

"Oh. White with blue trim."

"How original. Light blue or dark?"

"Dark."

"Cool." Sonny painted the boat the appropriate colors beneath Captain Casper then mentally blew the whole package to smithereens.

"What are you smiling at?" Casper said.

"I'm just thinking about you and your boat. It's gonna be great." The afternoon whirred and Milton pulled up in the Harmon Chevrolet golf cart. "You wanted to see me, Mr. Harmon?"

"Yeah, about this shrine."

"You want me to tear it down?"

"No, no. What I want you to do is build it up. Make it even better. Taller, wider, you name it. Bigger, fancier. Frame it up—whatever you have to do—just make it even more noticeable. More wood, stones. Heck, chrome, flags, and fireworks for all I care. A light show. I want it to make a splash."

"Why?" Milton said.

"Look, when I say fix a car you fix the car, right? You don't ask why. Now I'm telling you to trick out this piece-of-junk shrine. Just do what I tell you."

"All right. It's already pretty big."

"Bigger, Milton. Can you do it or not?"

"I think so. Maybe some flags on poles?"

"I don't care. Just make it happen. And drop everything else. I want it done by tomorrow. Spare no expense. Put anything you need on the Harmon Chevrolet account. My secretary will take care of that part."

"Okay."

"C'mon, Casper." Sonny walked around and climbed into the Escalade.

Casper climbed up, ducking to protect his perm. "I guess buying a little goodwill won't hurt."

Sonny tapped an Angel Lives flyer on his dashboard. "These things are everywhere. Every light pole, tree, bulletin board, shop window . . . Have empathy—rule numero uno when it comes to sales. We play this right—toss 'em an Angel bone—they'll be clamoring for Harmon Village. And Outback steak."

"Whatever you say. Just sell it. I think I'm getting an ulcer."

A horn beeped and Charles Faulks's tow truck rolled past, the long, pink Cadillac hoisted up behind it. Sonny started the Escalade and followed Charles around the corner and onto the car lot. Two workers on ladders struggled to attach a large sheet of industrial-grade plastic over the shattered showroom window. Sonny took in a long, slow yoga breath then released it. What he really needed was to match it with a drink. He felt Casper's beady little turkey eyes.

"How's that empathy working now?" the mayor said.

"The dead chick is one thing. I got other plans for her glass-for-brains, window-smashing drunk of a husband."

Milton zipped by in the golf cart and buzzed into the mechanic's bay.

"That Milton guy creeps me out." Casper said.

"He's a useful tool. He's big and scary-looking but he does what he's told. It's called a prison mentality."

"I hope you have a strong leash."

"Strong enough."

CHAPTER THIRTY-NINE

HONEY POURED PELLEGRINO SPARKLING WATER over some ice and stuck the bottle back in the refrigerator. She carried the glass out onto the back deck of her small apartment. She sipped, liking the feel of bubbles in her nose. *Not bad, New York. I could get used to this stuff.* A bass drum thumping an electrified sound check carried through the air. Later, when the band kicked in on the stage under the old oak, the whole town would be able to hear it. Then again the whole town would probably be there anyway. The dance bookending the last night of Miracle Days was one of Paradise's biggest events of the year.

Thump, thump, thump.

Matthias . . . Maybe she should avoid Jake for a while. Jake just complicated things. And at the moment she needed simple. She'd walked away from a good man in Honduras. She didn't want to make the same mistake twice.

Nope. Time to be happy.

And Matthias makes me happy.

She downed the Pellegrino in three long gulps, set the glass on her tiny patio table, and leaned forward on the rail looking down at her hands. Not a girl's hands anymore. A woman's hands—her mother's hands. Where had the years gone?

A bass guitar joined the drum. Then an electric guitar began tuning, matching string with string, vibrating with slight tonal dissonance.

The knock she'd expected sounded and the door opened. Matthias's voice, "Hello? Anybody home?"

"I'm out back," she called. "Help yourself to your fizzy water. It's in the fridge."

From the kitchen the cupboard opened and glasses tinkled. Then the sucking sound of the refrigerator door opening.

"You want some?" he called.

"I already have some."

His cologne preceded him onto the deck. "Hey."

Honey took in his shined boots, jeans, and narrow-cut black shirt with pearl buttons. "Wow, it's the cowboy fashion model from New York City."

"Is it okay? It's a dance."

"It's perfect."

"You okay?"

"I have my mother's hands."

He leaned next to her. "I love your hands."

"You're a nice guy, you know that?"

He grinned. "For a city cowboy, you mean? I'm trying."

A cricket sang somewhere in the yard below, his chirpy monotone melody asking questions of the gathering darkness, getting no answers. Honey hadn't played an instrument since her piano lessons as a little girl, but to her ears the cricket's song matched the guitarist's key as he kicked off "Sweet Home Alabama." When the whole band joined in she could no longer hear the insect's prayer.

"So, you ready to take me to a dance?" Honey said.

"Can I finish my fizzy water first?"

"Down it, mister. Let's go."

He did.

"You missing the Escalade yet?" she asked as he opened the passenger door of the Bronco for her and helped her in.

"Could have been a Camaro according to Sonny."

"No joke? You turned down a Camaro?"

"Wasn't easy. But he can drive it around and pretend he's chasing bad guys in Honolulu."

Honey smiled.

Matthias crossed and climbed into the driver's seat.

"Well, Sonny's a big fish," she said.

Matthias started the truck and dropped it into drive. "Uh-huh, just ask him. And now this whole Harmon Village thing's got everybody in a snit."

"He's used to getting his way." They drove with the windows down. Honey held her mother's hand out and let autumn slip through her fingers. "How's Gomez Gomez doing?"

"Back in the hospital, so far so good. You know, I kind of like the guy."

"He does grow on you."

As they turned the corner into the town center a resplendent glow engulfed them. Strings of white and colored lights—all shapes and sizes—laced through the enormous old oak without missing a branch. More light strings stretched between tall poles erected at intervals, strategically placed so not an inch of downtown Paradise lay in shadow.

"Wild. I bet they can see this from space," Matthias said.

"Biggest event of the year."

"No doubt. Glad I'm off the clock."

"How did you swing that, by the way?"

Matthias grinned. "It's good to be king." He did a slow loop around the square, drove through an open space in the low fence, and parked the Bronco behind the bandstand.

"I'm not sure this is a legal parking space, officer," Honey said.

"You think I'll get a ticket?" Matthias walked around, opened the passenger door for her, and held out his arm. She took it and hopped down. They navigated a riot of thick electrical cables, instrument cases, and a scattering of picnic tables as they rounded the stage. The music jumped several decibels as they passed from the rear to the front of the speakers. A temporary wooden dance floor roughly as large as an Olympic-size swimming pool stretched in front of the stage, full to capacity. Several couples danced around the edges, unable to fit onto the floor itself. Onstage, the band finished a song then jumped straight into another. "Running on Empty."

"Jackson Browne? I thought this was supposed to be a country band," Matthias said, talking loud into her ear.

"I think you call them *eclectic*. The Rio Kings from New Mexico. This is their first time doing the Miracle Days dance. Doc ran into them last year and told Jake. Jake told Katie. She's in charge of booking the band every year."

"Jake . . ."

Honey looked up at him. "And Doc and Katie. You okay?"

He shifted his gaze from her to the stage. "Let me ask you something. Is Father Jake going to come up every time we have a conversation?"

She felt a flash of irritation. "I don't know, is he? It seems to me you're the one who always wants backstory."

Matthias nodded assent. "You're right. I'm sorry. Forget it, okay? I think it's just something Gomez Gomez said getting to me a little."

"I just want to dance and have a good time. Can we do that?"

"Absolutely. Tell you what, I'll get us something to drink. You want anything?"

"Floyd'll have Mexican Cokes at his booth. He goes down and picks up cases of it in Nogales every year."

"Mexican? There's a difference?"

"Trust me."

"Two Mexican Cokes coming up." He moved off toward one of the concession stands lining the square.

Honey smiled as she watched the band. *Eclectic* definitely fit the Rio Kings. The singer, a huge bearded biker with a guitar, added a thick layer of desert grit to the song while a gray-haired African American gentleman in a pinstripe suit tickled away on an upright piano. The drummer and bass player might have been brothers. Both wore T-shirts and cowboy hats although the lanky bassist skipped jeans and boots and opted for baggy board shorts and flip-flops. The right side of the stage hosted what appeared to be an entire mariachi troupe complete with a horn section and stringed instruments of several different sizes. A sturdy blonde woman poured into a floral-print dress held a microphone in one hand and a trumpet in the other alternating between backup vocals and joining the mariachi horns for punctuating stabs of brass.

Jackson ended with a four-note swell and the biker played a few opening notes before the woman in the flower-print dress took the vocal lead on "Me and Bobby McGee."

Honey turned at a nudge on her elbow, expecting Matthias.

Katie winked at her, face damp with perspiration. "What do you think of the band, mija?"

"They're cool. They fit right in."

"I'm glad Doc found them. Where's Mr. Narrow Hips?"

"Went to get us something to drink. I think he's a little miffed. I mentioned Jake."

"You always mention Jake."

"That's what he said. And for the record, I don't. Sometimes he mentions Jake."

"Whatever. Leave Jake at home. Have fun."

"That's what I told him."

Matthias appeared, a couple of Coke bottles in hand. He gave one to Honey. "Heya, Katie."

"Hi, handsome. You ready to run away with me?"

"Where we gonna go?"

"You could show me Times Square."

"It's not all it's cracked up to be. Anyway, I already have a date."

Katie put a hand on his arm. "If you get bored, I'll be on the dance floor."

Matthias tipped his bottle to her. "You got it."

The band transitioned songs again. One of the mariachi musicians set down his guitar and took the microphone from the blonde and started in on a heavily accented rendition of U2's "One."

"Ha! I like these guys," Matthias said.

"So, ask me to dance," Honey said.

"What about our Mexican Cokes?"

"You think someone's going to steal the police chief's soda?"

"Maybe. I never underestimate the depths to which the average human can sink."

"So you'll get a new one. C'mon." Honey set her bottle on a table and reached out her hand to him. He set his bottle next to hers and took her hand.

On the dance floor he pulled her close. "I like Miracle Days."

"Me too."

He stiffened a little. She sensed as much as felt it. She pulled back.

"Something wrong?" she said.

"No. Nothing at all."

She turned her head and leaned into his chest.

And saw Jake at the edge of the crowd.

CHAPTER FORTY

JAKE WATCHED MATTHIAS LEAD HONEY onto the dance floor and did a pretty good job lying to himself that it didn't bother him. He looked at the band instead. A mariachi version of U2's "One." He thought about Doc and his wife dancing to this very band in some out-of-the-way bar in the New Mexico desert. Doc and his stories . . . He'd tell Jake to cut in on Matthias just for fun. And if Jake didn't, Doc would. He was like that.

But Doc wasn't a priest either.

Father Enzo elbowed him. "There's nothing that says a priest can't dance."

"Leave the boy alone," Lucille said.

"I'm fine," Jake said. "Just enjoying the music."

Father Enzo bowed to Lucille. "How about you, lovely Lucille? Will you dance with a priest?"

Lucille thought for a few seconds then took his hand. "What's the worst that could happen? Don't step on my feet."

Father Enzo led her to the floor, straightened his back, and took her into a formal ballroom stance. Lucille looked at Jake and rolled her eyes, but beamed as Father Enzo led out.

"It's like *American Bandstand* meets *The Twilight Zone*." Early came up next to Jake, a Styrofoam coffee cup in his hand.

"Where'd you come from?"

"Roaming the earth to see whom I might devour."

288

"You're a strange individual, you know that?"

"Thanks, dear." Early nodded toward a big video screen erected to the side of the stage. "What's with the drive-in theater?"

"No idea. Not on duty tonight?"

"Nah, all the underlings are covering the bases. I'm a free man unless there's an emergency and they can't live without me."

"No date?"

Early sipped his coffee. "Don't fence me in, brother."

"How many women did you ask?"

"Beside the point. Anyway, I have you."

"That's true, but I'm not much of a dancer."

"Don't have to be when you look that good in a dress."

"I'm not even gonna respond."

"You see Gomez Gomez today?"

"I tried. Looks like unless he wants to drug me and steal my robe I'm not all that welcome."

"A very Gomez Gomez move."

"I thought I was making progress with him. I don't know what to do with the guy anymore."

Onstage the band broke into some Texas swing. The big biker singer stepped up to the mic.

"Baby, pack up your clouds, you're blocking my blue sky
Take back your rain, 'cause it won't let the sun shine
It's a beautiful night with the stars shining clear
It's warm outside, babe, but it's cold in here . . ."

Katie approached. "The Lone Ranger and Tonto ride again."

"Hey, Aunt Katie," Jake said.

She shook her head. "You over here crying in your beer because your old girlfriend is dancing with someone else?"

"I'm not crying."

"Why you look all mopey then?"

"What have I done now?"

"You walk around all Jake-ish, that's what. You gonna back me up here, Tonto?"

"Not my circus, not my monkeys," Early said.

"It's warm outside, but it's cold in here
It's blowing heartache, it's raining tears
The weatherman's calling for sunny and clear
It's warm outside, babe, but it's cold in here . . ."

Against his better judgment Jake chanced a glance at Matthias and Honey. Honey's back was to him but Matthias's eyes met his, held, then moved on.

"These walls are fragile so, baby, don't throw stones
We all got closets full of dead men's bones . . ."

"I'm not sure your boss likes me," Jake said to Early.

"Maybe he's Baptist."

"I'm sure that's it."

Early drained his coffee and tossed the cup into a nearby trash can. "So you know why Baptists don't believe in premarital sex?"

"If I beg, will you please not tell me?"

"They're afraid it might lead to dancing."

"You had to do it."

"I only tell you so you'll know why I just converted to Presbyterianism. I feel like dancing. Adios."

In typical Early fashion, the big man opted to cut right through the middle of the dancers instead of going around. Charlton Heston through the Red Sea. He struck up a conversation with a pretty brunette in a red dress on the far side of the dance floor. A moment later he led her out and they started to two-step.

Jake watched Early and the woman dance. Honey and Matthias had disappeared. The night and crowd pressed. Sweat trickled down the back of Jake's neck and he tugged at his collar. Leaving the stage behind, he walked through the throng. It thinned the farther he got from the oak. He bought a Dos Equis at a concession trailer and found an empty picnic table far out past the border of activity. The bottle painted a slow, wet ring of condensation on the wood. He picked it up and took a long pull, trying to decide if Honey's face had looked happy out there dancing with Matthias. He hoped she was happy. He wished it for her. Because no matter how many times he turned the thing over in his brain, the situation remained the same—in the end the best he could hope for was her happiness. Something he'd never be able to provide. He loved her. He'd always love her. The robe and collar would never change that. But he would content himself with loving her from a distance.

An Angel Lives poster stapled to a nearby light pole caught his eye. He tipped his bottle to it. "I'm glad, Angel. You of all people deserve to be remembered. I know I've said it a million times, but I'm still sorry. It should've been me. Tell you the truth, I'm not so sure it wasn't." He took another long drink.

"You talking to yourself, father?" Honey always carried her bottle by the mouth, dangling off her index finger. The familiar sight brought Jake a smile.

"I'm the only one who listens," he said.

"I very much doubt that."

"You'd be surprised." He pointed at her Coke. "So Floyd made the run to Nogales again this year, huh?"

"Floyd and taxes. Two things you can always count on." Honey slid onto the picnic table bench opposite. She sipped and cocked her head at him. "Saw you over there. We used to dance. Remember those days?"

"Whether I want to or not. So clear it hurts. I don't think Matthias is my biggest fan."

"He feels threatened, but he'd never admit it."

"No reason for him to be. I only want the best for you."

"He'd never ask me to keep my distance . . ."

"But you're thinking it might be a good idea."

"I don't want to lose our friendship, I really don't. It's just—"

"I understand. You deserve a shot. Whatever you want."

She bit her bottom lip. "You did always know me best."

"Where is he now?"

"Back there. I asked him to give me a minute."

Jake picked at the label on the beer with his thumbnail. "He should know I'm no threat given the circumstances. And I don't want to be."

Her gaze held him, giving no quarter. "Maybe not physically. But emotionally I'm not so sure. You proved that when we talked at Finnegan's the other day. You made me feel things I can't feel. I gotta move on, Jake."

"You said that. I'd never hold you."

"I said it to you, but now I'm finally saying it to myself."

"Will he make you happy?"

She looked back toward the crowd and stage, the distance slightly muffling Benny Goodman's "In the Mood." "I think so. I'm getting there."

"The one thing I know is I want you to be happy. I always have."

"I know that." Her smile brought a familiar stab. "I want me to be happy too. He likes eighties hair bands. Is that weird?"

"Everybody's got their thing, right?"

"And bro country . . ."

"You might need to draw the line there."

The edge of her mouth curved up. "It's drawn."

"So he makes you happy. I'm glad."

"I think he could. If I really let you go."

Jake reached out and clinked glass on glass. "Go be happy, Honey. It's the right thing."

She stood. "Are you gonna be okay?"

"I'm gonna be fine."

"Bye, Jake."

"Bye, Honey."

Then the night took her.

Goodbye, Honey . . . Jake finished his beer and tossed the bottle in a trash barrel. It'd been a long day. He rose and hopped the low fence, deciding he'd take the sidewalk around the square back to the mission. Was he going to be okay? *No.* But at the end of the day what choice did he have? He wasn't like Erasmo who could go fight for a girl. *What choice do any of us have?*

From the stage, a woman sang, her voice sweet in the night. Bonnie Raitt's "Angel from Montgomery." The strings of lights overhead blocked the stars and lit the town, but as the song ended an even brighter presence flashed as the huge video screen next to the big oak blinked to life and filled itself with Sonny Harmon's face.

What in the world?

Mayor Casper Green shuffled to the front of the stage, microphone in hand. His voice pounded the evening. "Hey there, Paradise, you having a good time tonight?"

A cheer came from the crowd.

"How about these Rio Kings, huh?"

Another burst of enthusiastic applause.

"Let's all give a big thanks to our own Katie Morales for bringing in such a fine band to close out this year's Miracle Days!"

More claps and cheers.

"And, hey, how about giving it up for our corporate sponsor tonight, Harmon Chevrolet! Listen, Sonny Harmon is good enough to have sponsored the last five of these dances. Like me, he's a real lover and supporter of our little community. I'd like to invite Sonny up here to say a few words." He held out an arm. "Come on up here, boy!"

The crowd clapped, but with noticeably less vigor than they had for the Rio Kings. Curious, Jake re-hopped the fence and headed back into the crowd. He stopped at the edge of the dance floor. Onstage a soundman helped Sonny fiddle with a miniature headset microphone. Sonny kept mouthing the word "Check" but nothing came through the speakers.

Early approached, face flushed and beaded with sweat.

"You look like you've been having fun," Jake said.

"Katrina. Girl I met. She was teaching me how to swing dance."

"Did you catch on?"

"Enough to get a date with her for next Friday night. Guess I did okay."

"What's with Sonny, you think?"

Early shrugged. "Maybe we're gonna get his big fish speech en masse."

Sonny's mic kicked in right in the middle of a word sending feedback into the night, squealing off the surrounding buildings. The soundman brought the volume quickly under control.

"This thing on? You folks hear me?" Sonny said.

CHAPTER FORTY-ONE

"WE HEAR YA, SONNY," SOMEONE in the crowd shouted.

Sonny barely felt the ear-mounted mic. A new and surreal experience hearing his voice blasting through the big speakers on the sides of the stage.

"Good, good!" Sonny said. "Now listen, folks, we're gonna get right back to the dancing—"

"How about right now?" somebody called out.

Sonny kicked the nudge of irritation away, laughed, and held up his hands in surrender. "Yes, I promise! As your sponsor tonight, I just wanted to take a few minutes to talk to you. Kind of clear the air, if you will."

A murmur rippled the crowd. Good ripple or bad? Sonny tried to read them. Not his thing. But, hey, he was the big fish, not them. "I know there's been some concern in our community about the land I own adjacent to the car lot. Tonight I wanted to alleviate those concerns so we can all just relax and have a great time. The kind of thing we're so good at here in Paradise, right? Now, I know by now you've all heard about the little development I've planned to enhance our beautiful town."

"Wait a minute, Sonny," someone called out. "What do you mean the land you own? Isn't that public land?"

"It's Angel's land!" another voice said.

It's cool. Take a breath, you got this . . .

295

Casper Green stepped forward to a mic. "Actually, folks, Sonny's right. He purchased that land from the city last year."

"I don't remember a vote," the same person called out.

"It was a council matter. Not everything is open to public vote," Casper said. "Although anyone could've come to a meeting and voiced an objection if you so desired."

Sonny raised a hand, glad he hadn't blown Casper to bits yet. A time and season for everything. "Look, folks, the last think I want to do tonight is cause a problem. My plans for that land are for the town's benefit, not for mine. We're talking a cinema complex, outlet stores, sporting goods shop . . . Heck, even an Outback Steakhouse!"

Another voice: "What's wrong with the Star? I been seeing movies at the Star since I was a kid."

A rumble of agreement.

"And we already got Spur's," another added. "What do we need an Outback for?"

This is like dealing with children. "Outback's just a possibility," Sonny said. "Nothing set in stone. But Spur's doesn't have Bloomin' Onions, am I right?"

"Angel lives!" somebody shouted.

"Angel lives!" came a reply. The crowed rippled again.

Sonny clenched and unclenched his fists and focused on holding his practiced smile. "Look, Angel was a great lady, no doubt about it. We all miss her dearly, especially our friend Gomez Gomez. The good news there is he's finally in the hospital where he can get some help. That's why one thing I insist on is that we honor Angel's memory, God rest her soul. In fact, if you've driven by the lot today you'll see Harmon Chevrolet has invested a considerable amount of money adding to and beatifying the memorial some of you have graciously erected. That's why I've proposed that in the very center of the new construction we'll place a small grassy area and a stone to honor Angel's life and the impact she had on all of us."

"The whole place should be left alone," a woman said.

Early Pines standing off to the side with Father Jake cupped a hand to his mouth. "Yeah! The whole place should be left alone forever! Who cares about onions?" The detective winked.

Sonny seriously wanted to punch somebody. Blow up not just Casper's boat but the whole stinking lot of them. Why was he even talking to these hillbillies? *Everybody loves Outback, man!* He smiled through gritted teeth at the camera. "All right, I want to show you something! Because we all know seeing is better than hearing. So I've had an architecture firm in Phoenix make up a scale model of the whole property. I'm telling you, folks, you're gonna love this!" *You better, you morons. This thing cost as much as a new car.* "Just think, how would you like a place to bring your kids—your whole family—to get ice cream, see a movie, have some well-deserved fun? Restaurants, stores, a sports bar . . . everything this town needs. I'm going to bring it right to you."

He raised a hand and Casper and Milton wheeled out a huge cloth-covered table from the recesses of the stage. A camera pre-mounted to give a downward angle would show the entirety of the covered model on the big video screen. So lifelike it would leave these imbeciles speechless. Sonny offered his best fatherly chuckle, his dad's laugh. *Sells 'em every time, kid.* "Drumroll please! Paradise, are you ready?"

"Just show us already," someone shouted.

"You can do better than that! *Are you ready?*"

A smattering of claps. Yeah, he'd love to nuke the lot of them. But they hadn't seen his coup de grâce. The model the architect firm had mocked up looked like Disney on a sugar high. These people would wet themselves. He couldn't help teasing a little longer. "I'm gonna count down from ten."

"C'mon, Sonny!"

"Ha! All right then . . . Three, two, one!" Sonny yanked the cloth away just like he'd practiced, keeping his eyes on the crowd to gauge their reaction. A hush fell over the square. Man, even better than he'd hoped. A woman in front of the stage pointed at the screen and said something to the man next to her. Thrilled, Sonny glanced down at the model. His fixed smile slid off his face. *Impossible . . .* There, across his beautiful model of Harmon Village, someone had taken florescent yellow paint and sprayed in bold block letters ANGEL LIVES.

"Angel lives," someone called out.

"Angel lives!" another answered.

"Angel lives! Angel lives! Angel lives!" The chant started out quiet then swelled in volume until it filled the night and echoed through the square, five-hundred-plus voices shouting in unison.

Rage flooded Sonny's limbs, a great tidal surge of embarrassment mixed with adrenaline. Without thinking he gripped the edge of the model and lifted with every ounce of strength he possessed. It tipped and tumbled off the stage, booming onto the dance floor as people scattered.

"You're all idiots!" he said, voice rattling the speakers. "I was doing this for you. Trying to do something nice for this godforsaken wide spot in the road. And all you can think about is that crazy dead woman and that whacko piece of waste that used to be her husband. Well, guess what? You get Harmon World whether you like it or not. And I'll put a public toilet smack in the middle of where Angel's memorial was gonna be! Since I'm a nice guy maybe I'll even still put her name on it. *Angel's Toilet!* And how about this—construction starts tomorrow morning when I personally climb into my bulldozer and turn your Angel shrine into dust and sticks."

Silence gripped the square.

Sonny grinned. He felt better. "Thank you, Paradise. Good night!"

CHAPTER FORTY-TWO

HONEY STOPPED AT THE COUNTER to top off Matthias's coffee.
"The whole thing is crazy. Gomez Gomez drugging Jake. Driving
through Sonny's window. Sonny's big public tantrum. It's like some
movie where aliens are taking over people's bodies."

"You left out some good parts," Matthias said. "Don't forget Elvis
tagging along on Mr. Toad's wild ride. We should write a screenplay,
make a million bucks."

"You could finally get those Yankees tickets."

"Yup. Sonny's tantrum, that was crazy. I was up most of the night
dealing with that whole mess."

"You think he was just ranting or will he really go through with it
today? Tearing down the memorial and everything?"

"The guy's an egomaniac. The homecoming king gets snubbed. Last
night he told me he'll start with that shrine first then keep right on
going. I honestly wish I had some way of stopping him—he's an arro-
gant jerk—but Casper and the town council back him all the way and
legally my hands are tied. Somehow he actually did buy that land for a
dollar. Completely above board according to city records. I've checked.
The best I can do as chief is make sure nobody gets hurt and Gomez
Gomez gets the help he needs."

"It's gonna kill Gomez Gomez when Sonny wrecks that land. Like
wiping away everything he has left of Angel. I'm glad he's in the hospital and can't see it."

"Best place for him. He keeps talking about God and Venus and Elvis and someone named Bones. He's seriously a mess. Get him off the alcohol and hopefully he comes out of this with a sound mind."

"You never knew him before. I'm not sure his mind was ever all that sound. Angel was good for him though. She balanced him. She latched onto him and loved him like he was the only man on the planet."

Matthias blew on his coffee. "I've seen the signs. Heard stuff. But what was she really like?"

"Angel? How can I describe her? She was one in a million. Tiny, explosive, piles and piles of blonde hair, always singing. She loved everybody in her path. Didn't matter if they were rich, poor, or in between. All those signs? They're the real deal. She gave herself away every day without one complaint. I got tired just watching her."

"I'm sorry I never met her. She obviously still carries serious clout around here—which sucks for Sonny. I'm sorry for Gomez Gomez."

"He breaks my heart."

Katie banged through the kitchen door holding a plate with a hot pad. She scooted past Honey and slid the plate in front of a man in a plaid shirt and an Arizona Diamondbacks hat a few stools down. "Your enchiladas verde. Enjoy. Hot plate. Be careful."

"Gracias, beautiful," the man said.

Katie clucked her tongue. "Keep talking. Flattery will get you a lot of places but not to discount land." On her way back she stopped and looked at Matthias. "I'm gonna start charging you rent for that stool, *policia* man, it's busy today. You like the tacos?"

"Perfect as always. And I'm leaving. Sorry for holding your waitress captive."

"Tie her up and take her away, I don't care. As long as somebody makes her smile." Katie banged back through the kitchen door.

Matthias looked at his watch. "Any chance of seeing you later tonight?"

"It's Thursday. Tennis Ball Two Steppers night."

"What in the world is Tennis Ball Two Steppers?"

"Dance over at Golden Years. I'm kind of the unofficial DJ."

"Tennis ball?"

"On account of the tennis balls stuck on the back legs of their walkers."

"Ah . . . Why *do* old people always put tennis balls on the legs of their walkers? Seems like someone would've come up with something better by now."

"This is one of life's great mysteries. Ask me when I'm ninety, I'll probably know. Anyway, I'll be there tonight if you want to come."

"Is that an invitation?"

"I'm just saying it's a free country."

Music started playing in Matthias's pocket and he fished out his cell phone.

"Wait a minute, was that Robert Earl Keen?" Honey said.

"Matthias speaking. What's up, Lawrence?"

"Robert Earl Keen?" Honey mouthed.

"All right, I'm on my way." Matthias slipped the phone back into his pocket.

"Is your ringtone 'Gringo Honeymoon'?" Honey said.

"So? I like that song. What can I say? You won me over." He laid a few bills on the counter. "Gotta run, Sonny again."

"Is he starting?"

"Not sure. I'll call you later, okay?"

"Okay. See you when I see you."

He paused at the door. "Golden Years. I'll bring the tennis balls."

Honey watched him jog across the street to the police Bronco.

Just make her smile, Katie had said. Did he?

Yes. He does. And when he doesn't, smile anyway.

She'd said goodbye to Jake last night. And he'd said it to her as well. Both knew what it meant. There was finality to it. And she should feel free.

She should smile.

She *would* smile.

"Mija!"

Katie's head poked out of the partially opened kitchen door.

"You have to see this. Get in here," Katie said, her head disappearing again.

Honey pushed through the swinging door and found her boss staring at the old television with the clothes hanger antenna she kept tuned to KPTV on the shelf above the stove.

"It's Jake," Katie said. "What in the world is he doing?"

Rosa Perez's pretty face filled the TV screen. "Let me reiterate, Sonny Harmon, owner of Harmon Chevrolet, himself is the man you see behind me in the bulldozer. He's said today is the day he'll begin clearing the vacant tract of land many locals are calling Angel's place for his new Harmon Village project. Mr. Harmon came this morning intent on making a statement. And as you can see, it's a several ton statement. Sonny claimed first on his list is the memorial to Angel Gomez"—Rosa pointed a manicured finger at the shrine—"who was killed on this spot five years ago. But it seems Mr. Harmon has run up against a bit of a snag this morning. A snag in the form of a local Catholic priest, Father Jake Morales."

Rosa offered her megawatt reporter smile and stepped to one side, revealing a massive earthmover lined up facing Angel's shrine. The camera zoomed in on a figure in front of the huge tractor. Blurry at first as the camera jerked in and out of focus then steadied. There, tiny next to the mammoth machine, sitting on a folding lawn chair, wearing his inevitable old cowboy hat, robe flapping in the Arizona mountain breeze, was Jake.

"I have to go," Honey said.

CHAPTER FORTY-THREE

SONNY REVVED THE BULLDOZER'S ENGINE and let it creep forward a foot. How would it feel to flat out run over the guy? Look at the idiot! Sitting there like he didn't have a care in the world. A crowd had begun to gather next to the news van and that ditzy reporter Rosa Perez. Fine and good, let the whole world watch Sonny Harmon in action. But now stupid Jake sat there like a king on a throne, trashing Sonny's moment. *His* moment! Every nerve in his body sung, aching to tear into the trees, brush, and the ghost of Angel Gomez on the other side of this stupid, stupid, stupid, stubborn priest.

He revved again and jumped another foot forward. Jake didn't flinch. In fact, the moron almost looked asleep.

"Jake!" Sonny shouted.

Jake turned his face up.

Sonny stood over his seat, hands gripping the machine's controls. "What's the matter with you, you idiot?" He threw the tractor in reverse and angled back to come at the shrine from a different direction. Jake stood, stretched, and moved his chair into position to block Sonny's new approach. Sonny reversed and shifted over again. Jake mirrored him. Sonny pounded the dash.

Lights flashed and Galt's Bronco pulled up next to the bulldozer. Rosa Perez rushed up to him with her microphone and cameraman, but Galt waved her off. The police chief climbed up over the bulldozer track and knocked on the glass.

"Get off my tractor!" Sonny shouted through the door.

Galt knocked again. Sonny looked straight ahead. *Don't look at him and he'll go away.* Another knock. Sonny revved the engine. Galt knocked once more and Sonny gave him the finger. Galt pounded this time.

Sonny opened the door. "What?"

"Get down off the tractor."

"You get down. My tractor, my property. Why are you talking to me and not him? Arrest that moron!"

"Look, Sonny—"

"Mr. Harmon to you. Any chance at Sonny went out the window when you gave back the Escalade."

"Okay, Mr. Harmon, then. Look, tempers are hot right now. The best thing to do at the moment is move the tractor and let everybody settle down. Let the crowd and the newspeople leave. Can you do that for me please?"

"Get off my tractor! I gave them a chance last night and they made it very clear. They choose Angel's ghost over a brand-new Outback Steakhouse. They're hicks. Idiots. You're from New York, man, you should see that. What's the matter with you? I don't care what they say. I don't care what they think. Now you go tell the pope down there to move his butt because I'm about to turn him into a Communion wafer!"

"Mr. Har—"

Sonny shouted so hard spit flew. "Get off the tractor!"

Galt climbed down, shaking his head, and walked over to Jake. They talked for a bit. Galt scratched the back of his neck. They talked some more. Finally Galt came back to the tractor and climbed up.

Sonny waited, forcing the chief to knock before opening the door. "Well?"

"He's not budging. Says he owes it to Angel and Gomez Gomez."

"Can't anyone around here get it through their skull that there's no Angel? The woman is dead. She's a handful of dirt in a coffee can. Get that guy off my property. Arrest him and drag him away!"

"She's not dead to them. Angel lives, remember? They want to remember her. They love her."

Sonny rubbed his face with his hands. "That woman, ugh! I couldn't stand her when she was alive either. She was a weirdo then, she's even worse as a ghost."

"Look, why don't you just stand down for a little while, and we'll see if there's a way we can figure this out without anyone getting hurt."

"How very police chief of you. Why don't you do your job? You should've kept the Escalade, man. Then you'd cuff this moron and I could go play with my big toy in my big sandbox."

"You going to stand down?"

Two news cameras trained their big black eyes on Sonny along with several cell phones in the crowd. He tried his sales smile but was afraid it came out more like a grimace than anything else. "Tell you what. In the name of business I'll give it one hour. One hour for you to get everybody here off my property—"

"Technically everyone but Father Jake is up on the road—city property."

"Whatever you want to tell yourself. One hour. Get 'em gone. Then I'm starting my playdate. And I swear to you, without hesitation, I'll run over the moron. I'll smash him like an ant."

"And I'll arrest you for murder."

"He's trespassing. It's self-defense. Stand your ground law and all that. One hour."

"Sonny, you know you're not going to—"

"One." Sonny looked at his watch and held up his index finger. "Ticktock."

Galt climbed down, headed over to talk to the crowd. As he watched the chief go, Sonny reached behind his back and touched the butt of the .44 Magnum shoved into his waistband.

It felt good.

CHAPTER FORTY-FOUR

"Man, baby, that priest is a cat," Elvis was saying.

Gomez Gomez tore his eyes from the hospital room television. "He killed Angel. He ain't no cat."

Elvis made a show of studying his nails. "So you keep saying."

"What's that supposed to mean? So I keep saying! Open and shut. Jake wasn't watching the road and hit her head-on. Told me himself. He killed her. The end."

"I ain't heard no fat lady sing, baby."

"Then you must be deaf. Credits are rolling, man."

"Is it ever really the end?"

"You the old man on the mountaintop now? It was the end of Angel's story, that's for sure."

"Nah, man, Angel's story's just getting off the ground. You'll see."

"You know what I mean."

"What you mean is you need an excuse to be mad at the cat so you won't have to face your own self."

"I face myself every day."

"Nah, you run every day. The truth is you lost your friend along with your wife that day. But losing the friend was your choice, man."

"You think I shoulda just accepted his apology? *Hey, man, it was me, I killed Angel . . .* I shoulda said, *No problem, buddy*, and gave him a hug or something? I don't think so."

"Jake lost that day too. He lost a lot, baby."

"All I know is he killed her. All I need to know."

"Did you see it happen? Angel drove fast. Sure there ain't more to the story?"

"Why am I arguing with imaginary Elvis? He killed her. I got to spell it out for you?"

"Man, all you do is spell it out. But what I see right now is that cat sitting in a lawn chair cool as the other side of Priscilla's pillow, facing down a bulldozer. And why's he doing it, baby? You tell me that?"

Gomez Gomez scratched his chin. "I guess because he feels guilty 'bout Angel."

"Big no, daddy-o. The Jakester's doing it for you, baby. You think you're a cat sitting in here sucking lemon Jell-O between your teeth talking to the King, but that dude's tugging on old death's ear because of you. Because he loves you."

Gomez Gomez looked down at the half-eaten Jell-O on the plastic hospital plate. He *had* been sucking it through his teeth. "I just need to find Angel."

"You don't need that raggedy old can, baby. She ain't in there. She never was."

"He killed her. What was I supposed to do?"

"You were supposed to be his friend, man. Like he's doing for you now."

"It hurt too bad."

"Yeah, things hurt sometimes. But you know the guy. You could've been his friend instead of wallowing in bad booze and self-pity. Two things Angel would've hated to see."

Stinkin' Elvis. But the King was right. Angel would've hated what he'd become.

"I just wish I could see her again. Even if it's in a dream or something," Gomez Gomez said.

"You will, man. One day."

"I don't know. I'm an imperfect believer."

"Ain't no other kind, baby. You got your imperfect believers and you got your perfect doubters and you got everything in between.

Everybody's got a gig and it'll all shake down. You know the truth and it'll set you free, that part ain't about you anyway. Question is, what do you do now? While you're here? You gonna let old Jake hang in the breeze out there by himself?"

"It's his choice. Anyway, what am I supposed to do about it? I'm under arrest here. I got a guard this time too. It ain't like I can leave. I gotta watch it on TV."

"I think you'll figure it out. Now adios, baby, I got to split. The King has left the building."

"Figure it out how?"

But Elvis was gone.

Early walked in without knocking. "You talking to snakes again?"

"Nah, Elvis."

"You should've worn a helmet riding them bulls, you know that?"

"He says Angel's story ain't over."

Early pointed at the TV. "He may be a figment of your imagination but he's no idiot. She's prime time even as we speak."

"Jake's doing that for me, isn't he?"

Early dropped into Elvis's chair and put his boots up on Gomez Gomez's bed. "Yup, he is. He's Jake."

"He killed Angel."

"That line's tired, man."

"Yeah, it might be. You know all that time down there in that shack? Mad at him? After Angel, Jake's the one I missed the most. No offense."

"None taken. I miss him too. The thing with Angel broke him, and he was the one guy I always thought was unbreakable."

"And it turns out he's just an imperfect believer . . ."

"What?"

"Nothing. I got to talk to him, man. I been telling him how much I hate him for five years. Now he's sitting there in front of Angel's place telling me right back that he loves me, that I'm still his friend, and he's got my back even though I'm a crazy snake-talker."

"That's actually the sanest thing you've said in a long time, man. I've been trying to tell you for five years it wasn't his fault."

"But that's the thing. Maybe it wasn't his fault and maybe it was. It don't matter anymore. He's been telling me he was sorry all this time, and I just spit on him over and over. And that ain't no figure of speech. I mean I really spit on him. And look at what he's doing. For me."

"So what are you saying, amigo? What do you want to do?"

"I gotta get out of here. I gotta talk to him. Tell him I'm sorry too. I gotta do it now. Can you help me?"

Early grinned, then called toward the open door. "Hey, Lawrence?"

A thin face appeared in the doorway. "Yeah?"

"Take a break, man. Go get yourself some food or something. I'll watch the snake charmer for a while."

CHAPTER FORTY-FIVE

HONEY MADE A QUICK STOP at her apartment to change. After that it only took ten minutes to get across town to Angel's place. Already the crowd she'd seen on television had grown. At least fifty people stood along the side of the road near the news van. Several of them held Angel Lives signs. Sonny still occupied the idling bulldozer and Jake—implacable, unmovable Jake—sat on a lawn chair in front of the shrine. Cars and trucks lined the road for a hundred yards or so. She drove past them and backed onto the gravel on the opposite side of the street from the activity. She sat for a long moment staring out at the clean autumn without really seeing it.

In an instant it had clicked.

Life's puzzle pieces dropping into perfect order right out of the sky. The hard answer. The worst answer. But the only answer.

There in Katie's kitchen watching Jake on the TV. The path stretched before her clearer than any she'd known. But once she opened this car door and stepped out, there was no going back. No more dancing with Matthias, no more flirting over the counter. No more doctors in Honduras.

Just Jake.

Jake the priest.

Once she opened this door . . .

Then she did. She swung her legs out and stood. She walked to the trunk, searching out the right key on her ring.

"Honey?"

She'd expected him. She turned.

"I thought you were still working," Matthias said.

"I was but I saw it on TV and I needed to come."

"I don't understand. I think it'd be better if you weren't here. There's nothing you can do to help me. I've got it under control."

A car passed. Leftover breeze stirred a circle of dust around their feet. "I'm not here for you, Matthias."

Realization dawned in his perfect eyes. Honey inserted the trunk key and popped the hatch. She opened it and pulled out a folding lawn chair.

Matthias shook his head. "Honey, no."

"I'm sorry."

"Why? What good will it do?"

"I don't know. I just know I have to go."

Matthias took off his sunglasses, held them between two fingers, hooked his thumbs in the front pockets of his jeans, and leaned his weight on one leg.

"Sonny will back down. And Father Jake will be fine."

"I have to go. The thing is . . . I love him."

"What?"

"Yeah." There it was, right out in the sun.

"He's a priest, Honey."

"I know he is. But he's still him and I love him. I always have. I can't help it."

"What can you hope for here? What do you expect to happen?"

"I don't know. Nothing. I just know I have to do this."

Matthias sighed and looked out over the trees. "Unbelievable. Well, I can't let you go over there. It's dangerous. Seriously, I won't allow it."

"You know you're not stopping me."

"C'mon, this is crazy! Think about it. We have a good thing here. And there's no future with him. No future at all! Where is it supposed to go?"

"Nowhere. I know that. It's not like I haven't thought it through.

I have. But at the end of the day, no matter how many times I turn it over, no matter what angle I look at it from, it comes up the same. I just love him. It's ridiculous, it's senseless, it's pointless, but there it is. And I'm sick of fighting it. I was standing there watching him on Katie's TV and it hit me, you know? I've loved this guy since second grade. Since before he knew my name or even knew I was alive. I loved him then and I love him now. And if I'm honest I don't think I can ever love anyone else. So why try? It's not fair to anyone. You included."

"Okay, listen." He held up both hands. "I know I'm beating a dead horse, but I have to restate the obvious. He's a priest. You can never be with him. Don't you deserve—"

"Then I won't be with him. But I won't be without him either. I can still love him. And I will love him because I do love him. Even if it's from a distance. Or just pouring him a cup of coffee at Shorty's. At least it's something. And at least it's true—real. It is what it is. As long as my heart is with him, how can I give it, even part of it, to someone else?"

"Honey . . ."

"I've thought it through."

"But—"

"You did make me smile."

"But I'm not Jake."

"You're not Jake."

He gave a rueful smile and shook his head. "Well, who knows? Maybe I have a future with Katie."

She laughed, blinking back tears. "You've got a real shot there."

Matthias sighed. "All right then, c'mon. You're not going down without me." He led the way down the road and past the parked cars. Rosa the reporter spotted Honey's lawn chair and rushed toward them, microphone ready. Matthias fended her off with an outstretched palm. "Not now, Rosa."

Somebody in the crowd called out, "Way to go, Honey!"

Butterflies swirled inside her. *What am I doing?* But then again it wasn't a choice, was it? There had never really been a choice. Her heart belonged to Jake and nothing, not even a thousand years of Catholic tradition, would ever change that.

"You're sure about this?" Matthias said under his breath.

"You know I am. I wouldn't be here if I wasn't."

Jake sat up straight in his chair as they approached.

Matthias stopped in front of Jake, sliding a hand into his hip pocket. "Well, Father Jake the priest, very much against my will and strong protest, it looks like you have company on your little field trip to the woods."

Jake's eyes fixed on Honey, taking in her chair. "No, Honey. Sonny's a loose cannon. It's not safe."

"Gomez Gomez is my friend too."

"I can do this alone. One works as well as two here."

"One never works as well as two. Not when the two is you and me. You know it and I know it. At least I do now."

They looked at each other, neither breaking the stare.

"I thought we said goodbye last night," Jake said.

Honey unfolded her lawn chair and set it next to his. "Hi, Jake."

He smiled. "Hi, Honey."

CHAPTER FORTY-SIX

AT LEAST A HUNDRED PEOPLE—probably more—gathered now. Up on the road a few cars and a minivan jockeyed for parking. Rosa Perez kept busy with her microphone talking to one watcher after another, keeping her faithful cameraman in constant motion. They were too far away for Jake to make out what any of them said.

The breeze blew a strand of hair into Honey's face and she brushed it away with a finger. Jake studied the familiar line of her jaw. Every detail of this woman spoke to him. She smelled of lavender and sunlight. The clean white blouse. Her jeans had a small hole in one knee. Light pink polish on her nails. She held her hands in her lap, caressing one with the other.

"What's going on, Honey?" he said.

"I don't know. I saw you on TV and had to come."

"Honey—"

She met his eyes. "Okay, look, *Father* Jake, here it is. And it's ridiculous so don't say anything. You know how you told me you still loved me at Finnegan's the other day? The truth is . . . the very, very unfortunate truth is I love you too—which doesn't mean I don't still want to punch you in the face. I love you and that's why I'm not at work where I should be right now. And why I'm not thinking about a date tonight with a very nice and available man, which I also should be doing right now. Instead I'm out here with a guy I can never ever be with, sitting on a lawn chair looking at a bulldozer the size of a planet. Isn't it a beautiful day?"

"Honey—"

"Seriously, don't talk."

"You smell like sunlight and lavender."

"What part of 'don't talk' aren't you getting?"

"But—"

"Look, I'm sick of telling my heart not to feel. Because I do feel. I thought over time it would change but it hasn't, so here I am, get used to it. And there's no use going over the obvious. I can see your stupid robe and collar just like everybody else. Shoot, better than everybody else. But take off that hat, it's making me mad."

Jake took it off and set it on his knee. "Why is my hat making you mad?"

"I don't know, it just is. So, yeah, I know the situation, but some things are just bigger than situations, and what I feel is one of those bigger things. Sorry."

"I never should've said anything at Finnegan's."

"Little late now, bud. But I feel what I feel. It's always been there. Finnegan's or not."

"What now?"

Honey leaned back, closed her eyes, and turned her face up to the sun. "I don't know what's gonna happen. Nothing, I guess. I'll be a waitress, you'll be a priest, I'll pour your coffee, and you'll ask me how my grandma is. It'll have to be enough."

"I can't do that to you."

"It's enough, Jake. I love you and you love me. It can't be the first time in history this has happened, right?"

Early's old truck rumbled around the news van, honked its way through the crowd—temporary police light flashing on the roof—and parked. Early and Gomez Gomez climbed out, Gomez Gomez wearing a hospital gown over boots and old jeans.

"You kids on a date?" Early said as he approached. "When does the movie start?"

"Any minute. Where's your lawn chair?" Honey said.

Early pointed a thumb over his shoulder. "It looks like I'm working today thanks to Sonny's little freak-out. I gotta help Matthias keep you sixties protest types from getting pancaked. And GG here had to come talk to Jake."

"To me?" Jake said.

"Yeah, apparently he has something on his mind," Early said.

"You okay, Gomez Gomez?" Jake said.

"Hey, Jake, I . . ."

"It's okay. I know, man. I'm glad you came."

A single tear tracked Gomez Gomez's cheek. "Nah, man, it ain't okay. I don't know whose fault it was. Angel, you know? Maybe it was yours, maybe hers, maybe nobody's. It don't matter. What I'm saying is I don't want you to say you're sorry anymore. I shoulda heard you that first time. It shoulda been different."

"That means a lot, amigo. I've really missed you."

Gomez Gomez hugged his arms to his chest. "You got another chair?"

"I can find you something," Early said.

Gomez Gomez squatted and rolled into a sitting position next to Jake. "It's cool if you can't. I guess I been sitting on the ground for a long time anyway, huh? How you doing, Honey?"

"It's good to see you," Honey said.

"And I ain't drunk. I'm sober like Early. One day at a time and all that. He says he's gonna be my sponsor."

"Better me than Elvis and snakes," Early said.

"At least better than snakes—Elvis is cool," Gomez Gomez said.

A dove cooed.

The afternoon pressed on. The calm before the storm. Milton, Sonny's big mechanic, leaned against a tree near the dozer, taking in the scene with curious eyes. Over by the van, Matthias talked into Rosa's news mic, pausing every once in a while to point either at Sonny, still sitting in the cab of the bulldozer, or at Jake, Honey, and Gomez Gomez. Rosa leaned in, head cocked. A guy like Matthias probably made for great television.

"You know who would've loved this, don't you? Us being here? Doing this?" Honey said.

"Angel," Gomez Gomez said.

"Mostly she would've loved seeing you guys back together again," Honey said.

Early kicked the dirt with his boot toe. "You know what? I got one of those collapsible camp chairs in my truck. I'll go grab it." He headed off at a quick walk.

"I probably should've married that guy one of those million times he asked," Honey said.

"God definitely broke the mold," Jake said.

An engine rattled. Then the roar of the bulldozer shattered the afternoon.

CHAPTER FORTY-SEVEN

SONNY WATCHED ROSA PEREZ INTERVIEW Galt. The police chief naively thinking an hour of waiting would cool him down proved two things. First, Galt was a very small fish, and second, he didn't know Sonny at all. In fact, Sonny spent the hour fanning his smolder into a satisfying white-hot rage.

And, brother, his flames leapt.

Not only was Father Jake still sitting smack in the middle of Sonny's field of vision, now Honey Hicks and whacko Goober Gomez were there too. Exactly two seconds after the hour expired, Sonny fired and revved the bulldozer's diesel engine. Who did they think they were? Some noble hippie protesters? Save the whales or something? He was the only whale in this pond, thank you very much. He maneuvered the hydraulic controls, raised the huge blade high, then smashed it down. *Shake the earth. That'll put the fear of God into the stupid little fish—make 'em wiggle their tiny tails and scatter.*

But still, there they sat.

"That pass was on the money, you morons!" he shouted. He pounded the blade again. He cranked the big diesel up to a lion's roar. He saw the crowd out of the corner of his eye, felt the tension. And stupid Galt trying to wave him down, standing behind the open door of his police Bronco talking into a radio. Sonny revved again. He allowed the tractor to jerk forward, almost not believing he was doing it. What would it feel like? Just let the machine roll? Smash every little fish in sight?

His arms numbed with adrenaline. Outside the dozer's cab the world spun. Blurred. But one thing—one person—pierced Sonny's diminishing awareness with crystal-clear focus.

Glass-for-brains.

Nutjob Goober Gomez sat there cross-legged on the ground like some old Indian chief with every mystery of the universe stuffed into his pockets. *If it weren't for you none of this would be happening. You and your lunatic wife.*

And then it happened. The crazy whackadoo looked right up into Sonny's face and mouthed two unmistakable words—"Angel lives."

The earth lurched and rocked, fast-motion film. Electric energy rushed Sonny's body, shocked him as the scream inside his head seared his throat and slammed through his teeth, louder than the diesel roar in the cab. His arms and legs took on their own movement and he watched in fascinated amazement as they lowered the bulldozer's blade and slammed the tractor forward. *I'm really doing it! I'm gonna plow 'em!* Let the world watch. Put it on the five o'clock news. Why not? Go national, man. He was in it now. The power in that moment overwhelmed and blotted out everything else.

Something big and white flashed in his peripheral vision accompanied by a metallic smash. The bulldozer crunched, rocked, then stopped. Sonny reversed, then slammed the controls forward again. No dice. Galt's police Bronco, front end torn and twisted, wedged beneath the bulldozer's track. Metal on metal squealed as Sonny, screaming every curse word he could think of along with a few he made up on the spot, tried to force the machine forward. Galt rolled out of the Bronco's door, struggled to his feet, and rushed the bulldozer. Sonny's arms and legs pounded every lever and pedal with wild, adrenaline-infused abandon as he worked to dislodge the Bronco. Galt got a running start and leapt onto the lurching behemoth. He somehow made it to the cab and pounded the glass. Sonny waved him away and was answered with more pounding.

Galt, you idiot!

Angel's shrine filled his windshield. He gave the tractor everything it had. Metal grated against metal and the Bronco began a slow rollover. Galt pounded again, shouting something unintelligible. Sonny swiveled and looked directly into the lawman's eyes. Galt's face flushed red with anger. Who did this little fish think he was? More adrenaline—a flood of purest euphoria. Sonny reached back and yanked the pistol from his belt. In the same instant, the bulldozer broke free of the Bronco with a boom and the tractor lurched forward.

Galt pounded so hard the tempered glass rattled.

Sonny screamed, shoved the barrel of the gun against the glass, and pulled the trigger.

The shrine loomed in the windshield and the dozer blasted through it like the bullet through the glass.

CHAPTER FORTY-EIGHT

JAKE PICKED HIMSELF UP OFF of Honey and her crumpled lawn chair. She stood, brushing dirt off her clothes in a cloud of dust. Confused and frightened shouts filled the afternoon.

"Are you okay?" Jake said.

Honey's eyes were wide. "I can't believe he did it! Has he gone crazy? And I just froze. If you hadn't knocked me out of the way he would've smashed right over us. Is Gomez Gomez okay?"

Jake looked around. "I think so. I saw him roll the other direction."

"Hey! I need some help over here." Early knelt next to Matthias's crumpled form.

Jake rushed to them. "What happened?"

Early used both hands to press a wound low on Matthias's side. Thick black blood oozed through his fingers. "I was coming around my truck when Matthias rammed the dozer. He jumped up and tried to get into the cab. I can't say for sure but I think maniac Sonny shot him. And the cab is empty. He must've taken off on foot. Here, put pressure on this while I call in for an ambulance."

A lanky young guy in a KPTV jacket ran up with towels and a suitcase-size first-aid kit. "Let me get in there."

Some of the tension eased from Early's features. "Dean. I didn't know you were here."

"Picking up extra work with the news crew," Dean said. "We always carry first-aid equipment in the van."

"His breathing is shallow. Pulse seems good but he's not conscious." Early glanced at Jake. "Dean's a paramedic with PFD."

Dean pressed a towel against Matthias's wound while Early called for help. Within minutes two more officers arrived and began moving the crowd back and across the street.

Rosa Perez shouted across the distance, microphone in hand. "Early! Can you tell us what happened?"

Early held up a palm and shook his head. "Later, Rosa."

Siren lights flashed and an ambulance rolled up. Paramedics jumped out and joined Dean. Matthias still hadn't moved. They worked quickly, securing him to a board then up onto a gurney.

Tears streaked the dirt on Honey's face. "Do you think he'll be okay, Early?"

"I honestly don't know. That's a lot of blood. Right now I have another problem. Sonny's gone, and if I'm right he has a gun. John and Logan are the only other two officers on duty right now. They need to be here. I got a couple more coming but it's gonna be a while."

Jake did a slow three-sixty. "When Sonny came at us I saw his face. He's really lost it. And he was looking right at Gomez Gomez."

"I forgot about Gomez Gomez. Where is he?" Early said.

"That's the thing," Jake said. "He's gone."

"And so is Sonny . . ." Early said.

"Exactly. With a gun. I saw his face. Sonny's going hunting."

Early punched a button on his cell phone. "Lawrence . . . Yeah? Well, tell them to move their butts, man! I need them here *now*." He punched off. "I gotta go. If Sonny's after Gomez Gomez I don't have time to wait for backup."

Dean approached. "Early, we're moving him. He's not in good shape."

"Yeah, thanks. I'll come as soon as I can get things squared away here."

Dean nodded. "Roger that."

"I'm going with you, Early," Jake said.

"No way. It's a police matter."

"You think I'm going to wait here? It's Gomez Gomez. I'm going."

Early studied him. "Let's move then."

Honey grabbed Jake's arm. "Be careful. Don't do anything stupid. Please."

Jake put his hand over hers. "Go with Matthias, okay? He may need you."

"Please, Jake."

"I'll be careful. You know I will."

Honey hugged him then ran to the back of the ambulance where the paramedics were busy loading the gurney.

"Let's go." Early started off.

They passed the bulldozer and demolished shrine. Early cast around for footprints at the edge of the brush. A minute later he pointed. "Here. Gomez Gomez's boots for sure. Two more following, I think. Somebody's with Sonny?"

"Milton," Jake said. "He was watching the whole thing. And I didn't see him back there just now."

"Great, Sonny Harmon with a gun and now he's got his pet giant."

"Gomez Gomez knows this place like the back of his hand. He won't be easy to find."

"He's also unarmed and still detoxing. His odds aren't great. We got to stop this right now. You sure you're coming?"

Jake didn't answer, just started after the tracks, heading down the path toward Gomez Gomez's old camp.

CHAPTER FORTY-NINE

A DOVE COOED. ANXIOUS, SCARED. Gomez Gomez knew he was in trouble. Sonny's face behind the glass had said it all. Then Officer Galt jumping up and the muzzle flash in the cab. Gomez Gomez recognized it for what it was.

Sonny Harmon way past out of control.

Like the bull in his dream. The bull that wouldn't stop until it killed everything within sight.

So Gomez Gomez moved through the brush and trees as fast as his T-bird-deprived legs let him. He wanted a drink. He wanted a place to hide. He wanted Sonny to go away. He wanted Angel.

Jake and Honey had made it safely out of the way of Sonny's blade. He'd seen that much in the chaos. That was something.

Galt might be dead—probably was dead. The dove would cry over that. Galt had turned out okay in the end.

A hand grabbed his hospital gown and yanked him sideways into the brush. Gomez Gomez stumbled and went down in a heap. Bones stood over him.

"Where did you come from?" Gomez Gomez said.

"I saw you run. I figured you'd come this way."

"Sonny's after me."

"Yeah, I saw him. He shot that police guy. Crazy, man."

"I think he wants to kill me. He's probably mad about the Cadillac."

324

"He's probably mad about a lot of things. But mostly I think he just wants to kill somebody."

"What are we gonna do?"

"Try to get away, what else? Run. Hide. You got a better idea?"

"Not at the moment."

"We'd have a pretty good chance if we got across the river. But he might see us going across."

"I can't swim anyway."

"Really? We could try to loop back around to town, or even to Angel's memorial, or what's left of it, and get help."

"Yeah, but Sonny shot Officer Galt right in front of everybody. I bet he'd do the same to me. And somebody else could get hurt too."

"That's true."

"I got to find Early. Or Jake. They'd know what to do."

"Hey!" a distant voice shouted. "Glass-for-brains! You out there? Come on out and let me send you to your crazy wife right now. She's waiting, boyo!"

Bones held a finger to his lips.

"I know you didn't go far. Come on, let's get it over with. Quick and painless, right? I promise. Me to you. You have my word."

Bones motioned Gomez Gomez to follow with a silent hand gesture. Crouching, he led off through the bushes tracing a thin game trail.

Angel, what's happening here?

It seemed like only days ago they'd been so happy in their little house. Not a big house, but perfect for the two of them. But now Angel was gone. And he was following strange Bones through the bushes trying to get away from a maniac who wanted to shoot him.

Let me send you to your wife . . . Should I let him, Angel? Should I come to you now?

But Bones kept moving and Gomez Gomez's feet kept following. What would it feel like to get shot? Would it hurt? Would he even know when it happened? Maybe he'd just step into Angel's arms in a flash of light.

Something crunched in the brush off to the right and Bones drew up, cocking his head. Maybe the rattler was close by. Wouldn't that be something? The rattler biting Sonny before he could kill anybody else? Or biting Gomez Gomez even?

Another scrape in the bushes. Bones moved behind a thick ponderosa pine. Beyond it, sunlight dappled a wide clearing. They waited a long time. No more sounds. Where was Sonny?

Finally Bones whispered, "If we can get past this clearing and up the hill we'll hit the road. We could make it back to the shrine and find your friend the cop."

"What if Sonny's here someplace? Hiding and waiting? He'll see us for sure."

"We can't go around, it's too thick. We'd make too much noise. And we can't go back the way we came. What else we gonna do?"

Let me send you to your wife . . .

"Okay, kid, but I'll go first, cool? If something happens, you run and don't stop till you find help."

"Why would you do that?"

Gomez Gomez shrugged. "Because we're friends, man."

"We are?"

"Yeah, amigo. Thick as thieves, you and me."

"You never said that before."

"I know, Spaceman. But I'm saying it now. Friends for sure. And I couldn't ask for better."

Bones hugged him.

"I ain't much of a hugger, dude," Gomez Gomez said, then hugged the kid back.

"Be careful," Bones said.

Let me send you to your wife . . .

"It'll be cool."

The sun touched the tree line as Gomez Gomez took a tentative step into the clearing. No snakes talked. Elvis nowhere to be seen. He pulled a long lungful of cool autumn air in through his nose then released it through his mouth. Something glinted in the thick grass.

He stooped and picked it up—a Thunderbird bottle. Probably one of his old troops. Half full too. Or half empty?

The dove cooed, answered by another. Gomez Gomez dropped the bottle where he'd found it. Some things in life just got too heavy to carry.

He began across the clearing, sun on his face. He felt good suddenly. He started to whistle. "Can't Help Falling in Love," one of Angel's favorites.

He was halfway across when Milton stepped out of the trees in front of him holding a shotgun.

CHAPTER FIFTY

"WHERE'D YOU GET THE GUN?" All Gomez Gomez could think to say.

"Had it stashed. Thought I'd bring it along."

"Cool. You gonna kill me then?"

Milton didn't look mad, but as far as Gomez Gomez knew, guys like Milton didn't necessarily have to be mad to kill a guy. In fact, when he looked close, Milton seemed kind of sad beneath his tattoos. Still, he seemed like a guy that could kill somebody no problem.

"I guess it's okay if you have to," Gomez Gomez said. "No hard feelings, man. Big enough holes, right?"

The bushes parted behind Milton and Sonny strode into the clearing wearing a smug smile. "Heya, nutjob, ready to go see your lunatic wife?"

"Don't call her that," Gomez Gomez said.

"Man, all I wanted was to build something nice, you know? Bring this hole of a town out of the dark ages. Let me ask you before I blast your ugly head off, what's so bad about an Outback Steakhouse?"

"I don't know. I never been. I like steak though."

"It's crazy, I thought I ran over you. What a rush. But you must've scooted out of the way. Like a cockroach. You a cockroach, nutjob?"

"No. Just an imperfect believer."

"Well, you're a freak, and I'm gonna blow your head off. I'm pretty sure I already killed somebody today, so I probably have to go to jail anyway. I'm gonna take my time, then watch your head splatter just like that junkie on episode fifty-four of *After Sunset*. You ever seen that one?"

"Maybe. I don't think so."

"Too bad. Would've been a good visual for you. So anyway, yeah, I'm gonna shoot you. But before I do I gotta tell you something funny. You want to hear something funny?"

"You mean like a joke?"

"Exactly! Like a joke. So here it is—I'm pulling out of my car lot one day in . . . guess what?"

"A car?"

"Yeah, but *what* car?"

Gomez Gomez shrugged.

"In my pink Caddy! Wait for it, you'll see why this is funny in a minute. So I'm pulling out and I'm checking myself in the mirror. Little comb job, you know? 'Cause nobody feathers their hair right anymore. So I'm combing and pulling out and I hear something. What do you think I hear?"

"Got me."

"I hear brakes! Isn't that hilarious? I hear 'em screech out on the road and guess what?"

"What?"

"Your crazy wife goes swerving past to miss me. Are you getting it yet? Yeah, I can see by your face you're catching on. So your crazy wife fishtails, almost gets it back under control but overcorrects, and bam! Head-on into old Jake's truck. That cray-cray or what? Now here's the best part. The punch line, right? Me? I pull on out like nothing and take my beautiful pink Caddy over to Spur's where me and Casper Green knock back a few beers. Then I go home. Watch the whole deal on the news that night. Isn't that a good one, Goober?"

"You killed Angel?" Gomez Gomez said.

"Well, not directly. Doesn't do to point fingers. Or actually go ahead and point, I don't care. You're a whack job anyway." Sonny dropped a nylon backpack off his shoulder and opened it. "Hey, check this out! Brought it along in the dozer for fun. Like fuzzy dice. Seemed fitting."

The Folgers can caught the fading sunlight.

"Give her to me," Gomez Gomez said.

"Nah."

"Please . . ."

"No way, Jose. No final wishes for nutjobs on my watch."

"Don't call him that, give him Angel!" Bones charged into the clearing. Sonny's face blanched. "Jeremy?"

"You can't kill him. He's my friend," Bones said.

"Why'd he call you Jeremy? I thought your name was Bones, Spaceman," Gomez Gomez said.

Bones wiped his nose with the back of his hand. "He always calls me Jeremy. He's my dad."

"You're dad ain't in the jungle?"

"I wish he was," Bones said.

"He killed Angel . . ." Gomez Gomez's head struggled to catch up.

"I didn't know about that. I just know he wanted to run you out. I hear him talking all the time. He doesn't even know I'm around. Because he doesn't care about anyone or anything but himself."

"You're Sonny's son . . ."

"He don't care nothing about that. But you're my friend. That's why I started the Angel Lives stuff. And sprayed it on his stupid model."

Sonny looked dumbfounded. "That was you? My own son?" He leveled his pistol at Gomez Gomez. "You made my son as much a freak as you are. How my blood flows through those freaky little veins I'll never know. Look at him!" Sonny held the Folgers can up. "Hey, want to see me blast an angel out of the air? Check this out." He threw the can high.

"No!" Gomez Gomez said.

Sonny's pistol popped. The can tumbled to earth, landing in the grass.

"Hmm, missed," Sonny said. "Oh well, I'll get it next time. Set it on a fence or something. Never miss that way. For now my creepy son can watch his old man blow his new bestie's head off instead. Little freak. Always creeping around . . . I wish your loser mother would've taken you with her. Tell you what, prison will be a relief." He fixed a bead on Gomez Gomez's skull.

Gomez Gomez closed his eyes. Crashing brush made him open them again.

Early ran into the clearing, Jake behind him. Early's gun drawn. "Put it down, Sonny."

Sonny grinned. "Or what? Shoot me if you want. Any way it plays Goober Gomez is gonna die."

"Just put the gun down," Early said.

Gomez Gomez lifted a hand. "It's cool, Early. I'm already full of big enough holes. I wanna see Angel."

"See what I mean?" Sonny pulled the hammer back. The click loud in the afternoon. "Here he comes, Mrs. Gomez."

"Do it," Gomez Gomez said.

But then Milton moved.

The big man's arm jerked up and back faster than the rattler. His elbow smashed Sonny's face with enough force to put a hole in a brick wall. Sonny crumpled like a wet washcloth, gun sliding from his fingers harmlessly onto the grass. Milton kicked it gently away.

Early kept his gun leveled. "Milton, step away from him."

Milton did.

Gomez Gomez—in his mind halfway to heaven—pulled himself back to earth, struggling to make sense of what was happening.

"Keep your hands up," Early said.

Gomez Gomez closed the distance between himself and Milton in a few steps.

"Gomez Gomez . . ." Jake said.

"Nah, Jake, it's cool." Gomez Gomez looked deep into Milton's eyes. Sadness lived there. "You knew her . . . didn't you?"

Milton shrugged and nodded. "Long time ago. I was pretty strung out then. I robbed that place she was working down in Gila Bend. Even knocked her down on the way out. But Angel, know what she did? After all that she came and saw me in prison. She was nice. Real. Made me want to get clean. So I did."

"That was Angel all right," Gomez Gomez said. "Way she was."

"I was a real mess. She didn't care. Visited me in prison, man. Who would do that? That's why I wrote it on the sign."

Early lowered his gun.

CHAPTER FIFTY-ONE

OCEANOGRAPHERS HAVE SPENT DECADES PROBING, measuring, and mapping peaks, valleys, and vast plains hidden beneath the sea. Liquid sheen that covers three-quarters of our earth's surface. Down there, they tell us, mountain ranges thrust between bottomless, plunging canyons, all lost in that eternal, sunless ink. Challenger Deep in the Mariana Trench is more than seven miles down. So deep that if Mount Everest—the highest mountain on the planet—were scooped off its beach towel and tossed into that abyss it would still be covered by a mile of water.

And yet as marvelous as the ocean is, there is something greater. The Challenger Deep is nothing but a scratch on the surface of the sky above lovers' heads. And bigger still, too deep for oceanographers, too vast for astronomers, too wonderful for theologians—the human heart.

And such is love.

From his office window Jake watched a tumbleweed kick up dust as it bounced across the old baseball field.

So here he was again.

Two weeks since that day in the clearing at Angel's place. After they'd hauled Sonny to jail, Gomez Gomez hugged Jake and wept. They'd talked every day since. Still dripping from this baptism of reconciliation, Jake found great joy. The soaring flight of born again.

Gomez Gomez had moved in with Early the day he was released

from the hospital with no pending charges. He ticked off his sober days one by one on an Elvis Presley calendar and spent hours in the yard talking to his friend Bones, who was living with a foster mother who, according to Gomez Gomez, made the best chocolate chip cookies in the world.

Matthias hadn't made it back to work yet but at least was able to continue his recuperation at home.

This morning at Shorty's, Honey had poured Jake's coffee and he'd asked about her grandmother. Tonight they'd walk the town square together, talking, careful not to touch, just like they had every night since that day she'd sat down next to him in front of Sonny's tractor.

And tomorrow he'd have morning prayers, hear confession, make a few hospital visits, clean and organize . . .

How far would that tumbleweed go? Maybe down the mountain all the way to I-10. Then maybe down that ribbon of asphalt all the way to where it ended at the Santa Monica pier. Maybe it'd roll right into the Pacific, the tide taking it all the way to the bottom of Challenger Deep where Everest bubbled from its sudden dunk.

Maybe there it would finally find peace.

Honey . . .

A knock sounded and Jake turned. Father Enzo's dark hair and smiling face leaned into the room.

"You look lost in thought," Father Enzo said.

"Yes, sorry, father."

"Why be sorry? As far as I can see most of the world is lost in thoughtlessness. It is good to spend time in contemplation. God meets us in the stillness, yes? Sit with me, would you?"

The old man sank into one of Jake's leather chairs. Jake took a seat on the couch. "What can I do for you, father? More Superman?"

"Superman, yes, yes. How are you, Father Jake?"

"I'm fine, I think."

Father Enzo balanced his elbows on the arms of the chair and folded his hands in front of him, making a steeple with his index fingers. "I don't think you're fine. I think you are in love."

Jake looked deep for words. "I'm sorry, father. But I know my duty and I'll fulfill it."

"Again with 'I'm sorry.' Why are you sorry? Love—real love—should never make us sorry."

"I've prayed. I've asked God to take this. I have no excuse. But I haven't acted physically, father. I can handle it, I promise."

"You can handle love? It is a thing rarely done, in my experience. Hate, maybe. Lust can be overcome. Temptation can be mastered by God's help. But love? Love is who God is. Real love, pure love, is a part of him, do you know?"

"I think so."

"Tell me, did you enjoy my story? From the island of Corfu?"

The turn of conversation confused Jake a little. "Of course, father. You've got a great imagination."

"I have no imagination at all. Only memory. Memories of something that happened a long time ago in another world. On a beautiful island far away in the Ionian Sea."

"Another world . . . ?"

"That's right. In that world I was in love. And in that world I was not called Enzo."

CHAPTER FIFTY-TWO

LIGHT SLANTED A HARD ANGLE through the office window. Dust danced and twirled in the beam. Jake studied the old priest.

"Let me understand, she didn't choose you so you ran to the church?"

"I made my stand that night. I gave my argument, my plea. I thought, how could they not understand the love in my heart? It was greater than all else! But what could I do? In the end she made up her mind. I was mortified—ashamed. I knew a Catholic priest. A friend. He was kind and understanding. I went to him. I was of age and he helped me to go to Rome where I attended seminary and eventually entered the priesthood. That's when I changed my name. I wanted a fresh start. To forget the love I left behind. Then, as you know, for many, many years I served at the Vatican. Ten years ago I came to America. Here I am. Almost sixty years now since I was that love-struck boy chasing fish in the waters of Corfu."

"And you never went back?"

"A few times. But by then I'd settled into my new life. Eventually I became content. Eventually I found peace."

"You were able to move on. You got past her? So it can be done . . . That's what you've been telling me all along."

"No, son. What I'm telling you is there are times, rare times, but incredibly beautiful times, when love must not be denied. It must be attempted, whether it flourishes or fails. Like strands of rope wound tightly together. The strands make it strong. They are separate, yes, but they are also one thing—two parts making a whole. This kind of rope is never meant to be unwound. When it is forced apart there can only be sadness. Weakness. Think of a love ordained by a God who knows the very number of your days. This will be hard to hear, but I believe with my whole heart, Father Jake, that you took a wrong turn five years ago. You listened to your grief and your guilt over the accident with Angel Gomez rather than to God's whisper. You hid behind your robe and collar."

"You're saying I shouldn't be a priest?"

The old man leaned over and put a hand on Jake's arm. Deep creases lined his face. A face prone to outbursts of joy. "I've talked long with the bishop. To tell you the truth, he was not in agreement at first. These things are not easy. But I think he's come to see I am right on the matter. The process will take some time but that isn't something for you to worry about. As of right now, if you so choose, you are released. Laicized. We will take care of the details."

"I don't understand. Don't you think I can find peace in God?"

"Of course you can. And you must. There is no other! But you do not have to be a priest to have peace in God. In fact, sometimes it is God who makes us uneasy. Even miserable, if we've strayed from the path he has for us. I would be going against my conscience before God to attempt to convince you to continue down a path I don't believe is best for you. To force you to stay as you are. It is not what I believe. It is not what is right."

"I took a vow, father. To God."

"Did you? Or did you take a vow to yourself? Did you even give God a say in the matter? I wonder."

Jake tried to wrangle his reeling thoughts. "But what am I supposed to do?"

"Take off that robe and collar and go be Jake Morales."

"How can a person just pick up and get on with life after disappointing God like that? It seems too much. How can—"

"If you are truly asking that question you and I are not acquainted with the same God. You are not a disappointment to him. You are a joy! A robe, or lack of one, can never change that. Simply know him. Walk with him every day of your life. And take this woman whom you love so deeply with you. Now please go."

Jake leaned forward, elbows on his knees. Was this happening? Shackles fell. His spirit surged. Then a rush of sadness.

"What is it?" Father Enzo said.

"You. That love you had. That special, pure love. And your boat, your grandfather, everything. You had to leave it all. How can you stand it? Even after all this time?"

The old man's eyes shone when he laughed. "You're confused, my boy. Love always wins! It must. My name all those years ago was not Erasmo. It was Fabrizio."

CHAPTER FIFTY-THREE

A STRAND OF BLACK HAIR blew across Gomez Gomez's face. He pushed it away with the back of his hand. Hard, rough hands still unfamiliar with life indoors.

It was good being at Early's place. Regular food, a clean bed to sleep in. A solid, human world of brick and stone. Nothing like his old camp, the endless nights, shimmery spirits dancing at the edges of the campfire light. And the days when the air smelled of earth, lizards, and diesel fumes blowing down from the highway.

But now he was here, on the edge of the earth. A strange pair they must've made. Elvis, sequined jumpsuit brilliant against the dying sun, and Gomez Gomez in his stiff new Levi's and shirt Honey bought for him.

He should've told them all—asked them to come. Jake, Early, Honey, Bones. Bones would've liked to have been here. He was still Bones. Though the lady he'd been placed with actually cared where he was for a change. Yeah, Spaceman acted like he hated it but Gomez Gomez knew better.

In the end he hadn't invited anyone at all, wanting to come alone. But Elvis was Elvis. The King came and went as he pleased. And somehow him being here now seemed appropriate. And so they stood—King and wino—on top of Apache Drop with a hundred miles of Arizona desert stretched out beneath them in three directions.

"It's a nice evening for it," Gomez Gomez said.

"Would've been good for it five years ago, baby."

"I wasn't ready then."

"And you are now?"

"No." Gomez Gomez held up the shiny, fresh Yuban can. His hands shook. "She always liked Yuban."

Elvis put a hand on his shoulder. "She's happy, baby."

"She always said to get Yuban when I went to Harlan's Market."

"Good call. Smart lady. Yuban's good stuff."

A hawk circled out over the expanse, wide lazy loops.

"Let's do it, man. Whenever you're ready," Elvis said.

Gomez Gomez pulled in a deep breath then released. The plastic lid came off too easy, even with trembling fingers. He'd hoped it would take longer.

"Okay. Goodbye then. I'll always love you, Angel." *She always liked to keep things simple.*

He tipped the coffee can and let a handful of ashes escape. A handful only. A fraction of someone's life and dreams, everything they were. They spun into the updraft. Air rushing from the warm desert floor to the coolness of the deep blue. The ashes swirled and dipped, rising high into the air, falling, then climbing again. They whipped around Gomez Gomez and peppered his clothes. Small white specks of her. He didn't brush them off.

"She really knew how to die, you know?"

"Yeah, man," Elvis said. "You gonna do the rest?"

"I don't just mean at the end. I mean from the first day I met her. She knew how to die. I never did."

"I knew what you meant, man. Most folks don't know how. But that chick is something."

Tears came but Gomez Gomez blinked them away. She wouldn't want him to cry. He replaced the lid and tucked the can under his arm. He bent and picked up a rock and threw it over the edge. Jake would've thrown farther. Even when they were kids he'd had the best arm.

"They say her memorial was big. 'Cause she touched so many people.

Pretty much everybody showed up. The whole town . . . But I couldn't go. You know? I couldn't say goodbye. And all I had was that Folgers can. I went to the bushes instead. And I kept her with me."

"She loved you, baby. But you're here now. That's what counts. I think you should finish it up."

Gomez Gomez pulled the T-bird bottle out of the inside pocket of his coat. He removed the cap and took two steps forward. The liquid didn't pour as much as spray in the stiff updraft. He wound up and threw the bottle as far out toward the dropping sun as he could—not far enough. A strong gust drowned out the sound of it breaking below.

"I just want her to know . . ."

"She does."

"I think I'll stay a while. Just me and her. Then I'll do the rest."

"All right, baby. This was good. I'm proud of you."

The wind and the sun . . . "Thanks, King."

"You're a cat, you know?"

"Nah, I'm an imperfect believer."

"Exactly. You be good, son. The King loves you."

Alone with the fading desert, Gomez Gomez squatted, then sat, leaning his back against a rock ledge still warm from the day. Warmth that had traveled a hundred million miles just for him and Angel. He held the can on his lap.

"I miss you, Angel," he said to the sky.

He listened hard, but it wasn't Angel who answered.

"So you finally left us for real society?" The rattlesnake was curled in a crack of the rock, enjoying the same residual warmth, not a foot away from Gomez Gomez's face.

"Things change. I got clean. And I got a Yuban can."

"So I see. And no T-bird."

"I'm three weeks sober now."

"Well, I can't say I'm happy about it."

"Had to do it, man. I feel pretty good."

"You don't miss it?"

"Every second of every minute of every day."

The rattlesnake pulled his big diamond-shaped head back. "I feel bored with you."

"I thought you might."

"You know what I feel like doing, don't you?"

Gomez Gomez sighed and looked out at the endlessness of the desert. The snake struck twice and with great accuracy just below Gomez Gomez's jawline.

Funny, no pain. He'd heard the horror stories of snakebite. But nothing except a hazy peace.

And the sky and the desert.

And then Angel.

The sun behind her flashing through her blonde hair—a gleaming yellow torrent in the wind.

She smiled and reached for him.

CHAPTER FIFTY-FOUR

JAKE HELD HONEY'S HAND AS the two of them walked down the hill. Jake wore no robe now. Jeans, a dress shirt, and his old boots. Her hand in his—her skin—both familiar and forever mysterious. Jake carried the Yuban can containing the mingled ashes of Angel and Gomez Gomez in the crook of his arm.

"So many people came," Honey said.

"She touched them all. It's important to them. Like leaving the signs. And Gomez Gomez's loyalty to her memory is a testament they want to honor."

No less than five or six hundred people sprawled across the hill above the cliff. Jake picked out faces as they walked through. Charles Faulks, Aunt Katie and Uncle Lou . . . Milton, a familiar face at church these days, stood with Father Enzo and Lucille. Matthias leaned on a crutch, Rosa Perez holding tight to his arm, no news microphone in sight.

The four winds of the earth are fickle characters. Shifting on a whim with sunlight, tide, and fortune. Today no updraft whipped skyward from the desert floor. A gentle breeze blew from behind, intermittently tugging and releasing the clothes of those gathered with light and playful fingers. Jake held the Yuban can at the edge of Apache Drop. Honey, Early, and Bones stood with him. No sound system for amplified eulogies. No programs or guest book to sign. Everyone knew Gomez Gomez and Angel called for an organic affair. A memorial stone had been erected, silhouetted against the desert sky.

342

GOMEZ GOMEZ AND ANGEL
FOREVER MEANT TO BE

Wings were carved into the polished granite above Angel's name.

"I still can't believe he's gone," Honey said.

"Me neither. But it feels right, doing it like this," Early said.

Jake held up the can. "I'm gonna miss him, miss them both, but I'm glad they're together." He pulled the lid off.

"Wait, maybe Bones should do it," Honey said.

Jake looked down at the kid. Tear-streaked face. Glasses catching sunlight. "You okay?"

"Yeah, I'm cool," Bones said.

"You want to do it?"

Bones took the can. "He was my friend."

"Yes, he was. And that's saying a whole lot," Jake said.

Bones tipped the can and shook it. The mingled ashes fell into a sudden exhale of wind and floated out over the desert below. They tumbled and caught the sunlight, almost as if laughing at newfound freedom.

Bones's smile came soft through moist eyes. "Crazy guy. He always said they were beautiful."

Jake nodded. "He was right. They are."

EPILOGUE

Corfu, Greece—Modern Day

THE LITTLE BOAT BOBBED LIGHTLY on the calm Ionian Sea where the rocky bed dropped off to the blue and black of deep water. Dolphins finned. Always a sure sign of good luck. The old man sat on the rail, pulled on his fins, and spit into his mask. He swirled the saliva with his finger to prevent fogging. A woman came through the wheelhouse door, her swim gear in her hands, and joined him. She donned her gear.

"You ready?" she said.

He looked at her, something he never ever tired of doing and knew he never would. Pure white hair framed her beautiful sun-lined face. Eyes the color of the sky and sea.

"What a gas," he said.

She laughed and hugged him. "What a gas."

He took her hand and together they dropped into the blue.